The Titanium
(Destiny of Love)
Part One
(Book One)

L.T. Kenneth

DEDICATION

This is for all the people who believed in me, my family, my friends and everyone who inspired me to get this far.

ACKNOWLEDGMENTS

And to those who supported and prayed for me, know that I could have not done this without you. Your prayers and support mean a lot. And those who showed me God, I am forever thankful.

PROLOGUE

Imagine, suddenly everything was taken away from you. Your home, your belongings, even the sun. Sent to live underground, and you have to toil away in the mines for hours, the monotony of your efforts interrupted only by a sharp bark of a guard, a crack of a whip, or the drip of water from the dark ceiling above. Your food is as tasteless as it is colourless, but you eat to survive. Everything you do is to survive. Eventually, you have children, who grow up and learn how to survive themselves, long enough to have children of their own, who they then teach to survive. And with each generation, knowledge of the sun, trees, and fresh air, become bedtime stories told to help the children go to bed.

Sometimes, you'll find that you've been graced with a special talent. You are smarter than those around you, you have the voice of an angel, you're more beautiful than most. Try as you might to hide them, eventually you will inevitably attract the attention of a guard, and they will send you in for evaluation. If deemed worthy, you are sent to work the surface as a slave for the King, trading the cold, damp darkness for the warmth of the sun, trading your family for a life of slavery, never to return back to your home.

This is the life I have been born into, but it's not the life I am going to live. Survival is getting harder and harder, and my people are fading away into the darkness. I will be the one to lead them into the light.

"The Titanium (Destiny of Love Part one) ". A story of challenges, love, and self-discovery.

CHAPTER 1

"You there. 932." I was walking back from the well, my bucket dragging on the floor, heavy with water. I stilled after hearing the guard call my number, a few drips spilling over the side as the water splashed around in protest to my sudden halt. The back of my neck burned as the guard held the lantern behind me so he could read my numbers. Even though I've had them since I was a child, I still woke up in the middle of the night, the memories of the pain from that day they marked me refusing to leave my mind. I don't know if anyone else had the same nightmares. I've always been too afraid to ask, not wanting to appear any weaker than people already think I am. We all have our numbers branded on our neck. It's something we've all had to go through. Every man must wear his hair short, and every woman must wear her hair up so that the guards can identify us with ease. Down here, under the earth, we aren't supposed to have names. Down here, they tell us that Cethin is where the dirt belongs, and grains of dirt aren't important enough for names. Instead, they gave us numbers. Our individualism is a mere whisper when the coast is clear. The names we choose for ourselves are known only by those closest to us.

If you work hard enough, you can buy a real name. The King chooses your name, and with it comes a coloured cloak, stained with colours otherwise not found underground. The rest of us are consigned to simple, brown tunics. These men and women are among the leaders of our underground world. Well, as much as one can lead with the guards watching our every move.

To those that live above in Ahrenia, we are nothing but scum. Decades ago, after a great famine scoured the land, all the blame fell upon us, the marginalized in society. Anyone who didn't have enough money, anyone who suffered from illness or handicap, anyone who was not ideal, was a victim of the King's wrath. We were told that, if it weren't for the poverty we created, no war would be able to fester. They blamed every criminal act, every failure, every sorrow, on us. And so, in what has become known as the Great Purge, the rulers decided to send us all down to the mines, where we would work until the day we died in the darkness, never again seeing the light of the sun. Sending the strongest of us ahead to expand the mines, we built an underground village that was large enough to hold all the rejects of the kingdom. Collectively, we became known as Nethers, the ground-dwellers, the scum of the Earth. This was the beginning of Cethin.

Life on the surface of Ahrenia has returned to normal, continuing on without ever looking back to those that were lost. Any hope of a return to the surface has all but faded. We've learned to adapt, living off groundwater, tubers, and roots. The few things we can't grow or build for ourselves are brought by the guards in order to keep us alive. Otherwise, they wouldn't have anyone to do the hard labour. They would have to find some other way to support their luxurious lifestyle.

Being underground, we provide the mineral resources for the wealthy. In the centuries that we have been down here, the mines have grown deeper and deeper. Some take days to reach the bottom. Anyone who causes trouble with the guards is forced to work in the deepest pits, separated from their family and the few comforts we have left to us. However, those who follow the rules don't fare much better. Most of us are destined to work until death. Those that are special enough, the strong ones, the talented ones, the beautiful ones, are taken from Cethin to work above as slaves to the kingdom. Not a single one has ever come back. To keep us safe from this, our parents raise us to be lackluster, to blend in, not wanting to condemn their children to lives of slavery on the surface. But as much as we try to remain inconspicuous, to disappear in the darkness of the caves, the guards seek us out and beat us down, treating us like the filth they believe us to be. Admittedly, living in Cethin isn't a far cry from the life of a slave, but at least we can be slaves among our family. On the surface, one would be completely alone.

"923!" The guard pulled me up by the hair and spun me around. I dropped my bucket on the ground and lamented all the water that was wasted, now seeping back into the dirt. The guard grinned in a way that sent my stomach churning when he saw my face. "Ah, I knew it was you. My little cave flower has somehow managed to bloom in this waste heap. How's about you and me go back to my room, and you can show me a good time for all the hard work I've done here in this hell hole?"

"Excuse me, sir. I must bring this water back to my family." I kept my eyes down, watching as the last of the water disappeared into the earth, leaving the ground damp and dark; not much different than the rest of the soil around it. I looked back up at the pockmarked face of the guard, who was most likely in his early twenties. The young ones are the worst. They seem to think that they have the right to anything or anyone down here, overly-confident behind the power of their uniforms and the the sword at their side. The younger guards see us as little more than ways to amuse themselves in these dark, timeless caves. The older ones either grow quieter as the years go on, or they grow meaner.

"You speak as though you have a choice. I wasn't offering." Grabbing me by the arm, he began to pull me up the trail and towards the guard holdings.

"Hey, mister! Hey!" A voice caused the guard to turn around.

"What, kid? Can't you see that I'm busy?" A spindly boy was tugging on the guard's shirt.

"But down in the mine, there's a fight! 359 accused 973 of stealing his load, and then 973 punched him in the face, and there was a bunch of hollering and fighting and a pick-axe in the eye,"

"Damn! Can't you Nether scum just work like your supposed to? There's a reason your down here!" Muttering curses to himself, he ran down the trail. When the coast was clear, I turned and looked down at my rescuer.

"Really, Conor?" I whispered, making sure no guards caught us using our names. "An axe in the eye? I think you're having too much fun with the stories" I ruffled his dirty blond hair, and wiped a smudge off his pale face. Without the light of the sun, we don't have much colour. There are a few of us that still carry traces of dark hair and skin, but for the most part, we are unremarkable, fading into the earth around us.

"Well you keep getting stuck with nasty men! My imagination is pretty good, but sometimes my storytelling can't keep up with your troublemaking!" I realized the irony of the chastisement I was receiving from a boy little more than half my age. "I have to mix it up once in a while! Honestly Faradene, you get yourself in more trouble than any other girl around here."

I couldn't argue with that. It was true. It seemed like every time I managed to leave my room, I wind-up in some situation. But is isn't like I go looking for trouble, I just happen to attract it. I'm what one would call conspicuous.

Other than the few glimpses I've chanced at the well, I haven't seen my own reflection. I only know that my hair is the same dark brown colour as the table in my family's den, while my eyes are made up of the same green as the carrot leaves in our underground garden. These have singled me out from everyone else's mud-brown eyes and dirty blond hair, leaving me in a category on my own, which only serves to gain unwanted attention. The guards seem to think that they are entitled to anything they desire, and apparently I am in high demand. If not for the protection of my parents, I would have very early on become one among many women down here taken for the guard's pleasure.

"Then it's a good thing I have you around to rescue me," I replied to Conor. "Now go ahead and get back to your mother. Supper is coming along and she doesn't need anything else to worry about. I've got to return to the well and get more water. I'll be home soon." I bent down to pick up the bucket, sighing at the thought of having to go all the way back down to the well.

Well, I reminded myself, at least I'm out. Rarely did I get the chance to leave the "safety" of my family's den, which to me felt more like a prison, so I greatly appreciated all my small outings, even though I tended to get myself into trouble every time.

"Just don't take too long! I don't want to have to rescue you again!" With a wink, he scampered up the trail and down the dark corridor. The lanterns flickered in his wake, and I turned around to headed back down the trail.

CHAPTER 2

When I returned, I entered my family's den only to be greeted by Conor's apologetic expression. He was hiding behind my mother, who had a scowl carved into her face and her arms crossed tight over her chest. She closed the gap between myself and her, and before I could open my mouth in protest, sent a hard slap across my face, the sound ringing throughout the room.

" Faradene! You have no excuse wandering through the tunnels by yourself! Conor comes back nearly every week, telling me stories about the trouble you get yourself into. Haven't you learned by now that nothing comes of you leaving the den?"

"But I had to get some water for dinner," I began to protest before her stern face stopped me short.

"You know we can't fool around here. The King doesn't care about what his men to do us. There is nothing here to protect you!" She looked at me in earnest, her voice quieter, "I can't protect you." She grasped my arm, holding onto me as if, should she let go, I would be lost to her. "Come on and sit. Supper's ready."

I shot Conor a glare as he ran out of our den, and he cast me a sympathetic smile before turning the corner. I turned back around and made my way to the centre of the room. Our home consisted of one large, rounded out room with bare, brown walls and a scattering of mismatched rugs covering the floor. In the back sits a fire pit, and above it tonight cooked what I assumed to be another round of potato and carrot stew in a large cauldron. My mother handed me a clay bowl and I went to fill it up. I shuddered as another brown carrot slopped its way into my bowl, trying not to watch as it sunk under the sea of yellow broth. I took my seat at the table, and was joined a moment later by my mother. I pushed the carrot lump around in my bowl, not wanting to break the awkward silence.

"Go on and eat. I know it looks bad, but with the rationing, there isn't much to be done. We've got to use what we have, and only then can we ask for more. Besides, you don't want your father to see you turning your nose up at your food when he works so hard to make sure that everyone has what they need."

My father is one of the few members of our community recognized by the guards as an authority figure of Cethin. He often meets with other men and women in a council, working to provide some relief for their people. For a time, things were going well, considering the fact that we are underground. We had enough food to last us, the animals we that were occasionally brought down when a new group of guards came in were nice and healthy, and the guards themselves took their job a bit more seriously, giving us less trouble. But recently, the King has been sending more and more guards down below. The guards, unaccustomed to having to live with rations and the scarce resources of underground living, consume nearly double what we do. The little remaining food must be partitioned up amongst the animals and ourselves. As consequence, the animals have been getting thinner, and so have we. While the guards, on the other hand, have grown plump, with an attitude as large as their appetite.

The council meets weekly, and the King's guards always attend, to make sure nothing amiss is going on. The members discuss trivial things such as food count, mining revenue, and the status of the group latrine. To the guards, nothing seems out of the ordinary. But to the members of the council, every word has a double meaning, and through this code, we have begun to organize a revolt right under the guard's noses. None but the council knows the plan; even I am in the dark. But that doesn't stop me from trying to weave my way into the plot.

As my mother and I ate our supper in silence, my father walked into our den. He placed his blue-stained cloak across the doorway as a curtain, the symbol that all are home and resting.

"My sweet Miriam!" My father's booming voice resounded through the room as he swept my mother up into a mighty embrace.

"Hush, Anso, the guards will hear you! You know that they follow you closely!"

"Let them!" He boomed, turning his face back towards the opening. "I have nothing to fear from those weak, power hungry brutes. If they won't let us run our own colony, I should at least be able to run my own den. And that means that if I want to love my wife, so be it!"

"You're in a jolly mood, Anso. Did the council meeting go well?" My mother asked.

"Did it go well? Things will start changing for the better, I can tell you that. We just have a few more obstacles to face," My father stopped short with a stern look from my mother. He looked down at me, and I couldn't help but smile. My father was as jovial as my mother was strict, but when times called, his enthusiasm would just as quickly turn to a fueled passion for righteousness, in which his great strength seemed to have no bounds.

"Ah, Faradene, and how is my beautiful child doing?" He scooped me up into his arms as well, and wrapped us all in a tight hug.

"Ahh! Let go! I can't breathe!" I squirmed my way out of his grip, giggling, and we both sat back down to eat. My mother left to fetch him a bowl, and before I could think of a way to distract my father, she returned and sat down, her eyes trained on mine as she announced,

" Faradene got herself into trouble again. This time a guard nearly dragged her to his room to have his way with her."

"That wasn't my fault!" I protested before she could say any more. "It isn't like I asked him to grab me! We needed water, and you weren't here! I had only gone to the well,"

"Exactly!" She cut me off. "I've told you before, you are not to leave our den on your own! You demand too much attention, and we don't need to give the guards any excuse to hurt us more than they already have!"

"But you can't hold me up in this room forever! What am I supposed to do? Work needs to be done, and if all I have to do to is sit here my entire life, I'm going to go insane! Besides, it's not my fault I look like this!"

"Well the fact is, you do!" My mother took in a deep breath, trying to reign in her voice, which had rose to a shout. She continued in a much quieter, but equally demanding tone. "I don't want to lose you just because you were bored and looking for something to do. Your father and I are doing all that we can to protect you, but if you keep choosing to be reckless, there is nothing we can do to save you! Not only are you getting yourself in trouble, but you are also threatening the safety of Conor, his family, and everyone else you selfishly pull into your thoughtless attempts to distract yourself from boredom."

At this, my father put his large hand on my shoulder, concern in his eyes. "Faradene, I agree with your mother. You can't drag other people into your business."

Furious, I stood up, throwing his hand off me. "I've done nothing wrong except be born like this! I shouldn't be treated like a child just because of my looks! I am old enough to take care of myself and make my own decisions!"

"Eighteen is hardly old enough to know what is right and wrong! You think you know more about the way things work because your father is on the council, but you're really just a naive child. You don't know anything about the real world," my mother argued.

"Because you never let me see it!" I was enraged, and I couldn't help from raising my voice. We've had this conversation before, and every time it grew worse and worse. We always wound up talking in circles, never really communicating anything, hearing rather than listening, reacting in place of considering, never getting anywhere. Still, I couldn't help but fight back. "It's not enough that everyone avoids me, but you also trap me in this room! You're no better than the guards! All I want is to do my part! Just let me live like everyone else!"

"You can never be like everyone else! Why can't you understand that?" She stopped yelling and opened her hands towards me, reaching to stroke my hair. I warily backed away, but she continued advancing. "You are a beautiful diamond in this coal mine. Just let your father and I take care of you and keep you out of danger." I batted her hands away, moving more quickly out of her outstretched arms.

"No. You can't treat me like this any-more. Father is a councilman, and you work every day with the children. Everyone looks up to you two. But me, I'm nothing more than a pretty face that can't carry her own weight. I'm sick of it! I'm done sitting around!"

"Faradene,"

"No! I hate this face, I hate the guards, and I hate you!" I tore out of the room, getting tangled in my father's cloak. Unravelling myself, I let it fall to the floor. Looking up from the blue bundle now dusted with dirt, my eyes met those of my father, nearly unrecognisable in the grief that had so quickly replaced the mirth present a few moments ago. Tearing my eyes from his, I fled into the darkness.

CHAPTER 3

I tore my way through the tunnels, running past the well and into one of the abandoned mines. Down here in Cethin, we mine nearly every mineral the wealthy Ahrenians could desire. When the rich want crystals for their dresses, we find them crystals. When they need coal for their fires, we find them coal. They expect us to be able to summon a vein of ore at their whim, but in reality, we are forced to dig deep into the earth, tunnelling in a wide web until we stumble upon a trace of whatever they demand.

The old mine I found myself in is a simple marble mine. It's one of my favourites, because the simple marble has rose veins running through it, making the ordinary beautiful. But tonight, it just made me more upset. I wish that I could be just plain white marble, like everyone else, but instead I have pink streaks running through me, separating me from the rest.

When I was young, all the children would attend lessons until they were strong enough to work. My mother was the teacher, and she taught us the basics on how to survive. Which roots are safe to eat, how to dry meat with salt, how to make cheese from goats milk, and most importantly, how to blend in. How to avoid the guards at all times, and how to react should they catch you doing anything they decide you shouldn't be doing. On occasion, she would teach us about the history of our community. Why we are destined to live in the dark while the rich live above ground. These lessons were my favourite for two reasons. Whenever she spoke of history, she would speak about the outdoors. Although she has never been, knows about it from her great great grandmother, who taught her great grandmother, who taught her grandmother, who taught her mother, who taught her. They almost sound like legends, these things called trees and flowers, a sun that rises and falls every day to tell you when to start anew. Down here, we have little sense of the time of day. With no sun or moon, night and day are trivial anachronisms that the guards hold on to in order to keep their sanity while they work underground. Us, we are accustomed to the lack of day and instead rely on special candles that reach a bulb of gunpowder at every hour to let us know how much time has passed. These as well are more for the guards' sake than our own. We have all adapted, more or less, to be on the same schedule. We rise together, we work together, and we fall together. Everything we do is done as a group. Which can make it all the more evident when someone doesn't exactly fit in.

Another reason I loved history was that we studied independently. When we had practical lessons, everyone had to partner up, but I always seemed to be singled out. It was only much later, looking back on it, that I found out it was because all of my classmates were warned by their families to stay away from me, as I could only bring trouble to them. I was not only a hazard to myself, it seemed, but to anyone who knew me. I would always beg my mother to let me do it on my own, but she would scold me and say that everyone needed a partner. So I would end up being paired with the boy or girl everyone decided to avoid that day. The sick one, the rude one, the slow one, and even they treated me coldly.

This cycle continued until Conor started to attend class. His mother and mine were good friends, so we grew up together. When his father passed away during a mining accident, we adopted their family, helping in any way we could until they got their feet back on the ground. Although Conor's older brothers avoided me, he didn't seem to care much, and despite being four years younger than me, he was mature enough for us to relate. Tall and skinny for his age, he was nearly as conspicuous as myself, which, when paired with his mischievousness, always seemed to lead to interesting stories. He never failed to come by my den afterwards and relay to me his latest adventures. It soon became my favourite part of the day, and I would eagerly wait for him to come and break the monotony of my life.

As the years went on, I found myself the eldest in the class by 2 years. I became uncomfortably aware of how much older I was once my body started changing, and finally asked my mom why she hadn't let me go work like all the other youths that had been in my class before. My mother had sighed and sat me down, explaining to me that I was different, that she and father needed to protect me. To do that, I couldn't work like everyone else. Naively, I asked them what I needed protection from. Their answer was simply "the King".

That was when I learned that the King instructs the guards to send him notice every time someone extraordinary is born in Cethin. If the King finds them worthy, they are brought to work as slaves in Ahrenia. I couldn't understand why they had to protect me from a future in the light. From all that I had learned in the history lessons, the surface was a beautiful place. For one thing, there were colours all around. Here in Cethin, the only colours are the dyed cloaks that have been passed on through generations, some brought down by the original Nethers, others obtained from the King along with their name.

"So let me into the light! I can always come back, right?" I had asked them. My mother and father looked at each other, and my father released a heavy sigh. "Even though they let you into the light, it doesn't mean you are free to enjoy it. You are a slave to their demand, and you have no family to protect you. And a girl as beautiful as you would be taken advantage of far too quickly. I can't allow anything like that to happen to you. So, you must hide your face from the guards. Only let them know you as another number. Never let them know just how beautiful you are."

After that day, my mother didn't make me go to class. Instead, I was forced to do chores in the safety of our den. Occasionally, when my mother wasn't teaching the children, she would give me more history lessons, science lessons, and even taught me how to read and write, an impractical skill unless you are a member of the council. In these dark tunnels, nobody cares if you know how to spell your name, but for me, it was one of my only respites. My father would often come home with scrolls that the guards discarded so that I had something of interest to read. But the scrolls rarely contained anything significant; the majority dressed the population of our community, requests for more supplies, reports on births and deaths. Any letters of actual importance were burned before anyone ever got to them.

The only other respite from my prison was if I was needed to help with outside chores. These came very rarely, and my mother always treated them with the utmost caution. If I ever had to leave the den, she would put dirt on my face and dress me in our dirtiest tunics in order to disguise my appearance. It was almost as if my looks were a crime, and I was forced to hide them should the guards find out that I was guilty. I quickly began to see my appearance as a curse, responsible for my detainment.

Coming back to the present, I traced the rose vein running through the cool marble. In a sudden act of fury, I smacked the smooth plane, wincing as the pain travelled up my hand and into my arm. The jolt of pain triggered an idea, and suddenly, I knew what I wanted to do. Like the marble, I could be both beautiful and strong. I wouldn't let anyone hit me without hitting back. With a plan forming in my head, I made my way back to our den, taking more caution than I did on my way here. I didn't want to run into a guard just quite yet.

CHAPTER 4

I slowly crept up to my family's den, hoping that they would be asleep, but the flicker of candlelight indicated otherwise. As I crept closer, I heard the soft murmur of voices. Dashing to the wall, I leaned against the dirt and listened in.

"We can't let her run around, Anso. It's too dangerous." My mother's tight voice was all too familiar.

"But we can't lock her up in here either. She's right. She needs something to do. Maybe she could help in another way. The council and I were talking about it, and," My mother cut him off.

"No. The fact that you even considered involving her in the council's business is unbelievable. It is too risky, no matter your plan. I won't allow her to get hurt."

"But all we need is one person to go above, one person to get close to the King, and maybe we can change something. Faradene certainly is beautiful enough to reach the surface, and if we plan right, she could make it out safely. Listen, Miriam. A messenger just came in a few hours ago. Surely he would deliver Faradene to the King." I pressed my ear to the wall, hoping to hear more, but it was silent. Eventually, I heard a slight sniffle as my mother began to cry. The sound was muffled, as if she were crying into my father's shirt.

"I know it's hard, Miriam. I'm not saying it has to be Faradene. Maybe we will be able to find someone else. But we must do what is best for the whole colony, even if it's at the expense of an individual. But enough talk for now. Let's get to rest. I'll go out and look for Faradene while you sleep."

Quickly, I snuck around the corner into the neighbouring den, lucky to find everyone asleep. I peered through the crack in the cloak, watching and waiting until my father walked down the trail and out of sight. I turned back to my den, with my father's blue cloak covering the door, a symbol of his power, protecting us from the rest of the world, sealing us together as a family. I slowly walked towards it, my hand extended to meet it's coarse, but well-worn, wool. With tears in my eyes, I bunched it into my fist, taking it all the stains that it had accumulated throughout its history. I ripped a small strip off the bottom and tied it around my wrist. As I released it, I watched it sway gently in front of the opening, providing a final glimpse into my den. I now had an answer, a way to help everyone in the only way I could. Kissing my hand, I placed it on the wall and turned around. It was time to get myself into trouble.

As a child, I was always curious about sunlight. My mother told me that it's like a giant ball of fire, lighting up the entire world until it leaves the sky and darkness resumes. I used to tell her that I thought it was sad how the setting sun leaves everyone in darkness, but then she told me about the moon. Something like the sun, but not so bright. And around the moon are specks of light called stars that fill the darkness. I could only imagine what a world full of colours, light, and darkness would look like. Before all the students began avoiding me, we would draw pictures during breaks in my mother's class about what we thought was on the surface. Sometimes my mother would join us and draw pictures while telling stories that have been passed down through generations about the world above, always sure to draw a sun shining in the sky over the land and animals she had created in the dirt.

Here in Cethin, everything is lit by lamplight. All the fuel for our lamps is mined down here. Our eyes are used to the dim yellow light, having never seen the sunlight. It takes the guards a bit longer to adapt to the change; consequently, for the first few days of their service, they are tasked with no other duty than to walk around the tunnels. A few have gotten lost, wandering in the outskirts of the network. Some were lucky enough to be stumbled upon by a Cethin, but the majority were lost forever, most likely having run out of fuel for their lantern and wandered deeper into the earth, where they may have fallen into a crevice, a hot underground stream, or any of the other risks that come with living underground. Mother says that the men used to the sun can go insane if they have to stay underground for too long. That's why the King switches them out every few years, but with some, even a few years can be too much. That's what the sun-room is for. When my mother was a child, she had heard news of a sun-room being constructed in the guards' quarters, which would open a hole large enough in the ceiling for the sunlight to come through and fill the room with natural light. Unsurprisingly, this room was made to be off limits from all Nethers, and as such, my mother absolutely forbade me from trying to get a glimpse of it. Every child is warned to stay away from the sun-room, mainly out of fear of what the guards might do to a lost child. But, of course, as with all children, as soon as my mother said it was off limits, I was immediately entranced with the idea of an adventure to the sun-room, and for a long time, I couldn't think of anything but trying to find a way into the room.

As time went on, thoughts of sunlight became rarer and rarer, replaced by preoccupations with chores and other duties, and soon the forbidden room was forced into a small corner in the back of my mind. I forgot about my desire to see the sun-room, just like my ancestors. The first ones exiled down here were too busy trying to establish a way to survive to worry about things like sunlight. By the second generation, we didn't know any different. And so the cycle continued.

Tonight, I was going to break the cycle. Approaching this very room, I wiped the grime off my face with the sleeve of my tunic, let my hair down, combed it with my fingers, and stepped through the entryway. Not knowing what to expect, I put my hands over my eyes and looked around through the cracks in my fingers.

The first thing I noticed was that there were many shirtless guards sleeping on raised mats. There were whips, clubs, and swords hanging from racks along the walls. From what I hear, these weapons are used in abundance by the guards who watch over the mines. There was also strong odor in the air, which I attributed to the fact that the guards find themselves too high of rank to share a latrine with us. They must have one dug somewhere nearby. Sweeping the room with my eyes, it occurred to me that the room was lit by candles as well. I looked for the tell-tale crack in the wall, and saw just a faint blue glow coming through the ceiling. I wondered if this was what the sun looked like, or if I was seeing the moon. Puzzled, I dropped my hands and looked around for a brighter light. As I turned to search, I saw a group of men sitting around a table, all looking at me with wide eyes. I took a few steps back into the shadow of the opening.

"Oy! What are you doing in here? I thought this room was off limits to you people." A large-bellied man about my father's age spoke to me, his voice shaking me out of my startled paralysis.

"I□I□I'm looking for the messenger." I managed to form a complete sentence with my suddenly heavy tongue.

"What would a girl like you want with the messenger? Not a soul in Ahrenia would dream of sending a message to a Nether, I can tell you that right now. Go on and leave this room." The man grumbled as he turned back around to face the table. Upon it were small, rectangular pieces of paper, thicker than the scrolls my father picked up for me, with small numbers and symbols on them.

A pale man at the same table peered up at me with a familiar glint in his eyes, which were shadowed by eyebrows thicker than the hair on his head. "Hold on a moment, Gethro. Don't be having' her leave too quick, now. These old card games are getting dull, and I've been achin' for some real entertainment for a while now. Hey lassie," he mentioned me over to him by opening his legs and patting his thigh, but my feet remained planted in the ground, "why don't you come over here and join me? You could be my good luck charm."

"Isaac, I would quit running your mouth before you get ahead of yourself. What with you being so drunk and all, I doubt you would get very far before that alcohol gets the best of you. You'd just end up wasting her."

The men at the table sniggered, and the man named Isaac stood angrily, looking like he was about to fight, when he stumbled on his feet and instead fell into the mat behind him in a sprawl, which only heightened the men's laughter.

Hoping I could use the guards current good humour to my advantage, I asked again.

"I need to speak to the messenger. I believe I know something that may interest him."

This raised their attention. The large man, Gethro, turned back around to face me, leaning his arm against the back of his chair, one eyebrow raised.

"Is that so? Why don't you tell us and we will decide for ourselves."

With that, I stepped further into the room and into the candlelight. I felt the energy in the air shift as I came into view, the candlelight flickering across my face, illuminating that which I had been forced to hide for so long.

"I've come to ask for evaluation. If the messenger sees me fit, I wish to offer my services to the King and work on the surface."

Gethro stood from his chair and walked towards me. "Al-right. You say you want to see the messenger? Fine. I'll take you to the messenger." He grabbed me by the arm and roughly directed me towards another opening on the left side of the room. Pushing aside the curtain, he shoved me in front of him and into the room.

The room was much darker than the one we had just left, and it took a few seconds for my eyes to adjust until I could make out the man at the end of the room. The tall, well-dressed man I assumed to be the King's messenger was writing on a scroll at his table. He was much younger than I thought he would be, only a few years older than myself. Startled at our brash entrance, he looked up. He tucked a strand of blond hair behind his ear, which had fallen out of his ponytail. It rested against his tanned skin, an obvious sign that he was from the surface. Even the guards tent to wear a dull pallor, their colour having faded after only a few months underground.

There were strange, clear pieces of glass that the messenger held up to his eyes, making them appear very large and very blue. When he lowered the glass pieces, I had to hold back a chuckle, as his eyes now seemed too small for his face. His mouth was twisted into a grimace, as if he had just taken a sip of spoiled goats milk. The overall effect was less than intimidating.

"Can I help you?" He had an unpleasant, nasally tone that seemed to say, "I'm too important for you, why are you wasting my time?" I considered whether of not I wanted to spend my journey to Ahrenia with this man, or it I should wait for another, more amiable Ahrenian. Before I could make up my mind, Gethro shoved me further into the room.

"This lass here wants to be evaluated. Thinks she has what it takes to go to the surface." Gethro eyed me up and down appreciatively, making it all too apparent that at least he believed that I did, indeed, have "it". When his eyes trailed up to meet mine, he grinned suggestively. My face flamed and I looked away.

"I'll be the one to decide that," the messenger announced. He waited a few moments before clearing his throat. "Alone. You are dismissed." I kept my eyes down during this exchange, only looking up after hearing the flutter of the curtain that announced Gethro's leave.

"So you want to get out of here? I can't say I blame you. Now come over this way so I can see what you've got to offer. I can't see you in the dark." He stepped towards me and turned me around slowly, taking me in from every angle. I tried to suppress the chills running down my back as I felt his eyes rake my body, but when he put his hand on the back of my neck, I couldn't help but flinch. I heard him chuckle under his breath as he brushed my hair to the side, revealing my number. He asked me and I stepped closer, turning around so he could read my neck.

"923." He turned me back around, his hands starting at my shoulders, then trailing it down my sides. After reaching my hip, he rose one hand, cupping my chin firmly in his grasp, then used the other to pull me against him, so that his hand could slide all the way around and grip my rear. I pulled back a bit in surprise, but he kept his grip, rotating my face from side to side, his expression contemplative. "Your face is fair enough, and you have developed well. It's a shame you don't have more meat on your bones, though. I guess it can't be helped. I wouldn't expect you Nethers to know how to farm anything other than mud." He gave my rear end another squeeze, and I gasped in alarm, to which he simply commented, "It seems pretty firm. However, I'm afraid that I can't see your shape under that potato sack you're wearing. I don't suppose you would mind taking it off so I can get a better look?"

I glowered at him, and with every ounce of dignity I could muster, I told him, "That is up for the King to decide. He is the one who must evaluate me, I only need you to take me to him." At that, the messenger slapped me across the face, then caught it so that he was looking me directly in the eyes. I held his glare, refusing to back down.

"You have no right to speak to me that way. You are scum. Just another worm in the dirt. I don't have to do anything for you. For all I care, I could evaluate you right here, in whichever way I choose. Or, better yet, I could send you to the guards, let them decide whether or not you are good enough for the King." With my chin still in his grip, he used one hand to rip my tunic down, revealing my chest. His eyes tracked their way down, studying, and I wanted so bad to disappear, shame flooding my face. When he was done, he dropped my chin my face to the side, leaving me to pull my tunic back up over my shoulder. My eyes watered from both the shame and the slap, but I refused to shed a tear. Instead, I glowered at him, my eyes burning with hatred and anger. He tasked his tongue, turning back towards his desk.

"I have no doubt that, by looks alone, you would make a nice addition to the King's slaves. However, as far as your performance goes," he paused and looked at me in a way that had my stomach rolling, "well, I'm sure I'll get a chance to test that out on the way to the capital." He took out another scroll, and glanced back up. "923. That's you, is it not? Just another number."

Furious at this man for making me feel so ashamed, but determined to not let him see, I fisted my hands until my fingernails dug into my palms. If I wanted to help my people, I would have to be strong. So I held my tongue and just watched his hand as he wrote down my number as well as a few notes.

After the messenger finished writing, he peered back up at me.

"What, you're still here? I'm leaving an hour before sunrise. I don't want to see you until then. And bring your own supplies. Don't expect me to take care of you if you forget anything either. Now get out of my sight."

Flustered, I left the room, and once again found myself amidst a group of guards. The men at the table were still invested in their paper cards, so I was able to make my way out of the room without gaining any-more unwanted attention. Once I was back in the hall, I thought about what the messenger had told me. I needed to find myself some food, drink, and supplies for the journey. The problem was that I had no idea what to expect above ground, nor did I have access to my room to pack supplies. I paced around the hall, trying to form a plan in my head, when I remembered the supply room. I rejected it and tried to think of other solutions, but finally, with a guilty conscience, I headed down the hall.

CHAPTER 5

There was a storage room that my mother used to take her classes to on the days we worked with roots and animals, in which you could find not only food reserves but also mining supplies such as gloves and hammers. Although I hated to take anything from the already low provisions, I really had no other choice. I tried to justify this by telling myself that what I was doing was for the best of the colony, but I still couldn't shake the heavy feeling in my gut as I entered the storage room.

I stood in the entrance-way, astonished by how much lower the rations were compared to the last time I was here, taking inventory with my mother. Where the shelves used to be filled now had but a few items haphazardly splayed out They were spread out as if someone hoped that, by putting more space between the items, it wouldn't look so desperately empty. I tried to ignore the stone in my heart and think rationally. What would I need for a journey of an unknown length in an unknown land with unknown people? The reality of the situation hit me, and I fell against the wall for balance, knocking down one of the sacks from the shelves. It was sitting among some of the other sacks, most of which were nearly empty, but this one was still completely filled. It must have been on of the bags that was brought here long ago, out of the hope that we would be able to grow a larger diversity of crops. However, we never had much success, as the seedlings needed more sunlight than we could offer. We normally used these dormant seeds to feed our goats and chickens, but there were some seeds that were toxic to eat, so they were destined to rot on these underground shelves. The bag I had knocked down split open, and a waterfall of seeds began to spill out. Frantically, I tried to shovel them back into the sack.

I gathered the majority of the seeds back in the sack, and while I was picking up the last few seeds, I found one that had already sprouted. A small, green leaf was just beginning to emerge from the brown shell. I slumped against the wall, holding the seed in my palm, wondering about the fate of this delicate leaf. Would it would ever be planted? If so, would it even have a chance at life down here, never to see the sunlight? Sitting there, meditating on the seed, I found a reserve of strength that helped me push on. I dropped in down my shift and got back to business.

I browsed through the shelves, grabbing some potato buns, carrots and tubers, hard cheeses, a water skin, and a pair of boots, leaving my tweed slippers in their place. Condensing two bags of potatoes together into one, I used the now-empty sack to hold all my supplies. On an impulse, I grabbed a small, dull knife, and made my way back to the sunroom.

Even though I was sure that, at this hour, everyone would be asleep, I still kept to the less frequented, and consequentially less lit, tunnels. I slowly made my way around the corner, my hand extended to feel for anything in front, when it suddenly made contact with something warm and soft. I screamed and dropped my bag, spilling its contents across the floor. Hastily, I picked everything up before I even looked up to see who had caught me, until I saw a small hand pick up the knife. Raising my gaze from the floor, I was met by Conor's light brown eyes.

"What are you doing up so late, Conor? You ought to be in bed!"

"What am I doing? I think think the better question is what are you doing, skulking around the tunnels in the middle of the night? I'm notorious for my mischievousness. You're notorious for, well, getting yourself into trouble." I glared at him and he just shrugged. "Fine. Don't answer. It doesn't matter. I already know what you're doing." I felt my heart skip a beat. "You're probably going to go explore the old mines. Or, are you going down to the hot spring? Wait, I know, you're going to look for the body of that guard who got lost a few months ago!" I let loose an internal sigh of relief, realizing he didn't have any idea of what I was going to do. I decided to let him continue, convincing himself of whatever it was he thought I was doing. "Seriously, which one is it? I went to go apologize for telling your mom about the guard, and you weren't there. Your dad asked me where you were," he stopped and looked more serious. "He's looking for you, you know. Your parents are really worried about you."

I felt a rush of annoyance, followed by a pang of guilt. "Conor, you can't tell them where I am, and I can't tell you where I'm going, either." He opened his mouth in protest, but I shook my head and held up my hand. "You're not coming, and I really don't have time to talk. I have to go!" I reached for my knife, but he stepped back, keeping it out of my reach.

"No. I'm not giving it to you until you tell me where you're going." When I didn't respond , he lowered himself into a crouch, challenging, "I'm faster than you. I could run and tell your parents what you're doing." He and I glared at each other until I groaned and rolled my eyes.

"Fine! You're so stubborn, you know that?" He simply grinned and stuck out his tongue. "But you really can't tell anyone. At least not until I'm gone." I took a breath and braced myself for his reaction. "I'm going to Ahrenia. I'm going to the surface."

"Oh." That was definitely not the reaction I was expecting.

"What do you mean, oh? It's not like its everyday someone goes to the surface."

"Well, to be honest, I've been expecting it for a while. You aren't allowed to do anything down here any-ways. You can't be happy, even with me for company." He looked up to me with a sad smile,"I just wish you didn't have to abandon us like this."

"Conor, listen to me. I'm not abandoning you. I would never do something like that. I'd much rather live down here than with those stupid, selfish surface dwellers," I justified. Never before had anyone in Cethin volunteered themselves for inspection, but there was an unspoken consensus that it was one of the worst possible things someone could do. It would essentially be a renouncement of our people, a way of saying that the surface and all that they have done to us was justified, that their ways of living are correct. I shuddered to think that this was what people would think of me after today. But as much as I didn't want everyone to think I deserted them, I knew I couldn't tell anyone what I was doing for fear of them interfering. But still, the thought of being labelled a traitor, a deserter, stung more than I would have liked.

"Then why are you leaving? Did your parents force you out for what happened earlier? I could talk to them, tell them it wasn't your fault!"

"No, Conor, it isn't that. They don't know I'm leaving, and you can't tell them." My heart broke when I saw tears begin to form in his eyes. "Oh, I'm gonna miss you," I said, pulling him into a hug. When I released him, I hurriedly whispered to him my plan, and I asked him to tell my parents my plan after two weeks, so they wouldn't think that they've been disgraced by their daughter, but also wouldn't be able to follow me. We hugged again, and he wished me luck, handing me back the knife.

"Keep yourself out of trouble!" I told him as we split apart. Walking separate ways, I gave him one last wave and disappeared around the corner.

CHAPTER 6

I hoped that I wasn't too late. Or too early, for that matter. Honestly, I had no idea when the sun would rise. I figured that I was right on time when I walked back into the sun-room and there were more guards awake than before, getting ready for duty. Some guards had just finished their watch shift, which they still call "night duty", partly because they sill wished to maintain their routines from the surface, and partly because when everyone is in their den, we turn off most of the lanterns to save fuel. As I walked to the messenger's room, I passed under the slit and saw that the sky was darker that it had been before. I was disoriented, thinking that I had been mistaken, and that I still had more time before we would leave. Standing with my head tilted towards the crack, I was startled when the guard from the day before, Gethro, said from behind me, "It's always darkest before the dawn."

Confused, I spun around and asked, "What is?"

"The sky," he replied, and then left the room. I pondered this as I made my way towards the messengers' room, and with a deep breath, stepped in through the curtain.

The messenger was standing in front of the desk, assembling the papers in his pack, when I entered the room. He looked up at me and greeted, "So you actually made it. Well, it's good that you did, because I was about to leave without you." He closed his bag and swung a cloak over his shoulders as he walked towards the entrance. Wen he reached me, I shied back a bit, not wanting to get in his way and have a repeat of last time. He just raised an eyebrow and walked through the entrance, the curtain swinging behind him. I stood there, not knowing what to do, until he stuck his head back in the room. "Why are you just standing there? Come on, the horse is waiting."

Upon hearing the word "horse", my heart leapt. Did I hear him right? I had heard stories about the tall, elegant beasts that we had once ridden on the surface, and the tight bonds we formed with each animal, trusting them to get us where we needed to be, safely. Down here, we had no use for horses. The only livestock down here were sheep, hens, goats, and the occasional pig. Our cats were able to fend for themselves, staving off the rats and mice that occupy the tunnels with us. We didn't have the resources to spare for dogs, and anything else would impractical.

"Are you just gonna stand there and stare at me like an imbecile? I swear, you Nethers have the mental capacity of a shrew." Still stunned by the idea of seeing a horse, it took me a few moments to realize that he was insulting me, but it didn't make a difference. I was still going to see an actual horse!

"I'm sorry, did you say we would ride a horse?" I had to make sure I heard correctly before I let my excitement get the best of me.

"Just when I thought you couldn't surprise me with your idiocy. Are you daft? I'm not letting you on my horse. You can ride the baggage mule." With that, he pulled his head back out of the room. Having little other choice, I followed him through the sun-room and out a tunnel I hadn't noticed before. I turned around to give the sun-room one last glance, and noticed that the crack in the wall seemed to be faintly glowing, the dark blue colour from before having changed to a lighter grey. Wondering what was ahead, I jogged to catch back up with the King's messenger and stuck close to his heels, my footsteps in time with my racing heart.

The tunnels leading to the exit twisted and turned, weaving around in a puzzle used by the King to keep us from escaping our underground prison. Anyone who tried to flee the tunnels would end up getting lost in the maze. As children, the adults told us tales of people going insane, finding themselves at dead ends that all seemed to be the same until eventually they would collapse from exhaustion. There was no water in this part of the cave, and I was glad that I had brought my water skin along with me. Not knowing how much longer we had to go, I tried to ration it wisely. I was walking behind the messenger from a safe distance, having learned my lesson from when we had first set off. Upon entering the darkness of the tunnel, before he had lit his torch, I extended my hand out to find him, when, without warning, he pulled me into his chest, pressing me against him, his hands squeezing my rear. With a shout, I shoved him off, and he simply smirked and told me to mind myself. In these dark tunnels lit by only his lamplight, I had no choice. So I trailed behind at a distance, barely close enough so that I didn't loose him in the darkness, but far away enough to assure he wouldn't be able to lay his hand on me again. I couldn't help but wonder how the he didn't get lost, that is until I saw the small map he held in his hand which he would consult every few turns. Curious, I tried to look over his shoulder to see where the map was taking us, but he very quickly caught on and hid his map from my sight.

And so we travelled on, in what seemed like an endless circle. I kept thinking back to the stories about the men and women loosing their mind in these tunnels, now beginning to understand how maddening it was when you had absolutely no idea where you were headed. After what seemed like an eternity, the messenger finally spoke up.

"Are you just going to creep behind me this entire time? Don't get me wrong, I wasn't planning on you being an interesting companion. I mean, you probably wouldn't be able to sustain a conversation for very long what with all that dirt stuck in your ears and all, but I figured you would at least know how to talk." He glanced over his shoulder at me, and I stared down at the path. He laughed and kept walking, talking all the while.

"Fine. No matter if you won't speak with me, I can still talk to you. I've got plenty to say." He proceeded to tell me, in vulgar detail, about his collection of lovers. He especially enjoyed explaining the lovemaking, and by the middle of the third story, this one taking place in the bed of an unknowing duke, I was seriously considering taking a wrong turn and getting myself lost just to escape his ramblings.

"That pretentious duke, he thought he could make me look like a fool. Well, me and my lass showed him. While he was off on another one of his fancy dinners-I swear, that man ate more than the pigs served at the feast-I grabbed one of the servant girls and we had ourselves a jolly time in his bed, if you know what I mean. What she lacked in brains she made up for with beauty and a willingness to experiment. We didn't waste any time, either. Her blasted gown had so many buttons, so in a feat of strength fuelled by the passion of the moment, I managed to cleanly rip the back of her gown open. What can I say, duty calls!" He looked at my horrified expression and winked. "Ha! Maybe I should have myself a girl before a wrestling match! I would undoubtedly win, the power of love flowing through my veins and giving me strength." He flexed his muscles and boxed with an imaginary enemy, throwing his hands up in apparent victory after a few jabs, celebrating with the invisible crowd. "Any-ways, once we got that dress off of her, I grabbed,"

"That's enough!" I protested. "Fine! What do you want me to talk about?"

"Aha! She speaks! Go on," he prompted.

"I doubt there's little you want to ask me. Ahrenians already think that they know everything there is to know. They also seem to think that we don't know how to do anything other than dig. So I don't see why you want to talk to me, unless you're interested in learning how to mine. If you Ahrenians would just open your minds a little, you would realize that you're not as smart as you think you are."

"Is that right? Well then, why don't you enlighten me on how advanced you ground-dwellers are."

I considered picking up one of the many stones on the ground and chucking it at his head, but instead I answered, "We do plenty. All those gems on the dresses of your lovers, or on the coats you wear to all your parties. Where do you think the gems came from?" I huffed.

L. T. Kenneth

"So you can pick up a heavy hammer and smash rocks. Big deal. We have slaves that could do that for us."

"But do they know exactly where in the rock the best ore will come from? Or how to extract it without bringing down the entire cavern? Do they know how to tunnel so far underground that an entire community of people can survive without seeing the sun? Do they know where to dig a latrine so the water washed the waste away downstream without polluting everyone's drinking water? Do they know which roots are safe to eat and which ones kill with even the slightest touch of the lips? Your slaves don't know anything. We don't just survive down here. We are able to make a living." The echoes of my rant echoed through the tunnels, and I fumed in the silence, opening and closing my hands into fists. Never had I encountered anyone who could make me so angry so quickly.

"Al-right, I'll admit it. I'm slightly impressed," He said, putting his hands up in surrender. We took some steps in the momentary silence, myself thinking that I had finally shut him up, but then he opened his darned mouth again. "So how do you do all that?"

My new-found confidence from my small victory deflated. "I don't really know. I was never allowed to go out and work because people like you were always there to cause trouble." Determined to impress him, I added, "But I do know how to read and write. I only get to read the scrolls that you bring the guards, which aren't very interesting by the way, but it helps me pass the time. I also know a lot of stories about the surface, but I don't know how many are true."

The messenger looked over his shoulder at me again, with an expression I hadn't seen before. This smile was less menacing and more sincere. "The name's Croxley. If you want, I can answer some questions about the surface before we reach it. That is, if you still know how to use your tongue." He turned back around, taking us around another corner.

Astonished, I didn't know whether or not he was pulling my leg or being sincere. But by the way he allowed me to think in silence, I figured his offer was genuine. I thought about the stories my mother used to tell me, but had trouble thinking of which question I wanted to ask first. Finally, I gave up trying to pick just one and replied, "Tell me everything about the surface. What does it look like? Is the sun so bright that it burns your eyes? How many colours are there? I hear that there are about thirty species of animals. Also, what do you,"

"Whoa!" He cut me off, and even though his back was turned to me, I could hear his smile in his voice. "Um, let's see. No, the sun doesn't burn your eyes, just don't look directly at it for too long. There are lots of colours depending on what you are looking at. And on the surface, there

24

is a lot to look at. There isn't just one surface. There are deserts that are just sand, with the occasional bush, and these tall, spiny things called cacti. Then there are mountains. The highest ones get this white, powdery, cold stuff called snow that falls from the sky. Most mountains are forested, which means they have a lot of trees and bushes and flowers. Ahrenia has a few mountains, and is mostly forested. Only a few areas get snow in the winter, but we get rain all year." He tapped his thumb against his lips, thinking about what else to say.

Animals love the forests, and trust me, there are far more than thirty species. You've got deer, rabbits, these nasty things called skunks, and tons of birds, which fly around the trees. There are also a lot of bugs, most of which are devil spawn, but some are tolerable, like the butterfly. And then you've got the ocean, which is an endless span of salt water. I can't really tell you much about that because I actually haven't been there. But apparently there are these enormous animals that swim around, and they battle sea monsters that take down fishing ships." He stopped and looked back, and I made no attempt to hide my amazed expression. He smirked and asked, "Am I going to fast?"

I couldn't stop smiling. So much that I had learned about the surface was true, and those was only the basics. There was more than I could ever imagine to this new land, and it was both exciting and overwhelming. My heart lifted a little, and I prepared another round of questions.

"Can you explain flying? Is it like running? And how does water get salty? What do you-"

Crowley started laughing at my rapid fire of questions, and it struck me just how nice of a laugh he had when it wasn't directed towards making me feel insignificant. "Look who's talking now! I knew I could get it out of you. Before you ask any more questions, let me ask you something. What am I supposed to call you?"

"923", I answered automatically.

"I'm not going to bother to try and remember those numbers. You must have something else for me to use."

"I don't. My number was given to me by the King, and it is has been my only name for my entire life."

He peered at me, and I couldn't tell if he believed me. "Fine. Then I'll give you a name," he announced. "Let's see☐I had myself a girl named Beatrice one time, she was impressively flexible"

"No. That is never going to happen." I tried to come up with a way around being named Beatrice without giving away the fact that my parents had illegally given me a name. "I guess you can call me Faradene. I read the name in one of the reports and thought it was nice."

"Oh yuck. That's worse than Beatrice. Here, I'll give you a nickname. Instead, I'll call you: Fara. She was a beautiful, hard-headed woman who fought valiantly against invaders during a magnificent battle a few centuries ago. You seem to be just as obstinate as she. Plus, Fara sounds like fair. Yup. I like it. Fara it is."

Despite myself, I actually liked Fara. A new name for a new beginning. But deep down, I knew I would forever in my heart be Faradene. I won't forget who I am and what I'm meant to do. "Fara is better than Beatrice," I decided. "Now, about the ocean"

CHAPTER 7

"I promise you, that's the best way to explain it. Clouds are like floating clumps of wool in the sky. Some are thin wisps, others are thick enough for you to sleep on. If you look long enough, they can change shape to look like animals, castles, whatever you imagine."

"How can something so big float in the sky?" I had been asking questions for the last few hours. Well, really, I had no idea how much time had passed, but since I started asking questions, I lost track of how many turns we had taken, how long we had walked down each tunnel. My feet seemed to have picked up a rhythm, my steps carrying me forward as if with a mind of their own. While my body moved on it's own accord, I was able to focus my mind on forming a picture of the world above.

I was grateful to Croxley for being so forthcoming, but I still didn't trust him. I'm sure that his interest in me came from pure boredom rather than kindness. Nonetheless, that didn't stop me from monopolizing on the wealth of knowledge he had about something that was so distant to me.

Just as I was about to ask another question, he held up his hand. It suddenly occurred to me that the cave had gotten significantly brighter. The light from the lantern was barely discernible from the light in the tunnel. I hoped this meant that our journey was coming to an end.

As if reading my thoughts, Croxley announced, "We are just about there. I've got the mule and the horse tied up in the next room."

The last tunnel seemed endless in my anticipation. In my excitement I started walking so quickly that I ended up in front of Croxley. "Where do you think you're going," he called out. I turned around to look at him, and he smiled. The corner of his eyes crinkled, and something in his expression made my stomach turn in a way that wasn't entirely unpleasant.

But before I could really think about it, the feeling was replaced once again by repulsion. Keeping in character, Croxley slapped my rear as he passed from behind me, whistling a tuneless song as he finished the curve and left me in the tunnel. With a groan, I walked into the cavern, ready to give him a piece of my mind, but my reprimand was cut short when two large beasts came into sight.

Croxley was placing a blanket on the back of the larger beast while it drank out of the water trough in front of the post it was tied to. I assumed this one was the horse. It was magnificent, majestic. A deep, chestnut brown, its coat had a splatter of white spots on its rear. Along it's neck was a thick mane, much more impressive than those of our goats, and on its rear a tail that was braided much like my own hair. Around its hooves were thick, white cuffs that gradually blended into the deep brown of its long, elegant legs.

My eyes were soaking up every detail of the horse, memorizing each curve of its muscular frame, every glimmer in its shining pelt. When I finally was able to remove my gaze from the horse, I turned it to the mule. This creature was more comical than majestic, with tall ears and a short mane that stood straight up. It was a rich rust colour, with a big splotch of white on its nose. As I walked up to it, it swiftly came up to me, pressing its nose into my hand and flexing its lips over my fingers.

"Ahh! What's it doing?" I yelped, yanking my hand back and checking it for all five fingers.

"He's just looking for a snack is all. Hey, it looks like he found some! Atta boy, Samuel!"

I turned around to find the mule's head in my bag, pulling out the carrots I had packed for myself. "Hey, give those back!" I yelled, jumping forward and grabbing the carrots by the leaves. Fighting against the mule for the carrots, I finally gave up when I felt his drool dip down the carrots and onto my arm.

"Yuck!" I exclaimed, shaking my hands towards Croxley, purposefully flinging the goo in his direction. He dodged, but I still managed to get some in his hair, which he picked out and flung towards the ground. "What did you call him," I asked as I was wiping the rest of the drool off my hands onto my shift. "Samuel?"

"Yeah. It's really a bad joke. Get it, Sam the Mule? But good 'ol Sam doesn't mind, do ya boy?" Croxley reached out and gave Sam a hard pat on the shoulder, and I watched as a cloud of dust rose from his coat. Croxley returned to loading his gear onto to the horse's back, and I slowly crept up behind him, getting as close as I dared to this intimidating animal.

"And the horse? What is its name?"

"This isn't just any horse, it's a stallion. And he happens to be named Sir Thunderclap Fire-bolt."

I stared at him in disbelief. "There is no way I'm calling him Sir Thunderbolt Fire-spout, or whatever it is, even if he is a stallion□by the way, what exactly is a stallion?"

"Well, basically, he hasn't had his manhood removed. So, like me, this handsome guy can get to all the women he wants." He looked back towards me, standing in a position I assumed was supposed to be impressive, but with traces of mule drool still dripping from his hair and dirt from the tunnels dusting his clothes, I couldn't help but laugh. And once I started, I couldn't stop. I felt like all the stress from the day seemed to be escaping with every laugh, and so I let myself go into the moment of joy, knowing that my high spirits probably wouldn't last.

"What are you laughing at?" He frowned at me, tightening the strap around Sir Thunder's waist. I tried to answer, pointing to his hair, but each laugh was pulling me closer and closer to the ground, until I was sitting there, breathless, hiccups interrupting my slowing chuckles. He sighed and rolled his eyes. "Fine. You just sit there while I load up all of the rest of our supplies on Sam, and then we are leaving."

Croxley had us walk Sam and Sir Thunder, which was my nickname for the stallion, through the last length of tunnel. It had gotten much brighter to the point where we no longer needed the lantern. I felt my legs tremble with excitement, my imagination aflame with all the new information Croxley had given me, mixed with what I had already known before.

As we left the tunnel, the sudden light attacked my eyes, and I shielded them against the sensory onslaught. Blinking rapidly, I tried to clear the blinding glare of the sun out of my eyes. While they were still clearing, my ears picked up on a confusing array of sounds. My mind supplied me with a few answers, telling me that the soft whispers I heard was the wind, and the subtle babbling was water flowing over rocks. Others were lost to me, like the high-pitched whistles echoing through the forest. To add to the over-stimulation, my poor nose, used to the slightly metallic smell of the mines and the stale air of the caves, was suddenly attacked by a wide array of scents. It reminded me of when we would till the garden underground, revealing the dark soil and sprinkling it with animal dung, but on a much larger scale.

"Welcome to Ahrenia! Don't worry, you'll get used to the sun. It just takes a few minutes." Croxley had been walking in front of me, but now I could barely make out his shape.

"Will the sun always do this? I can't see a thing!" I stretched my hands out and grabbed onto Sam to keep me from tripping.

"Excuse me, what are you doing," Croxley said, and I feel his mouth move under my hand.

I squinted, mortified upon the realization that I had placed my hands directly atop Croxley's head. "Oh! Sorry! I thought you were the mule!"

"Is that supposed to be an insult?" He teased, pretending to be offended. "No matter. Don't cover your eyes, it will only make the process much longer. Just keep them open and they'll adjust."

Gradually, through squinted eyes, my vision returned until I could make out my surroundings. I was flooded with colours, so many different shades of greens and browns, and even some reds and yellows. The assault on my senses left me feeling strangely vulnerable. Used to having the walls of the earth to protect me, being out in the open instilled me with a fresh sense of fear and vulnerability alongside a renewed vigour for adventure.

"I thought that trees were supposed to be green. Why do these have red and orange leaves?" I walked up to a tree and rubbed its leaves between my fingers. The underside was soft, velvety, while the upper side was waxy. It broke off in my hand, and I gasped. "Oh no! I'm sorry, I didn't mean to do that! What's gonna happen? Is it going to die?"

Croxley chuckled and removed another leaf. I gaped at him, distressed for this giant plant we were slowly torturing. "Don't worry. I don't think losing a few leaves has ever caused a tree to die. Besides, this one looks like it's about to lose its leaves any-ways."

"Why? Is it sick?" Concerned for the tree's health, I inspected its thick trunk, troubled by the bits of bark peeling off.

"Hardly. It's just changing seasons. It's autumn, which is when many trees lose their leaves to prepare for winter. Before the leaves fall, they change colours. It's really quite beautiful."

"Oh." That was all I could muster. I looked around and saw many different types of trees losing their leaves, alongside trees that had long, sharp, dark green needles coming out where the leaves should be. There seemed to be plants of every size and colour. Some of them even had flowers, which were like nothing I had ever seen before. While scanning the landscape in front of me, my eyes suddenly stopped on a bush with small white berries. My mouth began to water as my mind processed what it was seeing. I was accustomed to a few kinds of tubers and vegetables, but underground we couldn't grow fruit. The sweetest things we had to eat were carrots. I examined the bush, wondering how they would taste. Croxley must have noticed, because he called out a warning.

"I wouldn't touch those if I were you, Fara. Those are poisonous."
My spirits deflated, and I wondered if I would ever be able to taste the food that had always made my stomach rumble when learning about

them in my mother's classes. While I was lamenting my lack of berries, Croxley jumped up on Sir Thunder, making it look effortless. He looked back at me as if he expected me to do the same.

Sam and I just stared at each other. I hadn't the slightest idea how I was going to get on. "Um, pardon me, Sam. I'm just gonna climb up on you now." As I tried to pull myself up, Sam moved forward, causing me to lose my balance. "Just hold still!" With an effort, I jumped up and landed with my stomach laying across his back. Okay, I was on the mule, but now what? Swinging my body around, I tried to sit up, but my tunic wouldn't let my legs split. Shooting a look at Croxley, I noticed he was watching me with an amused grin pasted on his smug face. I scowled and he turned and urged Sir Thunder forward.

Abandoning all modesty, I hitched my frock's skirt above my knees and put my legs on both sides. "Go on. Walk. Move. Forward, Sam. Go!" My efforts were useless. Sam just sat there, chewing on some grass.

"Just kick him in the sides," Croxley called back to me.

Kick him in the sides? I was suspicious that Croxley was trying to get me thrown off, but I wasn't having any success my way, so I lightly tapped Sam with my heels. Not surprisingly, he didn't move.

"Harder! He would have felt a fly before feeling that kick!" Croxley called back, having turned Sir Thunder around to watch me struggle.

"Um, okay. Sorry, Sam!" With more power this time, I kicked him and was nearly thrown off his back when he surged forward. "Ahhh!!!"

"Fara, come back!" Laughing, Croxley kicked Sir Thunder into a run to catch up to us. I grabbed onto Sam's neck as he slowed down to a more leisurely pace, while Sir Thunder settled beside us. Sam just huffed and resumed chewing on the grass he still had in his mouth.

"See? Easy!"

I shot him a glare. "Al-right, I will admit this is somewhat enjoyable." I tried to let my hips sway to the rhythm of Sam's gait, finding it a bit more comfortable as I grew more relaxed. After a while, though, I could feel a pain radiating from my tail-bone into my hips. "How long until we get to the capital? A few hours?" I asked Croxley.

"Try a few days," he called back over his shoulder.

My shock must have been obvious, because he continued with, "Don't worry, time flies much faster here than in the tunnels."

Wondering what I had signed myself up for, I realized that I really didn't think it through before running off. Hoping that I could find a way to help my people, I resigned myself to a long journey.

"This isn't so bad, is it?" I patted Sam on the neck as I gave one last glance towards the cave before it disappeared into the forest.

CHAPTER 8

This was bad. I don't think I have ever been in this much pain. After riding all day, I felt like I would never be able to sit again. When Croxley finally announced it was time to set up camp, I groaned with relief and nearly threw myself off of Sam. Rubbing my sore end, I was baffled at Croxley's ability to slide off Sir Thunder so gracefully, not seeming to have any ill effects from the long ride.

The only thing to distract me from my aching behind was the sunset. It was absolutely breathtaking. The trees broke to reveal a pink sky, the sun casting long shadows on the trees below as it disappeared behind the mountains in the distance. I stood there, as I certainly couldn't sit, until the sun disappeared completely. Within a few minutes, the sky began to fade into a dark blue.

Watching the sunset gave me a pang of homesickness. I thought back to the time when I had told my mother that I would be sad when the sun set, and I couldn't help but smile as I corrected my seven year old self in my mind. Yes, the departure of the sun was sad, because all the wonderful things it revealed would soon be clad in darkness, but it gave such a beautiful goodbye that I couldn't help but feel like a wonderful gift would come with the new day.

Before I could even begin to miss the sun, small, bright lights began to dot the sky. I watched as more and more appeared, and I connected them in my head, forming pictures in the night sky.

"Fara, I lit a fire. Now that the sun is down, it will begin to get much colder. Not to mention the predators start to come out," Croxley said, coming up from behind me and pulling my attention from the sunset.

Giving one last glance towards the sky, I turned away from the ledge and walked to the fire. Croxley had tied Sir Thunder and Sam to a tree next to our supplies and was sitting on his cloak near the fire. He was eating some kind of dried meat with a loaf of bread. Having rationed my food throughout the day, I still had some roots and bread left, but I couldn't say that I was excited to eat it.

To be honest, I missed my mother's stew.

Following Croxley's example, I sat near the fire, wincing as my rear end touched the ground. "How can you sit so easily? Aren't you sore, you know, here," I asked, motioning to my rear area.

"No, I'm used to riding. I'm very good at it, you know. Hence, messenger." He gestured towards his apparel, and then added suggestively, "But if you'd like, I can massage you, make it feel better, get you nice and loosened up." I glared at him, and he shrugged in response, ripping apart another piece of meat. I tore a piece of my potato loaf and put it in my mouth, taking a drink of water to wash the dry bread down. Then I picked up the root, about to take a bite, but stopped at the bewildered look on Croxley's face.

"What?"

"What on earth are you eating? It looks some form of animal waste."

"It's a tuber. When the King forced us all underground, we had to breed special vegetables that could survive with little light. We mostly eat root vegetables, and we have some livestock for milk, eggs, and cheese. I did have some carrots, but your mule stole them." Sam grunted from his tether as if he understood me. "Yes, I'm talking about you," I called back to him. I took another bite of the tuber, making a performance of it, keeping eye contact with Croxley the whole time. I celebrated a mini-victory when he shuddered and looked away.

"I don't care what you say. It still looks like you're eating poop. I'll stick to my meat."

Our banter faded into silence, the forest sounds taking over. Croxley added another log to the fire, and laid down on his cloak. "Be up early tomorrow." With that, he rolled over with his back to me, and within minutes, I could hear the steady breathing of a restful sleep.

Without his company, as obnoxious as it was, I had little to distract myself from the pang of homesickness that came with the sunset. Sitting alone by the fire, a sudden wave of fear, loneliness, and hopelessness settled over me. I had no plan. Let's say I get to the King. Then what? Who says he will listen to anything I say? I'm just another Nether with a fair face.

Alongside the homesickness came a sense of guilt as well. I left without telling either of my parents goodbye, with my father looking for me and my mother worrying about my safety. If there was any way I could tell them that I was safe, I would. With the pain of a sharp knife, I realized that part of what my mother had said was right. I was selfish. I failed to realize how my decisions impacted other people.

But I also knew that I have been more happy today than I can remember being for a very long time. I had no future down in Cethin, where I couldn't even leave the den for fear of attracting unwanted attention. Up here, I'm more likely to blend in. But more than the respite from the spotlight is the chance to prove myself worthy to my people. Even if I must be a slave, I know that I made the right choice in coming to the surface.

I will try and save my people. I will do my best. Repeating this mantra over and over in my mind, I finally drifted off to sleep.

I suddenly awoke to a blood-curdling scream. I had grown

accustomed to the sounds of the forest during the day; the beautiful bird-calls, occasional snaps of twigs, the sound of running water, they had all turned into a dull roar in the background of my thoughts, only audible if I focused in on them. In comparison, the sudden harsh silence sounded sinister. Pulling my knife from my boot and holding it in front of me, I surveyed the forest, but the fire was reduced to a small pile of glowing coals, leaving the edges of the camp shrouded in complete darkness. Suddenly, another scream echoed through our camp, this one sounding much closer. I felt the hairs raise on the back of my neck, my senses now on full alert. When a sudden whoosh of wind swept over my head, I screamed louder than I ever had before.

"What? Fara, what is it?" Croxley jerked up, woken by my scream, to find me trembling with my knees pulled to my chest. He ran up next to me and crouched down, grasping me by the shoulders, lowering my hand with the knife in its grip and gently taking it from me. He set it down at his side and looked into my pale face, trying to track my darting eyes for the source of what had frightened me. "Fara! What's wrong?"

"There was a phantom! I saw it! It swept over the camp, howling and screaming!" As I looked up, I saw it sitting in the nearby tree, its pale white body reflecting the moonlight, starkly contrasting two bottomless black which were undoubtedly staring straight at me. I pointed it out "There! There it is! Just watching us!"

Croxley's tight grip on my shoulders relaxed, and he sat back down with a sigh as he explained, "That's not a phantom, Fara. It is an owl. To be more specific, a barn owl. They are very common in this forest."

"But the scream! I heard it!" I couldn't tear my gaze away from the barn owl sitting in the tree. It looked menacing, its shoulders hunched over, wings spread open behind it, its beak slowly clashing open and shut while its head moved in a slow circle. It was equally as mesmerizing as it was terrorizing.

"That was just its call. Don't worry. Owls are completely safe. This one is probably hunting." He slid his hands off my shoulders, pressing them against his thighs as he stood up, obviously tired. "You know, many say that the owl is a good omen," he said, still peering into the forest.

Just as suddenly as it appeared, it left with a silent swoop of its wings. The only sound to give it away was another scream, which left my heart racing at an irregular, rapid cadence. Finally dragging my eyes away from the now empty branch, I caught Croxley's gaze, and felt my heart leap in different direction when I saw the concern in his expression. He looked away as soon as his eyes met mine, keeping himself busy with the task of rolling up his mat.

"Well, now that you're awake, we may as well get going. The sun should be rising soon." He began to gather his things, leaving me sitting there, feeling my heart slowly come back down to a normal cadence. Although every time I looked at Croxley, it seemed to speed up again.

I was confused about what had just passed between us. Yesterday, Croxley was a rude, arrogant man who believed that I was just a mindless pretty face with no feelings and no thoughts. But now, I wasn't entirely sure where we stood, or what I thought about it. Shaking my head as if it would shake all these thoughts out of my mind, I began to gather my things as well. In a short matter of time, we had packed up all of our supplies and loaded them on Samuel and Sir Thunder. Croxley kicked sand on the fire, and with the rise of the sun, we were off.

CHAPTER 9

Woken with such a start, I didn't realize how cold it had gotten overnight. But now, as we slowly made our way through the forest, I wished I had something warmer to cover my arms. Cethin didn't have what one could consider weather. It consistently ranged from humid warmth near the underground springs to a cooler dampness in the mines and the dens. For this reason, I had little use for thick coats or furs. Our thin tunics served us fine underground.

Here on the surface, however, the biting chill penetrated through the thin fabric and found its way deep into my bones. I kept rubbing my hands up and down Sam's neck, managing to keep them warm in his thick fur. My face, however, did not fare as well, and soon my lips were dry and chapped. Wrapping my cloak tighter around my shoulders, I considered asking Croxley for an extra blanket, but quickly turned that thought down. Most likely, he would mock me and accuse me of not bringing the proper supplies. And even if he did lend me a blanket, he probably wouldn't let me forget that I owe him a favour. And the last thing I wanted was to be even further in his debt. So instead, I sat in silence, shivering in the frigid wind.

As the sun rose higher in the sky, I warmed up considerably. With the sun on my skin, I was quickly able to shake my chill and pay more attention to my surroundings. Now that I understood a little bit more about the forest, I was able to find birds where I had only seen leaves before. I was able to recognize some trees and flowers, and even spot a few squirrels scurrying up the trees as Sam and Sir Thunder wove their way through the forest.

Out of the blue, I spotted another berry bush, this one with large, purple berries. Remembering what had happened yesterday, I pointed the leaves out to Croxley and asked if they were edible. After a moment of consideration, he nodded.

Eager to taste the sweet fruit, I jumped off Sam and ran to the bush. Reaching out to grab a handful, I cursed when all I ended with was a bunch of scratches from its thorns. Frowning, I reached out again, slower this time, and managed to grab a large, plump berry. I looked closely, examining it for any obvious indication that it might kill me on the spot. Finding none, I popped it in my mouth.

I nearly swooned at the rush of sweet juice that burst from the berry. It had a faint sourness to it, just enough to be refreshing. I reached out again, careful to mind the thorns, and soon I had collected nearly all of the berries from the small bush, holding them with the skirt of my frock. I glanced over at Croxley, who was still on his horse, and held up my findings. "Don't eat too many at a time! Your stomach won't be too grateful," he cautioned through cupped hands as he moved Sir Thunder closer to where I stood. "Give some here!" He held out his hand, but I firmly protected my bounty.

"Bring your own supplies, remember? I can't take care of you! Get your own berries!" Turning around, I searched the bush for any purple orbs that I may have missed, when suddenly I spotted two animals across the way, emerging from a wall of tall bushes, heading towards the pond a few steps ahead of us. They had smooth. short brown fur, thin legs, and atop their long, slender necks were narrow heads that were scanning the forest for any signs of potential danger. One, which was slightly larger, had what looked like branches growing out of the top of its head. Crouching below the now-bare berry bush, I turned around towards Croxley and gestured for him to stay there.

I watched the animals stretch their long necks down, entranced by their beauty. As one lifted its head and cocked its ears, I felt Croxley crouch down beside me and whisper in my ear, "Dear-"

My face flamed at the unexpected comment. "Dear what?"

"No," I heard him sigh under his breath, "That is what they are called. Deer."

"Oh." I turned back around to face the deer, but to my dismay, we had scared them away. No longer bothering to whisper, I glared at him. "Now look what you've done!"

"Me? What on earth did I do?"

"You and your obnoxious, nasally voice scared them away!"

"Nasally□what?" He exclaimed, "My voice is not nasally!"

"Oh please, it sounds like someone's shoved a clod of dirt up your giant nose!" His hand darted up to his face to cover his nose, and I celebrated my small victory. Mimicking his tone, I pranced around with my skirt full of berries, announcing, "I'm the King's royal messenger, sent to perform his errands throughout Ahrenia, showering my grace on everyone I meet. I think that every woman is dying to give herself to me because of my dashing good looks. Oh, and even though I'm beyond charming, I can't seem to get myself to share my supplies with my travelling companion, despite the fact that she is nearly freezing to death in the cold wind!" I looked back at him, ready to unleash another torrent of insults, but stopped short at his crestfallen expression.

"I□didn't know you were cold. You should have said something," he said in a quiet voice. Turning around, he headed back to the horses, which were where we had left them, grazing on the grass.

Despite all that he had done to me, I still felt a pang of guilt that he felt bad. This was quickly followed by anger at myself for feeling guilty. Why should I feel bad? He needed to get his ego checked. I wrapped my berries in a wad of cloth and put them in my pocket. When I made my way back to Sam, I noticed that there was a cloak laid out on his back. I turned to look for Croxley, but he was already on Sir Thunder, riding deeper into the forest. I grabbed the cloak in my hands, holding it for a few moments, watching him move further away. Wrapping it around my shoulders, I climbed onto Sam's back with more ease than before, and kicked him into a steady trot.

As we continued down the path, my hips swaying in time with Sam while we meandered down the path, I pondered the man in front of me as I ate my berries.

"Is my nose really that big?"

"What?" Croxley's question pulled me out of my daydream. I was wondering whether or not Conor had told my parents of my plan. I hoped that they understood my choice. Although I had no idea what fate lie before me in the city, I knew that it would be more meaningful and rewarding than the one I had lived before. And if I am lucky, I will be able to save my people from their fate, although I still had yet to develop a plan. Again, I cursed myself for not finding out more about the Council's plan before leaving.

"Fara?"

"What? Sorry. Um, your nose?"

"Forget about it. We are going to stop up ahead at the river." Gazing past Sir Thunder, I saw a slice of blue breaking up the thick blanket of green. The river lazily flowed through the clearing, with a few red and yellow leaves spinning in its current. As we got closer, I heard the pattering of the water over the rocks, a familiar sound that had very often lulled me to sleep back in Cethin.

When we reached the river, Croxley jumped off Sir Thunder and walked toward the water. Following his lead, I slid off Sam's back and made my way to the edge of the river. Grabbing my water skin, I bent down to refill it, but it was still more than half full, and I wondered why we had stopped at another river so soon. Standing up and closing my water skin, I lookup around and was stupefied by the sight of Croxley in his undergarments.

"Um, excuse me! What are you doing?" I quickly averted my gaze and concentrated on repositioning my water skin at my side. When I looked up again, Croxley was in the water, his hair undone, fanned around his head as he bobbed on the surface.

"I'm bathing. You cave dwellers ever bathe? No? That explains why you stink so bad!" He grinned and dunked his head before I could respond. When he popped back up, I threw a rock at him, but he dodged, and the resulting splash wasn't as rewarding as a hit would have been.

"I bathe! Honestly! Just because we live underground doesn't mean we can't have hygiene!" I huffed and walked towards the water. Still, I realized that our arguments now stemmed from good-natured teasing rather than from hostility. I wonder when that happened, I thought to myself.

Taking off my shoes, I dipped my toe into the water, and immediately pulled it right back out.

"Are you insane? This is freezing!" In Cethin, we use hot springs for bathing. The heat helps sooth the muscles and wash the grime away. This water, on the other hand, was barely warmer than ice.

"What do you expect? We are descending a mountain! This water comes from the melting snow of the mountaintop that collects into streams and rivers as it falls down the slopes." He splashed some of the freezing water towards me, which I ineffectively tried to block with my hands. "I find it refreshing!"

So it is freshly melted ice.

"He finds it refreshing," I mumbled to myself as I walked along the bank towards where the river curved around and out of sight.

"Where are you going?"

"Unlike you, I prefer privacy." Considering my company, I added, "And if I catch you peeking around the corner, I will kill you."

Croxley reassembled his face into an attempt at a frown. "But who will protect you from the scary owls and other creatures of the night? No matter, I wouldn't want to see your nether-body any-ways. One time was enough for me. And who knows what you look like in the actual light of the day. You might have a second bellybutton that I couldn't see in the dim cave lighting." He winked and slunk under the water.

I rolled my eyes and walked around the bend. Once I made sure I was out of sight, I stripped down and braced myself for the cold. Standing at the waters edge, I dipped my toe in and quickly pulled it out. "Come on, you can do this," I told myself. But as much as I tried, I couldn't force myself in. Deciding I would have to take a more drastic approach, I backed away from the river's edge. Closing my eyes, I ran full speed into the water, releasing a shriek when the cold water slapped my face.

Pulling my head under the water, I quickly scrubbed my fingers through my hair, rubbed my hands over my body, and retreated out of the water. Shivering, I jumped up and down until most of the water dripped off, and threw on my frock.

Walking back around the bend, I saw that Croxley had gotten dressed as well. When he saw me, he gave me a queer look.

"What?" I asked self-consciously. Hoping that I put my frock on correctly, I patted down any loose folds of fabric.

"How was your battle with the water? Did you win?"

Realizing that he was speaking about my shriek, I put on a stern face and said seriously, "Yes. I proved victorious, and now all of its watery subjects must bow to me. So next time you enter the water, beware." And with as much dignity as I could muster, I climbed back onto Sam, my hair still dripping cold water down my back. I tried my best to hide my shiver and demand nobly, "Shall we go?"

Croxley mock-bowed and hopped onto Sir Thunder. Once again, he made it look infuriatingly effortless. "Yes, oh mighty mistress of the sea."

CHAPTER 10

"Here we are! The royal city of Stonewall."

Croxley and I had reached the end of the forest. We were greeted by a small, grassy field leading up to the city. Seeing the massive stone wall made with bricks of many different shapes and colours surrounding the city, I could see why it was called Stonewall.

In total, our journey had taken around 5 days. The rest of the trip was uneventful, stopping only to get more water, relieve ourselves, and sleep. I kept myself busy searching for animals, bugs, flowers, and, of course, berries, which I ate more slowly than I did my first batch. I wouldn't admit it to Croxley, but the berries destroyed my stomach. Croxley's method of passing the time, on the other hand, was by inventing different, more effective ways to get on my nerves. At first, it took little effort on his part to infuriate me, but as time grew on and my comebacks became sharper, his game grew less entertaining and he finally gave up. Occasionally my mind would wander back to Cethin, and with a pang of homesickness, I would imagine my family going on with their lives without me. Other times, I would wonder what future lie ahead of me in the city, often forgetting that I had submitted myself to be a slave.

At the base of the wall, it suddenly occurred to me that I never thought about what would happen if the King evaluated me to be unfit for the surface. Never in our history had someone come back down to Cethin from the surface, not including the guards.

"Croxley?"

"What do you want, Fara?"

"What would happen if the King doesn't see me fit for the surface?"

"Well, you would probably be executed," Croxley stated matter-of-factly. When he turned around, he saw the worry on my face, and quickly added, "nothing big, though. Just a quick beheading in the dungeon, so don't worry."

"Oh. Okay. Thanks." Not knowing what else to say, I absent-mindedly braided Sam's mane, weaving his strands of hair in and out in an effort to distract myself. There's no use worrying about the future, I told myself, whatever happens, there is nothing you can do but go on.

Entering Stonewall was no easy task. There was a crowd of people at the entrance, each one being checked by a guard for papers and weapons. I had hoped that Croxley, being the King's messenger, would be able to bypass the crowd, but one glance at his concerned expression told me otherwise. We dismounted and waited in line, moving at an agonizingly slow pace. Although the day was cool enough, I was quickly sweating amongst the crowd of people. Croxley didn't fare much better. I could see his blond hair plastered down on his forehead, and he growled at a passer-by who stepped on his foot. Looking around, I was surprised at how many stunning faces I saw. Croxley was right. Here, I was no longer extraordinary. I was just another pretty face.

I didn't know how I felt about that. On one hand, I have always wanted to be like everyone else, no longer singled out for my looks, no longer imprisoned by my appearance. On the other, I had little more to offer other than my fair face. What else would I bargain with?

When we finally made it up to the guards, they began to search our bags and our persons. Croxley showed them his papers from the King, and explained to them that I was up for evaluation. Once the guards had heard I was from Cethin, I noticed that they handled me much more roughly and with much less respect. When one guard let a hand linger too close to my chest while searching my person, Croxley grabbed his hand and stood in front of me, blocking me from the guard's reach.

Shocked, I looked at the guard's cross expression, his hand in Croxley's grip, and then at Croxley. Turning his head to look behind at me, he held my gaze as he shoved the guard's hand down.

"I think you've searched enough. Are we good to go on?" His voice held a threat, implying that there would be a problem if they held us any longer. Luckily, things didn't escalate, as the large crowd demanded the guards' attention. We walked through the entrance and I was relieved to find it much calmer than our previous setting.

Wagons were being pulled in the street by the most elegant horses, some so large that their nose alone was the size of my head. Maidens strolled the city in extravagant dresses, and merchants had stands set up on every corner. But most incredible were the buildings. In Cethin, we slept in dens, with only the most necessary pieces of furniture. We had no use for walls of wood or stone because the earth provided us with everything we needed. But here, the buildings were at least three horses high, packed together so tightly that, had they been people, would have been standing shoulder to shoulder. Each building was made of its own material, as they were all in competition be the most original structure.

Some were made of wood, with intricate carvings over the doorways, different stains colouring the wood with unnatural shades of blues and reds. Others were made of bricks, with shackled roofs that promised a dry head when the rain came. There were even some buildings made of granite and marble, most likely mined in Cethin. The marble had been transformed into pillars and statues, while the granite floors had been polished to make every individual speck shine.

In awe, I couldn't help but wonder how everything was kept so clean. That was, until I saw a horse relieve itself. From an alley in the building, a manservant dressed in very plain garb came out unnoticed by everyone, save me. He quickly scooped up the waste, brushed the area clean, and returned back to the alleyway. This entire scene played out in less than a minute, and try as I might, I couldn't keep track of the man after he walked more than a few steps.

Is this my future, I thought to myself, to become invisible?

"When do we see the King?" I asked Croxley, who was guiding Sir Thunder a few steps ahead of me.

Without turning around, he answered, "Most likely tomorrow. The King is very busy. We will have to stay in an inn for the night. Once we check in, I'm going to leave and make an appointment with the King."

"What's an 'inn'?" Croxley stopped and turned around, and I shrugged to indicate my ignorance. He was obviously surprised that I didn't know what an inn was, and began to explain.

"It's a place where you pay to eat and can often-times find a place to stay overnight. Some are very nice, while others are well, we'll avoid those ones," he said, turned back around. "Follow me. I know a good one."

As we passed through the city, I couldn't help but stare at those we passed. Nearly every citizen appeared special in some way. The women ranged from small and delicate to large and volumptious, and even the worst-dressed of them stole your attention. Your eyes couldn't help but linger on their beauty. The men were equally varied, with a mix of men of smaller, almost feminine stature to large, muscular individuals who appeared capable of pulling a carriage on their shoulders, and all those in between. We walked south to the plaza and on the corners were performers; women contorted with their feet curling over their back, men swallowing swords, instrumentalists, vocalists, a whole menagerie of impressive feats. Once again, I wondered what would become of me in this city where I was little more than another face, and a dirty face at that.

We arrived at the inn, which happened to be a tall, white building, black and gold trim framing the doors and the windows. There were windows on both the ground and higher up on the building, and through a higher one I saw a face. I wondered how someone managed to get their face all the way up there.

I noticed a sign atop the door. The lettering was white on a black background, with gold detail etched around the edge of each letter. The Golden Inn.

Well that fits.

As we walked in, a mouthwatering aroma swept over me, and I could barely stand it. Having finished the last of my food this morning, with only a few berries to tide me over, I was famished. By the look of Croxley's reaction, he was hungry as well. As he spoke to the man at the front counter, my attention drifted elsewhere. I was hypnotized by the plates of food that walked out of the kitchen and into the main room, where groups of people sat at tables waiting to eat. There were dishes I could recognize, like stew and bread, but never had I seen such meals so artistically arranged. In addition, there were plates that had food I hadn't even known existed, trailing scents behind them that left my stomach growling. Then, when I thought it couldn't get any better, a dish like no other passed under my nose and had be salivating. Filled with what looked like my forest berries was a shallow bowl made of bread, it both looked and smelled like heaven.

"Fara. Fara!" Embarrassed, I realized that Croxley had been calling my name. I turned towards him.

"What?"

"I'm taking our rides to the stables. After-wards, I'm going to head over to the castle to inform the King of your impending evaluation. It won't take too long. Now," he said, adjusting the bags and handing them off to me, "if you could take these bags to our room, it is upstairs, two doors to the left. Here is the key." He handed me a small, golden key, which I rotated around in my palm. Even the keys to their doors were nicer than the finest jewellery we had in Cethin. All of the gold, jewels, and stones that we mined were immediately sent back to Ahrenia, and if we were found hoarding any of it, the punishment was severe. "We'll meet back in here, and then we can get something to eat."

I turned around and tried to figure out how to get on the second floor. Having been distracted by the food, I hadn't noticed the stairs behind the innkeeper, leading upwards. Carrying our bags, I walked up the stairs and found our door. I made it to what I assumed was our door and put the bags down. I tried to open the door, but it was locked. I pulled and pushed on it, not sure how to work the door. In Cethin, we only had cloaks and the occasional slab of wood separating one room from another. This one, however, wouldn't budge, no matter how hard I pushed against it. Feeling slightly foolish, I searched for some hint on how to open it. Then I remembered the key in my hand, and saw the small round metal knob sticking out of the door, which had a small whole underneath it. I managed to jam the key inside the hole and moved it around until the lock finally clicked and the door swung open. Balancing a bag on my chest, I couldn't get a good view of the room, which is why I nearly tripped when I ran into the bed.

In Cethin, we slept on mats made up of a few blankets laid over a pile of soft dirt. So when I saw the bed, lifted off the ground like the clouds that floated in the sky, I immediately dropped my bags and threw myself upon it. It felt heavenly, my body sinking into its warmth, the soft sheets caressing my skin, the pillow cupping my head in its gentle grip. All troubles forgotten, I could have laid there for the rest of my life. Eventually, the smell of food wafted up through the still-open door, and my empty stomach protested against my immobility. With a groan and a stomach rumble, I dragged myself off the bed.

Descending the stairs, I scanned for Croxley.

"Fara!" I spotted him, waving his hand in the air to catch my attention. He was sitting at a table with a large plate in front of him. I approached him but stopped when I saw what was on the table. I eye-balled at the plate expectantly, mesmerized by the duck stuffed with bread, surrounded by potatoes and carrots.

"That looks delicious," I told him, my mouth watering.

Croxley just looked at me. "You don't think I'm buying you a plate, do you?"

"Oh, um right. Sorry."

Croxley held my gaze for a few more seconds, and then broke it with a laugh. "Fara, I'm sorry. I was just kidding. Here, sit down," he said, pulling out a chair for me. I sat down, my emotions in a whirl, while Croxley motion a servant over, who came with another plate of food. "Dig in," he announced.

And I did.

CHAPTER 11

After our dinner, which was by far the greatest thing I'd ever eaten, we returned to our room. Sitting on the edge of the bed, I took off my boots, and then fell back with a resounding "oomph". I rubbed my hands over my distended stomach, which, for the first time in my life, was full to the point of bursting. I sighed with pleasure as I felt the soft mattress curve to the shape of my body. Interrupting my bliss, I felt the bed shift under Croxley's weight as he sat down beside me. It was only then that I realized there was one bed, and two people. My mind unsuccessfully reached for a way to address the situation, and I squirmed away from Croxley as much as the space of the bed would allow.

"Comfortable?" He asked me, laying down next to me.

"Um, yeah. We don't have anything like this in Cethin."

"If you want to see a real bed, you should try the castle. You could lay five people in one bed! Talk about a good time." Croxley chucked, but stopped when he saw the concerned expression on my face. "Not that I'm thinking about that here. Um, I'll take the floor and you can have the bed." With that, he got up, took the top sheet from the bed, and lay it on the ground.

I felt compelled to offer him the bed, since he was paying for the room, but the longer I lay on it, the deeper I sunk, and the harder it was for me to keep my eyes open. In an effort to stay awake, I rolled on my side, propping myself up on my elbow to peer over the edge of the bed at Croxley, who was laying on the floor.

"Croxley? Are you still awake?"

"Just barely," he replied. I arranged myself into a somewhat seated position,, a thought buzzing in the back of the head that I knew would keep me awake all night if I didn't voice it.

"What made you change your mind about me? Why are you suddenly being so, well kind? I mean, you helped me with the guard, you bought me dinner, and now you're letting me sleep in this bed while you sleep on the floor."

Croxley rolled over onto his back, his hands behind his head and his face turned to the ceiling. "Honestly? Because you've proved to me that

Nethers are indeed worth more than dirt. At home, they tell us as children that your people are the cause for all the wars of our past, the ones to blame for illness, poverty, and sadness. They describe Ahrenia as it was before the purge and compare it to the Ahrenia of today. I mean, you saw the city today. It was nearly spotless, and everyone was content with themselves. And I can tell you, it gets much nicer as you get to the castle.

With this in mind, it's no wonder the guards treat you like trash. Indeed, we know what goes on down there. But you have to understand, the idea that Nethers are little better than the worst criminals is one that is shared among all Ahrenians. It's just how we are raised. But you've shown me that you're the same as us, if not better. There's no reason that you and your people should be stuck underground, when you've done nothing wrong. When I saw that guard touch you like that, just because he had found out that you are a Nether☐I realized that I had been no different. What I did to you in the cavern," he looked at me and paused, "for that, I am sorry."

As far as the meal and the bed go, I figured that after your evaluation, you'll not have a chance to enjoy the city. I wanted to show you that the surface isn't completely bad."

Stunned, I couldn't figure out how to respond. I mumbled a quiet "Thank You", and rolled back over onto the bed. With those kind words, he just may have helped raise my opinion of Ahrenians. On the other hand, he also lowered my hopes of changing anything with the King. If the King taught his people to hate us so thoroughly, was there really any chance that he would help my people get free? To add to the noise in my head was the threat of the evaluation hanging in the near future. Forlorn, I closed my eyes and struggled to calm my mind. Somehow, sleep won the battle with my thoughts and I was able to sink into a sweet oblivion.

I awoke to the sunrise. Despite everything that I've been through, the sunrise still managed to lift my spirits and prepare me for the new day. When I sat up, I noticed that I had somehow acquired a blanket during the night. Threading it between my fingers absent-mindedly, I looked through the window at the sun rising over the city. I rolled out of bed, stretching deeply, enjoying the lack of pain and soreness that had been haunting my muscles throughout the journey. As I arched my back, sighing in pleasure, I heard a moan and quickly turned back around. I held back a snigger as I watched Croxley ease himself into a seated position, looking more like an old man than one in his youth. He cracked his joints and slowly stood up.

"Sleep well?" I piped, not able to pass up a perfect opportunity to tease him.

Croxley just growled at me, his messy blond hair drooping in front of his face. "Next time you get the floor."

I laughed and thanked him while I gathered the few things that we had brought with us. In no time, we were ready to leave.

"Your evaluation with the King is in an hour, so we won't be able to eat breakfast. Make sure to ask the innkeeper for some fresh rolls when you check us out so we can eat on the way." He picked up our bags and walked to the door, but I remained standing where I was. I can't say that I had forgotten about the impending evaluation, but when he mentioned it so plainly, a pang of nerves coursed through my body, making my stomach swirl. He must have noticed, because he set his bags down and walked back to me, placing his hand comfortingly on my shoulder. "Listen, you don't worry about the evaluation. I'll do what I can to help."

"What could you do?"

"I just might be able to have some influence in the decision." Before I could ask him what he meant, he went back to grab the bags and said, "I'll meet you outside! Don't forget the bread," as he ran down the stairs.

I took extra care preparing for the day. I braided a small section of hair near my face, tying it with the strand of blue fabric I had taken from my father's cloak, and left the rest down to show off its length. With a wet cloth, I scrubbed my face to give it a healthy glow, pinching my cheeks to make them slightly pink. But as for clothing, I didn't have any other option. I scrutinized my frock, covered in mud and grass stains. My shoes didn't fare much better, the toes of my travel-worn boots peeping out from underneath my frock. I had my knife tucked into my boot, hoping that I wouldn't have to use it but not fully knowing what to expect. I guess this will have to do, I thought, shrugging.

There was a maid sweeping the kitchen, preparing for breakfast, and I asked her for a bag of rolls. Then I turned to the counter and rang the bell to summon the innkeeper. He popped out of a nearby room, his stomach making its way around the corner before he did. His round face was slightly ruddy but otherwise appeared kindly. He gave me a gracious smile after he noticed me at the counter, and I held up my hand to offer him the key.

"Leaving already? How was your stay," he asked.

"Wonderful. The bed was very comfortable and the food was delicious."

"Now I know you're lying to me! This inn is nice, but the food is utterly bland," he looked over his back, then leaned in towards me. In a low voice, he whispered, "but don't tell my wife that, she's the cook!" He gave me a playful smile and then asked, standing back up, "By the way, where are you from?"

"Oh, I, uh□" Desperately, I searched my mind for any names of cities other than Stonewall that Croxley may have mentioned, but I wasn't able to come up with any. Meanwhile, the innkeeper scrutinized me, going over my muddied gown, my fingernails with their ever-present amount of dirt staining them, and suddenly his eyes widened. I watched as his expression turned from gracious to repulsed as he accused, "Don't tell me you're one of those damn Nethers!"

The maid in the kitchen dropped her broom, but the innkeeper didn't notice. He was too busy chasing me out onto the streets. "How dare you sleep in my inn! You must really have some nerve, polluting that room with all your Nether diseases and bugs that you carry around with you. Now I'm going to need to replace that bed." I frantically grabbed my bags and ran out the door, breathless. As I stumbled down the steps, the man called out after me, "I don't want to see you stepping foot anywhere near my inn!" He slammed the door shut and with the resounding clang, my knees went weak and I collapsed on the stairs.

I remained sitting on the steps, waiting for Croxley, angrily trying to prevent the tears threatening to form in my eyes from spilling over. Don't let them see you cry, I told myself, you need to get used to this. It's only going to get worse. I hugged my knees to my chest, pressing my eyes against them, when suddenly my stomach rumbled. I realized that I had forgotten the bread.

After everything that happened, this seemed to be the breaking point. I curled my head and quietly cried into my knees, oblivious to the occasional passers-by odd stares. When I could finally control myself, I glanced up to see the maid from the kitchen holding out a bag of fresh buns. Wiping the tears from my eyes, I reached up to grab the bag. "Thank you," I sniffed.

"Don't mention it. Seriously, don't. If my boss knew what I was doing□" she let her words trail off as she checked to make sure nobody was watching. She started back up the steps, but I grabbed her hand.

"Wait! Why did you help me," I asked, confused by her kindness.

"Dirt sticks together, right?" Before I could ask what that meant, she ran up the steps and slipped back into the inn without a sound. As she went in through the door, Croxley came around the bend. I quickly tidied myself up, hoping that my eyes weren't red, and distracted myself with Sam. I double-checked all of his gear, the last week of travelling providing me with enough experience to tell me what to look for, what to tighten, to make sure to triple check the saddle belt. A few days back, I had slipped upside-down, hanging on for dear life to my saddle under Sam's stomach after I had failed to tighten the belt all the way. Jumping up onto Sam's back this morning, I was surprised at how much more limber I was than when I had first ridden him. Although my bottom was still aching, it was more of a dull, steady pain than a sharp, fiery burn. But what hurt more than the pain was the thought that this was the last time I may ever ride again. As this sunk in, I watched Croxley jumped onto Sir Thunder and take off. With a click of my heels, Sam and I trailed behind.

Making our way around town, I found that the crowd grew larger as the sun rose higher in the sky. I tried to keep myself preoccupied by reading the names of inns that we passed, but in a manner of minutes, I found that I was once again worrying about meeting the King. After what Croxley had told me, that the King was responsible for this dirty image of Nethers, paired with the reaction of the innkeeper, I couldn't help but expect the worst. I was all I could do but hope that I was found beautiful enough to be used as a slave. What an odd desire.

Travelling through the city, I realized how strange it was not being singled out amongst the crowd for my appearance. But come my evaluation, I would be singled out because of my home. It seems I was never meant to fit in. Looking at Croxley, who was proudly showing me around the place he called home, I couldn't help but think, with a tinge of envy, that this is where he belonged. He appeared to be completely at ease, even greeting the occasional stranger who strolled by. Not for the first time, I wondered just where in this city he came from. He never really told me much about his upbringing, and all I knew of his position was that he was the King's messenger. I didn't know how to ask him about his family, so I just sat in silence as Sam pattered down the paved road.

If I thought that the first part of the city, which Croxley called the "lower part", was spectacular, then the castle itself was absolutely breathtaking. The castle was constructed out of dark, shining stone, one that I had never seen before in the mines. As I approached, the sun glinted off the stone and created a halo around it, as if what I was looking at was just a trick of the light. When I got nearer, I couldn't help but marvel at the seamless stone, interrupted only by a large wooden door, the wood stained a deep red. It had been polished to perfection, no errors to be found. It was perfect, in a menacing sort of way. I thought it fit the tales of the King perfectly.

We were met by another set of guards at the door, and I noticed that these guards were not only dressed much more sharply in a more impressive uniform, but they also possessed a serious, confident manner that the guards in Cethin lacked. Croxley presented them with his papers, and when they turned to me, he simply said "evaluation". They gave a quick, synchronized nod, relieved us of our horses, and then split apart, unblocking the doorway. The clack of our heels broke the silence as we walked down the empty corridor. The floor was made of black marble, while the walls carried portraits, weapons, and other decorations.

When we were out of earshot, Croxley muttered "Pompous prudes." I looked up at him in surprise, and he just rubbed the back of his head. his eyes looking up, "We have a history. They, um ... let's just say they don't like me very much."

"That's hard to believe," I said sarcastically. We passed down another hallway, this one adorned with a rather large display of weapons surrounding a tapestry depicting their bloody purpose located in the center of the room. Motioning with my arm, I indicated the decorations on the walls.

"I like the décor. Very ... cheery,"

"You get used to it. But I agree, I think they would look much more regal with bright green walls and feathered lamps around every corner." He looked at me seriously before we both broke face and chuckled. As we walked the rest of the way in companionable silence, I thought back to what Croxley had said, about the guards not liking him, and getting used to the castle. I started to wonder just how much time he has spent here.

"Croxley," I asked, looking at him from a side glance, "how do you know all this stuff about the castle?"

"I pretty much grew up here. My father was the King's messenger, and his father before him. We are like an extension of the royal family. When my father was out on errands, I would wander the castle, and I got to know a lot about its nooks and crannies, hidden corridors, and most importantly, the guests' secrets. You see, lots of important people are invited to stay in the castle for different balls, negotiations, those sorts of things. I know more about the going-ons of this kingdom and those around it than some of the King's advisors." Before he could continue, we arrived at a door, looking to me like all the others we had passed. Little did I know that this seemingly plain door held the key to my fate.

"After you, Fara."

CHAPTER 12

"Your highness," Croxley bowed before the King, and I followed suit. We remained kneeled for what seemed like an unnecessary long time, until the King told us we could rise. I surveyed the room before once gain resting my eyes on the King, who was sitting on a large throne made of dark wood, embellished with a deep red cushion. He wore a white, stiff collared shirt under a dark blue vest with embellished patterns threaded in silver. Across his chest lay a sash adorned with badges and medals. His cloak was heavy and thick, lined in white fur, contrasting the dark blue colour of the fabric itself. I fleetingly thought how drab my travel-worn, tattered brown frock must appear to him. His face seemed ageless. His dark brown eyes bore the knowledge of a lifetime, but his skin was smooth and unwrinkled, save for the deep frown in his forehead. He was unquestionably handsome, in a frightening, intimidating way. When those dark, endless eyes met mine, I quickly looked away to focus on those sitting beside him in the room.

On one side stood a woman, old but graceful, holding herself up with dignity. I wondered who she was, knowing that the Queen had passed away many years ago. I noticed she wore a stern look upon her face as she ran her eyes up and down my appearance. On the other side of the King sat a young man around Croxley's age, dressed in a fine blue shirt that made his green eyes shine. He had a strong, handsome face, with eyes that held all the energy of a child's. He was slightly tanned, and his thick auburn hair was streaked with highlights, suggesting time spent in the sun. To my surprise, his eyes went directly to Croxley, who returned the look with a nod, but it was so slight that I thought I wondered if I had imagined the whole thing.

Shocking me into awareness, the King spoke for the first time. His voice reverberated through the room, bouncing off the marble. "You wish to be evaluated? Well then, step up closer. Don't worry, I won't bite," he joked, although his tone suggested otherwise. The King grinned, but the smile never reached his eyes. I knew right then and there that he would never try and help my people. I would have to find another way.

I took a few steps towards him, and he leaned forward in his throne. Standing here presenting myself, I couldn't help but think about Croxley's evaluation, and the humiliation and hatred I felt towards him. Looking at Croxley now, I wondered if I had began to trust him, as the only person I knew up here, to take care of me. His eyes met mine, but quickly looked away.

"Turn around," the King demanded. Keeping my eyes on Croxley, confused at his response, I spun around slowly, holding my stomach in and slightly lifting my chest in the way I had seen the women in the city do, hoping that I was satisfying whatever requirements the King had. After I completed my circle, I searched his face for a reaction, but I had no luck. His face appeared as if it was made out of stone, not a single crack in his calm, serious demeanour, as if he knew that he had complete and absolute control of the situation. Instead, I looked to the woman for any hints. She still had a stern expression on her face, but her folded arms had finally been released and were now relaxed at her sides. If I was correct, her eyebrows were turned up slightly in interest.

Sliding my eyes over to the man seated next to the King, I felt a rush of heat as he ran his eyes up and down my person, apparently just now noticing me.

When his eyes reached mine, I couldn't seem to drop my stare. He held my gaze for what seemed like minutes, and the entire time I held my breath. I sunk into his deep green eyes, glimmering with a hint of mischief, as well as something else. I tried to peer in further, to figure out what I saw. Next to me, I heard Croxley clear his throat, jolting me out of my trance. I quickly lowered my gaze, cheeks flaming. I stood there for a few more minutes, looking towards the ground, the silence agonizing. My palms had grown sweaty, and I had to stop myself from rubbing them on my frock. Finally, the King leaned back in his throne. "What do you think, Headmistress Mathelda?" The stern woman, Mathelda, gave me another appraisal. Without warning, she rose from her chair, approached me, and grabbed my wrists.

"Hmmm .... " She turned them over In her hands, which were cold and bony. "Her hands are soft. It looks like she hasn't done any hard work in her life. Unusual for a Nether. Her hair is long and glossy, and her skin is unblemished." She took hold of my chin, and pulled my face down. "Her eyes are quite unique. I think she will fit in with my girls just fine. Oh, but this will never do." Mathelda pulled my knife from my boot, smirking and holding it up for all to see. "There will be no weapons for you." She handed it to Croxley, who held it from himself at a distance as if it carried some disease or curse. The King caught my eyes, tasking his tongue, and I looked down, my stomach in a whirl.

"What say you, Prince Erik," the King asked after a few moments of painful silence. My already-frazzled mind stumbled over the word " Prince". In Cethin, we don't hear much news about Ahrenia, or any of the other nations, for that matter, only able to pick up a few snips from the guard's conversations. I had only heard them mention a Prince briefly, and it was always in tandem with discussions of palace balls and parties.

"I find her interesting." Prince Erik's voice had the same nasally pitch that seemed to be shared by all Ahrenians, but rather than making his voice sound obnoxious, as it did with Croxley's, it created a musical undertone. "I say we let her stay. Have you a name?"

Before I could answer, the King laughed mockingly and declared "Of course she doesn't have a name. She is from the pits of the earth. What is your number, girl?"

"923" I responded automatically.

"Your highness, if I may," Croxley spoke up for the first time since entering the room. "I have taken the liberty of naming her myself, just to make the journey with this scum more bearable. I call her Fara, and it might be less confusing to the poor dullard if we keep her name the same."

Scum? The power of his words sent me reeling. Did I hear him correctly?

"So you gave her a pet name? Fara, is it? How cute," the King repeated, rolling the name around in his mouth. Hearing my name in this man's intimidating voice made my insides squirm, and I had to fight to keep my trembling hands hidden from his sight. "It'll do. Mathelda, if I am correct, I would say this girl belongs in the royal brothel."

"That was exactly what I was thinking," Mathelda concurred. I wracked my brain for the meaning of the word brothel, and with a sudden understanding I knew that I wanted more than anything to be placed somewhere else.

"Pardon me, sire," Croxley waited for the King's gesture before he continued on, "this girl has experience with horses. I think she would fit in much better surrounded by beasts than she would with the wealthy lords who visit the brothel. I know from first-hand experience that she makes for lousy company. Not to mention the fact that the guards told me that she is equally lacking in bed. If you were to put her in a brothel, you would more likely end up losing money and angering guests that making any profit." He waved at me dismissively. "Really, she would be a waste of time to try and clean up, and a waste of money for any nobles who want to get to know her a bit better."

Hurt as I was by Croxley's complete betrayal, I was distracted by the King's reaction. A flash of skepticism leaped across his face, and then his eyes widened with a knowing smile. All of this happened within the course of a few seconds, and once again, I wondered if the stress of the whole thing was causing my imagination to run rampant.

"Is that right," he finally conceded. He drummed his fingers against the armrest of his throne. Leaning back, he concluded, "it seems as though we have a new stable hand. Mathelda, she is yours to take. I myself have better things to do. Come along, Erik." We all kneeled as the King and Prince stood and left the room, and before I could fully straighten and stand up, Mathelda yanked me by the wrist

"Come on, up with you. I haven't got all day." She dragged me towards the door, and I walked passed Croxley. I caught a whisper, I'm sorry, as I walked out the door.

CHAPTER 13

"This is where you will eat. Breakfast is at sunrise, dinner at sundown. You are in charge of keeping your own time, as nobody will bother to wake you up. If you miss a meal, it is nobody's fault but your own, and you will just have to make due. In addition, you must check in every day before you leave and when you return from work. And I will warn you, should you miss check in, I will be most displeased." From the tone of her voice, I knew that the last thing I wanted to do was see Mathelda displeased.

After we left the evaluation room, Mathelda dragged me down a series of corridors and a flight of stairs, at the end of which we found ourselves below the castle in the servant's chambers. Once again, I was underground. A few servants whisked past us carrying trays, pillows, letters, always in a hurry. I wondered how many of them were from Cethin, and how many of them were Ahrenians, forced to work out of punishment for a crime, debt, or deformity. When we made it to the main room, there wasn't a soul in sight. It seemed like everyone was too busy to rest. Without a doubt, I would soon join them.

The room itself was walled with dirt, with only a few lamps casting light in the centre of the room. Despite the dread rooted deep in my belly, I felt a sense of comfort at being underground, protected by the earth, no longer out in the open, vulnerable to the seasons, the forest, and the creatures that inhabit it. However, I knew that there was much more danger for me here than there was out in the forest.

The centre of the room contained five long tables, each with a pair of benches that could easily seat 20 bodies. In the back was a tall stack of bowls and plates, with a cluster of spoons piled nearby.

Having had only eaten one of the small, stale loaves of bread for breakfast, I was in desperate need for something to eat, but I didn't dare ask.

"Hurry up, no dawdling!" Mathelda called over her shoulder as she exited the main room though a narrow corridor. I ran to catch up to her, and as soon as I fell in behind her, she resumed her orientation. "As Headmistress, I have a lot of business to attend to, which doesn't include worrying about the servants. So don't call any attention to yourself, and make sure that you stay out of trouble."

This hallway forked into many smaller tunnels, and we followed it all the way to the last branch, which took us to a small room, furnished with two cots and a small chamber pot in the back-right corner. At the foot of one of the cots was a light blue dress and a thin pair of slippers. There was a small opening in the opposite wall, where thin beams of light shone through to light up the room. "This is where you will sleep.

Change into your uniform and report back to the dining room, and I'll take you to the horse stalls." She turned around to leave the room, but on her way out she paused and added over her shoulder, "On second thought, leave your boots on. I don't want you to dirty up the slippers. I might have you use them for another job later," and then left the room.

I set my bag on the cot and gingerly pulled off my shift. The sweat from the day had mixed with the absurd amounts of dirt already in the crude fabric from my days in Cethin and the week spent trekking through the forest, making it even more of an effort to get off. Peeling it off my skin, I had actually begun to pant a little by the time I was finally able to get free. As I was shaking it out, hoping to rid it of at least some of the filth it had collected during the journey, something fell out and bounced behind my cot. Curious, I set my shift down on the cot and crouched to look behind it. Along with an intimidating amount of spiders and dust, I found the seed that I had absent-mindedly taken from the storage room.

A twinge of guilt ran through me for forgetting the seed and letting it go without light or water for the entire duration of our journey. In a way, I felt like this seed was a direct connection to home, and in abandoning the seed, I had abandoned my people. With this realization came a wave of doubt that I had come not as a voice for my people, but in an attempt to escape from the dull routine of my life in Cethin. Was I really that selfish? My mother had though so. Tenderly, I set the seed on the ledge of the small gap in the wall, deciding at that moment that I was going to do all that I can to help my people, to put them before me, and to prove my mother wrong. My first step, albeit small, was to care for this seed.

Realizing I was wasting time, I hurriedly pulled the dress on and left the room. I ran through the tunnel, hoping that I was going to correct way.

When I finally made it to the dining hall after a few wrong turns, I saw Mathelda waiting for me, her face bearing its seemingly permanent scowl. "Now that you're finished wasting my time, may we go?"

"Yes, ma'am. Sorry."

Mathelda dumped me at the horse stables, leaving me in the hands of a tan, burly man who went by the name of Heathrow. "But you can call me Heath", he said with a firm handshake. He flashed a smile, showing off his laugh lines and the creases around his light blue eyes. I couldn't help but smile in return. "And what do I call you?"

"923, sir."

"That ain't no name for a person. Nope, that won't do. Come on, I know you've got something better."

"I go by Fara, I suppose," I said with a shrug of my shoulders.

"Fara? That's much better. Now, what's a young lass like you doing in a place like this?" He gave my hand, which was still in his tight grasp, a soft squeeze before releasing it. I subtly tried to shake it out, the blood rushing back in with a sharp tingle.

"I'm here to work with the horses. I was just...ah, evaluated. They told me I was to work with you." I watched his face as I explained the situation, but if Heath was at all concerned about my heritage, he didn't show it.

"How much experience do you have with horses, Fara?" He asked me.

"I've been riding for little over a week. Well, actually, I was riding a mule, but my□" I paused, stumbling over the word "friend" in reference to Croxley. After what happened in the evaluation room, I wasn't sure who Croxley was to me. "My escort", I finally decided on, "rode a stallion."

"And they sent you to me, eh?" Heath scanned my thin arms and soft hands, his expression skeptical. "Well, I'll take yah, as long as you're willing to work."

"Absolutely, sir. I'll try my best."

"That's what I like about you Nethers. You work harder than Ahrenian servants, and you don't complain nearly as much!" Heath clapped his rather large and calloused hands together, the sudden movement and loud sound scaring the nearby horse. He patted its neck, his hands gentle for a man of such large size. "Come on in, I'll introduce you to everyone. "

Entering the stables, the first thing that hit me was the smell. It was obvious that a large number of animals resided here. My distaste must have registered on my face, because Heath laughed and told me I'd get used to it after a while. He walked me through the stable, introducing me to the horses as we passed, giving me time to let each one sniff my hand, feed it a sugar cube, and, as he put it, "get acquainted."

We made our way down the row, and I was surprised at the variation of horses in the stables. There were many brown horses like Sir Thunder, though none with the same speckled bottom. There were also white horses, black horses, spotted horses, and countless other combinations. When I thought I had seen it all, the last horse proved me wrong.

"It's beautiful," I whispered, standing in front of a horse whose fur shined like the gold we mined back home. I slowly held out my hand like I had with all the other horses. It hovered its nose in front of my palm, the warm breathe making me shiver. After a few moments of hesitation, it finally leaned its nose into my hand and motioned its head down, as if asking for a rub. I happily obliged, gently rubbing the top of its head.

"She sure is. This mare's name is Elana. Looks like she likes you!

Here, give her a sugar cube. That's a girl."

Heath looked at each horse like they were his pride and joy, but his eye twinkled just a bit brighter when he spoke about Elana. "I raised this one as a foal. You should 'a seen her, all leg and no body. But she filled out nice, didn't she? If I were a stallion... " He waggled his eyebrows suggestively, and I laughed.

Elana put her head down, over the edge of the stall, and I rubbed my hands along her cheeks, then ran my fingers through the tuft of mane hanging on her forehead. The tips were sun bleached, nearly white, while the roots were a rich, golden blonde, creating a most unique gradient.

"Well, now that you've met everyone, it's time to get the real work done. Since you came so late in the day, you're getting off easy this time. All ya gotta do is shovel their stalls and give them their nightly feed. Here's your shovel," he handed me a heavy, wide headed shovel and a wooden bucket. "When you're done with that, just toss the rubbish in the fire pit and come to me so I can show you where I keep the hay."

He left me with the shovel and bucket and headed out of the stables.

Shovelling the stalls was a smelly, dirty job, but one that I could handle without too much difficulty. Once I got the hang of carrying the shovel back to the bucket without losing all of its load, I was able to finish in little over two hours. The horses barely seemed to notice my presence in their stall as I cleaned up their messes.

When I got to Elana's stall, she prodded me with her head the entire time I cleaned, probably hoping I would give her another sugar cube.

"Sorry, Elana! I don't have any-more!" I patted her neck and backed out of her stall, tugging the bucket along the ground, now that it was heavy with waste, when I bumped into someone.

"Sorry!" I turned around to apologize, and found myself staring straight into the shining green eyes of the Prince. "Oh!" In my surprise, I stepped back, tripping over and falling into the bucket. "Yuck," I moaned. After multiple unsuccessful attempts to pull myself free, I realized with fallen spirits that I was stuck.

The Prince's spirits, however, seemed to be in good sorts. He was doubled over, fanning his hand in front of his face and plugging his nose, all the while laughing uncontrollably. When he finally gained control of himself, he reached out his hands.

"I'm sorry, I'm sorry! Here, let me help you up," he offered breathlessly. Before I could refuse, he gripped my hands and pulled me up, straight into his chest. For a few moments, I just stayed there, a warmth creeping in through my body, until I realized what I was doing, and pushed myself away. "Sorry," I exclaimed.

"You said that already," he chuckled, the smile revealing a gap between his two front teeth that I hadn't noticed before. In a way, it made his regal features less intimidating. Regardless, I still didn't know how to respond, and I wracked my brain for something to say that would fill the increasingly awkward silence.

I finally blurted out, "What are you doing here?"

Brilliant.

"What am I doing here? What are you doing with my horse?" He shot back.

"Elana is your horse?" I asked, incredulously.

"Yes, she is my horse, thank you very much. And I would appreciate it if you didn't fatten her up by feeding her sugar cubes all day!" He looked confused by my fowl temper, and I berated myself for being rude, but I just couldn't help it. His presence essentially was turning my mind to mush.

I scowled and turned around to pick up the bucket. "If you don't mind, I need to get back to work." I shoved past him, dragging the waste-laden bucket to the fire pit. I held my breath while dumping it into the fire, but to be honest, it smelled much better than the latrines at home. That was one thing I definitely didn't miss.

The Prince was still following me, making it impossible to think. "What?" I finally cried out, exasperated. It had been a long day, and my small burst of energy that came with meeting all of the horses was quickly fading.

"Look, " he said, grabbing my arm so that I faced him, but after seeing the fear in my face, he quickly let it go.

"I'm sorry," He said, puling his hands back to his sides, "thank you for your work with the horses. I appreciate you taking care of Elana."

I grumbled a "your welcome," and went out to meet Heath, leaving the Prince standing alone in the stalls.

"Ah, so you've finished up-good lord! Now what have ya gone and done to yourself? Turn around," Heath commanded upon seeing, and most likely smelling me. I obeyed, and Heath released a loud guffaw, "I don't even want to know what happened here!" He considered it, then said," Well, actually, it might make for a good story, but we'll save it for later. You've still got some work to do!" He pushed himself up from the table he was working at and motioned for me to follow.

We walked to the back of the barn to a large pile of hay.

"Now, what you wanna do is take this pitchfork here," he picked up the thick tool and handed it to me. I nearly dropped it, its weight coming as a surprise. "Be careful now! Al-right, go ahead and stick that in the hay, and when it comes out, use your hand to hold it against the fork. You're gonna want to give each horse a stack about the size of your head.

Good luck!" He patted me on the shoulder and returned to his work, leaving me standing there, hopelessly comparing the size of the haystack to myself. I was definitely the smaller one.

Straining under the weight of the pitchfork, I was panting and dripping in sweat by the time I finished giving the horses their food. The Prince must have left while I was getting the hay, because he was gone when I returned. Although it wasn't as though I was looking for him, I tried telling myself, but I knew in the back of my head that I would've liked him to see me working. Why, I have no idea. That fact alone infuriated me, and I exhausted all my confused emotions by stabbing passionately into the haystack with my pitchfork. Finally, I put the pitchfork back where Heath had gotten it, the hay stack now closer to my size, and fruitlessly tried to tidy myself up a bit before returning to the stables.

"Heath! I've finished up!" I found Heath in one of the stalls, picking dirt out of one of the horse's hooves. He lifted his head and said, "Go on and get yourself a good rest. I've got some hard work planned for tomorrow!" I hurried on my way back to the servant chambers, not wanting to be late, racing against the setting sun while my stomach growled in anticipation.

CHAPTER 14

"How dare you come back here looking like this!" In my rush to get to the main room on time, I had forgotten about the mess that was made of my dress. To my horror, Mathelda noticed it immediately and stormed across the dining room. Before I could react, she grabbed my ear, pulling me out of the dining room and back into the entrance corridor. She whispered into it sharply, "Do you have any sense or are you completely daft? You've gone and ruined your dress, and yet you still have the audacity to come in, late, and interrupt our meal."

Releasing my ear from her grip, she told me to go directly to my room without supper, before I "fouled up the place."

Anger made my eyes water, but I refused to gratify her with my tears, so I held them in and walked across the room with as much dignity as I could muster. The girls seated at the tables in the dining room craned their necks to peer into the entranceway where Mathelda had dragged me, and I had to endure their their mocking laughs, their sneers, and their harsh words as I walked back through the dining room and out through the back corridor. With laugher at my back, I finally reached the exit.

As soon as I was sure I was out of sight, I hitched up my skirt and started to run, no longer trying to hold back my tears. All of the memories from my youth at the schools, where the girls would ridicule me and single me out, came flooding back. At the end of the corridor, I turned into my room and threw myself onto the cot, exhaustion, hunger, and shame taking over. Quiet sobs racked my body, and I buried my face into the pillow so no one could hear, lest I get reprimanded for that as well.

Eventually, I ran out of tears, and I was able to calm myself down. It was only then that I felt another presence in the room. I looked up, and to my astonishment, there was another servant girl in the room, standing at the foot of the bed.

The shock of recognition stopped my tears short. It was the maid from the inn!

"Are you done yet? I don't mean to be rude, but that's my cot you're crying on."

"I'm sorry, I didn't know!" I quickly pushed myself up and off her cot, now standing awkwardly in the middle of the room.

"Don't worry about it, I've just had a long day and need to get these shoes off my feet. I'm Jean, by the way," she said, setting down her bag as she sat on the edge of her cot. She sighed with pleasure as she removed her slippers, massaging her feet for a few moments before looking back up at me. I stared back, dumbfounded, and decided that I should say something else to my new room-mate.

"Um, hi. I'm Fara," I offered.

"I know. I was at the inn, remember? You caused quite the stir."

"Of course! I could never forget your kindness! Thank you for that."

"Yeah, well that kindness got me fired." I opened my mouth to apologize, but she just shook her head and said, "No, really, it's okay. That man treated me badly any-ways. It was just what I needed to get myself out of a troublesome situation. And now I'm going to return that favour." She pulled the bag to her lap and took out a thick slice of bread, followed by a slice of cheese and an apple. My stomach rumbled in anticipation.

"For me?" She nodded and handed me the food, which I took gratefully and began to eat, right there in the middle of the room.

"Whoa!" She said, "Take a seat before you drop it all! That wasn't easy to steal!" I sat on the edge of the bed, unable to speak because of all the food I had shoved in my mouth. She watched me with an amused smile, her chin in her hands, then began to braid her hair and prepare for bed.

When I finished eating, or rather, inhaling my food, I laid back on the bed, waiting for my stomach to realize that it now had food in it. From my position, I could see the small opening in the wall, and through it the changing colours of the sky. I watched the clouds pass by for a moment, and then remembered the seed I had placed on the ledge, which I went to pick up. Scooping some dirt from the ground, I formed a small mound on the ledge of the opening and placed the seedling in the middle, careful not to hurt the tiny sprout. I made a mental note to find a cup and some water for the sapling tomorrow. I took another glance outside the window, and then sat back down, on the correct cot this time. I was incredibly tired, and as much as I wanted to fall asleep, I knew I had better change my dress before I got my cot covered in horse poop.

I swiftly undressed into my undergarments, grateful that Jean granted me some privacy focusing on her braid, and then laid back down on my cot, pulling the thin sheet over my body. I shut my eyes, willing sleep to overcome me, when, like a jolt, a memory flashed through my head. Dirt sticks together, right? No longer tired, I sat straight up, startling Jean in the process. "What did you mean, 'Dirt sticks together?'"

"What?"

"When you helped me at the inn, you told me 'Dirt sticks together'. What does that mean? Are you from Cethin?" I thought back to my childhood-she didn't look much older than me, and I didn't recognize her from my mother's classes. Furthermore, if she were to have left Cethin, I would have heard about it. People don't leave very often.

She sighed. "Do we really have to get into this now? I'm tired." When I refused to lay back down, she gave in. "Fine. No, I'm not from Cethin, although where I'm from isn't too different. My home is Grundale. We live in the tunnels south of Stonewall."

My mind was spinning. "I thought Cethin was where they had banished everyone during the Great Purge. You mean, there's another colony?"

"There are many more. During the purge, when the King banished the marginalized, he didn't realize how many of us there were. They considered killing us off, but there were too many of us. It's the only reason they even bothered to let us live. That, and they needed some extra labour in the failing economy. So they separated us into groups and sent us underground, choosing,"

I finished for her, whispering, "the strongest of the poor to tunnel ahead and make a living underground." I crawled closer to her, bewildered. "How do you know all this? In Cethin, the elders told us we were the only ones."

"They told us the same in Grundale. But when I was sent up here, I met slaves from different colonies. Most of the girls here are from the colonies, and there are a few men working throughout the castle that are also from the colonies, but most of the men from the colonies are either working on the outskirts of the city, constructing and expanding, or are forced to serve in the King's army. But I don't really know that much about the other colonies, because they are always watching us, listening, waiting for one of us to slip up. They don't want us talking about where we are from. I'm sure you can imagine why. We all think that we are the only ones. I think that's why they won't let us back home once we come up here. They don't want us to spread the word that there are others."

"Why not? What would it hurt, us knowing that we aren't alone?"

Jean's voice suddenly turned cold. "It's simple. There is power in numbers."

Chills tore through my body as the true meaning of her words sunk in. With more Nethers, there was a chance of a stronger revolt. More people to fight, more passion to fuel the fires for change. I thought back to my original mission, to find freedom for my people. With this new-found knowledge, my seemingly impossible plan now seemed plausible.

"Jean, can I trust you?" I peered into her hazel eyes. She held my gaze, and firmly nodded. I sucked in a breath, and told her in a rush, "I wasn't sent here. I left Cethin. I chose to be evaluated." I watched as she recoiled in disgust.

"You abandoned your people? You betrayed them!" Her reaction, although hurtful, was natural. It was the same as Conor's, and I'm sure of everyone else in Cethin. During the trip, I often had to stop my mind from wandering to my family back in Cethin, and how they perceived my disappearance. Did they think me a deserter? I thought of my peers from my mother's classes. Yes, I'm sure they did. But Conor? No, he knew why I was going. Hopefully he told my family why I left, so that they still thought of me in a good light, or perhaps, a better light.

"Let me explain. I came here for freedom. Not just for me, but for my people. For your people, for all of us." I prayed that she would believe me, that I wouldn't lose my only friend down here.

Her hackles still raised, she asked skeptically, "How do you plan to do that?"

I sighed, having asked myself the same question every day. "Honestly, I don't know. But I knew I had to try. You know what it's like, being different from everyone else, being singled out. I couldn't stand it. And my father was talking about a revolt. He said that all we needed was someone on the surface. So that's what I did." Jean's suspicious expression softened into one of sadness.

"Well, you've wasted your time," she said.

"But don't you see? You said it yourself! There is power in numbers! If all of the slaves, servants, and Nethers from every colony got together to fight, nothing could stop us! All we need is someone to help lead us! Someone to tell the colonies that they aren't alone!" In my excitement, my voice had grown stronger, all traces of my exhaustion gone. Jean shushed me, and I whispered, "We could change things!"

"But how would we get back to the colonies? How can we tell them? Once you're up here, there is no way back." She added in a despondent whisper, "I'd do anything to send at least a message back home, to let them know I'm okay." With these words, a face appeared in my mind. Croxley? I don't know if I could trust him. He said that he was on my side, but after what happened during the evaluation, I can't be sure. Either way, a solution had to exist. "I'll come up with something. I'm not just going to give up," I firmly declared.

Jean and I sat in silence for a while longer, until she spoke quietly, staring into her hands. "You know, things weren't that hard for me back home. I'm not ugly, but I'm not near as beautiful as you. The guards didn't really cause me that much trouble. My true talent is singing. I used to sing at colony celebrations, around the mines, whenever it was safe. But, one day, the guards heard me and took me away from my family. It was the most terrible thing that had ever happened to me. I cried for hours, until the guard finally knocked me out to make me quiet. And to think that you just left them...I can't decide if you are brave or heartless." She looked up at me, tears welling up in the corner of her eyes. "I miss them," she said. I felt my own tears beginning, surprised that I had any left. I admitted to her, "Me too. I could have never imagined how much I would miss home." In an effort to stave off more tears, as I had shed enough today, I asked Jean, "Would you sing for me? A song from Grundale?"

Jean smiled and nodded. "I'll sing you my favourite. My mother sang it to me every night, and it was the last thing I heard before I left." In a quiet, pure voice, she sang a haunting tune that reached deep into my heart.

When the birds you can't hear
And you're lost in dark silence
Don't fret, I'll be near
To protect you from violence
No matter how hard
They try to break us down
Together, we stand strong
We will always hold our ground
Each day, as we work,
And they beat us and bite us,
We know, in our hearts,

That they can never fight us.
The distance may be far
And the times may be rough
But we know who we are
And who we are, we are tough
So when I've come and gone,
Just know, in your heart,
That when you sing this song,
We will never be apart.

The tears I had been trying to hold back now flowed freely, but not out of sadness. Rather, it felt like the hole in my heart that had been growing larger in the past few days was now on the mend. I noticed that Jean was crying as well. With silent tears streaming down both of our faces, we embraced, letting the unspoken grief and fear dissipate in the warm comfort of our new friendship.

As soon as I laid back down, the exhaustion from before took over. I was barely able to thank Jean before my eyes closed and sleep consumed me.

CHAPTER 15

The next day was much easier. Jean woke me up early so that I could clean my dress before breakfast. I pulled my reluctant body out of bed and laced up my boots, wearing my old travelling dress and carrying the soiled one. Walking to the wash-room, I passed by many girls, some who smiled friendlily, others not paying me any attention. I was surprised at how many girls Jean knew. Most of the girls we passed exchanged greetings with her. When a group of girls huddled together, sneering and laughing at me, Jean walked over with her head held high and told them something that I couldn't overhear. But whatever it was, it was effective, as it brought their tittering to a stop and sent them walking away.

The wash room turned out to be a small, round room with two large barrels filled with water in the centre, and a bunch of smaller, empty buckets scattered around the room. Jean told me that the first barrel had clean water, which you scooped up with a bucket and did your washing in. When you were done, you were supposed to dump the dirty water in the other barrel.

I followed her instructions, and managed to get most of the dirt out of my shift from the journey, as well as the horse poop out of my work dress from the day before.

I wrung out my work dress as tightly as I could before pulling it over my head. It was still damp, but bearable. I looked over at Jean, who was washing her uniform as well. Her dress looked a bit different from mine. "That reminds me, what job do you have now that I got you fired?" I asked her, still feeling guilty about making her lose her job at the inn.

"I told you, I was meaning to quit any-ways. So stop worrying about it. Now, I do some work in the kitchen, basically delivering food and the like to those staying in the castle. And, sometimes, Mathelda has me, um, entertain some of the guests." She kept her eyes trained on her skirt, which she was scrubbing intently although it was already clean.

"What do you mean, entertain? What do you do?"

"Well, you know, I □ " she stopped speaking as some other girls walked in the room, and, shooting me a meaningful glance, picked up her things and walked out.

I followed, but she didn't expand any further on the subject. Dropping off our wet clothes in our room, we made our way to the dining room.

"I hate that old man. 'Duke Ermingham the third.' As if the first two weren't horrid enough." Jean and I were eating breakfast at a table with some other girls whom Jean knew, and one in particular had not stopped complaining since we sat down. I was fine with it, though, because it meant I didn't have to do any talking, and could pay full attention to my food. It wasn't anywhere near the meal I had eaten at the inn, it was better than nothing. I mopped up some of the vegetable broth with my bread, hoping to catch every last drop. I was so concentrated on the task at hand that I was able to tune out most of the girl's ranting.

But it seemed that the other girls at the table weren't as content to listen to the girl's complaints. Finally, one changed the subject as the complainer paused to take a breath.

"Have you heard about the Prince?" Despite myself, my interest was immediately sparked. My head shot up, bread forgotten. "I heard today that he was engaged to a princess from Ethera. The King is attempting to make some kind of alliance."

"I think her name is Lena. Everyone is saying that she is absolutely beautiful," another girl chimed in. It seemed like I was not the only one whose interest was piqued. Soon, the table was filled with chatter.

"We'll see if the Prince can handle being tied down, if you know what I mean." The other girls nodded, but this joke went over my head.

"I don't," I answered, now fully engaged in the conversation. One of the girls sniggered, but I ignored it, thirsty for more information.

"You know, the way he always has a different women on his arm," the girl on my right answered. "Not to mention he is always running off on 'adventures'. I'm surprised he finally decided to settle down."

By the end of breakfast, I had learned plenty about Prince Erik. There was a lot for me to ponder as I made my way to the stables. From what I heard, he was a notorious flirt, always reeling in women with his charm and good looks. It also doesn't hurt that he's a Prince, I suppose. Apparently, he leaves all the time, shirking his responsibilities as a Prince, only returning to the castle when he needs more money or to throw a great party. To be honest, the more I learned about him, the less I admired him.

But still, the news of his engagement stung more than I would have liked. Get over it, I chastised myself, your one encounter in the stables was nothing special. He's probably forgotten all about it. And you should, too. I slurped dow the rest of my soup, and stacked my bowl on the way out with a decisive clink.

"Good morning, Heath," I called out in greeting as I walked into the stables. I searched around, but couldn't find any sign of him. "Heath? Where are you?"

"I'm back here!" I heard a loud oomph, and made my way towards the direction of the sound. I found him by the fire pit, his arms full of wood and his face black with soot. I tried to hold back my laughter, but my attempts proved futile. My giggling announced my presence, and Heath turned towards me, his face now in full view. This new angle sent my giggling into a full-blown laughing fit.

"What happened to you?" I walked up and removed a few pieces of wood from the large pile he held, although I was hardly any help, my laughter making my arms weak. Heath rolled his eyes at me. "Enough, enough, lets get this wood down and then I'll set you up with your job today."

I helped him set down the rest of the wood in the fire pit, careful not to drop any too hard. I still ended up with black soot spotting my dress and skirting the edges, and I groaned inwardly, thinking that, at this rate, I would probably have to wash my dress every evening before dinner if I wanted to be on good terms with Mathelda, though I wasn't completely sure that was possible.

"Since you're here early, I'll let you brush the horses and clean their hooves. I normally do this every morning, but I haven't had the chance yet. The brushes and picks are over there," he pointed to the rack against the wall. "I'll be in the back unloading hay if you need me." Heath walked out of the stables, and I grabbed the brush and hoof pick.

Approaching the first horse, I glanced at the name plate, which read "Mac."

"Good morning, Mac," I told him as I squeezed into the stall and began brushing his fur. When he was good and clean, I looked down at his hooves. I tried to remember how Heath had cleaned them, and bent down to pick up his hoof. It didn't budge. "Come on, Mac, help me out!" I tugged at it, pulled at it from many different angles, and finally, the horse raised his hoof, more out of irritation than obedience. I awkwardly held his foot between my knees while I scraped the dirt out of his hoof, and moved on to the next one. He seemed to know what I was doing, because his other three hooves proved much easier. Making my way down the line, I found that I enjoyed brushing the horses much more than I did shovelling the stalls. I noticed that some of the horses had been shifted around, and that there were some new members while other stalls were empty. Much to my disappointment, Elana's stall was among the empty ones.

After I finished that job, I went to find out what Heath needed me to do next. I found him out back, unloading hay from a cart. The cart was hitched to a mule, and a man sat at the front of it.

Heath saw me and motioned for me to come to him.

"Ah, Fara! Come 'ere and help me unload this cart!" I hustled over and started grabbing bales of hay, walking them to the growing haystack. In no time, Heath and I had cleared the cart. I noticed that the merchant never once offered to help us unload. Then again, his arms were so thin that I couldn't imagine him being able to carry more than two.

"Al-right, thanks for waiting." Heath dusted off his hands and held one out for a handshake. The merchant just scowled at the hand as he said, "That will be 5 silvers." Heath, unbothered, smoothly slipped his outstretched hand into his pocket to pull out the man's pay.

"On second thought," the merchant interrupted, "you could let just me take your barn girl out for a night."

Unaware that the merchant had even noticed me up to this point, I was startled by his request. Heath, however, remained composed. "She is not up for offer. Take your silvers and leave."

"Are you sure, old man? She's a Nether, am I right? She's not even worth a bale of hay, but I'm willing to cut you a deal. A night with her in exchange for free deliveries for the month. I'll even throw in some apples and alfalfa. Still want to refuse?" The merchant looked confident, and, to my horror, Heath seemed to be considering. I begged him with my eyes, but he wasn't looking my way. The merchant, on the other hand, was looking at me with a slimy smirk pasted on his face, pleased with his apparent conquest.

Finally, Heath spoke. "Nope, I don't think that will do. She works for me in my stable, and that work is worth more than a few apples and bales of hay. Now move along, before I tell your wife what you've been up to, tormenting innocent girls and such."

"You wouldn't dare. I have connections with people much higher than you. You'd want to consider getting on my bad side before doing anything rash." Heath shrugged off the threats, which only seemed to further enrage the merchant. "Well, I'll be back, just wait. I'll wipe that smug grin off your face, Heath. You'll see." He whipped his mule into a walk and pattered down the road until he was out of sight.

I exhaled a shaky sigh of relief, and admitted to Heath, "I thought you were truly considering the deal!" Heath said nothing. "Truly, Heath, where you?" Heath just shrugged his shoulders.

"I'd be a fool not to. It was a mighty fine deal. But some men in this town think that they own any women who hasn't already been married off. It's time someone showed them otherwise. Although it'll prove a hassle to find another merchant to sell me hay, it was worth it to teach someone a lesson." He looked angry as he considered, "I know if anyone tried to get to my daughter like that, I would be on him with a branding iron before he got past the first button."

"You have a daughter?" For some reason, I couldn't imagine Heath's large, strong hands carrying a small child. But then I thought back to how gentle he was with the horses, and knew at that moment that he must be a good father.

"Oh boy, set myself up for that, didn't I?" Heath took a seat down on the hay we had just finished unpacking, clasping his hands together and watching his thumbs twirl as he spoke. "My dear wife Erna, bless her soul, gave me three good, strong boys many years ago, and they've grown to start families of their own. Some years ago, she became pregnant again, but this time the pregnancy hit her hard, and she passed shortly after child birth. She had finally brought us the daughter she'd always wanted." Heath sniffed, and I watched a fat, swollen tear roll down his cheek, carving a trail through the leftover soot. "Now, little Shawna is my heart and joy." He looked at me as if from a distance, and then announced, "Actually, she reminds me a lot of you. She'll grow into a stubborn, beautiful girl, capable of carrying her own."

I smiled bashfully at Heath, and the burly man's face reddened underneath the soot. He stood up and turned around, rubbing his jaw. "Enough jabbering, we've got work to do," he declared gruffly, and then walked off. Still smiling, I followed after him.

CHAPTER 16

The days turned into weeks, and I grew accustomed to the routine of life here in the city of Stonewall. Wake up, go to breakfast, go to work, leave work, wash for supper, eat, go to sleep. Of course, it was adorned with conversations with Jean and her friends, as well as joking with

Heath. During the day, I had little time to think about anything other than the work I had to do. But there were some nights when I would be laying in bed, unable to sleep, and those were the times when my homesickness would sneak up on me and I would fall into its grip. Eventually, it got easier and easier to pull myself out, to tear myself away from the grief I associated with leaving and focus more on what I am here to fight for.

Through Jean, I met many girls from different underground colonies. Some were more akin to living on the surface, never looking back to those they left behind. But most of the girls were like me, missing home and wanting to do something to help. In the back of my mind, I was constantly thinking about the revolt, gauging whom I could trust to help when the time arose. I had to be careful, though, and didn't actually say anything about my plans. If I told the wrong person, if I made the mistake of telling a girl loyal to Mathelda, it would all be over. I couldn't imagine the consequences, nor did I try to. So instead, I spoke to the girls in an easy, conversational manner, hoping to gleam some hints on where they came from. But for all my talking, I still had yet to find a way back to the colonies, a way to tell them that they weren't alone, and that, together, we could fight. Whenever this problem arose, my mind always flitted back to Croxley.

Even if I could trust him, and I didn't know if I could, I hadn't seen him since he left me here, so I had no way to ask him for help. In an odd way, I missed him. What's more, the Prince hasn't returned. Every day I went to the stables, I found myself checking to see if Elana was in her stall, but it was always vacant. It had been empty for nearly a month. I briefly wondered if it was I who set the Prince off, if my rudeness made him leave, but then I remembered what the girls had said about the Prince. That he loves to run off, go on adventures. Plus, he had just been engaged to marry. That's enough to make a man run off.

I chastised myself for imagining that I was important enough to be the reason for his sudden disappearance. Please, you're just a stable hand, here to pick up horse poop. I shook myself of my reflections as I approached the stables. By now, I knew what to do and where to go. I called out a greeting to Heath and made my way to the brush bucket, grabbing a handful of sugar cubes on the way.

"Hello Mac. Here you go." While Mac was chewing on his sugar cube, I cleaned his hooves and brushed him down, then moving on to the next horse, settling into the familiar rhythm of the day. That is, until I saw Sir Thunder.

"Sir Thunder," I exclaimed, "and Sam, who I found in the next stall. I threw my hands around Sir Thunder's thick, muscular neck. Apparently the excitement wasn't mutual, because as I was holding him, he careened his neck around over my shoulder to grab the sugar cubes from my dress pocket. I laughed and pushed myself off of him, giving him a cube, and then went to Sam, who showed me the same amount of interest. I cleaned their hooves and brushed them with extra care, noting that they was exceptionally dirty.

"Now where did Croxley take you two," I wondered aloud. Then it hit me. If Sir Thunder and Sam were back, that meant that Croxley was back. I mulled this over in my mind with mixed emotions as I moved from one horse to the next.

As if one shock wasn't enough for today, after making my way down the majority of the stalls, I saw the fair, golden head of Elana peek out of the stall at the end.

"Elana? You're here too?" I greeted her with the same I enthusiasm I gave Sir Thunder, although her reciprocation was much better, her chin nuzzling my back as I stroked her beautiful mane. I noticed that she, too, had a thick film of dirt embedded in her coat and mane. Before I could begin to wonder where she had been, someone came from behind me and snaked their arm around my waist.

"Excuse me!" I exclaimed as I turned around, instinctively reaching out to slap whoever it was behind me. My mind didn't process that it was Croxley's mug until my hand reached his cheek with a resounding smack!

"And hello to you too, Fara," he said, rubbing his jaw. "I guess I deserved that."

"That was just the beginning! What are you doing here? Where did you go? Why did you leave?" My mouth was spewing out questions before I could even think of them, and I knew that I must have sounded like a bumbling idiot, but I couldn't help myself.

Croxley laughed and pulled me into an embrace, sending my stream of questions to a halt, my mind now preoccupied with trying to figure out what was going on. "Glad to know you're still curious! I've missed you," He stopped laughing and pulled out of the embrace, his grin softening into a quiet smile as he looked at me tenderly. My mental gears were still processing what had just happened and the swirl of emotions that came with it. Before I managed to form a coherent sentence, Heath appeared. His eyes immediately went to Croxley's hands on my shoulders, which were quickly dropped, and then directed his gaze to me.

"Fara, the missus wants to see you. I believe she said it was important." Confused, I walked outside, leaving Croxley and Heath behind, only to find Mathelda waiting at the entrance.

"Come with me, girl." Without any further explanation, she walked away, back towards the castle, leaving me little choice but to follow. The whole way, I wracked my mind for an explanation as to why she came for me. After that first day, I had been very careful to stay out of her way, and for a while, I thought that I had been successful. With a shock, I realized that it must be about the plans for the revolt. Someone must have realized why I was so curious about the colonies, having asked one-too-many questions, and now I was going to pay for it. I swallowed the nerves rising in my throat and clasped my hands together, hoping to hide their shaking.

She took me back to my room, and before I had a chance to ask what was going on, told me to wash up and to put on my good slippers and the clean dress I saw lying on my cot. I waited for her to leave, but she made no indication of moving. Turning myself around, I slipped out of my dirty uniform and pulled the rag out of the bowl of water at the side of my cot. After I had wiped most of the grime away, I slipped into the new dress. It sent shivers of pleasure down my spine, goosebumps raising along my arms as the smooth fabric, unlike any I had felt before, shimmered down my skin. It was a vibrant green, which contrasted against my pale skin and dark hair.

Mathelda looked satisfied, but I couldn't imagine why she would have me wear such a thing. A morbid image appeared in my mind in which I was swinging from the gallows, an execution victim dressed in the finest gown so that, even in death, I wouldn't mar the beauty of the royal city. My nervous eyes flitted around the room, stopping at my plant on the windowsill. Having watered it every night, it had grown much larger in the past month. Its leaves were thick and green, with a round stalk that pointed towards the sky. It had become a symbol of hope for me, and I could only hope that Jean would continue to care for it.

"Hurry now," Mathelda barked, and once again I followed her through the tunnels.

We were walking through one of the residential hallways where nobles normal stay when she explained to me, "You have a request."

"A request?" I didn't understand.

"I was expecting one sooner or later, but I have to say that I was surprised by your first customer. For your sake, I hope you entertain him well." And with that, she shoved me through one of the doors in the hallway and left.

I turned around, and to my horror, I saw the hay merchant from a few weeks ago laying on a bed, his spindly appendages poking out of a blanket covering only the lower half of his body, while his upper half was unclothed. He beckoned me forward, but I felt like a deer caught by a predator, my legs stiff and my eyes wide. Suddenly, I knew exactly what all the other girls did for work. Memories of my times in the tunnels, when the guards would try to take me back to their rooms, paired with more recent memories of girls coming back to the dorms late at night, whimpering in their rooms, flooded my mind. Images like that of Jean gingerly sitting on her bed, removing her dress that looked as though it had been put on wrong. All of them came together, and the harsh reality that I had tried so hard to avoid was now facing me, point blank, and it was all too obvious.

The slimy merchant laughed darkly. "I would tell you not to worry, that I won't hurt you, but from what I hear, I can't make any promises. I believe I'm your first client, yes? I paid good money for this, you know. Girls like you are a rare commodity." He paused and a smug grin appeared on his face. "I told you I would be back, didn't I?" He stood, the blankets falling from around his waist, and I saw that he was still wearing thin briefs. This offered little relief, though, as he was walking towards me, and I had no where to go. I was trapped. In what seemed both like seconds and hours, he closed the short gap between us and stopped in front of me. He ran a hand through my hair, pushing it behind my ear, and I flinched, moving to take a step back. He grabbed me by the shoulders, locking me in place. My mind flitted back to earlier today, when Croxley's hands were in the same spot, and I wondered at how the same position could make me feel so different depending on who was holding me.

The merchant kept his grip on my right shoulder with one hand, while the other moved up to caress my cheek. His breath smelled foul and rancid, and as he sighed, the tell-tale scent of alcohol wafted up my nostrils. I felt like I was about to vomit. He abruptly planted his lips on mine, and stuck his tongue in my mouth.

I bit down, hard.

He howled and pulled back, wiping a hand over his lips, and I noticed with slight satisfaction that I had drawn blood. My satisfaction was short lived, however, as his hand darted behind my head to grab at the hair at the nape of my neck. He tugged on it, pulling my head back, and I whimpered out of pain and fear. He hissed, "So you want to play it like that, do you? You like it rough? I can give you rough." Pulling me to the bed, I was sickly surprised at the strength of this scrawny man. He threw me on the bed, and thrust himself on top of me. Tears began to stream down my face, but I couldn't wipe them away because he was pinning my wrists to the bed. Keeping one hand on my wrists while his legs straddled over me, he struggled to undo the top laces of my dress. I closed my eyes, not wanting to watch him any-more, when suddenly, his weight was lifted off of me.

I heard him curse, and when I opened my eyes, he was in the grip of a guard. "What the hell is this," he exclaimed. "I paid good money for this girl!" I quickly squirmed my way off the bed, getting as far away from him as possible.

Another second guard came from behind me and announced, "I have an order from the King. She is needed." Before I could react, he spun me around and pushed me out the door. I glanced back into the room, and I saw the other guard struggling with the merchant, finally resorting to slugging him on the head which succeeded in knocking him out. The guard hustled towards the door and closed it behind himself. I could only stare at him with wide eyes, the shock being the only thing that kept me from going completely hysterical.

They moved at a quick pace, herding me up a staircase and into another room. This one had a fireplace in the corner, a large bed with a canopy, and some chairs seated around a table. I didn't see the King anywhere, and for the umpteenth time today, I wondered just what exactly

was going on. The guards locked the door behind them, and then slumped against it, putting their hands on each other's shoulders.

"What is going on?" I yelled, finally reaching my breaking point. "Let me out of here!"

"Calm down, calm down!" The guard in front of me took off his helmet, and I had to blink a few times to make sure I was seeing things correctly. Underneath the helmet was none other than Croxley. Not knowing what else to do, I collapsed into the chair next to me, staring at him with a completely blank face. Croxley followed and crouched down in front of me. "Relax, you're okay. We came to rescue you ."

"We? Who is that," I motioned to the other guard, who was putting more fire on the fireplace. He set the poker down and walked towards me. He took off his helmet, knelt down, and, taking my hand, kissed it and then looked up at me.

"Nice to meet you," he said, his bright green eyes locking with mine. "My name is Erik."

CHAPTER 17

"Y-y-your highness," I stuttered, attempting to pull my hand back, but he held it tight, clasped in both hands. He kept my gaze, and before I could get lost in it, I reminded myself about his reputation. "You're engaged," I blurted out.

Smooth.

He laughed, a melodious, carefree sound that sent my already racing heart into a sprint. But behind the laughter, I sensed a pang of sadness.

"Croxley, is she always so blunt?" He looked at Croxley, who shrugged, and then looked back at me. "Engaged. That I am. And to the most beautiful maiden in all the lands, for that matter. Princess Lena of Ethera. What a lovely name." He sounded less than sincere. Mocking, almost.

Croxley, however, was much more frank. "Lena. What a horrid woman. Sure, she looks fine on the outside, but I couldn't spend more than a few minutes in her presence without wanting to dump a glass of water on her swollen, arrogant head." He shook Prince Erik's shoulder companionably, and looked so forlorn for his friend that one would of thought he was the one engaged to the Princess. "Sorry, old friend, but it's true."

The Prince stood up and careened around the room, declaring in a snobbish manner, "and yet, it is all part of the Prince's duty," Prince Erik continued, droning about how a Prince must "make sacrifices for the kingdom, get his priorities lined up and learn how to separate himself from the commoners," and so on, obviously repeating something that had been drilled into his head since birth. The longer he went, the more ridiculous the demands became.

"Do not bathe on Tuesday mornings, unless the maid has already washed the tub, or else you will have to wash again the next hour in a different room. You may not wear a purple cloak with red trousers, else you may start a war. If you have a guest who would like to sit on your right, you must drape your cloak over your left shoulder, unless you are not wearing a cloak, in which case you may only sit with guests on your left side. And if you find the food to your disliking, spit it into discretely back into your soup spoon, not your meal spoon, else you will offend your guest." The Prince sat on the edge of the couch, looking exhausted just by thinking about all the complex rules he had to follow. "Honestly, whoever said being royal was easy obviously hasn't had to take lessons from my tutor."

Croxley and I remained quiet, sympathetic but not knowing how to ease his grief. Prince Erik cleared his throat, uncomfortable in the silence, and pushed himself up with his hands on his knees. "I'm going to check on the guards. You two stay here in the room," he announced and exited, leaving Croxley and I alone. I awkwardly looked around, sitting stiff and straight, not knowing what to say, but Croxley didn't seem to share the same inhibitions.

He came and sat down next to me, sighing as he relaxed into the sofa. With his eyes closed and his hands clasped over his lap, I was able to relax my mind, and my questions from when I first saw him earlier today resurfaced. l took a few breaths to try and form a coherent question, not knowing which one to ask first, so l eased in with the simplest question I could think of. "Why didn't you tell me you knew the Prince?"

"Why are women so caught up with the Prince? I swear, mention the Prince's name once, and suddenly everyone wants to be your best friend." He glanced at me, then laced his fingers behind his head. "Honestly, I didn't mention it because it wasn't important." I scowled. Fair enough.

"Okay, next question. Where were you?"

"I'm a messenger. I deliver messages. It's kind of what I do. The Prince decided he wanted to come with. Nothing interesting. Stayed in a few inns, scared off a few phantom owls," he teased. "The usual."

"Did you visit another colony," I blurted, my cautiousness thrown to the wind as my curiosity got the best of me.

"What?" Croxley's eyes widened. He obviously wasn't expecting this sort of question. "There aren't any..." I cut him off with a hand in the air. "Don't lie to me, I know that Cethin isn't the only place where people are forced to live underground."

Croxley's expression of false ignorance was replaced with one of accusation. "How do you know this," he asked, his posture suddenly erect, no longer resting into the seat.

"Answer me first. Did you go to another colony? Did you go underground?" I wasn't about to let him bully me into dismissing the questions I so desperately needed answered.

"No. I'm not allowed to take anyone to the tunnels except for guards or banished criminals. Not even the Prince. Now, tell me how you found out about the others."

I looked at him, gauging whether or not I could trust this man. I had before, but after what he had done during my evaluation, followed by his sudden disappearance, I wasn't completely sure. His eyes bore into me during my silence until finally I admitted, "In the slave rooms, some of the other girls share stories about their homes. We all miss them, Croxley, and in sharing our past, we are able to bring them back to life a little bit."

Croxley shook his head, as if he didn't want to hear it. "Fara, you have to be careful. If someone were to hear you talking about Cethin, not to mention other colonies, you could get into serious trouble."

Suddenly, I was enraged. "Who are you to care about what kind of trouble I get myself into?" I stood up, my hands in fists, my voice raised. "You are the one who left me here, basically turning me over into the hands of that horrible woman. Look where that got me!" My anger left just as quickly as it came, replaced with the sting of betrayal. "I thought that you were my friend. But you were just playing with me, using me to get what you wanted," I accused, my voice barely above a whisper.

Croxley grabbed my fists, pulling me down into him. "Why do you think that Erik and I came for you tonight? Because I didn't care for you? Fara, you must realize, during your evaluation I had to pretend like I didn't know you, like I didn't care about what happened to you. Otherwise, we both would have been punished." He spoke gently, his tone soothing. "I tried to save you from this," he gestured to the room, which I understood as a reference to the situation with the merchant earlier tonight, "by putting you with the horses. But your beauty must have caught someone's eye, and I'm afraid that you got yourself into a mess that was practically inevitable for someone like you to end up in."

I couldn't look into his eyes, rather, I cast my gaze downward and furiously tried to keep my tears from spilling over. The entirety of the situation was frustrating. No, I corrected myself, it's the surface which is frustrating. All these stupid rules, these condescending laws and legislations. I've had enough of it. And I knew that my mission wasn't just about me. It was about all the other colonies who had to live in the dark, all the girls who are forced to be man's slave, all the children forced to grow up without being able to see the sky, the clouds, to feel the warmth of the sun upon their face.

Croxley lightly cupped my face in his hands, which were calloused and travel-worn. I looked into his eyes, and in that instance I knew what he said was true.

"Croxley, I need to tell you something." He kept his eyes trained on me and nodded. Preparing myself, I released a deep sigh and began.

"The reason I volunteered for evaluation wasn't because I was sick of Cethin. I wasn't cast out, I didn't abandon my people, and I didn't leave everyone behind to see the surface. Sure, I've always wanted to see what it looked like. Every child always dreams of seeing trees and the sky and the water and," in my nervousness, I was rambling, but I forced myself to get to the point. "the point is, I volunteered for evaluation so that I could bring my people to the surface."

Croxley's hands fell away from my face, but in earnest, I grabbed them and held them tight, not wanting him to leave before he heard it all.

"I didn't really have a plan. To be honest, I still don't really have a plan. I thought that I could convince the King to let my village come to the surface, to let us live like we used to, but now I see that it would be impossible to reason with him. But then the girls started telling me about their homes, that there were other colonies, and I realized that, if we all managed to team together, we could convince the King to give us our freedom. 'Strength in numbers', or something like that." I took a pause, preparing myself for the reaction I knew would come after the next step of the plan.

"This is were you come in. I was hoping that you could teach me how to get back, so I can tell the elders what I've found. While I work with them, you could send messages to the other colonies, telling them all to rally together. Maybe I can come along to help convince them. If we all work together, we should be able to achieve-" Croxley cut me off, his tone low but severe.

"Fara, you don't have any idea what you're asking for. Everything you just mentioned is treasonous to begin with, not to mention the shear impossibility of it all. You can't begin to comprehend how difficult it would be for me to even deliver a message to a colony without the guards knowing, let alone escort people in and out under their noses. It's never going to work."

Suddenly, the door flung open, startling Croxley into a fighting stance in front of me, sending me behind his back.

"Relax, it's just me," the Prince said, closing the door behind him. "The coast is all clear. I don't think that man will be asking for your service again any time soon, Fara." He lounged on the couch across from us, propping himself up on one elbow, his eyes bouncing between Croxley and I, quizzically trying to make sense of our position. Croxley stood out of his crouch and released his protective grip on me. We just stood there awkwardly, avoiding each other's eye contact, when finally Prince Erik broke the tension.

"By the way, I heard you two talking through the door. I'm on board."

Croxley and I gawked at each other, our mouths gaping open. Croxley was the first to move, bringing his palm to his face, shaking his head. "My friend, you don't seem to understand. This wouldn't be just another adventure to keep you from getting bored. Those were different. There was no risk. This, though, this could cost us not only our lives, but also the lives of thousands of families."

"Your words hurt, Croxley. Do you honestly think me so selfish?"

"No, I think you're naive. You haven't been exposed to the real world. Honestly, you've never even ventured into the slums of this city. You have no idea how to handle poverty. The colonies are much worse. The guards have lost all notions of manners, their actions brash and crude. The people of the colonies are desperate for any chance for salvation, practically throwing themselves at you for any word of the surface. There are rats and filth everywhere, and that's once you actually make it to the colony. The journey there is often long and filled with trials not worth the destination." Croxley looked at me, his eyes apologizing for his bleak description of my home. He doesn't have anything to apologize for, I thought, it's all true. The Prince, on the other hand, had more trouble believing it.

"It cannot be that bad. If your job is so terrible, why do you keep it," the Prince asked, sitting up from his position.

"In truth? Because it was the job of my father, and his father before him. The King at that time had chosen my grandfather's line to do this job, and we've had little say since then. You don't seem to understand the absolute power the King has over the lives of the commoners."

Prince Erik stood, his voice growing intense as he walked closer to Croxley. "You don't think I know the effects of his control? I've been living with his tyranny my entire life! What kind of childhood do you think I had? While you were off going on your little trips with your father, or playing with the other boys, I was stuck in the castle learning how to navigate the court, the history of the kingdom, or being forced to entertain some snotty rich child from another noble family. Ever since I was a child, my father has defined my life for me, and now I am being told who to marry for the so-called 'good of our kingdom'. So I apologize for being selfish, for wanting to escape all of this and feel like I actually have control of my own life for a change." Prince Erik ended with his face in Croxley's, both standing on the edge of a fight. I hid inconspicuously in the corner, all too aware that I had no part in the conversation happening before me.

However, from my corner, I empathized with the Prince. I understood how he felt, the child of someone in power, always expected to put the community first, having to grow up separated from your peers, sheltered. To think that he, who walked with an air of confidence and a careless demeanour, suffered from the same insecurities as I. I wanted to let him know that I understood, but this was neither the time nor the place. Instead, I stood in my comer with my arms crossed, waiting for the tense air to dissolve. Croxley was the first to crack. His fists relaxed and he sighed, turning around and walking back to the couch, where he stood with his hands gripping its arm for support, as if the conversation had drained him of the last of his energy.

"I'm sorry, my friend. We both have our burdens, and I would like to keep mine to a minimum. I just can't find a way to do this without putting our lives at risk."

"What's life without a little risk?" The Prince paced around, thinking. "I'm sure I could come up with a solution. I mean, I was taught by the brightest men of the kingdom!" Croxley and I both looked at each other, sharing the same thought. It looks like our Prince has recovered his confidence.

"If I may," I looked at the Prince for permission to speak, and he nodded, while Croxley let out an exasperated groan, collapsing into the couch. Choosing to ignore him, I proceeded. "I have a few ideas myself, and I know some of the girls would love to help,"

"No, the less people that know, the better. If we do end up doing this, and I still highly recommend against it, then we need to make sure that none of this information leaks." Before I could protest, Croxley continued, "I know those girls better than you do, Fara. You may think you can trust them, but most of them will manipulate you just to get what they want. Be careful around them. Don't let a single soul outside of this room know what we've been discussing." My thoughts flicked to the girls I had spent hours with reminiscing about our homes. How am I supposed to keep my plan to myself when I would see the despair in their eyes every time I spoke to them? I sighed inwardly.

For now, I'll keep quiet. At least Croxley seemed to be considering it. Perhaps later I can convince him to let me bring others in.

Croxley kept his eyes trained on me, as if he could hear my internal debate, so I nodded and assured him, "Okay, I promise I won't tell any of the girls." Croxley raised his eyebrows, not entirely believing me, but I didn't have enough energy to argue. Suddenly, all the emotions of the day, all the shocks and surprises, crashed down on me and I found myself exhausted. I yawned and wobbled on my feet. Both Croxley and the Prince rushed to my side to support me, and if I had not been so tired, I would have been amused by their sudden chivalry. Instead, I pushed them off and headed towards the door, when it occurred to me that I didn't know where I was going. "How do I get back to my room?" I asked, eager to get back to my cot.

Croxley put his helmet back on his head and checked the hallways. After a few moments, he motioned for me to follow. I kept my eyes trained on his back as we returned to the servant corridors, turning around for one last glimpse of the Prince as the door shut behind us.

CHAPTER 18

I woke up to the sound of birds chirping, the sun shining through my eyelids. I rolled over and stretched, enjoying the pull on my stiff muscles, when I suddenly froze mid-stretch. "I'm late for work!" I jumped out of bed and rushed to put my dress and shoes on, while memories of the night before rushed through my mind. I saw my nice dress laying crumpled in the corner, and chastised myself for not taking better care of it. As if Mathelda won't already have enough to punish me for.

I picked it up and dusted it off, trying to banish it of any mud clumps before they could create stains. Laying it neatly on my bed. I dashed out of the room, running straight into none other but Mathelda herself. I was able to catch my balance before falling down, but she wasn't as lucky. I offered my hand to help her up, but she angrily shooed it away and clumsily stood back up, mud dripping from her backside.

"What on earth do you think you are doing, you little imbecile," Mathelda scolded, but mid-scold, she paused and attempted to reassemble her face into a smile, succeeding in what was best described as a grimace. "Forgive me," she offered in a voice barely above a whisper, "I was in the way."

Maybe it was the dumbfounded look on my face, or the fact that I couldn't utter a single word in response to this sudden change in character, that prompted her to continue talking.

"I assume you haven't eaten this morning. I had the cook save a plate for you." She turned around and walked towards the kitchen, leaving me standing alone with my mouth hanging open. Shaking myself out of it, I followed her into the kitchen, suddenly aware of the grumbling in my stomach.

Mathelda presented me with a plate of bread, gruel, and, to my surprise, an apple. Putting my manners aside, I greedily shoved it all down, half-starved from the day before. Halfway through, my throat caught as my now-fed brain began to process what was happening. What on earth is going on? I thought to myself. Why did Mathelda bother saving me a plate?

Why didn't she get madder when she fell? I choked on a piece of apple as the dreadful reality revealed itself. She's poisoned me. That's it. She doesn't want me around any-more, so this is her way of getting rid of me. Coughing, I stared at the apple in my hand out of disbelief that such an innocent fruit could commit such a heinous deed. Mathelda must have wanted to speed up the process, because she hit me hard on the back, and dislodged the piece of apple.

I cleared my throat and managed to say "Thanks" through my coughing, while in my head it occurred to me that I was thanking my killer. Thinking I might as well get it out in the open, I asked her why she saved me a plate.

"Well, I just felt like doing something nice for one of my hardest workers. I thought you deserved the rest after such a long day yesterday."

"Work? I'm late for work! I need to go to the stables!" Poison forgotten, I began to stand up, but Mathelda motioned for me to sit back down. I slowly sunk back down onto the seat, watching her, waiting for this façade to break.

"You don't need to work in the stables any more, my dear. I think we have found your place."

"What do you mean, 'my place'?" I completely gave up trying to figure up what was going on. Nothing was making sense anymore.

Mathelda forced what I presumed to be a laugh, which came out as strange, strained sound that seemed as though it had endured years of disuse. "You are so humble! Well, if you insist on acting dumb, I may as well tell you. You're to be a private service. To the Prince." She looked at me excitedly, the expression sitting awkwardly on her sharp face. When I failed to reciprocate her excitement, she sighed and explained, "The guard who dropped you off last night told me of the Prince's orders. He asked that I put you on reserve. He specifically stated that you aren't to see any other clients. How, may I ask, did you manage to catch the Prince's eye?"

"Oh, well, I, uh ... " Slowly, everything began to come together. Croxley must have made her think that I was servicing the Prince in the way the merchant hoped to be serviced last night. No wonder she didn't yell at me! If that were true, and the Prince was my elite clientèle, I'd be making her more money than all of the other girls combined!

"I, rem, tend to his horse," I offered as an explanation.

Mathelda replied wryly, "If that's what you want to call it," and I flushed in embarrassment as it occurred to me what she thought I meant. "Well, whatever you've been doing, you must have been doing a fine job. Although I can't say that I approve of the timing, what with his impending royal marriage and all. Never mind that, I'm not one to involve myself in castle affairs. I've been pushing my girls towards him all this time, and to think that he chose you," Mathelda ran her eyes up and down my figure, as though she was trying to see me through the Prince's eyes, but by the way she creased her eyebrows together, I assumed she was having difficulty finding anything that made me special. She finished her examination with a "hmph" and then directed her eyes towards my food, which I took as an indication to finish my plate.

Once I was done, my stomach more than satisfied, I awkwardly looked around the room, empty of all but Mathelda and I. I was unsure of what I was supposed to do next. Mathelda, on the other hand, seemed to know exactly what she wanted to do with me, and after calling the cook to come collect my plates, she motioned for me to stand up.

"Oh dear, I should have warned you before you finished your meal. You'll probably regret having eaten so much, but no matter. I'm taking you to the tailor to fit you for some new gowns. I can't have the Prince see you in these hand-me-down rags. And afterwards we will get you trimmed and polished. You could really use some shape to your eyebrows, and lit looks as if you're hair hasn't had a real brushing for a while," she said, holding my knotted hair out and letting it fall against my back.

I shuddered as the air hit my neck, its cold fingers brushing over my number. Or maybe it's because of Mathelda's sickly sweet double personality, I thought to myself as I followed her out of the dinning room.

I sprawled myself out on my bed, groaning and rubbing my hands over my poor stomach. Like Mathelda said, I regretted eating so much this morning once I had seen the tailor. Apparently, Ahrenian fashion demands that your waist is pulled so tight that your stomach has no place to go, while your breasts are practically sent plunging over the low neckline. The heavy skirts just added to the weight, and I felt as if I were swimming in a sea of fabric with every step I took. Although I can't complain about the material, I thought, reminiscing about the feeling of the silk running through my fingers as Mathelda helped me pick out different patterns and fabrics.

I say help, but it was more like demand. If I had it my way, I would have chosen only the softest fabrics in the simplest colours. A rich green that reminded me of the I first sight I had of the forest, another piece in the same deep purple of my first handful of berries. The only one I convinced Mathelda to let me keep was satin of the deepest midnight blue. Mathelda's eyes practically shone as she held it up to my face, and when she called the tailor over, they began to jabber excitedly about different embellishments and jewellery, a language that I didn't speak, while I just glazed over and absent-mindedly rubbed the fabric in-between my fingers.

Much to my dismay, the tailor was only the beginning of my worries. After they had finished trying to squash my ribcage into a "more ladylike physique", Mathelda dragged me to another form of torture, this one involving more traditional instruments of pain: hot wax and needles. When they were done clearing my face, arms, and other sensitive regions of hair, they allowed my poor, puckered, red body to sink into a soothing tub. Thinking the worst was over, I allowed myself to settle into the warm water, a luxury that brought back memories of my journeys with Croxley.

Before I could slip away into my revelries, however, the same tortures from before came in and instructed me me to stand up, exposing my bare skin to the freezing air, which she then proceeded to scrub raw with a rough rag and brush. To top it off, by the time I was free to sink back into the tub, the water had gone cold.

Finally, I was able to step into a dry, clean shift and simple gown, which hung lightly off my frame, the fabric caressing my battle-worn skin. The only thing left to do was try and tackle my hair. I was able to handle this with little protest. As a child, my mother would braid my hair to pass the time, finding different ways to keep it up so that it wouldn't cover my number. Thinking back to those times, I couldn't help but run my fingers over the brand on the back of my neck, once again exposed now that my hair was intricately assembled atop my head in the courtly fashion. After all this, after everything that's happened, I'm still 923. I wasn't able to decide if that was a good thing or a bad thing. Either way, I thought, I still miss home.

By the time I was released, the day was nearly over. I found myself wondering how Sir Thunder, Sam, Elana, and all the other horses were doing. I should go say hello to Heath, I told myself, but the thought made its way to the back of my mind as my body sunk into the bed and I drifted off to sleep.

"Hey. Fara. Wake up." I awoke to Jean nudging me awake, the setting sun sending an orange glow into the room. I groaned and stretched, my body still sore from all the events of the day.

"Morning, Jean," I yawned, propping myself up into a seated position. Jean sat back on her own bed, looking exhausted. "What's wrong?"

"Oh, nothing. I was just wondering how you were. I heard about your job yesterday. To be honest, I was wondering when they were gonna start putting you out there. Most girls start on the second or third day." Jean looked at me with a strange mix of compassion and envy.

"Well thanks for warning me," I said, hurt in my voice. If she knew this was going to happen all along, why didn't she tell me? Is she jealous that it took so long for me to meet the same fate as everyone else?

"Hey, don't get mad at me," she said, her hands up in surrender. " I wanted to tell you, but honestly, what good would it of done? You would've just been worried about it, waiting for it to happen. That doesn't help, believe me. You just have to put it in the back of your mind, don't think about it until the time comes."

"And just let yourself be violated? This isn't right!"

"Save it. You've only had to deal with this reality once. I've been dealing with it since I got here. We've all been dealt the same fate, so now you'll just have to get used to it. Besides, you wanted this life."

"Hey, that's not fair," I began to argue, but stopped when Jean turned her face and wiped her hands under her eyes. "Jean, I'm sorry. You're right. I shouldn't get mad at you, it isn't your fault." I got off my bed and patted her shoulder, but she flinched away. I remembered the many times that she had come home with bruises and had just waved them off, only telling me they were from work. In my ignorance, I failed to realize what she was truly struggling with. Determined now to change that, I pulled her into a comforting embrace. After a few awkward moments, I felt something in her break and she melted into my arms, openly crying. Now that I looked back on it, she wasn't the same joyful, open girl who helped me get through my first few days here. She seemed jaded, yet strong. I also felt guilty for her compassion. Nothing had really happened to me. Compared to her, I've got it made easy. Especially after today, when Mathelda spent the entire day pampering me. And I thought to complain because my tailored dress was too tight? Once again, I berated myself for my weakness. Meanwhile, my motivation to find freedom was rekindled with an even greater favor.

I promise you, Jean, I will find a way to save us. I sat there, holding her until her tears stopped, and she pulled away, a gentle smile forming on her tear-stained face.

"Sorry you had to see me like that," she said, as she stood up. "Now, lets grab I some food," she said, sniffling through the last few tears as she tried to put a cheerful smile on her face, "I'm starved!"

CHAPTER 19

The next day, I made sure to wake up extra early so that I could catch up with Jean and the other girls. They all treated me differently, aware that I had faced the harsh reality of life as a slave girl, and although I felt guilty for their misplaced sympathy, I couldn't afford to tell them the truth about what had happened.

As we chatted during breakfast, one of the girls from Mathelda's table approached us. Mathelda dines with a select group of girls. Most of them are girls who were born in Ahrenia and somehow made their way into slavery. Whether their parents sold them to settle a debt or they got themselves into trouble, nobody knew, but either way, they seem to think that their heritage trumps their position. Even though we are all slaves down here, they act as though they have superiority in this subterranean hierarchy. Among them are the some of the most beautiful girls here, the ones with the palest skin, the longest hair, the nicest teeth, and all of them are snobs. For the most part, I've been lucky enough to avoid them. Make any one of them angry enough, give them any reason to feel threatened by you, and you'll notice your life steadily gets worse and worse. And now, one of them was walking towards our table.

"Fara, Mathelda wants to speak to you." This girl, Lacy, looked directly at me as she spoke, as if I were the only one at the table. I looked nervously at Jean and the rest of the girls, who shrugged, then back to Lacy.

"Um, okay," I muttered, following her back to the table.

"Fara, come sit, my dear!" Mathelda gestured for the girl next to her to move so that I could sit next to her, but I just stood with my hands clasped behind me.

"No, that's okay. I'm fine." I just wanted Mathelda to tell me whatever it was she wanted to so that I could get back to my table. I could practically feel their curious stares at my back.

"I wasn't asking. Sit," she demanded, and I obeyed. "Besides, you shouldn't have to sit with those girls any-more, now that you've proven yourself worthy of some investment. Speaking of which, our Prince requests your company again today. Your dresses aren't finished yet, so I'll just have you wear one of Lacy's gowns. You appear to be the same size." I heard Lacy protest, and groaned inwardly. It looks like my life just got a whole lot more complicated. Mathelda didn't seem to notice, because she kept going.

"After you finish eating, get dressed and I will call for a guard to escort you to the
garden." She motioned towards the food on the table, but in my discomfort, I was unable to eat. I looked back to Jean and the other girls, but they had resumed their chatter, no doubt talking about me. So I sat at the table, awkwardly silent as the girls around me gossiped about their newest gown, what gifts their clients had bestowed on them, how their hair had refused to behave this morning. All topics that were completely foreign to me.

"Hey. Excuse me," I was startled out of my daydream by the girl sitting across from me. "Can I ask you how you keep your hair so smooth?"

"I don't know." The girl was obviously unsatisfied with this answer, so I went on. "I guess it's because I braid it before I sleep."

"What a great idea! Thanks!"

"Um, no problem." Her enthusiasm was so high that I couldn't tell if she was mocking me or genuinely really interested.

"Fara, right? I'm Lydia." She smiled, her pink lips opening to reveal bright teeth, her flushed cheeks dimpling. Her blonde hair was streaked with highlights of gold, while her tan skin practically glowed against her peach dress. Next to her, I felt pale and drab. It was easy to believe that she brought Mathelda good business. What I couldn't believe was that she was speaking to me so readily. "I room with Lacy. You're done with your food, right? Come with me so we can pick out a dress."

I could feel Lacy glaring at me, probably wishing a sudden and painful death upon me before I could lay my hands on her clothes, but I decided there wasn't much I could do about it. I just smiled at her apologetically, to which she sniffed and turned her head.

"Don't mind Lacy. She hates sharing," Lydia told me as we walked to her room. We passed Jean and the girls at our table, all of whom had curios looks on their face. I'm definitely going to hear about this from Jean later tonight. We left the main dining hall and turned down one of the tunnels. Lydia was still jabbering, telling me about the time she wore one of Lacy's powder blue dresses and her patron spilled red wine on it.

"You should have seen her face when I showed her! I mean, sure, I felt bad for getting the wine on it. Well, technically, it wasn't my fault, it was the King's messenger, what was his name? Conley? Crosby?"

"Croxley?" I asked, suddenly interested.

"Yes! Croxley! Any-ways, Croxley spilled this red wine all over the front of my, well, Lacy's, gown, but it wasn't that bad. I mean, most of the wine was soaked up by the mattress, which wasn't either of ours, by the way, but a Dukes ... "

Lydia finally stopped, both walking and talking, and gestured to one of the rooms. As we entered, I had to shield my eyes at the sunlight shining through the window. When my eyes adjusted, I let out an audible gasp. Her bed was thick and lifted off the ground, like that of the needs back at the inn, adorned with soft linen sheets. The room also contained a plush woollen rug, a mirror, a small desk with rows of lip stain, hair combs, accessories, and most noticeably, a large collection of gowns bursting from a cabinet standing against the wall. The variety of colour and style was second only to my visit to the tailors yesterday.

Lydia just giggled at my obvious shock, thrusting her arm towards all the gowns as she exclaimed, "Aren't they lovely? Now let's see, I think this one will suit you just fine!" She held up a deep blood-red gown with gold embroidery trailing down the side.

"Oh no, I can't wear that! It's much to fine! How about something else?" I looked for the simplest gown I could find, hoping for something inconspicuous, but Lydia laughed and put the first dress I found, which was a soft blue colour, back in the cabinet.

"No, silly, Lacy wouldn't even wear that to sleep!"

Things went on like this until we finally compromised on a pale green gown with subtle silver trim. Before I could leave, Lydia insisted on doing my hair, wanting to practice her braiding. I ended up with crown of braids, as apparently one wasn't enough for Lydia, and with that, I was finally set free. Mathelda grabbed me as soon as I entered the main room and ushered me to the guard waiting in the hallway. To my dismay, it wasn't Croxley in disguise, but an actual guard, who kept leering at me the whole way through.

We eventually made it to the garden through a series of twists and turns that I hadn't known existed. Despite having been at the castle for nearly two months, I still found myself lost quite often in its labyrinth of corridors and passageways. I had mainly spent my days working with Heath at the stables, with no leftover time to explore the castle.

Heath! My heart jerked as I thought of Elana, Sam, and Sir Thunder, all still waiting for me at the stables. Perhaps I can convince the Prince to take me to see them. I'll have to make sure I grab some sugar cubes or apples on the way there. Elana loves apples! I hoped Croxley wasn't pushing good ol' Sam too hard. My thoughts wandered off as the guard, myself in his wake, ventured further into the garden. My eyes widened as we wandered further and further in. It was like a hidden paradise! There were flowers of every kind, trees with fruits I had never seen, bushes with leaves of every shape and colour, all somehow able to evade the chill of winter that was causing all the other trees outside to lose their leaves. I wanted to run and twirl through the groves, but I wasn't about to make a fool out of myself in front of the guard. Instead, I let my gaze wander through all the flowers, making a mental note to find out the names of each one.

All my inhibitions about appearing foolish in front of the guard disappeared, and I couldn't help but gasp when I saw a bush shaped like a horse. When I looked down that row, I discovered a variety of animals. Some shrubs were recognizable, such as those shaped like birds and cats, but most of them were creatures I had never seen before. One was a large animal with what looked like second tail in place of its nose and ears larger than dinner plates, while another had a neck longer than I imagined was possible. There was even a horse with a sharp horn coming out of the front of its forehead. I wondered whether or not these creatures were fictitious or if it was just my sheer lack of experience on the surface that caused them to look foreign.

My mind lost in the moment, I didn't notice the guard stop until I had nearly run into him.

"The Prince is around the corner," announced the guard, who then promptly walked off through another branch of the garden, leaving me standing there alone with the plants. An unexpected nervousness rose in my stomach. I was so caught up with the beauty of the garden that I hadn't given much thought to what came next. I tidied my skirts and patted my hair, instantly feeling ridiculous for doing so.

Rounding the corner, I saw the Prince before he saw me. I caught myself admiring him from behind, his broad solders outlined by his thin shirt, the muscles faintly discernible, his profile striking against the backdrop of the garden. When he saw me, he smiled and waved me over.

"Good morning, Miss Fara," he greeted as I made my approach. He bowed and kissed my hand when I reached him, then swept his arm over the garden. "So, what do you think?"

"It's absolutely beautiful," I sheepishly answered, fully aware that I was speaking more of him than of the flowers. I rambled on, nervousness running my tongue.

"I never knew there were so many different kinds of flowers! Where do they all come from?"

"I'm glad you approve! Well, some of them come from Ahrenia, they just normally grow in different seasons, while others were shipped in from distant lands to make the collection more exotic. Here, I'll show you my favourite one." He pulled me over to the fountain in the middle of the clearing, which up until this point had completely escaped my attention, absorbed as I was in the Prince, and pointed to the thin vine climbing the statue. The flowers were a deep violet, some spun open while others were still twisted shut.

"These are called morning glories, so named because they bloom in the morning and, by the end of the day, close themselves up and die. They're actually a weed that the gardener is trying to uproot, but they just keep coming back. I admire their persistence. But don't try to pick one, or else they'll wither and die." He looked over the flowers at me and took me in, as if he was just now noticing me. "You look beautiful, by the way."

I blushed and looked towards the statue, following the vines with my eyes. When I reached the head, I turned my gaze back to the Prince.

"Thank you, your highness, but the gown isn't mine"

"You don't have to call me 'your highness', you know. Erik is fine."

"But I'm a servant! And a Nether, for that matter. I'm much too low in rank," I protested. The Prince groaned in return.

"Rank, rules, regulations. Honestly, I'm growing tired of it all!" The Prince paced out his frustration. "Before the engagement, I never really had an issue with any of I it. All the riches and luxury, I took it for granted. And I'll be the first to admit that I never really did my duty like I was supposed to. I merely enjoyed the title of 'your highness' without all the work, my ego fanned by the girls fawning over me and lining up to dance at the balls. But now, I'd much rather have a life like Croxley, who can come and go as he pleases, nothing to bind him down, no one to depend on him." He ran his hand through his hair, and suddenly looked self-conscious. "I'm sorry, I don't mean to burden you with all this. It seems as though I've already told you my life story, venting all my troubles, and yet I barely even know yours."

"That's not true!" Croxley's voice startled both the Prince and I, and we jumped apart, just now realizing how close we had gotten. "You were asking about her our entire trip!" Prince Erik cast his eyes down and rubbed the back of his neck, embarrassed. Croxley walked up and gave the Prince a companionable pat on the back, then wearily sat on the fountain's rim. He combed his hands through his hair as he sighed, and I noticed that, as he lifted his head back up, his eyes traced the line of my dress. "Fara, that gown suits you well," he told me quietly.

At this point, my face felt like it was about to melt off. I just nodded, not knowing what to do with all of these compliments. Croxley cleared his throat, brushing his hand through the water while speaking to us.

"Sorry I'm late, I was busy getting materials prepared for my next trip. Before you get all worked up, Fara," he cautioned when he saw my face light up, "I'm not going to a colony. I'm just going on some standard rounds to the surrounding towns. And no, Erik, you can't come with me this time either." Erik and I both looked dejected, which made Croxley laugh and exclaim, "Honestly, you two, what would you do without me? Speaking of which, have you started working on any plans yet, or do you finally agree with me that this is a completely foolish idea?"

"I've actually got some good ideas," Prince Erik said as he sat besides Croxley.

And so, we began brainstorming. At first, the plans weren't very practical, but the more we bounced ideas off each other, the more developed the strategies became. We decided that Croxley would start with the furthest colonies, because it would take longer for reports of rebellion to reach the castle. Should everything go according to plan, however, the guards should be out of the colonies and far enough away before the Nethers leave so as to not notice anything.

"Ahrenia is currently in conflict with Lucendorff. If we tell the guards that they've been chosen to fight for the King's army, they'd jump at the promotion without question."

"But wouldn't the generals be suspect of all the men suddenly coming in from no where?" Croxley asked.

"Good point," Erik concurred.

"I have an idea," I ventured. "What if they don't show up to the actual army? What if we position a false army in the opposite direction, sending them instructions that would keep them busy outside of Ahrenia? Tell them they are preparing the way for an important mission of some kind."

"What would we have them do?"

"Have them pave roads or something! Anything that will keep them occupied and unaware of what's really going on," I offered.

"That just might work," Prince Erik considered. "I could write some letters for verification's sake, and we could use them to perform some much-needed handiwork around the country. Kill two birds with one stone!"

"Precisely! And then, once we get the guards out, we can have the colonies group together. How many are there again, Croxley?"

"There are 7 total. Two in the north, one in the south, and two on either side of Stonewall." In the dirt, Croxley drew a map of Ahrenia, with Stonewall in the middle. Around it, he drew the colonies. To my surprise, Cethin was the closest to the royal city, on the western side. The northern colonies were in the mountains, while the eastern colonies were more spread out. Two were along the western coast, while another was directly south of Stonewall. That must be where Jean is from, I thought to myself. The northernmost colony was almost on the border between Ahrenia and Ludendorf, so we decided that Croxley should go there first.

"This is where the guards feel the most pressure from the Ludendorf conflict, so it would probably help to start there. Once we get the troops assembled, we can send them to repair a bridge that fell a few years back, telling them it is part of the invasion plan. The bridge is located a few miles north of the colony, so they will be out of the way when I guide Nethers to this colony," Croxley said, circling Cethin. "This should be the best meeting point. My only question now is, once we get them there, what are we going to do? What good will any of this do in regards to earning your people their freedom?" Both Croxley and the Prince looked at me expectantly, and I flailed for an answer.

"I don't know. I was hoping that if we could get enough of us together, we could all just ask the King. With so many of us, how could he refuse?"

"Easily." Surprisingly, it was Prince Erik who shot me down, not Croxley. "My father has no regard for Nethers. He often complains that you absorb more resources than you put out. I fear that, by gathering everyone in one place, you are setting them up for an easy slaughter. If you want to get something accomplished, you'll have to take it by force. That is the only language my father seems to speak."

"Surely you're not suggesting an attack on your own kingdom," Croxley panicked, concern written all over his face.

"Of course not. I am the Prince of Ahrenia. If I acted against my father, I would be branded a traitor, and the people would throw me out. But I can't say that violence won't occur. Should things develop into that, it would be because of my father's stubbornness, not because of any treason on my part."

"If we have a chief from every colony come into the castle and demand an audience, it would appear very poor on his part to ignore them," Croxley offered.

"Well, we can only hope." Prince Erik stood up from the fountain and clapped his hands together. "Anyhow, all this planning has made me hungry enough to eat a horse. Shall we go out for lunch?"

"Horse!" I exclaimed, jumping up into a standing position, receiving a peculiar look from Croxley and the Prince. "I've been dying to see Elena, Sir Thunder, and Sam! I miss Heath as well. He is bound to be worrying about me. Could we stop by them afterwards?"

"And get your gown all tattered?" Croxley admonished.

"I'll be careful, I promise!" I assembled my face into an expression I had seen Conor pull on his mother whenever he was being disciplined, making my eyes wider and pouting my lip just a bit. Aware of the low cut of my dress, I even went as far as to gently squeeze my breasts together. I cringed inwardly at my shameless behaviour, but I couldn't help it. I needed the peace that the horses always brought to me after all that had happened today.

Erik slung his arm around Croxley's shoulders, graciously exclaiming, "I don't see why not! Let's get going, then."

After a rich lunch at one of the nearby inns, we headed over to the stables. On the way, we picked up a bag of apples and small tin sugar cubes, which Erik proceeded to munch on the whole way there.

"Hey, leave some for the horses!" I chastened, my excitement building with every step. When we finally got there, I ran into the stables and straight down to Elana, standing as regal as ever. After brushing her down, I moved onto Sir Thunder, and then Sam. When Croxley and Prince Erik came wandering in, I was bouncing back and forth between the horses, trying to give them all equal amounts of attention.

"Look at her! She looks like she's about to sprout a third arm," Croxley joked, leaning in to feed Sir Thunder an apple.

"If it isn't Miss Fara!" Heath boomed, emerging from one of the stalls. He quickly walked up to me, wiping his hands on his pants before pulling me up off the ground and into a hug.

"You had me worried! You just up and went missing for days! I couldn't help but suspect the worst. It always seems to happen to the girls they send me sooner or later. ·

"Thanks Heath, nice to see you too," I choked out, his crushing embrace squeezing the air out of me. "But could you let me go? I can't really breathe."

"Oh, sorry las." Heath cleared his throat and gruffly set me down, patting me on the head. I smiled at this gentle giant. "What's got you dressed up so nice and proper?"

"Heath, you're never gonna believe what happened."

"I'm sure I can guess. Either way, forget I asked. I don't want to know. The less I know, the less trouble it causes me." I understood what he meant. It seems like I kept getting myself deeper and deeper into trouble here with every new thing I find out. But do I regret it? I can't say I do.

We spent the rest of the evening in the stables. Heath made us a fire to sit around and we helped ourselves to some stew, laughing over our meal and relaxing in each other's company. As much as it was comforting, it also made me a bit homesick. The scene was far too similar, reminding me of the bland meals we used to share around our small fire pit, our curtain held open for any neighbour to come in and make themselves at home. I missed Conor, with his smart remarks and his endless mischief. I missed his strong mother, who disciplined with a hard hand, but loved with an even softer heart.

Most of all, I missed my parents. The way my mother would braid my hair on top of my head to show my number. I ran my fingers along my neck, feeling the raised scar of the numbers 923. Its as much a part of me as my real name, my family, and my life underground as Faradene. It sever as a reminder of what I came up here to do. And now, I thought, I'm actually doing something. I'm planning with the Prince, of all people, to liberate not only my family, but anyone who has been condemned to live underground.

I can only hope that our plan will work.

We bade goodnight to Heath and the horses and made our way back to the castle. But when we got to the main road, we ran into a large group of people blocking the street. There was a loud clamour in the group, and they all seemed to be watching something.

"What are they all looking at?" I asked, having to raise my voice over the crowd. Croxley looked just as confused as I felt, but when we looked to the Prince, we noticed that he looked troubled. Before we could ask him what was wrong, he shot off into the crowd, just as a group of guards pushed through on the other side.

"You, Messenger," one of the guards approached us. "Do you know where the Prince is?"

"Why? What's going on?" asked Croxley.

"Her highness is here, Princess Lena. The Prince's bride-to-be."

CHAPTER 20

So that's why he was so keen on keeping himself busy yesterday. Princess Lena was coming, I thought to myself as I scrubbed my clothes clean the next morning. After Croxley pointed the guards in the opposite direction of the Prince, we forced our way through the crowd to the front, where we had a perfect view of the Princess's caravan. I have to admit, she knows how make an impressive entrance. Each of her wagons, and I lost track after the first 6, were led by white horses, their ropes embellished with rubies and sapphires. The carriages were trimmed with gold, and the woodwork was adorned with intricate carvings. The final carriage had a window in the back, through which you could faintly make out its precious cargo, Princess Lena. From what I could tell, she had long, dark hair, thick, pouty red lips, a soft nose, and a slender neck.

She was beautiful.

The rest of the day, I couldn't get her face out of my head. Or, rather, I couldn't get her face next to Erik's face out of my head. I know he said that he couldn't stand her, but now that she was here...

I convinced myself that the only reason I was I concerned about Princess Lena's arrival was because I was worried about her finding out about the plan from Prince Erik. Not to mention that now it'll be a lot harder to talk to him, what with her hanging on his arm.

I beat the images out of my head as I attacked a particularly stubborn stain in my gown. Tonight, there is supposed to an official welcome feast in honour of her arrival, and all of the servants have to work the kitchen and dining hall, which means I have to dawn my pale blue uniform once again. As much as I hate to admit it, I was growing fond of the fine fabrics Mathelda was dressing me in.

Oh well, I thought to myself, at least I'll be able to spend some time with Jean and the other girls. We had both been assigned serving duty, so we would be able to talk in between meals. From what Jean told me this morning, the rich love to eat. Their appetites are inexhaustible, which means that we will constantly be running between the kitchen and the dining room to replenish the exorbitant amount of food at the feast.

"They eat themselves sick," Jean had said earlier when she was explaining it to me. "And if they haven't eaten themselves to the point of explosion, the wine will do it. It 's absolutely horrendous! Here we are, our families starving in the tunnels, living off of bland roots and vegetables, while they are up here, wasting food like it grows on trees." With that, I gave her a look, and she sighed and rolled her eyes at me. "Oh, you know what I mean!"

Despite her complaints, I found myself eager for the night to begin, excited to see all the dishes that the cooks would come up with. The best thing I have eaten since coming to Ahrenia is still the meal that Croxley and I shared at the inn before reaching the castle, but I was sure that this food would be of much better quality. Imagining different plates and tastes in my head, I finished scrubbing my dress and hung it near the hearth to dry, not in the least enthusiastic about my dull breakfast of gruel.

"Do people actually eat this?" I gaped in disbelief after we returned from bringing in the third round of dishes. So far, there has been cow stomach filled with poultry giblets, fermented chicks served in little egg cups, and what looked to be a stew of snails and mushrooms.

So much for delicious meals.

"Honestly, if this is what they are eating all day, I say let them have it. I'll stick to my gruel, thanks." I told Jean.

"I would hold your tongue until you see the desert. Usually there are leftovers, so we can sneak a few plates at the end. By then, most of the kitchen is drunk from all the wine they 'taste' before they send it out, so it shouldn't be too hard."

Out of all the jobs and errands I've had to do since coming to the castle, I would have to say that dining duty was at the top of my list, second only to working the stables. As it turns out, royals love to gossip over food, so I've been able to pick up quite a few rumours over the last three meals. Most of it was trivial hearsay, such as the news that Sir Button had taken up a new sport known as tennis, or that a new style of headpieces were coming into fashion, or, most commonly, who seemed to end up in whose bed. But occasionally I passed by two bent heads discussing political matters, such as the increasing tension at Ahrenia's southern border.

Perfect, I thought, that might distract them even more while we are moving everyone from their colonies to the city. I kept my ears open for the rest of the night, but I didn't catch much else.

As much as my ears were open, so were my eyes. I couldn't help but look for the Prince and Croxley as soon as I entered the room. I found Croxley sitting near the far end of the table, quite a few chairs down from Prince Erik. He was engaged in conversation with his neighbours, and I thought he was enjoying himself until he caught my eye and pulled a face that indicated otherwise. Prince Erik, on the other hand, was seated next to Lena at the end of the table, fully absorbed with her presence, holding Lena's hands in his and leaning towards her, as if he were disclosing some scandalous secret. I turned my eyes away, trying to focus on something else, but that didn't stop me from hearing his melodious laughter fill the hall. Before I could dwell too much on the way it sent sharp pangs through my stomach, an unhappy bark brought me to attention.

"Hush! Serving girls don't talk when they are on duty!" Mathelda berated a group of giggling girls nearby before continuing on in my direction. "Oh, Fara, how are you, my dear? I'm sorry you had to work today, but we needed all the girls on staff." She reached out and tweaked my hair around until she was satisfied, while I stood completely still, holding my breath, as though she were a snake that would attack should I make a wrong move. She frightened me more when she was like this, wearing a mask of kindness, than she did as her regular, dictating self. "Jean, why don't you take Fara's next plate out for her? I'm sure she is getting tired from all this hard labour," she said, apparently having just noticed Jean for the first time.

"It's al-right, Mathelda, I can carry it," I tried to argue, but Mathelda shushed me with a stem look. I gave Jean a quick sympathetic look before she left, but she wasn't facing me.

"Now that that little minx is gone, I'll tell you something important," Mathelda said, turning to face me, her eyes sparkling. "Even though the Prince's bride has come, and let's be honest, no amount of work put into you will ever get you close to her beauty, I refuse to let our most important customer back out now. I want you to get as close to him as possible. Do everything you can to seduce him. Your gowns came in today, so you don't have to borrow from Lacy any more. Oh, and speaking of Lacy, you are going to move into her room. She has the largest closet, so

you can put all your new gowns in there. Lydia seemed excited to have you as a room mate anyhow. This way you don't have to deal with that Jean girl any more."

Horrified, I could only watch her back as she walked away, leaving me standing alone with a polite refusal stuck in my throat.

This was bad. Not only was I making enemies with Lacy, which is bad enough in itself, but I'm also leaving Jean behind. I knew that she was growing tired of my sudden rise in Mathelda's little hierarchy, and this would certainly push her over the edge. I needed her on my side, especially since I was going to need her help get to the colonies.

"What was that about?" Jean startled me, returning from her last shift.

"Um, well," might as well get it out, "Mathelda is going to move me to a different room. Into Lacy's room." As expected, Jean's face hardened.

"Oh. Okay."

"Jean, please don't take it that way. I honestly don't know why Mathelda is being so nice to me. Okay, I do know why, but that doesn't mean that I enjoy it. I mean, it's really not what you think. I wish I could just tell you ... "

"Tell me what? That you are sick of me and all the other girls? That we aren't pretty enough for you, especially now that you got all close and personal with the Prince? Yeah, we all know about that. Mathelda's been bragging about it nonstop. Well, you know what? Good for you. Looks like you don't need my help any-more."

"No, Jean, you have it all wrong! I do need your help, more than you know. I just can't talk about it here. But listen! I don't want Lacy's wardrobe or fancy clothes, I don't want any of this. I just want us to be free!" I shut my mouth before the last words could make it all the way out, worried that someone had overheard us, but everyone was too busy rushing in and out with dishes. Jean looked at me strangely for a few moments before shaking her head, closing her eyes and putting her hand up, as if she were giving up the entire situation.

"What are you even talking about? You know what? I don't even care any-more. I'll see you later. Oh yeah, I guess I won't. So long, Fara. Enjoy your new life." With that, Jean stomped out of the kitchen, while I stood there motionless amidst the bustle of the kitchen, not even trying to stop the tears from falling down.

Jean wasn't in the room when I came to move out. Then again, it wasn't like I had very much to move. I folded up my clothes, noticing that the ones I had worn on my journey here weeks ago still smelled faintly of the forest. I wished that I could just rip off my gown, throw on these clothes, and escape back into the forest, where everything was easy. Grabbing those and my boots, the last thing I had left to take was my plant. It had grown quite nicely. The stalk had shot up and a there was a thick head of leaves at the top, as well as a small white flower bud. I had no idea what it would grow into, what it would become. All I knew was that it had grown with me, something from Cethin that flowered in Ahrenia. With all of my belongings in my arm, I turned around and left my room.

When I reached Lydia's, or, I guess, our room, Lydia was sitting on her bed, apparently waiting for me. She squealed with excitement as I entered, jumping off her bed and pulling me into a tight hug.

"I am so excited! You know, I knew that you and I would get along the moment I saw you sitting at our table. I thought, 'Wow, that girls is pretty, in a weird, colourless kind of way.' And I have a lot of colour! So, we are like twins, but opposites! Plus, you won't complain as much as Lacy did, or get mad at me when I want to borrow your clothes. Right?"

I glazed over during her monologue, thinking back to Jean and what she must think of me. She probably thinks that I'm a traitor. First I leave my home, then I leave my first true friend. Is this all really worth it? It took me a few moments to notice that Lydia had stopped speaking and was looking at me expectantly, excitement lighting up her face.

"Um, yeah. I'm excited too. I guess," I offered non-committally. I stood there awkwardly, holding all of my belongings in my hands, not knowing where to set them. I don't know where I belong any-more.

Lydia must have noticed my exhausted expression because she grabbed some of the things in my hands. She set them on a desk, informing me that now, it was my desk, and motioned for me to sit on my bed. I put my plant in on the windowsill, noting that this room had an actual window rather than just a hole in the wall. Lydia was looking over my shoulder, and when I turned around, she asked about what kind of plant it was.

"To be honest, I don't really know. I brought it with me as a seed when I left."

"Left from where?" Lydia asked.

"From my home, from Cethin."

"Oh. You're from down there." Suddenly, Lydia didn't I seem too talkative. My curiosity sparked, and although I knew it was a risk, I just couldn't help but ask.

"Are you from a colony, Lydia?" I asked her quietly, as if I might spook her away should I ask anything too personal.

"A colony? Oh, you mean underground. Yes, I was born down in the dark. But I'm up in the light now, and I don't have to think about that any-more." What does that mean? Most girls talked about their home either with longing and homesickness or with scorn and a "good riddance". Lydia seemed to be frightened of her memories in the colonies.

"Lydia, what happened? How did you get up here?" I asked, gently prodding. Apparently, it wasn't gentle enough, because Lydia abruptly shook her head and jumped off the bed, a smile plastered on her face that didn't quite meet her eyes.

"Come on, let's look at your new wardrobe. They put all of your dresses on this side of the closet. I promised myself I wouldn't peek at them until you arrived, but now that you're here, I can't wait any longer!"

After Lydia dragged me to the closet, I lost all sight of the timid personality she had shown me. I made a mental note to try and get her to open up about her past, but for now I allowed her to dive into my new selection of clothes.

CHAPTER 21

Early the next morning, I awoke to find Lydia staring at me, unblinking. Once my heart stopped racing, I quietly called out, "Lydia? What do you need?" To my surprise, instead of answering, she let loose a loud snore and rolled over. She sleeps with her eyes open? Weird.

There was no way I could go back to sleep now, and besides, the light of the moon shone through the large window, brightening the room more than I was used to. I rose from my bed and left to relieve myself. Other than a few early risers, the quarters were eerily quiet. I took my time strolling through the tunnels, reflecting on everything that had happened in the past few weeks. Perhaps that's why I didn't realize that Mathelda was walking straight towards me until it was too late to hide.

Honestly, did this woman ever sleep? She approached me with a sense of purpose, and I could only imagine what she had planned for me this time.

"Oh, Fara. I'm glad you're awake. I have an important day planned for you. I thought it would be nice if you accompanied the Prince and his new fiancé on their errands."

"Are you sure? I wouldn't want to be in the way. They must have a lot to get done."

"My naive Fara, that is precisely the point. We don't want the Prince to get too far ahead in his marriage. He still has some time before they tie the knot, and I would like to milk all the profit we can out of this little arrangement we had set up so nicely."

"But what of the King? Surely he wouldn't allow a slave girl to accompany the royal couple on their duties." I honestly didn't know why I was arguing with Mathelda, because she would undoubtedly win.

That's not true, I admitted to myself, you're arguing because you don't want to see Erik and Lena together.

"What the King thinks is none of your business," Mathelda reprimanded, and I caught a glimpse of the familiar, uptight woman I had known her to be before all of this madness began. "Now listen here. I will only say this once. I own you. I don't know why you think that suddenly you have a say in what you do. Perhaps I have been too easy on you. Need I remind you, I am in charge of what you girls do, and like it or not, you have no say in the matter. You do what I tell you, and you don't ask any questions. Otherwise, I might just send you back to the stalls to work for the horses, and let all the other customers who are demanding your attention have their way with you. I can promise they will not have the same sense of, how should I say, civility, that you have become accustomed to. Do I make myself clear?" Mathelda's eyes glowered, and I knew that I had overstepped my boundaries.

"Yes, Mathelda," I replied, my head bowed. I would have to be more careful if I wanted to avoid a repeat with the merchant.

"Good. Now I want you to go to your room, get dressed, and come back here by the time the sun rises. The royal couple is planning on enjoying a quiet breakfast in the garden. I assume you know where that is?"

"Yes ma'am," I curtsied, then turned around and headed towards my room.

When I got back to my room, Lydia had woken up and was sitting in the bed, rubbing her eyes and quietly complaining that they were dry. I wonder why, I thought dryly, thinking back to the lovely sight I had been greeted with earlier.

"Good morning," I said, rummaging through my closet for something to wear.

"Mmmm....hello, Fara," she said, stretching her arms over her head and then sliding out of bed, sitting at the desk in front of a mirror. "What are your plans for today?" She asked as she combed through her long, blonde hair.

"I'm, ah, supposed to be accompanying the royal couple," I admitted, knowing she would find out sooner or later. I waited for her to let out an excited squeal, or some other Lydia-esque reaction, but all I got was a murmur of recognition. Turning around, I looked at her to see if anything was the matter.

"Lydia? Is everything okay?" I asked her, wondering if she was still upset about what we talked about last night, but if so, her face didn't show any emotion.

"Oh yes, I'm sorry. I'm just tired. Not much of a morning person, I guess. What about you? You are up pretty early. You were already gone when I woke up."

"Something woke me up and I couldn't go back to sleep," I purposely skipped the part about her strange sleeping habits, not wanting to embarrass her, "so I decided to walk around the tunnels." Hoping to lift her spirits, I did the only thing I thought might help. "Lydia, could you help me pick out something to wear for today?"

"Of course!" Her face literally lit up, while I, on the other hand, suddenly felt uneasy. This is what I get for being a nice person. I ended in a lavender gown with ruffled sleeves that cut open at the elbows, draping fabric down my arms and creating an admittedly nice effect. I convinced Lydia to let me wear my hair down, but she insisted that I borrow her silver hair clip, pinning the sweep of my hair to the side over my shoulder. She finished just as the sun began to climb in the sky, so I thanked her and quickly made my way to the main room.

As I entered, I found Mathelda at her usual table, her fingers rapping against the desk in an impatient manner. Inwardly, I flinched, knowing that she was probably upset at me for being a few minutes late. And I'm sure she hasn't forgotten about the conversation we had earlier.

When I made it to the table, Mathelda offered me an apple, which I politely declined, instead deciding to drink some water in attempt to calm my nerves. Every time I thought about having to follow the royal couple around, my stomach twisted further into a knot.

"I've organized for Bentley to come and pick you up. He will take you to the garden, where the royal couple is going to be enjoying their breakfast. I want you to find a way to join them. I assume that, having come from underground, you haven't the slightest amount of social skills, but somehow you have been able to hold your own with the Prince, so that means that he must genuinely appreciate your company. So, use the little charm that you seem to possess and remind Prince Erik what he has been missing out on these past few days."

"What if they refuse my company," I voiced my worries, knowing that Lena would almost assuredly not welcome my intrusion.

"Failure is not an option. I expect you'll do your best if you don't want to experience what we had talked about this morning." Mathelda said, standing up and nodding to someone across the room. I turned around and saw that it was the guard, who I assumed to be Bentley. My stomach in knots, I rose and approached him. He nodded a greeting and indicated for me to follow. On the way out, I looked back to see Jean entering the room. We caught each other's eyes, but only for a brief moment, as she quickly turned her head around to face someone else, acting as if she hadn't seen me.

Now I had to deal with the guilt of betraying Jean on top of everything else. Somehow I had managed to get myself completely reversed. Instead of helping free those stuck in the colonies, as well as all the Nethers enslaved up above, I was working with Mathelda. Instead of trying to plan the mission with the Prince, I was being used to try and interrupt his engagement in order to bring Mathelda more wealth.

Walking down the hallways, I realized that I had become a tool of the palace, succumbing to the same jealousies and intrigues that all the other Ahrenian nobles revel in. If I didn't watch myself, I would soon continue down the same path and become no better that the rest of the Ahrenians. Actually, I would be even worse, because I would always be given the dirtiest jobs, the least respect, the lowest standards. No matter how hard I worked, to them, I would always be a Nether.

That's right, I thought to myself, I would always be a Nether! In spite of everything that I've done and may do, my family and friends will always be there, supporting me with what little they have to provide. That will forever be more than anything the court could ever offer me. And since when is being a Nether such a bad thing? If anything, it's made me a better survivor than the Ahrenians. With this revelation, a sudden idea formed in my head, the sure way to make the King listen to us.

Nethers supply the kingdom with most of their materials. Without us, Ahrenians wouldn't have half of the necessities, not to mention luxuries, that they use day to day. If we we're to create an embargo, just for a few weeks, then people would have to admit to our importance, and eventually the King would have to see us! I mused over this idea for the rest of our trip. When Bentley and I enter the garden, I was so excited to tell Prince Erik my plan that I had forgotten my anxiety. That is, until the moment Bentley exited, leaving me standing awkwardly in the middle of the clearing, picking the edges of my sleeves as I made my way to the royal couples' table.

Prince Erik gave me a strange look, his eyes asking, or more like accusing, "what are you doing here?" I returned his gaze with an "I'm sorry" as I cleared my throat to introduce myself.

"Good morning, Prince Erik, Princess Lena." I bowed, feeling my face flame, raising it only after the Prince's dismissal.

"Good morning, Fara. Lena, this is Fara, a" he hesitated briefly, then went on "servant who often comes to help me. What do you need?"

Servant.

I'm just a servant.

The words sunk in, biting and deep. Suddenly, my pep-talk seemed irrelevant. All of the plans I came up with, as well as the confidence that came with it, disappeared. But I hid it, tucking the hurt away for another time, making sure to keep my mask of politeness on.

"Pleased to meet you, Princess Lena. My lady advised me to come and offer my services to you today. She would want nothing more than for you to have a comfortable welcome to the palace."

Lena took a few moments to respond, giving me a full appraisal, as if considering whether or not I was worth addressing. I must have passed the test, because she eventually flicked her hand dismissively and said "Well then, make yourself useful. Fetch me a drink."

I bowed again and walked to the table, where a delicious array of food had been spread out. Plates of cheeses, breads, and some dried fruits were laid out, surrounded by an assortment of fine wines. Picking one at random, I poured her a glass as I wondered internally about the similarities between Princess Lena, Mathelda, and Lacy. They were all undeniably attractive, but their personalities had about as much appeal as a venomous snake. I wondered if this was the norm in Ahrenia. If so, I'm glad that Cethin was kept out of it all. I would much rather be surrounded by beautiful souls than beautiful people.

"My lady," I said, offering the glass to the princess. She accepted it without so much as a glance my way, so I stood off to the side as her and the Prince politely conversed over trivial things like the weather and the latest ball.

Eventually, Princess Lena grew bored of the back and forth, so she asked to be shown around the garden. At that same moment, Bentley returned to summon Prince Erik, handing him a scroll. After reading it, the Prince looked up and asked if I could show Princess Lena around instead.

"Fara is familiar with the garden, perhaps she could show you around while I attend to this matter," he said as he rebound the message and followed Bentley out of the garden, leaving us alone.

The Princess and I looked at each other, neither of us excited with the proposition. In the end, her boredom must have exceeded any disgust she held for me, because eventually she sighed and replied, "Alright, show me around."

I took her through the garden, stopping at fountains and other monuments along the way. I could tell she wasn't thrilled to have me as an escort. Honestly, I probably knew little more about the garden than she did. I was in the middle of telling her about a yellow rose bush, with little more detail other than it was yellow and had thorns, when she suddenly declared, "I'm tired," and sat down at a bench on the side of the path. After wiping her forehead and fanning herself a little bit, she asked me,"So what exactly is there to do around here? So far I have only been taken to the garden or to dinner parties. Honestly, it's all getting quite dull. I would expect the royal capital of Ahrenia to have more luxury. If I had wanted to walk around gardens all day, I would have stayed back in my home country." She checked to see if I was still listening, so I assembled my face into an empathetic expression, which she took as encouragement to go on. "The Prince is disappointing as well. Sure, he is polite enough, but I thought he was supposed to be charming and spontaneous." She pulled a rose off of the bush next to her, yanking it roughly so that the bush recoiled back, which caused some petals to fall off the other flowers. I lamented those that fell, making note to collect them and bring them back to my room so they wouldn't go to waste.

"1 guess a good thing is that the guards here are all fairly handsome. I'd say your King knew what he was doing when he sent all the poor, ugly sods to live underground, didn't he? And I will admit, there are a few guards here that have taken my fancy. Especially that one guard☐What was his name? Bentley? Perhaps he will show me a better time than the Prince." She grinned deviously as she picked the flower petals off the roses one by one, pausing when she got through the last of them, after which she threw the stem carelessly over her shoulder.

I held my tongue, aching to reprimand her for her destruction of the garden, as well as for a few other, more personal, things. Instead, I simply replied "yes, my lady", hoping that my face appeared as impassive as my voice sounded. Inside, I however, I was quickly growing tired of this spoiled noblewoman. I almost lost it when she decidedly stated, "I think I'll play a little with Bentely. He seems willing, don't you think?" Before I could tell her what was really on my mind, I heard the Prince and Bentley making their way towards us.

"Erik!" She squealed, running up to him once he came into view, gripping his arm. "I missed you! Next time, I want you to show me around the garden!" I fumed, turning around so that they couldn't see my face.

Once I felt the fire in me cool down a little, I turned around and asked Prince Erik and Princess Lena if I could have their leave, stopping the Prince when he motioned for Bentley to walk me back.

"That is okay, I can find my way back on my own, thank you."

I walked through the garden, finding it much more enjoyable now that I didn't have to worry about entertaining an unwelcoming audience. I didn't realize where my legs were taking me until I was halfway to the stables. I wouldn't mind seeing Heath again, along with Elana and Sir Thunder. And who could forget Sam. I thought about picking up some carrots, but I didn't have any money nor anything to trade, so I picked wild alfalfa along the road to give them instead.

When I came to the barn, I didn't see any of the horses outside in the arena. There was a pile of hay stacked up against the front wall, so I picked up a barrel as I entered through the door.

"Heath?" I called out. I waited for a response, then tried again, but to no avail. I set the barrel of hay down and looked around, dusting my hands off on my the front of my gown, inwardly cringing when I saw the trail of dirt they left behind on the pale fabric. "Hello?" I couldn't think of a time when Heath wasn't at the barn. Maybe he's outside, I thought, but before I made it to the door to go and check, a large man emerged around the corner.

"What're you doin' in here?" He asked me, and I noticed he was holding some large branding tools, still red from the heat. I cautiously took a step back and answered,

"I'm looking for Heath." The man must of noticed me backing away because he put the brands in the nearest bucket, speaking over the hiss of the heated metal on water.

"Heath ain't here no more. The bank took this here barn away from him and sent him packing."

I couldn't believe my ears. "What? Why?"

"Don't ask me, Miss. Must 'a made the wrong person angry." Instantly, my mind shot to the merchant. That slimy rat!

"Do you know where Heath would be?"

"Last I heard, him and his daughter lived down in the southern edge of the city. It isn't too hard to find." He peered at me through squinted green eyes set in a dark brown wrinkled face. "I 'spect that you're gonna go looking?" I gave a small nod in affirmation, and the large man continued. "Heath's a good friend of mine. When I heard they was selling the barn, I bought it up before any halfwit could get their grubby hands on it. He runs a good place here. Let 'im know I'll take good care of it. I'm Brussel, by the way." He offered a large, calloused hand, which engulfed mine as we shook.

"Fara, and I'll tell him. " As I left, I remembered the alfalfa in my pocket, and walked back to give it to Brussel, asking of he could split it amongst Elana, Sir Thunder, and Sam.

"I can give it to Elana, but as for Sir Thunder and Sam, they aren't in the stables any-more. That palace messenger fellow took them this morning. They looked like they were ready for a few weeks worth of travelling at least."

"Really? Well, thank you for all your help," I said, wondering where Croxley might have gone at a time like this. I remembered that he said he had an assignment to do, but was it really so urgent that he need leave without another word? He knew that we were right in the middle of planning, and with the Prince basically out of the picture, I needed his help.

"Don't mention it," Brussel replied with a wave of his hand, as if trying to bat my gratitude out of the air. "But make sure you stay safe out there on the streets. The south side ain't any place for a pretty lass like yourself."

After I left the barn, I looked around to try and figure out where the south side would be. One would think that, having spent a few months here, I would know more about the layout of the city, but I've spent most of my time in the castle. Other than coming to the stables, I haven't seen very much.

Based off of where the sun was in the sky, I figured out more or less the general direction of south, and made my way down the road. Apart from the occasional cart that would rumble by, I was on my own, walking through the quiet town. Everyone must be avoiding the chill winter air. It was enough to make my nose drip, and I kept having to wipe it away with the back of my numb hands.

Eventually I came to a fork in the road. On a whim, I chose the path to left. Six more "whims" later, however, I had gotten myself lost and stuck at a dead end. By now, the sun was falling behind the homes, casting long shadows, and I was exhausted. I wished I had eaten breakfast this morning. I haven't had a single thing to eat all day. As if to remind me, my stomach gurgled, and I rubbed it absent-mindedly, as if I could comfort it into silence like one does with a babe. I sighed, rubbed my hands together to warm them up, and sat in a squat against the back wall. Looking at my dress, I saw that the bottom had become tattered and dirt-stained, worse for wear than I was. Mathelda's gonna kill me, I thought to myself. That is, if I ever find my way back. I rested my head in my hands as I tried to figure out how to get myself out of this mess. I made up my mind to ask the next person I saw how to return to the castle. I would just have to find out how to get to Heath another day. Maybe if I had more time to prepare some supplies and get some directions, I would be more successful.

At the sound of rustling, I popped my head up, looking around to find the source of the sound. A nearby cat had been eating some of the garbage left on the side of the alleyway and suddenly dashed away, spooked off by an unknown threat. Peering down the alley back up the way I came, I saw a group of shadows pass across the street. I got up and chased them down, calling after them, "Excuse me! Excuse me!"

The closest figure turned around and, seeing me, called for the rest of the group to stop. They turned out to be a group of 5 young men. One was picking his teeth with a toothpick, and when he saw me, he threw it down, spitting to the side. He peered down at me, his mouth forming into a smile that sent a chill down my spine.

"Pardon me, Miss, you appear to be lost," he said, running his eyes down my figure as though he could see right through the many layers of my gown.

"Um, actually, never mind. I'm sorry to bother you." Any concern I had about being lost was replaced by a sudden desire to be as far away from him as possible. I began backing away, but he mimicked my steps away with forward steps of his own.

"Aw, how sweet. But you don't have to worry, you aren't being a bother. May I ask your name?"

"I...I actually have to get going. Thank you for your help," I said as I turned to walk away, but the group of boys began to circle around me, tighter. I tried to get through the gap, but their bodies formed a wall, leaving me with no place to go.

"Aw, come on. We just met! I would love to get to know you," he brushed his fingers down the side of my face, and my heart leapt into my throat, racing with fear. He walked up closer, and I could smell his breath, thick with alcohol and smoke. In fact, they all reeked of alcohol, probably on their way from one pub to another. They wore very classic garb, not too flashy but obviously more than rags, appearing to be of the middle class of Ahrenia. I imagined that their fathers were businessmen, giving their sons just enough money and free time to get themselves into trouble. And they sure seemed like they were looking for trouble, something which I was all to afraid they would expect me to provide.

"Not in the mood to talk? Don't worry, I'll start. My name is Andrew. This is James, Derrick, Shannon, and George. We were just looking for a fun time, and you came along." He glanced down my dress and winked, saying "I think it was fate."

"Fate? I'm not too sure...I'm actually just trying to get back to the castle. If you could point me in the right direction-"

"Ah, so you're one of the castle girls, huh? You must know what you're doing, then." Andrew looked at the other guys, and I watched as their expressions changed from that of entertainment to pure hunger.

One of them chuckled and said, "I didn't know they extended their services out here. Hey Shannon, isn't your sister one of them?"

"Yeah, she is," murmured Shannon.

Then another added, "She works pretty hard, too. How'd she learn to be so flexible?" They all sniggered, and Shannon's face grew red.

"What the hell, George!" He exclaimed, pushing close to George's face.

"Calm down, man. It's not like I'm the only one whose helped her practice," Andrew said.

"That's my sister!" As they fought, I tried to seize my chance and escape amidst the distraction, but the fight ended as fast as it began when one of the men noticed me leaving. Once again, I was the centre of their attention. Andrew's playfulness faded away and he grabbed me by the arms, shoving me against the wall.

"Now listen here, bitch. I'm not playing around any more. I know what you do in that big castle of yours, and I'm not gonna let you get away without giving us a taste of the good life. Think of it as a way to expand your repertoire." I tried to squirm out of his grip, but he held me tight. He groped my breast, looking back at the group for encouragement. I whimpered, but didn't say any more out of fear. The rest of the men watched eagerly, as if imagining what they would do once they got a hold of me. Desperately, I looked around for someone to help, but there was no one on the street, which was now completely dark, as the sun had set and the sky turned black.

Andrew must have caught my eyes wandering, because he grabbed my face by the cheeks with his other hand and made me look him in the eyes. "You're going to let us have our fun, and if you scream, I'll make sure to have James get you quiet nice and quick. Understand?" He forced my head up and down in a nodding motion and then shoved me up against the wall behind us, practically smashing himself into my body. He dove his face down into my cleavage, and I responded by kneeing him in the groin. For a moment, his grip weakened, and I took the chance to scream. I barely managed to get a sound out before he recovered, slapping me across the face, sending my head in a whirl that left me sprawled on the ground, knocking the back of my head against the stones on the way down. He pinned my arms with one hand and send the other under my dress. When he leaned over me, I slammed my forehead up to meet his, which proceeded in stunning both of us, but I continued to struggle, desperately trying to break out of his grip. Some of the other men got involved, forcing me down every time I gained a little leeway, ensuring that they would all have a chance to have their way with me.

Finally, I curled in a ball, trying to protect myself as they attempted to pull me apart. They grabbed my legs and arms, opening me like a flower. A kick in the side knocked the wind out of me and put an end to my cries for help. As my vision clouded from the pain, I sent my hand out to find the rock that I hit my head on. Once I found it, I held on tight and swung my arm out, hitting the man closest to me and sending him to the ground. The small victory gave me a chance to dash towards the nearest building, pounding my fists against the door, begging for someone to open it, but I was pulled away before anyone answered. As they dragged me by the hair, I dug my heels into the ground and reached back to scratch at whoever had me. A mixture of blood and tears were streaming down my face and blinding my eyes, and my exhausted body was quickly gave up its last bit of energy.

Suddenly, I heard the slam of a door and I was dropped, sending dirt into my eyes and my mouth. Pushing myself up, I saw a large form grab two men by the collars and shove them against the wall, growling something at them that I couldn't hear. After letting them go, they went running down the road, looking behind them with fear in their eyes.

"You bastards better run," was the last thing I heard before I succumbed to the pain and let darkness wash over me.

CHAPTER 22

The first thing I noticed when I woke up was my aching side. After a few deep breaths, I was able to push that to the back of my mind, making room for the smell of fresh baked bread to register. Suddenly, I became very aware of the fact that I was starving, which provided the motivation I needed to open my eyes. Squinting against the bright light, I looked around, realizing that I had no idea where I was. Suppressing the waves of inner panic that came as all of last night's events rushed back, I took deep breaths and tried to collect myself before I lost all ability of rational thought. I noticed that I had been wrapped with a bandage around my waist and was wearing a loose nightgown, tucked into a bed of soft blankets with obvious care. So, wherever it is that I am, I must be safe, I reassured myself. Pulling myself out of bed, I slowly walked out of my room and followed my nose to find the source of the mouthwatering scent.

I passed through a few rooms until I found the bread sitting on the table in the middle of the kitchen. Looking around, I saw no one else. Well, after all the care they've given me, they were probably intending on giving me some of this too, I justified to myself as I lunged towards the bread, ripping open the loaf, burning my fingers but not caring in the slightest as the warmth filled my body and expanded in my stomach. I was diving into the second half when I heard someone exclaim, "Goodness gracious! Well, good morning!"

Embarrassed and guilty, I turned around. With a full mouth, I mumbled back, "Hello," and, after swallowing, I added sheepishly, "thanks for the bread."

"I see you helped yourself. Oh, don't worry about it, it isn't a problem. I have more coming out of the hearth as we speak. I imagine that you're thirsty as well, am I correct?" She asked with a knowing smile. I nodded, and she brought me a pitcher of watered-down ale "for the pain."

As I drank, I watched her expertly kneed the dough on the counter across from me. She looked to be in her later years, dark skinned and comfortably plump with strong hands and glossy black hair pulled back under a white bonnet. She was humming to herself as she worked, and I was reminded of my mother and her similar joy of cooking.

"Now that you're awake and nourished, would you mind telling me your name, child?"

"My name is Fara, ma'am."

"Fara? You certainly lived up to your name last night." My mind flickered back to the tale Croxley told me about the source of my name, the stubborn maiden who fought great battles for her people. "My name is Veloria. Most call me Val. Well, Miss Fara, may I ask why a palace girl like you was wandering the streets so late at night?"

"I was looking for a friend, you may know him. His name is Heath." I saw recognition of the name flash across her face.

"Ah, so you are Heath's stable-girl, then? He's spoken a lot about you. Well, you're in luck. His home is just down this street. You were very close to finding him before those boys, because we both know they don't deserve to be called men, caused a ruck-us. I'll let him know that you're here when my husband comes back. In the meantime, I recommend that you get some more rest. You took quite a beating last night."

As if my body was agreeing with her, a sudden rush of tiredness washed over me. She helped me up out of the chair and back to my room, where my eyelids fell as soon as I hit the pillow.

I awoke to the sound of laughter in the kitchen, deep belly laughs that could come from none other than Heath. With more ease than before, I made my way to the kitchen and found Heath, Val, and a tall, dark man who I assumed to be her husband.

"There she is!" Heath stood up and gave me a tight hug. I gasped out in pain but didn't protest too much. When he finally released me, he looked at me shyly and patted my shoulder, saying, "I've uh, missed your help."

I laughed and told him I missed him as well.

"So I heard you got yourself into a bit of trouble. You seem to be good at doing that," he told me, shaking his head. "I'm glad to see you're still in one piece. You're okay, right?" He looked at me, concern in his blue eyes.

"I'm okay," I reassured him "It seems like trouble has come to find you as well. Did you really lose the stables, Heath?"

At that, his face fell and he looked away. "Yeah, it's a shame. I'm gonna miss all those horses. But I 'spect you met Brussel. I trust him to take good care of the place. I had to protect my family, especially my girl, Shawna, even if it meant giving up the stables without a fight. Speaking of, she came with me today. Let me introduce her to you." While he left to get Shawna, I made my way to the table where Val and her husband were sitting.

"Sir, I expect you're the one I should thank. I can't begin to explain how grateful I am,"

"No need to get all sappy, girl. I did what any honest man would have done." He spoke gruffly and shortly, then abruptly left the kitchen. I looked at Val in surprise. They couldn't be more different, Val's warm personality and his surliness. But Val just smiled at me and shrugged. "Don't worry about him, Mr. Harris is just afraid to show emotion. But it's there, trust me, and I'm sure he appreciated your gratitude. If not, then I'll accept it for him."

At that moment, Heath and his daughter came into the room. "Shawna, I'd like you to meet Fara. Fara, Shawna." A girl around seven or eight years old poked her head around Heath, and he shoved her forward. "Don't be shy. Go on and shake hands!" I smiled at her and held out my hand, which she approached and shook surprisingly firmly. She had the same brown hair as Heath, and a very similar facial structure, only softer. The only difference was her beautiful hazel eyes, which I expect she got from her mother.

"Hello Shawna, nice to meet you," I told her.

"Nice to meet you too," she returned. We both stood there awkwardly, not knowing what to say, until Val came to our rescue and announced that dinner was ready. She had prepared a large turkey surrounded by potatoes, carrots, and other vegetables. We all swarmed the table, Mr. Harris included, and dug in. The meal loosened our tongues and we chatted long into the night. Eventually, Shawna went to the other room to fall asleep, and we turned our discussion to more serious matters, such as the stables.

"Heath, what exactly happened with the stables," I asked, and he sighed and told me what I had assumed, that the merchant decided to take his anger out on Heath, but what I didn't expect was that Heath had been accused of sedition.

Hearing that, I wondered if it was more of my fault than I initially realized. I know that it was the merchants anger and embarrassment that caused him to lash out, but now that Heath mentioned sedition, it had me wondering if the merchant somehow knew about what Prince Erik, Croxley, and I were planning.

"Heath, I'm sorry. I feel like this is because of me."

"Now don't be ridiculous, lass. How could this be your fault?" Suddenly, the whole table looked towards me quizzically. I knew I should hold my tongue, but my guilty conscience pushed me forward.

"I'm the one who made the merchant mad. He came to see me, and he wasn't happy with the service, or rather, lack of, that I gave him. He must of taken his anger out on you to get back at me."

"But that doesn't explain the accusations of sedition and treachery," Val said.

"No, something else does." I paused. I knew I could trust Heath, but I've just met Val and Mr. Harris. Taking a leap of faith, I decided that if Heath could trust them, then so could I. "You know that I am from Cethin, correct?"

Heath nodded, while Val and Mr. Harris let out a sharp exhale. They looked at each other, Mr. Harris's eyebrows raised, and Val sighed. Even here, the prejudice was deeply rooted. I took a deep breath, hoping that they could hear me with open ears, and went into my story, telling them everything about my life in Cethin. The horrible guards, the life without colour, sunlight, life, and the plan I have to change it all. At first they were skeptical. I kept looking at Heath throughout my tale to check on his reactions. If he had any resentment towards me, he wasn't showing any signs of it. Rather, he looked very pensive the whole time.

"I think that somehow the merchant figured out what I was up to, and reported it, using it to get revenge on Heath. Heath," I said, turning to him, "I take full responsibility for what happened to the stables. I don't know how it happened, but I know that it's my fault." With all my secrets out in the open, I felt refreshed, but also slightly naked, liked I've removed a layer of armour that left me more vulnerable, but also more free.

When my confession was over, we sat in silence for a few moments. I picked at my nails, not knowing what else to do. After what seemed like an eternity, Heath cleared his throat and said, "So, where do I sign up?"

Dumbfounded, I didn't know how to respond. The best I could give was, "Uh...what?"

Heath stood up out of his chair and began to pace the kitchen. "I have a confession myself. I didn't tell y'all cause I didn't want everyone giving me handouts, but I didn't just lose the stables. I lost me home too. I have just a week to find a new place for Shawna and I, and what's more, the officials that took the horses said that they would give me trouble if they saw me around town again. Now, I'm not worried about myself. I could give them guards a run for their money. But I can't risk Shawna. You know what they would do to her if they managed to get a hand on her." Heath stopped pacing and faced us, "So, what I'm saying is, I want to help you, Fara. I've got nothing left to lose. Everyone already thinks I'm a traitor, so I might as well put some truth to the rumour."

"Heath," I started, "I'm so sor-"

"Stop apologizing to me, lass!" Heath said, cutting me off. "It ain't your fault! What's done is done."

"Well," said Val, leaning back in her chair with her arms folded behind her head, "I have to say, I'm not to sure how I feel about all this, especially now that is been brought into my house. I think I'll give it a little time to sink in before I decide what I want to do about it all. In the meantime, let's get ourselves a much-needed rest and we can talk about it again in the morning. We don't want to make any rash decisions now, do we?"

At that moment, my body reminded me of everything it had gone through in the past twenty four hours. Exhaustion swept through me and I found myself barely able to keep my head up as the kitchen exchanged goodbyes. Heath stood in the doorway, a sleeping Shawna in his arms, and told me, "Just let me know how to help you, Fara. I'll do anything to keep my Shawna safe, which means I'll have to do even more to make it so more people don't have to go through the same I did. You're right. The way they run things here isn't right, and it's about time that someone changed it all around. I'm too old to change anything myself, but I'll help you in any way I can. Now get some rest, lass, and I'll see you in the morn."

With the last few drops of energy, I dragged myself to my bed, and slept a deep, dreamless sleep.

CHAPTER 23

Shawna woke me up the next morning. I opened my eyes to see her leaning over my bed, studying my face with a deep wrinkle set between her eyebrows, as if concentrating on something. When she noticed my eyes were open, she jerked back, looking downward to avoid my gaze.

"Good morning," I said, pushing myself up into a seated position.

"Um, good morning," she replied n a quiet voice. "I'm sorry, I was just□well, my pa always talks about you, saying you remind him of me, but you don't look anything like me." She played with something on the ground with her toe, keeping her eyes towards the ground, but I could just see them through her bangs as she looked up and said, "I'm nowhere near as pretty as you."

I sighed as I thought about how deeply the ideas of Ahrenia were engrained in its citizens. This poor girl already feels like the only thing that matters is her appearance. "Now that's not true. You and I just look different. I would love to have the rich, tan skin you have, and your hazel eyes are lovely." I reached over and brushed her hair behind her ears, and said, "besides, if I'm right, there's much more to you than your looks. Your father tells me all the time about how smart you are, and how you always fight for what's right. And," I added, giving her a playful nudge with my elbow, "he told me about how all the neighbourhood boys have been chasing you."

"Really?" She asked, her eyes growing wide. She sat there, thinking it over, while I got myself out of bed and pulled some warmer clothes over my dress. I was feeling much better this morning, my side only aching slightly as I pulled my layers over my head. I could probably make it back to the castle today, although I can't imagine what Mathelda will say. I shuddered and put the thought aside.

"Oh, I forgot to tell you. Breakfast is ready. Val's a really good cook, too. I always ask my pa if we can eat here," Shawna motioned me closer, then whispered in my ear, "my pa always burns the food, and what he doesn't burn still taste terrible. But don't tell him I said that, he thinks I love his cooking."

I reassured her that her secret was safe with me. She looked me over, as if judging my character. She must have decided she liked what she saw, because she smiled and pulled me out of the room and into the kitchen by my hand.

At the kitchen table sat Mr. Harris and Heath, while Val bustled about preparing everyone's dishes. I realized that there was another figure sitting at the table with their back to me, and it took me only a few seconds to figure out who it was.

"Jean?" I exclaimed, bewildered. "What are you doing here?"

She turned around, a scowl deeply etched on her face, but made no attempt to explain her sudden appearance, or, for that matter, how she knew I was here. Heath squirmed a little in his seat, and was relieved when Val set his plate down in front of him so that he could feign interest in his food. I sat down in the only available seat, right across from Jean, where I was under the attack of her burning glare.

"All right, dig in," Val announced once she had gotten everyone plated. I lifted my fork to my mouth, uncomfortable under Jean's gaze, but also ravenous. But before I could take a bite, Jean suddenly struck her fist down on the table.

"What do you think you are doing?" She exclaimed, making both the plates on the table and myself jump. "How could you completely betray me like this?"

I just stared at her, dumbstruck, not knowing how to answer or where this was coming from. Okay, that was a lie, I knew where it was coming from, but why now? And why here?

"Betray you? What are you talking about? And how did you know I was here?"

"Heath told me," she said, pointing at him with her fork but keeping her eyes locked on mine, while Heath put up his hands in front of him in defence against Jean's accusatory fork.

Heath looked at me with his hands still up in surrender and explained, "She came to the barn looking for you. Brussel told her you went to find me, so she appeared knocking on my door threatening me to tell her where you were."

"How could you lie to me?" Jean said, the hurt evident in her voice and on her face.

"Jean, you don't understand-"

"What don't I understand, you b-" Val stood up in a flurry, covering Shawna's ears, pointedly announcing to Heath and Mr. Harris that breakfast was over.

Mr. Harris, who had remained impassive the entire time, suddenly looked exasperated. "Can't a man just eat his breakfast in peace? I've got too much to do today to listen to you girls-"

"Mr. Harris!" Val barked sharply, and he stood up, pushed his chair in with a huff, and stomped out of the kitchen. Heath, Val, and Shawna followed in a much less dramatic procession, leaving Jean and I alone in the kitchen. I sighed, knowing an explanation was needed, not having any place start. After attempting to arrange my thoughts, I broke the tense silence.

"Jean, I don't know what it is you think I've been up to, but I'm almost positive that it isn't what's really going on."

"I know exactly what's going on. You could never accept that Nethers are lower here, for some reason thinking that you were better than the rest of us, so you decided to kiss up to Mathelda and become another puppet in her group. Once you caught the Prince's attention, you suddenly felt like you were one of them, an Ahrenian. You even became friends with that horrendous Princess Lena. We□I□wasn't good enough for you. You wanted the castle life, the money, the power. Well, guess what, you might've had it, but after your little stunt in which you disappeared for a few days, Mathelda's put a price on your back and has got a harsh beating waiting for you."

The way she said it, with so much anger and pain, shocked me. It made me realize just how dumb I was, to ignore Jean and the others who really made me feel at home the first few weeks I was here. After considering what she said, I asked, "If you hate me so much, why did you come looking for me?"

"Because I'm an idiot, and for some reason I was worried about you," she replied in a quiet voice.

I sighed, trying to figure out what I could do to fix what I had almost broken. "No, I'm the idiot. You're right, I did completely ignore you, but not for the reasons you think. Jean," I sighed, preparing myself to reveal my secret for the second time in a less than 24 hours. At this rate, it won't be a secret any-more. "The reason the Prince and I have been meeting up has nothing to do with what you, or Mathelda, for that matter, thinks. The Prince, Croxley, and I are planning a revolution. We are trying to free all Nethers from the King's abusive exploitation." I continued to explain our plan, about how we were going to visit the different colonies and work together to stage an embargo around the city, forcing the King to release us from his control. "At least, that's what we were planning to do, until Princess Lena came to the palace. Since then, I haven't been able to speak to Prince Erik alone, and Croxley was sent out on some errand, so I decided to go and find Heath for some help. But really, now that I think about it, I know I should've come to you first."

Jean just looked at me for a long time, until finally she slapped my arm, exclaiming, "Well duh! I can't believe you didn't tell me!"

"I wanted to, believe me, but Croxley and Eric didn't want to risk anything-"

"Eric? You mean the Prince?" She gave me a meaningful look. "Oh no, don't tell me that you've□you can't have actually□you like him, don't you?"

Startled by where the conversation had suddenly turned to, it took me a few moments to formulate a coherent answer, and even then, it ended up coming out as a spluttering of "Me? No, the Prince, he and I, we just, I mean, he's a Prince! And Lena, and, no!" Jean smiled at me suggestively, waggling her eyebrows. I laughed and decided that it was time to be honest, both to her and myself. "Yeah, I guess I do like him. I've never really let myself think about it that much, but□when I do, I can't help but smile. But, it's not like anything can happen. He's royalty, and even if we do manage to free everyone, I'm still just a girl from Cethin. He is the Prince of Ahrenia."

"Don't you mean the King?" Jean asked.

"What do you mean, the King?"

"Well, you said you were starting a revolution□there's no way you can be successful if you keep the King alive. He'd never let us live freely."

"Prince Eric isn't going to kill his father."

"Why not? His father hears one word about this plan and he wouldn't hesitate to kill the Prince."

"No, our plan is going to work, and nobody is going to die. You'll see."

She gave me a skeptical look, then nodded as if resigning to some inner decision. "Al-right, al-right. So tell me, how can I help?"

"Well, first, I need to get back to the castle," I told her, and she flung her hands up in exasperation.

"Are you kidding? I wasn't just trying to scare you when I said that Mathelda had something terrible waiting for you. If you go back to the castle, you won't be able to leave the quarters for a long time. "

"But I need to talk to the Prince somehow! Or maybe Croxley. I wish I knew where he was!"

"Hmmm" Jean said as she scooped some of her until-then forgotten breakfast into her mouth. Her thoughtful "hmms" turned into hums of pleasure as she ate more and more, and I decided to eat some of my plate as well while we mulled it over.

"I can try and sneak you in. I have a few friends among the guards who might be able to tell me where the Prince is, and I can try and get you to him without letting anyone else find out"

"I don't want you to get yourself in trouble, Jean."

"Don't worry about it. I've gotten myself in and out of trouble plenty of times. I can handle it. If I remember correctly, I've also gotten you out of a few situations as well."

"That's true. That bread is still the best tasting bread I've had," I told her, reminiscing back to my first days in the city with Croxley, and the shock of the prejudice, mistreatment, and injustice against Nethers. I never could have imagined back then what the future held for me.

"We might be able to get a few of the other girls in on the plan as well, " Jean said, and I mulled it over in my head. It was risky telling too many people, but I figured that at this point, the more help, the better.

Jean and I continued to plan out our slip into the castle, but our responses took on longer and longer pauses as we became engulfed in our food, hunger overcoming us. Heath, Val, and Mr. Harris must have been listening in, because as soon the tension eased and we began eating, they came in and resumed their spots at the table, Mr. Harris eating with such gusto that we all couldn't help but laugh.

CHAPTER 24

Jean and I decided that the best time to sneak into the castle was just past sunrise, as the night guards were at their most tired and about to be switched. Right as they swapped guard, we would run in through the servant entrance and hopefully avoid Mathelda and any of her posse. We left Val and Mr. Harris early in the morning, and I told Heath that I would give Brussel a message as soon as we found out what the next step was.

"I'll send Shawna along to pick up the message. I can't show my face around the city any-more, and I 'spect the guards are soon gonna show up at my house to boot me out soon," Heath had mentioned when I explained the plan. I still felt guilty for Heath's situation, but there wasn't much I could do except keep moving forward.

We arrived at the castle a bit before dawn, giving us some time before sunrise to find the best opportunity to sneak in. We hid in front of the servant entrance, watching the guards as they made their rounds, their feet dragging and their eyelids drooping from the long night. When a guard appeared that I didn't recognize, Jean and I both eased out of our hiding spot a bit down the road and walked steadily past the guard, hoping that he didn't recognize either of us and wouldn't bother us much. We managed to make it past him and into the tunnels, where there were only a few other guards posted, but they were too busy talking with each other to notice us slip by. I thanked my good luck and gently squeezed Jean's hand as she pulled me quickly back to her room.

"I haven't been assigned a new room-mate since you left, so you can hide here while I figure out a way to reach the Prince," she told me, sitting on the edge of her bed while I sat on mine.

"Lena isn't much of an early riser, so we have a better chance of reaching the Prince alone. You might be able to find him in the garden. If he is there, tell him to wait for me by the morning glories," I said, thinking back to our walk through the garden.

"Al-right," she replied, standing up and heading towards the exit. "I should check in for breakfast-hopefully Mathelda didn't notice me missing yesterday. I'll talk to some of the girls and send them your way so you can fill them in on your plan. I'll try and pick some out of each colony so that you can learn a little bit more about where they are and if their leaders are willing to join us."

"Thank you, Jean. I can't tell you how much it means to me. Oh, and be careful!"

"Yeah, yeah. Wish me luck!" And with that she left, leaving me alone in my old room.

I sat around for a while, swinging my feet back and forth from my perch at the edge of the bed, running my mind over what I would say to the Prince when I see him. All that succeeded in doing was making me nervous, so I got up and began pacing around the room, trying not to get nasty with anticipation. I couldn't help but feel excited about the prospect of seeing him again, especially without Lena around.

What was I thinking? I chastised myself, don't let yourself give in to his charm. It's all an act for him. Just look at how he behaves around Lena-so charming, but you know just how he feels about her. For all you know, it could be the same for you.

All this circling around in my mind was driving me crazy. I needed to get out of this room.

I popped my head out into the hallway, checking primarily for Mathelda. Nobody else would really notice that I was here. With so many servants around, it was hard for the guards to keep tabs on us all. As I meandered around, stopping by the wash-room and bathhouse, I decided to stop by Lydia's room to pick up some things I might need.

The first thing I noticed when I walked in was the seed I had brought from Cethin and planted my first night here. It had grown nice and large, its leaves spread out to absorb the little light spilling out on the windowsill. I walked closer to it, gently feeling its leaves in between my fingers, and I noticed the small, white bud was blooming from the tip of the stem.

"I've been watering it for you."

I jumped in my skin, turning to find Lydia standing at the entrance of the room.

"Hi," she said in a quiet voice.

"Um, hi," I replied, and we stood there looking at each other, myself not knowing what else to say when she suddenly ran up to me and gave me a tight hug, running through a stream of questions.

"Where were you? I haven't seen you in days! Mathelda keeps asking me if I knew where you went, but I didn't, and I told her so, but even if I did, I wouldn't tell her, unless it wasn't a secret, but even then I probably wouldn't because she doesn't need to know everything and I would hate for you to get in trouble." She paused to take a breath, and wailed, "Oh, but you are probably going to get in trouble any-ways. I'm sorry."

I practically had to pry myself loose from her grip so that I could get a good breath. "I wasn't gone that long Lydia!" I told her, laughing. "But I missed you too!"

"Well, so many girls go in and out of this place, I wasn't sure if you were gone for good. But I guess I should've known, because you didn't say goodbye or anything." She smiled sweetly, and I couldn't help but marvel about how someone could be so kind in our circumstances. Almost everyone else I met has grown harder, a little meaner, a little more selfish. Especially the ones that were born in Ahrenia and were enslaved for punishment. Although they had it just as bad as the rest of us, at least Nethers were used to being pushed around, being told what to do.

"Lydia, can I ask you a question?"

"Okay," she replied, sobering at the tone of my voice.

"Where are you from? A colony, right?" She nodded her head slightly, her casting her gaze down. "Which colony are you from?"

Her eyes watered up and I watched a tear roll down her cheek. She swept her hair to the side, and showed me the tell-tale sign of enslavement. The number 2391 was tattooed on the back of her neck, numbers that have up till this point remained hidden beneath her long, thick curtain of hair. She took a few deep breaths, and I let her sit in silence until she was ready to begin.

"I'm from the colonies, but not one that you've heard of. You probably never will."

"What do you mean?"

"My colony was destroyed."

"Destroyed? How?"

"The King," she had to stop, her eyes wandering around before they focused on a spot on the ground, "he King ordered that everyone be killed. It was horrible, Fara. Some of the villagers decided that they didn't want to work for the guards any-more. It seemed like every time new guards came in, they were meaner and crueller, giving out harsh punishments whenever they felt like it, always changing the rules and expecting us to know what they wanted us to do.

"One day, a woman was beat unconscious, to the brink of death. She was pregnant. When everyone else found out about it, well, it was the last straw. They decided to fight back against the guards, using whatever weapons we had lying around. But we were no match. The guards just kept pouring in. We didn't know at the time, but our colony was one of the closest to Stonewall, making it easy for the King to send in reinforcements.

"The guards were ruthless. They took everyone, man, woman, child- no exceptions. And the smiles on their faces while they did it...Fara, they are monsters. I watched them take the women," she let out a quiet sob, whispering "they raped my ma, right in front of me. Then they made her watch as they did the same to me. After they were done, they killed her. Sent a knife right into her heart. The only reason they saved me was because the captain said he wanted someone to help him pass the time on his way back, and he was sure he could get a reward for bringing me to the King to work as a slave after he had his time with me.

"So they bound my hands and walked me through my home, blood spattered across the walls, the bodies of friends and family strewn across the floor. At first, I searched desperately for life in their eyes, but after seeing none, I kept my head down, unable to witness any more.

"When we got back to the castle, the captain kept me in his room, coming in twice a day to have his way. It was horrible, degrading. I hated myself. Eventually, though, he had to go back to work, so I was handed over to Mathelda. I know you don't think so, but compared to everything else I've gone through, Mathelda's the best thing that has happened to me. She lets me have more control over things, and I've become good at what I do. It was what I was born to do. It's what you're supposed to do, too. That's why we were born pretty."

I couldn't decide what upset me more; the misfortune that Lydia has had to live through, or the acceptance of her new fate as the only alternative. I didn't know what to say. "I'm sorry" seemed flat and weak, so instead I just pulled her into an embrace, Lydia's occasional sniff into my shoulder breaking the companionable silence.

"Lydia, you know you don't have to settle for this. We can do so much more."

"What do you mean? Mathelda said that this was our duty. Nethers don't have the brains to keep up with the Ahrenians, so we have to rely on our beauty and talents to keep us afloat. My parents said the same thing, always telling me I couldn't afford to work or do the things everyone else did."

I completely understood what that was like, feeling like you had nothing to offer. And now, because I knew different, I kept pushing Lydia to open her mind to something more.

"I happen to have met quite a few Ahrenians that aren't nearly as smart as half of the Nethers I know. Would they know how to grow vegetables without the light of the sun, or how to find the richest minerals in the depths of the earth? How to avoid the noxious gas and where to find the pockets of clean air scattered throughout the mines? Just because we have different lives and abilities doesn't mean we can't live together."

Lydia pulled herself away from me, as if the idea repulsed her. She just sat there quietly, shaking her head from side to side. "Stop it. There's no use in thinking that you can change things," she said in a voice that was quite and cold. I was so used to her cheerful attitude that I couldn't help be taken aback by this new stiff, resolute character.

"But we can change things! Listen to me, Lydia," I dove in with little hesitation, "not only can we change things, but we will. I will. I'm already working with some other girls trying to get our colonies together to fight back, to make sure that things like this never happen again."

Lydia's expression grew darker, the opposite of what I was expecting, and her voice rose to a yell as she exclaimed, "What don't you understand? You have no chance! You will just get everyone killed! The guards are relentless, the King even more so. You aren't fighting for the good of the people, you are fighting for yourself!" Her voice just as quickly sunk to a whisper. "You just want to feel important. What you're doing is selfish. "

"But we have the Prince on our side!" I retorted back, anger loosening my tongue. At this point, I would tell her anything to get her to see the folly in her reasoning.

Lydia stood from the bed and turned away. "I'm done talking about this. I'm late for breakfast. Goodbye, Fara." And with that, she left me sitting on the bed, watching her walk away down the corridor, back to the only life she knows.

CHAPTER 25

After my encounter with Lydia, there was no way I could just sit around until Jean showed up. I had too much restless energy inside to simply wait for things to happen, so I went back to my old room. Not finding Jean anywhere, I decided to search for the Prince. Things were escalating too quickly for me to just let them go. We needed to work on our plan, especially now that Jean and some other girls were going to help out.

Being extra careful to avoid any eyes, especially those working for Mathelda. I made my way to the garden, the first place I could think of to find the Prince. If I was lucky, Jean might have already found him and told him to meet me there.

I cautiously walked through the garden, checking around to make sure nobody was following me. I saw a few courtiers strolling around, but luckily I didn't recognized any of them. One pair was so invested in each other that I doubt they would have noticed me even if I had walked right up to them and introduced myself. As I made my way through the hedges, I saw two guards come around a corner. I cursed inwardly, recognizing them as two of Mathelda's favourites, whom she often posts in our quarters. They would definitely remember me.

I frantically searched for a place to hide, realizing that I had basically trapped myself in the maze of hedges. I didn't think I would be able to retrace my steps backwards without getting lost, and the only other exit was in the direction they were coming from. Knowing that if I tried to run, I would probably end up at a dead end, I decided that the safest option would be to sink deeper into the bushes and hope that they don't pay too much attention to what's around them.

Holding my breath, I held my crouched position as they made their way past me. They were walking slowly, and my legs began to tremble. The corridor seemed endless, each step they took coinciding with my heartbeat, growing louder and louder as they grew closer. I was sure that they would be able to hear it, the echoing thump thump, an audible betrayal of my hiding spot. Over the thuds ringing through my ears, I could hear their conversation.

"Did you hear that the King is making us widen the women's quarters? We're gonna be up all night trying to add extra rooms down there. One thing though, there's nowhere else to dig! They are already under the castle. Seriously, why do we need to make more room for them? Just shove them all in together. Its not like they care. They're used to living in cramped, dark spaces."

"Yeah, like rats them girls are."

"All the Nethers are rats. They breed like them too. That's why we gotta make the quarters bigger. Apparently a lot of fresh meat will be coming in the next few weeks."

"Meat?"

"You know, women. I'd like to get a first taste of them, if you know what I mean."

"Yeah, me too." The larger one on the left nodded his head, and then a sudden look of understanding crossed his face. "Oh, I get it. Yeah, a taste. I'd like to taste a few."

It was all I could do to not appease my screaming legs and stand up, risking discovery for relief. I tried to ignore it and focus on the discussion happening before me. More servants? That means that more girls would be coming in from the colonies, which means we better get working fast if we want to get the soldiers out. I gasped as the harsh reality dawned on me, covering my mouth just a second too late. The guards looked around, obviously hearing my exclamation of surprise.

"Ay, did you hear that?" The shorter one looked around, peering into the bushes. The other followed suit, looking into the shrubs on the other side of the lane. I froze, attempting to be invisible. The guard came closer and closer to me, his eyes scanning the bushes, until he was looking straight at me. He squinted, as if trying to determine whether or not I was a trick of the light. I watched in horror as his hand stretched out to grab me, just as another hand seized me by the shoulders and pulled me back.

"Shhh, don't make a sound," a voice whispered in my ear. "It's alright men! I've got her!"

"Your Highness, is that you? We'll be right there, sir!"

"No need to worry, I can manage! I'll take her back to the quarters myself. You can continue your patrol." I felt his hands move from my shoulders down onto my waist, and then just as quickly release me, as if realizing they had gone astray. I spun around, startled to find him so close, his eyes meeting mine.

They lingered for a few moments, and after I was released by their powerful grip, I noticed that they looked sad and tired, the creases in the sides less from smiling and more from lack of sleep. Looking away, he took my hand and pulled me from the hedge, steering me down an unfamiliar path. We continued to walk for a while in silence, until he finally broke it, coughing as if to clear his throat before saying, "So, how have you been?"

In a most unladylike fashion, I laughed sarcastically and rolled my eyes. "Really? After not speaking to me for days, you ask me how I am? If you must know, I've been to the end of the city and back, nearly getting myself killed on a number of occasions, I've found out that Heath, you remember him, right? Or did you forget about him too? Well, Heath lost both the stables and his home because he was charged with treason, and now he wants to help with the rebellion. Jean wants to help as well, but Lydia thinks I'm setting us all up for ruin, and now I've just found out that your father is sending a swarm of troops to the colonies in order to bring more young girls over to this castle, so that your men could steal their innocence in order to pass the time. Not only that, but it means that we have even less time to round all the Nethers up before the men get there, but we haven't been able to plan anything because Croxley has been off who knows where and you've been too enraptured with Lena to know the difference." I huffed, having unleashed it all in one breath.

However, it seems that my rant proved effective, because for the first time since I've known him, the Prince was speechless. He walked away from me, his hands holding his neck behind his head. He turned back towards me, inhaled, then sighed again and turned around. I waited as this happened a few times, until finally he sat down on a marble bench and said, "I'm sorry."

The way he said it, with so much weariness, had me apologizing for my sudden outburst. "No, I'm sorry. It isn't all your fault. You have a lot of responsibilities."

"That is true, but I also need to have priorities. And lately, they haven't been in order. Lena□she just takes so much out of me."

I gave him a look, not sure if I wanted to hear what he had to say.

"No, no, not like that. She is just so, I don't know how to say it, royal. You thought I was bad, living the palace life, going to parties and such. She makes me look like a shut in! All she ever wants to do is go out, and when she isn't doing that, she is getting fitted for a new gown, buying new jewellery, demanding that merchants from across the land come in and bring their finest decorations. If she is to be queen, Ahrenia will be in ruins before long." He put his head in his hands, as if just thinking about it gave him a headache. As bad as I felt for him, I couldn't help but smile inwardly at hearing how badly he was tolerating Lena. "I must be honest with you, when Jean told me you needed to speak with me, I nearly came dashing here to meet you. It took a while to lose my guards, but I just mentioned that Lena needed them, and half of them fled while the other half flocked to her rescue. That woman has the castle in quite a state of riot."

I filtered through this in my head, so many of the things he had said sending my emotions in directions that I didn't currently have time for them to go. "Well shucks, it sounds like I've missed out on all the excitement," I finally replied.

He rose from the bench and walked towards me until we were nearly touching. "Out of all the things in my life right now, you are by far the most exciting." We stood there in each other's company for a few moments, until he cleared his throat, announcing, "So, Jean said you needed to speak to me about something."

"I do. I mentioned that Heath was ready to help us out. He wants to come to the colonies with us to rally them up, prepare them for the revolt. Jean and I know a few girls that might help get things together on this end. If only I knew where Croxley was. He was the main mind behind this plan. He would know what to do, now that the soldiers are going to raid the colonies."

"Croxley, the cunning devil I know him to be, is most likely working things out from wherever he is. It's up to us to just follow the plan. But we have to start soon. When will you be able to speak to Jean and Heath again?"

"I can try to get the message out to Heath tonight, and I will see Jean when I return to the chambers."

"Good. Meanwhile, I will prepare the horses and the bags for our journey. I shall tell my father that all this wedding planning has driven me a bit mad, and that I require a short journey to clear my head. I'm sure he will understand. Or if not understand, at least not be suspect. I mean, it wouldn't be the first time that I just up and ran from my responsibilities." He grinned sheepishly, not in the least sorry for his past actions.

"Al-right. It isn't safe for me here, so I will have to return to the Harris's home after I find Jean. If you need to get to me, ask Jean how to get there." I pushed myself away from him, my hand pressing against his chest, which felt warm and strong. As right as it felt, I knew that we were pushing our luck spending so much time together in the garden. "We should get going."

"You're right." He put his hand over my own on his chest, pulling it off and setting it down at my side. "Fara, I truly am sorry for having ignored you. If circumstances were different...yes, well. I'll be waiting to hear from Jean." And with that, we went our separate ways, him back to the castle and to Lena, myself back to the chambers, underground.

CHAPTER 26

As I made my way back, the hallways were in a buzz. Courtiers were dashing between rooms, while the guards were walking from door to door. I navigated through the servant's corridors, hoping to stay out of sight, wondering all the while what had the castle in such a state.

Rushing around the corner, I smacked into someone, bringing us both to the ground. I hurriedly pulled myself up, only to be dragged back down by the arm as a group of guards ran through the hallway. "Fara, stay down."

"Jean? What's going on?" I asked when I saw that it was her hand on my arm. She was bowing her head so no one could recognize her and I followed suit, walking close to her while she filled me in.

"Someone ratted us out. I don't know who. I promise it wasn't me, and none of the other girls said anything, they all swore. But Mathelda knows. She knows what you are trying to start. She might even know about the Prince and Croxley. I'm not sure, but you need to get out of here, fast! She's looking for you, for me, for Prince Erik, she's even had the King send out all of his guards to get every servant back into their quarters so that they can find you."

I stopped in my tracks as everything came crashing down. How? How could this have happened? My mind provided the answer, but my heart didn't want to accept it. Lydia, she's the only one who would have told. You're being selfish. You'll bring everyone down, she had said. She must have thought she was helping me, helping everyone from a terrible fate.

As the last of the guards passed through the corridor, Jean pulled me up and pushed me out, whispering fervently, "Go! Run! I will try to tell the Prince, but you need to get out of here! If I don't make it out, they've either captured me and have me imprisoned, or□well, or I'll be dead."

"No, Jean, you need to come with me! I can't leave you behind, not again! I told you we would be together in this!"

"That doesn't matter! All the Nethers, all of the families, the children, they matter. You need to save them, and waiting around for me won't get you any closer. Just promise me, Fara, promise me you will find my family. Here," she pressed something soft into my hand, and I closed it tightly, placing it in the pocket of my skirt without looking at it. "Give this to my family when you find them." She looked over her shoulder, and then let go of my hands. "Now go!" She gave me a quick hug and I squeezed her tight, releasing her, then dashing towards the exit. Before I made it out, I glanced back and saw her leave around the corner, then watched a group of three guards emerge across from the hall. At the last second before they saw me, I heard a "Hey! Hey, you dumb dogs! Over here!" Thank you, Jean.

Running as quickly as I could, I tripped and stumbled over the cobblestone. I ripped off my impractical shoes and continued running, trying to figure out where I should go. Going over the conversation in my head, I realized that I hadn't told Lydia everything. She didn't know about Heath and Val and Mr. Harris. Pausing for a few moments to catch my breath, I heard the sound of horse hooves over the cobblestone, followed by guards shouting and metal clanking. I dashed off the side of the road, running down the slope so that the hill would help cover me. I crouched and ran along the edge until I reached a bridge, under which I hid and listened to the horses' hooves pound above me, keeping time with my heartbeat.

When the last one passed, I stealthily crept out from under the bridge and sprinted across the street. My feet were starting to blister and bruise from all the running, and I started to reconsider throwing my shoes away. This was no time for me to be rash and act without thinking.

I spotted the stables up ahead, and wondered whether or not there would be an extra pair of work boots in the shed. I opened the doors, finding it dark and empty inside. I could hear the horses neighing, restless and frightened. I grabbed a lantern and a match, slowly making my way through the stables until I reached the supply closet. Opening the door, I gasped and dropped the lantern. From the ground, it's light flickered over Brussel's body on the floor, his nose broken, his eyes swollen and dark. I nearly collapsed as I took in the pool of blood around his body, searching around until I finally identified the source, a deep stab wound in his stomach. I pushed down on the wound to try and prevent any more blood loss, even though I knew that at this point it was probably hopeless, but I couldn't not do anything. I knelt there, hands trembling, and he moaned in pain, but he wouldn't open his eyes.

"Brussel? Brussel!" I kept repeating his name, but to no avail. I looked around and, finding a pitcher, poured the cold water on his face. He spluttered, his eyes opening but not truly seeing anything. "Brussel!" I shrieked, no longer concerned about being discovered.

His wandering eyes finally found mine. Seeing me for the first time, he mumbled, "Fara, what are you doing here?"

"Brussel! What happened to you?" I answered, ignoring his question.

"Oh, this. This ain't nothing. The guards, they just," he grunted and coughed, some blood trickling out of the corner of his mouth, "they came and tried to rile me up. Get me to talk. Said you guys were working some mighty scheme. Well, I didn't know anything about no scheme, but I wouldn't have told them even if I did, and I told them so. Seems they didn't like that answer though, cause they done dealt me a good one." He coughed again and closed his eyes.

"No! Brussel, stay with me!" I shook him again, and he only opened his eyes a slit.

"It's al-right, girly. This is just a scratch. I've had worse," he coughed out the word "worse", and I cringed at the blood that speckled his beard. I gripped his hand, and he squeezed back weakly, as if it took all of his energy to do so. Slowly, though, I felt his grip weaken, until it was only my hands keeping his suspended. I gently eased them down, silent tears dripping down my face. Is this what I was fighting for? Is this what was waiting for us? Is this all my fault? Endless doubts, questions, accusations of guilt ran through my mind. I sat there in his pool of blood, mourning all the lives that have been lost because of the disparity, the unjust separation between the rich and the poor. Knotting my skirt in my hands, I felt a bulge in the fold, and remembered that Jean had handed me something. Pulling it out, I saw that it was a small fabric doll. Now covered in Brussel's blood, the doll took on an eerie appearance.

The sound of a door creaking open startled me out of my grief. I shoved the doll back in my pocket, stood, and hid behind the storage room door, peering through the crack. I saw a familiar form walk in through the doorway, and before I could stop my feet, I found myself running towards it.

"Erik! They killed him! They killed Brussel!" I sobbed as we met, my hands pressed against his chest, curling into him as though he could shield me from all that was happening around us. He dropped the bags he was carrying and surrounded me in his arms, and we stood there as I drenched his chest with my tears.

When I had calmed down, he pulled me away, and seeing the blood, asked quietly, "Where is he?" I pointed to the supply closet and Erik made his way towards it, his grip tight on my hand.

Upon seeing Brussel, or rather, Brussel's body, he knelt down and felt for a pulse. He cursed again, louder this time, making me jump. He closed Brussel's eyes and stood up slowly. "We better get going. They're bound to be back soon." He handed me a bag, explaining that he managed to get a few supplies stuffed in it in a rush, but it wouldn't be enough to last us for long. We walked through the horses, all pawing the ground, restlessly pacing in their stalls. Erik found Elana and tried to calm her down, stroking her face and holding her head against his shoulder. He quickly grabbed a saddle and riding gear and tacked her up, then went back to the storage room to get a second set of gear for the horse I was to ride. I chose a younger mare, Misten, one who I remember being kind and gentle but also strong and determined. She had a grey coat that shined like metal, freckled with light spots. Petting her helped me calm down, and before I knew it, Erik had her ready for me to ride. I tied the pack to her saddle and went to mount, only to remember that I still had no shoes. I decided not to say anything to Erik, as it would only slow us down and we had so little time.

We went out through the back exit, and I said a small prayer for Brussel, despairing that we had to leave his body behind. I stayed atop Misten, waiting for Erik to come out with Elana. He was taking a while, and I started to get nervous. In response to my nerves, Misten began stomping her hooves, and I tried to calm her with soft hushes. Finally, Erik walked out of the barn, pulling Elana with one hand and holding a lantern in the other. Once he reached Misten and I, he looked up at me with grief heavy in his eyes.

"Fara, we have to burn the stables."

It took a few moments for what he said to process. I could only look at him as he continued to explain. "I've already doused everything in oil, and the horses are all let out of their stables. It will catch quickly, and the horses won't be in any danger."

He went through all the practical steps of his plan until finally I interrupted, "Why? Why do we have to burn it down?"

The stables were my home away from home. Not the castle, not the servant's quarters, but the smelly stables, full of my horse friends and Heath, who always showed me the utmost kindness. I hated to see it all go down in flames.

"Fara," Erik held my face in his hands and I grew still. "We need to do this. It is the best way to distract the guards, and there aren't any houses nearby to catch fire. Plus, they will have to catch the horses after putting the fire out, which will give us time to find Heath, get the plan, and get out of town. So, can you help me?" I looked at him and could see in his deep, green eyes, that there was no other option. With his warm hands still on my cheeks, I nodded.

We tied up Misten and Elana and I let all of the horses out of their stables, herding them towards the door. Coming from behind me, Erik lit the oil he had spread around the hay and the thatches, and we ran out of the stables as it quickly took the flame. We dashed back to Elana and Misten, who were nervously pacing in reaction to the fire and the herd of horses racing past them. We jumped on their backs and took off towards the Harris's home. I stopped and looked over my shoulder, watching as the fires consumed the the stables. "Fara," Erik called, and I slowly spun Misten back around, hoping that we would reach Heath in time.

I could only hope.

We couldn't ride as quickly as we would have liked because we didn't want to attract any attention. Consequentially, the short trip seemed to take hours. It wasn't until we finally made it to the Harris' home that my heart was able to calm down to a steady pace. We tied the horses in the back so that no passing guards would be able to see them, and I walked through the back door, the situation too urgent for common courtesy.

We entered the house and I called for Val and Mr. Harris, hoping that I wouldn't find them in the same state I found Brussel. We went through the house, searching every room, and finally, I found Val. If the situation was lighter, I would have laughed, because we found her in the kitchen, practically climbing into the pot she was cleaning. When she pulled her head out, her eyes widened at the sight of Erik and I, and she rushed over to me and began to fuss over my clothes, the blood, and the missing shoes. Never breaking character, she berated Erik for letting me ride with no shoes.

"Respectfully, your Highness," she said with a sight curtsey, then getting back to business, "you really shouldn't have been so senseless as to let a lady go out without proper footwear", and made me sit down until she found me a pair of her own that would fit. After she made sure we had food in our stomachs, despite our protests of not having time to eat, she asked us about what had happened in the castle.

"All I know is that guards have been running through the neighbourhood, going through every home, using this as excuse to take whatever they want as 'pieces of evidence'. It's terrible." Val shook her head sadly, as though she was the mother of society and the guards were her unruly children.

"Val, where are Heath and Shawna? Are they safe?" I impatiently asked her after she had finished her motherly ranting.

"Heath is out in the back with Mr. Harris. They are working at getting things ready for you all to leave. Shawna is with another family, safe and sound. Come, follow me."

She led us out to the back where we found Heath and Mr. Harris going over the map I had drawn for them of the colonies. All seven were on the map, scattered around Stonewall, which was more or less in the centre of Ahrenia. Upon seeing Prince Erik and I, Heath grabbed us by the shoulders and shook them assuredly, telling us that they had it all planned out and ready to go. Before he could dive into his plan, Erik placed his hand on Heath's shoulder, and told him gently that we had to burn the stables. Heath's face fell for a few moments, and he nodded solemnly.

"its okay. It weren't even mine any-more, was it?" He gave a small smile and steered us towards the maps. "You see here, you two have to start with this one first." He pointed at Cethin, then moved towards the east. "Mr. Harris and I will travel to the two eastern colonies, while you and Erik can go to the north. When Croxley comes back, we can send him to the west-most colony, and from there he can go to the south. I'm figuring it will take about a month to get to all of them on each side, and then we can have them all organize in Cethin, the because it is closest to Stonewall. That means you, Fara, have to go to your family first, convince them to join the rebellion, tell them that they need to open their homes to the other Nethers until we have enough numbers to invade the city."

"Heath, we don't have a month." I told him about the soldiers being sent to all of the colonies, and how we had to beat them there, otherwise there wouldn't be any hope for us to succeed. "There's no way we would be able to rally the Nethers with so many soldiers amongst them all. And if we wait till after the soldiers leave, the Nethers will have no strength left to fight, all their supplies will be gone, their moral too low. Heath, we need to leave now, to beat the guards. In order to do that, we need to go fast."

"We can figure out diplomacy on the way there," added Erik, "and once we establish alliances with the leaders of the larger colonies, we can rely on them to send emissaries to the other colonies rather than having us do it ourselves. So that means that Heath and Mr. Harris, you need to go to this colony here", he circled the large colony to the far north-east, "while Fara and I will go here," he said, circling one in the west.

"We can't go there," I interrupted, remembering my promise to Jean. "We have to go to Grundale. I promised Jean."

I could see it in the tight line of his mouth that this was completely backwards and out of order, and may even put the plan in jeopardy, but I wouldn't back down. After everything Jean has done for me, I had no other choice. I gripped my hand tight around the doll in my pocket and stood firm. Erik looked at me for a few moments, finally surrendering with a solemn nod.

"Al-right. After Cethin, we can go there. But we need to try and reach as many as we can. Val," he said, turning towards her, "I apologize having to ask this of you, but we require a few more supplies for our journey. I understand you're possessions are little, but should we be successful, I will make sure you are rewarded."

She waved his promise away with a flick of the hand, not out of ingratitude but out of sincerity. This woman didn't need any reward for doing what she thought was right. She reminded me so much of my own mother. I could only imagine a place and time when we could all be together and they could meet each other.

While Erik and Heath put together the final arrangements, Val and I put together the supplies. Although we were moving as rapidly as possible, she was still able to work in some motherly advice.

"You and the Prince make a strong team. But Fara, don't let your heart get in the way of your duty. You have to be cautious with who, and what, you give your heart to. Just make sure it's the right thing."

We waited until nightfall to leave the city, using the cover of darkness to our advantage. Luckily, only two groups of guards came by the Harris home, making it obvious that they doubted the Harris family was of any importance to the Prince. While they were inspecting the house, Erik, Heath, and I managed to hide in the cellar, out of sight. However, Mr. Harris went out to check on the rest of the neighbourhood, and came back reporting that Heath's home was completely destroyed. Heath said little for the rest of the night, directing all of his attention towards his work. I marvelled at how strong he was, knowing that he must feel deeply aggrieved at losing both his home and the stables, and yet he was still able to push himself to do what he believed needed to be done.

After we had everything ready, Mr. Harris, Heath, Erik, and I, pulling along Misten and Elana, went to the edge of the city, finding the wall heavily guarded. Rounds of guards were patrolling the exits, and we watched in the shadows as they marched back and forth. Standing in an alleyway across from the exit, we were all wearing cloaks, the hoods drawn over our heads, thankfully not attracting any attention.

"How in the bloody hell are we going to get out of here," Mr. Harris muttered, looking to Erik and I for ideas. Erik shrugged, while I looked around for a clue. I felt Misten nuzzle my shoulder, and I rubbed her cheek absent-mindedly, when an idea suddenly came to me.

"Here, hold my cloak," I said, handing it to Heath while I walked over to Misten. "Now Heath, I'm going to hang under Misten's belly, and you are going to drape my cloak across her back to hide me." I soothed Misten, hoping that what I was about to do wouldn't spook her. Slowly, I manoeuvred myself so that I was hanging from the saddle straps, grabbing onto Misten's stomach. Everyone was looking at me like I was a fool, but I knew this would work. "Okay, Heath," I grunted, working to keep myself up. He threw the cloak over Misten and I asked, "Can you see me?" I waited a few moments until the cloak was pulled off Misten.

"No, lass, ye were completely hidden," Heath said, and Mr. Harris snuffed, trying to appear unimpressed.

"Good," I replied, easing myself off of Misten, who waited till I was completely off before shaking and stomping her feet a bit, obviously uncomfortable with the whole situation. "Heath and Mr. Harris, you two aren't nearly as conspicuous as Erik and I, so you should be able to pass through the gate without much issue. Erik and I will ride on the underbellies of our horses and, hopefully, the guards won't check them." I looked at Erik to see if he was on board, only to find that he was already taking off his cloak and positioning himself under Elana.

Heath and Mr. Harris headed towards the gate, and I was unable to see anything other than the ground moving beneath me. Suddenly, we stopped, and I heard murmurs around us. I saw a new pair of feet walk around Misten, and I held my breath, trying to ignore the trembling in my arms as I held on tight around Misten's girth, which, luckily, wasn't too large. Just when I thought I was going to fall off, my arms screaming, Misten started walking again, and I watched the ground change from cobblestone to dirt. Eventually, we stopped again, and I just barely waited for the cloak to come off before releasing my grip and falling to the ground.

"Alright, we made it," Heath said, helping me up and dusting me off. Erik put his arms our for Mr. Harris to help him up, but Mr. Harris just scowled and folded his arms.

"Well, we must be going. It won't be long before they realize we are no longer in the city. Heath," Erik said, putting his hand on Heath's shoulder, "thank you for all your help. You've done so much for me all these years. I hope to see you again soon. And Mr. Harris," Erik went to put his hand on Mr. Harris' shoulder as well, but he took a step back and frowned, so instead Erik stuck out his hand, which Mr. Harris firmly shook, "thank you as well for opening your home up to Fara and I."

Mr. Harris looked at me at the mention of my name and returned Erik's gratitude with, "Yeah, well, just keep her safe."

I ran up to hug Mr. Harris, who stiffened but let me hug him for a few moments before pushing me away, a gentle smile on his face, and then I did the same to Heath. I didn't trust myself to say anything, so instead I just squeezed him tight, hoping to convey all that I was feeling in that moment.

We pulled apart and I mounted Misten, Erik mounted Elana, and with one final wave, we separated into the forest.

Now that we were out in the forest, we travelled slowly, the darkness not allowing for any faster mode of travel. The last time I was in the forest, it was the start of autumn, and the trees were beginning to change colour. Now, near the end of winter, the forest looked bare, menacing even. I shivered despite my cloak, seeing faces and creatures in the dark. I'm sure most of it was the stress of the day, of the week, of this entire journey, wearing on me. I wanted nothing more than to go back home, sink into my parents' arms, and have them tell me that everything would be okay. But that would mean throwing away everything that I've stood for, everything we have all worked for, sacrificed, and lost. Perhaps it was selfish, like Lydia said, but I wasn't able to let that all go.

"I've never actually been to a colony," Erik eventually admitted somewhat later, pulling me out of my thoughts.

"Really?" This honestly surprised me. I would think that, after having been on so many adventures with Croxley, he would have found himself in a colony at one time or another.

"I never really wanted to go to one. Even if Croxley had to go deliver a message or something, I would wait outside for him to come back. I felt that, if I didn't see it, if I didn't know what was going on, it wasn't really happening. Somehow, in my mind, that justified it all." He kept his gaze forward and he rode in front of me on Elana, so I could only see his back. Although I couldn't read his expression, I could hear the regret in his voice. This didn't, however, keep me from getting angry.

"How does that justify anything? You had to have at least some idea of the terrors that were happening down there! All the stories didn't mean anything to you?"

"You don't understand. In Ahrenia, we don't hear about the guards locking you in the mines without lanterns, we don't know about the women and children starving as the guards eat all the rations. They don't let us know. From what we can tell, all Nethers, whether from Cethin or Grundale, Weldar or Sprokil, Fyzen or Laurevell or Montill, are criminals, outcasts, and misfits that offer nothing to society other than what they can mine. They deserve whatever punishments they get."

"How can you say that?" At the sound of my voice rising, he stopped and turned around.

"I can't! At least, not any-more. Because now I know the truth, I know the lies. I□I know you." He tried to look me in the eyes, but I avoided his gaze. I looked away, at the ground, in the trees, anywhere but at him. But the darkness didn't offer much respite, and eventually I ended up focusing on Misten's neck as he continued his apology.

"It was you, Fara. You pulled me out of the parties, the drinking, the mistakes. You made me want to take responsibility. For once in my life, I actually began to act like a Prince, not just some spoiled palace brat. I saw in you kindness, compassion, and hope. You had passion and independence, a mind of your own, where as all the other girls I had ever met simply agreed with every word I had to say. Once I got to know you, I realized that I could no longer sit on the sidelines. I couldn't allow my father to wreak havoc on your people, innocent of all crimes other than being born a Nether, any longer. I had to do something. Because of you, Fara, I am actually doing something."

At some point during his confession, my gaze drifted up from Misten's neck and into his deep green eyes, and I felt my heart budge. I watched as he got off his horse and walked towards mine, holding his hand out to help me down. I looked at it for a moment, my heart beating loudly in my head, both from anger and from□something else. After a few beats, I gave him my hand and he eased me off Misten, right into him. He kept my hands in his as he pulled me closer, and I was sure he could feel my heart beat against his chest. Embarrassed, I looked down, but he gently turned my face back up to his.

"Fara, I'm not sure what's going to happen once we reach the colonies. We may be successful, or we may be too late. But I want you to know, that no matter what our chances are, you will always be my inspiration."

He gently leaned in closer, his head slightly bending to make up for our difference in height. Before I could catch on, he caught my lips with his, a slight pressure before pulling away. Suddenly, I felt like I lost something, and I pushed my lips against his, trying to get it back. This time it lasted much longer, our kiss growing deeper, until we seemed to melt into each other, fitting together seamlessly, no room for fear or anxiety, memories of the past or worries for the future, to come between us. It was just us, and it was perfect.

Eventually, we pulled apart, Erik leaning his forehead against mine, his breath heavy and warm. "I think we should make camp," he whispered into my hair.

"Okay," I finally responded once I was able to pull my thoughts back together. He walked away, his hand cradling mine until he was too far away, and my hand slid out of his gentle grasp. My hand felt empty without his, and I folded my arms around myself as I just now realized how cold it was. "I'll make the fire," I offered, and searched around to find enough kindling and dry logs, my mind replaying the kiss over and over again in my mind. I was glad it was dark enough that Erik couldn't see me smirking like an idiot.

We didn't say much to each other while we set up camp, comfortable in the shared silence. We had our mats placed on opposite sides of the fire, and I looked at him over the flame, the light dancing over his face. We said goodnight, and with a smile on my heart, I tucked in and fell asleep.

CHAPTER 27

"Fara! Wake up! Fara!" I woke to see Erik above me, shaking me awake, panic in his eyes. "The soldiers, they are close! I went to look for food and heard them in the forest. Their camp isn't too far from here, and from what I could tell, they were getting ready to pack up and move out. Which means we need to get out of here, now."

I jumped up and bundled my sleeping mat, not taking the time to fold it or roll it, and quickly covered the fire pit with sand, spreading the hot coals around until the last signs of it disappeared. Working quickly, Erik and I packed everything away on the horses and got ready to go.

"Wait, Fara," Erik grabbed my wrist before I was able to mount Misten, "We need to split ways. The guards are obviously looking for us, and I know this forest better than you do. I can easily get them off our trail. Here," he handed me the map but I pushed it back towards him, not wanting to split up. "Fara." I looked up at him, his eyes pleading. Taking the map, I folded it up and tucked it into my shift. "I have it memorized, so don't worry about me getting lost. Just go as fast as you can to Cethin, and I will meet you there. I promise." He kissed my forehead and then pushed me back, the quiet sound of horse hooves becoming audible. "Now go!"

I jumped on Misten and hesitated, turning back to him, but he slapped Misten on the rear with a "Hya", sending her into a gallop, leaving himself and Elana behind. We crashed through the forest, weaving through so as to create as little a path as possible. The same branches that had brushed my face before now whipped against my skin, splitting my cheeks open as I sped through them. I prayed the birds of the forest wouldn't give us away as we scared flocks of them into flight. For a while, all I could hear was Misten's panting in time with my own. When I felt like I had created a wide enough gap between the soldiers and myself, I slowed her down to a trot. I pulled the map out of my shift and tried to find my location. Even in winter, the forest canopy was too thick with leaves for me to use the sun to get my bearings. Instead, I had to rely on my memory in order to decipher the map's instructions. Once my mind cleared and my heart calmed, I was able to find a discernible trail that would lead me to Cethin. Our fast pace last night led us much further than I had initially thought, and to my surprise we were only a few hours away from the same caves that Croxley led me out of months ago. With both nervous excitement and anxiety, I spurred Misten along and continued our journey.

After navigating the caves for an hour, my nerves were beginning to get the best of me. I had left Misten behind at the entrance, and without her, I had no one to keep me company in the quiet darkness of the tunnels. I quietly hummed to myself the tune that Jean had sung to me, my song bouncing off of the walls of the tunnel, creating a chorus of echoes.

Scenarios of my welcome kept running through my head, visions of varying emotions, ranging from warm welcomes and embraces to violent accusations of treachery, haunting my every step. I told myself to calm down, that whatever was going to happen would happen no matter what I did at this point, but this did little to stop my nervous hands from gripping the lantern so tight that my knuckles turned white.

Eventually, the inevitable came, and my journey deeper and deeper into the tunnels brought me to the entrance of Cethin. Erik, Croxley, and I had spoken before about how to navigate past the guards: I had an order signed by Erik demanding that they leave the tunnels to join the King's forces in the south. Hopefully they don't run into the guards chasing us, I thought to myself. As the entrance to Cethin required passing through the guard's quarters, I had no choice but to face them head on. I could only hope that none of them would recognize me. Then again, I thought, I've changed quite a bit. All those days working in the barn with Heath had made me stronger, given my light frame some muscles that I wasn't able to build back when I was forced to stay in my room all day. The sun, too, had left its mark on me, lightening my dark brown hair and giving my skin a slight tan. My hair was longer now, too. I had let it down to cover my number, 923, and it nearly reached the small of my back, slightly tousled from the braid I had kept it in during the ride here. I was even aware of the changes in the way I carried myself. No longer walking through the caverns with my neck bared, eyes on the ground, I now had a new confidence that kept my head high. I could only hope that this confidence didn't crumble at first sight of the nightmares of my past.

My test came quickly. After only a few minutes of wandering the guard's corridors, I ran into a fat, pasty man struggling to tighten his belt.

"Oi! Who goes there?" He barked, obviously embarrassed about his current state, but more so surprised at my sudden appearance. "What do you think yet doin down here?"

Before he could grab me, I held the order up in front of him. "I come from the capital of Stonewall with an order from the King." He motioned to grab the parchment, but I pulled it back, knowing that I most likely wouldn't see it again should he get his hands on it. "Let me speak to the General in command."

He eyed me up and down, suspicion in his squinted eyes. Finally, he grunted and turned, motioning for me to step in front of him as he walked behind me. I felt his gaze bore into my back, but I just stood strong and walked on.

"Sir, we have a messenger from the royal city," he said when we reached the General's tent, motioning for me to remain outside.

"Al-right, send him in." The general's voice sounded familiar, and I cursed my luck when I realized that they hadn't changed him yet. Normally, the generals only last a few months, maybe a year, tops, but this one had been in command for nearly three years. I tightened my resolve and hoped that he wouldn't make the connection between the young woman standing before him today and the girl he had seen wandering the tunnels many months ago. My naïve world has been completely shattered, my childish desires replaced with much more serious concerns.

The guard let me into the tent, and the General exclaimed, "Well, look at that. The King is permitting women to work now? Seems to me that he has lost some of his sense, don't you think, Gruss?"

The chubby guard at my side laughed and replied, "Yes, sir. Them lasses are only good fer a few things, and they ain't got no place in the palace."

"Right you are, Gruss. If you ask me, they either belong in the kitchen or in bed." The men laughed together, thinking they were incredibly clever, but I maintained my composure.

I let them laugh the joke out, and when it had died down, I announced with as much authority as I could muster, "If you are done, General, I have an order from the King."

"Al-right, let's see it. Give it here, girl." He snatched the parchment out of my hand and scanned it carefully, reading it once, twice over. "This isn't signed in the King's name," he said after looking up.

"No, it was signed by Prince Erik. He has been put in charge of the King's armies for this mission."

"The Prince? That playboy? You've got to be bloody joking. There is no way he would be able to lead an army. He can barely lead himself out of bed, unless it's to a party!" The general turned towards his desk and took a swig from the bottle resting atop. From the grimace that followed, it must've been hard liquor. "Well, my right mind tells me to ignore this order if it means we have to deal with that dullard, but if the daddy's in charge, I guess I can't do anything about it. Gruss, start spreading news of the order. I want to be out of here my tomorrow midday at the latest. I'll leave behind 3 of my best men to watch over things." The General stopped collecting things at his desk and looked up. " And no, Gruss, that's not you." Gruss turned red in the face, his shoulders slumped and eyes cast downwards in disappointment. The general watched him for a few moments, then slammed his hand on the desk, startling Gruss out of his self-pity. "Well? Are you going to just stand there? Go!" Gruss practically ran out of the door, and I took my chance to leave with him. I didn't make it very far before the general called me back. "And where do you think you're going?"

"I, uh□need to evaluate the colony. Make sure everything is running smoothly."

"I can assure you, I run everything perfectly," he said, each step bringing him closer to me. "Instead of wasting your time snooping around, why don't you stay here for a while and keep me some company? I haven't been around a woman in a long time. These Cethin rats aren't even of the same species as you Ahrenian beauties," he said as he reached around my waist. I slapped his hand away and he pulled it back, cradling it in offense. I watched as his embarrassment quickly turned into fury.

"I would think before touching me again, General. When the King finds out how you are handling his officials," I tried to keep my voice steady, but memories of fear came rushing back, and I could feel a slight tremble in my voice.

"Oh, shut yer trap. We both know how you worked your way to the top, love. I just want you to show me a little of that□persuasion as well." He pulled me around so that my back was to his chest. I felt his breath against my neck, and I shuddered as he brushed my hair off to the side, exclaiming, "I knew it! I knew you looked familiar. We've only had one looker down here in a long time. You think you could come back here without me remembering you?"

I pushed myself away from him, hiding my trembling hands behind my back. "I'm warning you, stay back. I'm protected by the King himself. He ordered me to come down here and have you do your duty to serve the kingdom."

The General made his way towards me, his intent clear. I tried to step back, but I was already against the wall. I knew that if I were to run, he would easily catch me. All he would have to do is call the guards to help him, and I would be his. "You know, for some reason I don't believe that."

"How about I confirm it for you, General?" I nearly collapsed in relief when I heard Erik's voice. He was standing in the doorway, a few bruises on his cheek but not much worse for wear.

"Your highness, what are you doing down here? I mean, er, welcome, sir," The General stumbled over his words and bowed his head, looking like a guilty child caught stealing sweets.

"I can vouch for her. She is part of the palace court, and demands your respect."

"So you're the one who is getting special treatment," the general muttered, jealously eyeing the Prince.

"I'm sorry?" Prince Erik regarded the General with a challenge in his eye, and they looked at one another like two tomcats sizing each other up before a fight. After a few brief, tense moments, the General turned away and went back to his desk, sitting down and taking another swig of his drink. "Nothing, you're highness", he said as he swallowed the drink down, "I simply said I have a lot to get done, so if you must make your rounds through my colony, go ahead and please get out of my way. I look forward to being under your command, sir."

Erik gave me a quick quirk of the eyebrows. His being in command wasn't part of the plan, but he had enough sense enough to go along with it. "Thank you General, and good work. Come, Fara," he said.

"You might call her Fara, but she will never be anything more than 923. Try as you might, you won't ever be able to wash all the dirt off her," the General called after Erik as he was leaving.

I saw Erik's eyes flash with anger, but I caught his gaze. It's not worth it, I pleaded. He clenched his fists and left the room, and I quickly followed.

When we got far enough from the guard's quarters, I reached for his hand. "It's okay, it's fine. I'm used to it. I've grown up here, remember?" He still seemed angry, his back to me, looking towards the office. I knew he needed to keep his head on straight if we were to convince my father that he was on our side, and that we needed his help with the rebellion. "Erik, look at me." He turned his head, but his attention was still focused on the door. "Are you okay? Are the soldiers following you? What happened?"

That seemed to do the trick, because he finally pulled his eyes away and looked at me, reporting "No. Most of them never caught up with me, and I took care of the few that did." I reached up and touched his swollen cheek, feeling him flinch under my touch. "It's fine," he mumbled, and placing his hand over mine, closed his eyes and pressed into my hand. "It's fine now," he repeated, and I had a feeling he wasn't talking about his injuries.

"Erik, are you ready?"

"If you are," he replied. He went to take my hand, but I retracted.

"I think it would be better if I went in first, alone. I don't know how they are going to react to me, and I surely don't know how they will react to you. It's better to minimize our risks." I pulled my hand out from under his and made my way down the caverns, knowing that Erik was keeping pace just a few steps behind me, hidden in the shadows.

I slowed down when I heard the sound of people talking, having reached the main cavern where we would have group meals, meetings, festivals. It was the only space large enough to fit all of us at one time.

Peering around the edge, my heart leapt when I saw my father sitting at the head of the table. The first thing I noticed was that his hair had greyed, and his eyes were more tired than I had ever seen them. I felt a pang of guilt, knowing that I was most likely the cause.

I watched as my mother approached him and put her hand on his arm, which was resting on the table. She looked just as tired as he, and I could feel her grief from here. I felt my courage wane, wondering if I was doing the right thing. Do they really need this? I thought, knowing that a rebellion would bring countless amounts of bloodshed and grief should things turn badly. I felt that, after leaving their lives so suddenly, I had no right to re-enter in the same sudden manner. Who was I to suddenly reappear and ask everyone to make the ultimate sacrifice for people that they don't even know exist? All these doubts, these thoughts of anguish, swirled through my head, and I didn't notice at first that the chatter was dying down. But when the harsh sound of fervent whispering reached my ears, I snapped to attention and saw that my parents were staring straight at me. Actually, everyone was staring straight at me. I didn't know what to do, so I just stood there, my skin literally burning under their gaze.

Unable to move an inch, I felt like I was going to melt into a puddle. I scanned the crowd, purposefully avoiding my parent's eyes, and I saw familiar, if not friendly faces, some painted with looks of confusion, others contorted in anger and suspicion. While my eyes wandered around the room, I was caught unaware when a hand was placed on my shoulder. I looked up and saw that it was my father. For a few moments, he held me at an arm's distance, and then, with a sigh of relief loud enough to shake the whole room, he pulled me in to a tight squeeze, and I felt my mother join in, until we became a single crying unit. My mother kept kissing the top of my head, and my father repeatedly pulled his head back to look at me, as if he were looking for some trick, some slight that would prove this was a dream, that I wasn't really here.

I was beginning to think that I was going to suffocate under their embrace, when my father finally released me and said, "Welcome home, Faradene."

Acting the part, my mother quickly followed up with, "Where were you? Don't you know we've been worried sick? I can't believe you would just up and leave like that! Have I taught you no sense of responsibility? I-"

"Miriam," my father interrupted, rescuing me from the stream of reprimands my mother was about to release on me. "Faradene, what your mother says is true. You had no right to leave in the manner that you did." I began to interrupt, but he held up his hand. "True," he said, "you did tell Conor, who was smart enough to tell us just where on earth you had gone, but regardless, what you did was reckless and selfish. For months your mother and I wondered if we would ever see you again. We," he sighed, "began to lose hope. That is a terrible conclusion for parents to come to. Do you understand, Faradene?"

"Yes, Father. But you have to understand as well," I looked from my mother to my father, "you both have to understand, I did what I had to do. After being cooped up in our den for eighteen years, I needed to do my part. And, Father, you won't believe what I found out." I looked around, aware that we were still in the main cavern. Although most had returned back to their meal and conversation, I was still nervous about revealing too much. "Can we go back to the den? I need to talk to you in private." My parents conceded, and as we walked towards the den, I looked over my shoulder, hoping that Erik would be able to follow us without causing too much trouble.

"I'm not sure if you know this, but we aren't alone," I said once we had returned back to our den, my father's cloak over the doorway in the same way it was the night I left. I faced them, their backs to the entryway.

"What do you mean, we aren't alone," my mother asked.

"Cethin is just one of nine underground colonies. That means that there are eight other groups of people forced to live underground and suffer the same way we do."

I watched as the implications of this sunk in, my parents looking at each other with wide eyes.

"How do you know this? Faradene, where did you get this information? What were you even doing all this time?"

I took a deep breath and tried to summarize the past months into a few short sentences. "I was on the surface. I went with the messenger-his name is Croxley-and I became a servant in the castle. Most of the other girls that work in the castle come from colonies too, and I have a group of them that want to help fight for their freedom. Heath and Vil and Mr. Harris all want to help too, and they are going to go to the other colonies to try and gather forces. Pa, we are going to start the revolution."

It took my father a few minutes to respond, but when he did, it wasn't the response I had been expecting.

"No, we aren't Faradene. We can't. Even with the other colonies, there isn't any hope for us. When you were gone, the other councilmen and I tried planning and strategizing, but no matter how hard we worked, how much we argued over what was the best route to take, we always came to the same conclusion. Once we get our freedom, what then? We would have no place to go. Live in the cities? We would be cast out like the garbage they think we are. We would be putting ourselves at risk for nothing."

"That isn't true! Father, I've lived in the cities. True, most of the people believe the prejudice, and yes, we will have to break the stereotypes and create a new reputation for ourselves. But once they actually get to know us and realize that we are very much the same, they, for the most part, seem to accept us. I'd even venture to say that some of them like us." As I spoke, I saw the cloak ripple as Prince Erik snuck in, my parents backs to the entrance. I turned my eyes back towards my father. "We already have support among a few of them, Father. Whose to say we wont find more?"

My father shook his head solemnly, pitying me for my false hope. He walked towards me and cupped my shoulders in his large, calloused hands. "My sweet Faradene, I cant deny that you've matured since leaving. You've truly turned into a beautiful young woman. I don't know everything that you've seen, but in spite of it all, you are still very naïve. I'm sure you've found some friends on the surface, but a few commoners and slaves will not be enough to help our people win their freedom."

"Well, sir, I'm sure it would take some royal effort, but it can be done, I assure you."

CHAPTER 28

My parents whipped around, and before anyone else could respond, my father lunged and grabbed Erik in a choke-hold. Erik's face began to turn red as my father threatened, "I don't know what you heard, you filthy guard, but I'm not letting you leave this room so that you can go squeal to your friends. I have no choice but to-"

"Father, no!" I ran up to him, beating him on the arms until he released Erik, who sunk to the floor, coughing and gasping for air.

My father looked at me, adrenaline pumping, and protested, "Faradene, he is just going to report us and put our entire family at risk of being executed. We can't trust him to keep his mouth shut!" This side of my father frightened me, the side that was willing to do anything to protect his people.

"Father, how many guards have you had to□take care of?" I looked at him in a whole new light. The thick, muscular frame that has been used to support my family by working the mines every day now looked like a finely-honed weapon, the large hands transformed from gentle, loving hands to strong, powerful tools.

"I've only done what I had to do to protect my family and my people," he stated, and this was the only answer I needed. At first, I stared at him in fear, but when he looked into my eyes, I saw the memories. I saw the faces of all the guards he had to kill, and I knew that they must haunt him every time he closes his eyes. My father wasn't a cold-blooded killer. He was a man fighting for those he loved, and I knew at that moment that I could depend on him for anything. My mother too, I realized, would fight for me till her dying breath. And now, that was exactly what I was asking them to do.

"Father, you don't have to protect us from him. He is a friend." I helped Erik stand up, who had stopped coughing but was still rubbing his neck.

"Pleased to make your acquaintance," he said, but didn't extend his hand for a handshake. I didn't blame him.

"Faradene, who is he? Is he from one of the other colonies?" My mother asked, taking in his auburn hair and rich green eyes.

"No, he's um," I looked at Erik, not sure if he wanted me to reveal his rank. He met my eyes and nodded, taking over.

"Actually, I am from Ahrenia. My name is Erik. Most know me as

Prince Erik."

"Prince? Faradene, how did you manage to bring a Prince down here?" My mother looked at me, bewildered, while my father seemed unimpressed.

"Fara can be very convincing when she puts her mind to it," Erik said, a smile tugging on the corner of his mouth but otherwise keeping eye contact with my parents, who raised their eyebrows at the nickname. "She's opened my eyes to the suffering of your people, and I am eager to help you get the freedom you deserve."

My father spoke up. "Prince Erik. I've heard of you. You're the boy who is always up to no good, spending the palace's money on the grandest parties, shirking your duties to go on adventures whenever the desire hits you. I appreciate your offer, but with your reputation, I don't think you will be able to help us very much. I especially don't think you can help my daughter. And if I am correct, are you not engaged to be married soon? I would appreciate it if you would leave my family alone and let my colony rest in the little peace I am able to manage."

"Father!" I exclaimed, bewildered at his behaviour. Was he really willing to let all chances of freedom go because of his overprotection?

"No, Faradene. This young man has no sense of responsibility. He says he will help you now, but at the first sign of adversity, you can be sure he would leave you to struggle on your own."

"With all respect, sir," Erik cut in. "I will be the first to admit that I have been reckless and selfish. I took everything I had for granted, and worried about nothing but my own happiness. But because of your daughter□" he looked at me long enough for my cheeks to warm, and then back to my father. "Because of your daughter, I saw that everything I knew about the colonies, about how unintelligent, lazy, and criminal you are, is completely wrong. And I know of others who feel the same way. So, I pledge to you my help against the injustice that you have been subject to for centuries. I can only hope that you accept it."

My father looked at him skeptically, then to my mother, then to me, then back to him. Finally, he groaned and said, "I don't want to accept it, but it isn't up to me. We must let the rest of the councilmen. I can organize a meeting with them later tonight, but until then, you and Faradene need to wait here. I don't know how you got back here, but I'm sure the guards are already suspicious." I looked at Erik, who looked back at me and shrugged, as if saying, He'll find out eventually. My father sighed and turned around, heading towards the exit. "That means that the guards are going to be extra critical today, making things even more difficult." Pulling the cloak aside, he turned his head before he left, saying, "Faradene, I am very glad to see you home," and then let the cloak fall behind him.

My mother cleared her throat and clasped her hands together. "Well, since you're here, you may as well help me prepare supper. Faradene, you know where to find everything. And your highness, welcome to Cethin. I expect you to get your hands dirty."

Conor ended up meeting us for dinner, as his mother was on the council as well, which meant that he would spend the night helping my mother with chores, most likely taking stock of the storage rooms or weaving blankets. By the look on his face when Erik and I left for the meeting, he knew what he was in for.

When he first saw me, he had been telling my mother about how the missing turnips from the storage room weren't his fault. He stopped in his tracks, his dialogue trailing off, and just stared at me, as if he couldn't believe I was in the room. It only took a small wave on my part, and he came running into my arms. I held on a bit too long, and he soon squirmed out of my grip. I couldn't help but grab his cheeks and marvel at how much he had grown in the months I had been away. He looked as though he was still getting taller, although he still had yet to put an ounce of muscle on his bones.

"Faradene! Why are you back here? Are you here to save us? Did you do what you wanted to do? How is the surface? Why is your skin darker?"

His long stream of questions had me laughing, while Erik looked at me with a sense of bewilderment. I introduced them to each other, and when Conor heard the word "Prince," his mouth gaped open and he looked at Erik in awe. After a few seconds of silent appreciation, he delved into questions asking about princely life, and Erik looked flustered. Luckily, my mother interrupted his string of questions by placing a plate of food in front of his face, and he decided to sacrifice his curiosity in order to satisfy his stomach.

"Do you always eat that?" Erik asked, presumably referring to the dinner we had, the usual gruel made with potatoes and carrots, with a loaf of stale bread to soak it up.

"What else would we eat? In case you haven't noticed, we don't have a wide variety of choices here." I knew it tasted bad, but I couldn't help but give him a hard time. "It might not be up to your standards, but it's better than nothing. And trust me, I've had plenty of nights with nothing. I'd take gruel any day." I stopped walking and looked back at Erik, who had fallen behind. "What?" He was staring at the wall in front of him, chewing on his lip. After a while, he looked at me, concern on his face.

"What am I supposed to say to the parliament? How am I supposed to win their support if I don't know anything about them except for the stereotypes I've been raised with? They'll look right through my appeals and see me for exactly what I am, an immature Prince looking for a way to prove himself a hero."

"Give yourself some credit. You're much more than that," I encouraged. "Besides, this isn't a contest, Erik. You can't win them over. What you can do is be honest, be humble, and be respectful. If you show them that you truly care for their well being, are truly concerned with their freedom, then they will support you. Don't worry, you can do it," I walked closer to him and brushed his hair aside, my hand lingering on his cheek. "Erik, you can do this. And believe me when I tell you that you don't have to prove yourself a hero." He gently took my hand off his cheek, kissing it before interlocking his fingers with mine.

"If you are with me, then I can do it." Keeping a grip on my hand, he started walking down the tunnel. "Let's go to the meeting."

"Al-right. But Erik?"

"Yes?"

"You're walking the wrong way. The council room is in the other direction."

"Oh, right. Um, maybe you should lead."

"Good idea." And with that, I walked to the council room, Prince in tow.

CHAPTER 29

We released our grip on one another's hands before entering the council room. You could hear the buzz of discussion, some voices imbued with passion, others with anger. Prince Erik readjusted his shirt, then his hair, then his shirt again, and I smiled at his nervous gestures. "You've given plenty of speeches before. Why are you so nervous?"

"Because this time I'm actually working towards something I care about." He looked at me and I felt my cheeks warm. Taking a deep breath together, we entered, the room.

"We've suffered too long, Anso. We can't afford to lose more food to the guard's greedy mouths." A heavily bearded man was speaking. I think his name was Serrus. My father used to complain about him while we ate supper. "My family is growing too thin. Just look around. None of us can fill out our clothes. They drape across our shoulders, speaking of a time where things were better. Well, things are only going to get worse."

"That doesn't mean that we should put everything and everyone at risk," another man retorted from the other end of the circular room. This one I recognized better, as he had often come to visit us. His name was Broderick, and he was a kind soul with a gentle heart. "There has to be a diplomatic way to solve this. Perhaps we can call for a hearing summons with the general or even work our way towards Stonewall to speak to an audience. I say, if the Prince can help us get there, who are we to deny his offer?"

"Diplomacy would never work." This time is was Conor's mother, Julianne, who spoke up. "An entire civilization of people were subjected to live as slaves underground. What makes you think anyone on the surface cares about what happens to us down here?"

"I believe that's where I come in." Every head turned to look at Erik. As he walked to the centre of the room, he introduced himself. "As Prince of Ahrenia, I can vouch for a handful of people, myself included, who want nothing more than to see your freedom. I agree," he said, turning to look at Broderick, "diplomacy has to be our first goal. But I speak truthfully when I say that my father will not so much as give you a second glance if you approach him as you are now. In order to get his attention, we need to band up, work with the other colonies so that together, your voice can be heard."

"How many are you asking from us? We can't afford to send too many, for if you haven't noticed, we are already running low on supplies. If we lose any more hands☐well, it won't matter if we are granted audience because we will all be dead," a younger woman, one who had just joined the council a few months before I left, spoke up timidly.

"I understand you are hard-pressed. But to truly have any chance, we would need as many men and woman as we can get. In the next few weeks while we are rounding everyone else together, we can work to gather supplies so that the young and elderly can have something to survive off of while the stronger ones are gone. "

"What about these other colonies? How do we truly know they exist?" Serrus challenged.

Before Erik could respond, a quiet but strong voice spoke out. "Don't trouble the boy. They exist." The voice belonged to old Maguire, an elderly man who had been on the council since before anyone could remember. He doesn't often enter the dialogue, rather he observes with a keen eye, heavily considering both arguments before voicing his opinion. But when he did speak, his words were not taken lightly.

"Back when I was a young boy, my grandmother had told me stories about the Great Purge. She spoke of how her family was divided, how her and her mother were separated from her father and brother. She hoped that they had been allowed to remain on the surface, over the alternative of being killed as punishment for resisting. Years later, after her mother passed away, she overheard some guards speaking about a father and son who had been put to death after trying to escape from the colony. Confused, as no such attempts had been made in Cethin, she listened to snippets of conversations for days until she managed to put the whole story together.

What she found out was that her father and brother had been sent to a different colony during the Great Purge, and after they realized that the rest of the family hadn't made it with them, they plotted an escape plan. Other families that had been split up wanted to join them, and soon guards found out about the attempt and identified the son and father as the leaders of what they saw as a rebellion, putting them to death in order to quell any future attempts. Although it pained her to know of her family's demise, she finally had some closure. She guessed that there were more than just those two colonies, but by that time she had a family of her own and didn't want to endanger them by sneaking around for more information. That didn't stop her from telling her children and grandchildren the story, giving them a promise of hope in exchange for the promise to never tell another soul. Now, I won't put complete faith in you, Prince Erik, but I will put complete faith in my grandmother." Maguire folded his hands in his lap, apparently finished with his contribution.

"I guess that settles that. But we still don't have a plan," my father said.

"Well, we were hoping that Cethin would serve as the way-point for the other colonists, perhaps allowing us your quarters to house everyone until we are ready to enter the city."

Everyone started speaking at once, and questions like "how can we support all the other Nethers if we don't even have enough resources for ourselves," "what are we going to do about the guards," and "how do we even know this is going to work?"

"Everyone calm down!" My father pounded his fist on his chair's armrest to get everyone's attention. With everyone's feathers ruffled, it took a few moments for the voices to settle. "Now, from what I gather, your Highness, you intend on having Cethin house all of the volunteers from the other colonies, and once we have all assembled, we are to follow your escort into the city?"

"Yes. And if the King ignores our requests, then we will set up an embargo around the city. Add this to the fact that, with all of the colonies no longer running, supplies will quickly run out in the city and they would have no choice but to listen to our requests."

"Your highness, we can't afford to lose good men. If the King responds with forces and attacks our men, what then?" Julienne, who knew the sting of losing a husband, looked deeply concerned about the notion of other families feeling the same grief.

"I can make no promises," Erik conceded, his eyes never leaving hers. "But I will do everything in my power to prevent something such as that from occurring. As we speak, guards from the other colonies are being sent to work in the southern border on a project that should keep them busy long enough for us to enact our plan. We have nearly everything set up. We are only waiting on your confirmation." Following this, chatter spread throughout the room, and I stood in the corner, trying to gauge in which direction the conversation was going. From what I could hear, the council still sounded apprehensive, and I was growing nasty just standing and listening.

Finally, my father held up his hand to call for silence, announcing, "We will admit that you present a strong argument. We have for many years been trying to revolt ourselves, but the scale of which you mention is much larger than we had ever imagined. We will discuss it and let you know our decision within the fortnight."

I couldn't take it any-more. Although I had no place to speak, I walked into the centre of the room next to Erik. My father made eye contact with me, his eyes bright with warning, reminding me just how out of place I was, but I ignored their flame and spoke in a compelling voice. "Respectfully, council, we do not have the time to sit and converse. The King is-" I was interrupted by Serrus.

"Who is this girl and why does she think she has the right to speak in this council?" He leaned forward to inspect me, recognition widening his eyes. " Anso, is this not your spoiled daughter who thinks herself too good to work the mines like the rest of us? Who, until recently, had been living on the surface, leaving us behind to labour until our hands bleed?" He turned to look back at me. "Why don't you just return to your little den and leave the discussion to the adults? Honestly, child, what makes you think you know anything about the situation?"

My eyes stung, but I stood firm. "I'll acknowledge, sir, that I have been raised in seclusion, not out of vanity, but out of protection. However, I took it upon myself to break this seclusion when I presented myself for evaluation and was sent to work on the surface. For months I was ridiculed, used, abused, and had to endure more than you can imagine. But I was also aware, observing the court, planning and plotting, so that when I returned, I would be able to free my people. So I have come back with a plan for you." I challenged Serrus, holding his stare. "Now, if I may, I would like to have your audience."

Julianne spoke for me, saying, "I know this girl. She isn't just a delicate flower, she has thorns and can stand on her own. I believe we should listen to what she has to say."

"Thank you, Julianne." She smiled encouragingly, and I continued. "I understand that we are asking a lot of you, " I looked around the room, catching everyone's attention, "but we do not have time for the normal discussion, debate, and voting process. Before I left Ahrenia, I had heard some soldiers speaking of a project the King has in mind, a project that will require many hands to be taken from the colonies. According to them, a huge expedition is under-way in which the King's soldiers are going to raid the colonies in order to get more labourers." I paused to let this sink in, watching as members of the council make eye contact with each other across the room. I went on, warning "This means that we only have a short gap between when the guards leave and the soldiers come. And when they do come, you'll have wished that our guards were still here. I can promise you, the soldiers will destroy the little that we have, taking the able-bodied and leaving only the sick and the weak behind to fend for themselves. If we can reach Stonewall before the King sends out his troops, we can prevent more than just this from happening. We can make sure that nothing like this will ever happen again."

I stopped speaking, my heart pounding loudly in my chest from my impassioned speech, and I watched the faces around me for any sign of reaction. I was greeted with none, and I stood, forlorn, looking at my father in desperation. "Father, please. You know this is what is best for the people."

"Faradene, while your words may speak true, you are not a councilman. Therefore, your words are off the record and have no weight here." I opened my mouth to protest again, but closed it, not knowing what to say. He spoke the truth. "Because this is a special situation, however, we will consider your addition. Now, if you please, we will continue our discussion in private. We ask that you and Prince Erik leave and wait for our decision." I nodded, knowing that this was the best I could hope for. Before I could leave, my father motioned me to where he was sitting. He put his hand on my shoulder, speaking quietly, "And Faradene, thank you. I couldn't be more proud of you."

I repeated those words over in my head as we walked out of the council room and back through the corridors to the den. My father is proud of me.

CHAPTER 30

After the meeting, Erik and I returned to the den. We sat at the table, not saying much to each other. The only noise in the room came from nervous fingers rapping on the table and the crackling of the fire. When we had first returned, Conor and my mother swarmed us with questions regarding the meeting, but we weren't really sure what had happened ourselves, so didn't have much to report. After a while, Conor grew tired of helping my mother weave, so she took him back to his den to go to sleep.

Sometime after she had left, Erik's hand crept across the table and took my hand in his, pulling me from my thoughts. I looked at him and smiled. "You did a good job," I told him.

"We'll have to wait and see," he replied.

I nodded, and resumed my daydreams. My mind had been drifting though our plans, thinking of the next step and who would be playing in our dangerous game. My wanderings brought me to Heath, Mr. Harris, and eventually Croxley.

"I miss Croxley," I announced.

"Me too. I'm used to him going on long journeys, but he normally tells me where he goes first. This time he left without a word."

"What would make him do that?"

"Well, actually, we had an argument the night before☐" Erik trailed off, not willing to say more.

"About what?" I prompted, and Erik avoided my eyes, suddenly becoming occupied with tracing a knot in the wood of the table. "Erik, what did you fight about?"

He looked at me, then sighed and looked back down, avoiding me eyes. "You. We fought about you, Fara,"

"Really? Why? What did I do?"

"You didn't do anything. It wasn't really about you☐it was more over you."

"Over me? I'm not some piece of land you can decide to stake a claim in!" I felt myself grow defensive.

"That's not what I meant!" He sighed, then started over. "Fara, we were fighting because we both have feelings for you."

Now it was my turn to be speechless. "Um☐what?" My mind was still spinning around the idea that the Prince had feelings for me, and now Croxley? "No, Croxley was always making fun of me, and talking about all the women he made love to"

"That was his way of trying to impress you, or perhaps make you jealous. He's not used to courting women. It's one of the downsides of living in a world where you can get anything you want. You forget how to work for what really matters."

"Oh." I sat there, dumbfounded, running through all my memories with Croxley over in my head in a new light. "So, what happened?"

"Well, I told him that I though you were fascinating," I raised an eyebrow. "Yes, I actually used that word. I still think you are fascinating, by the way." He took my hands in his, inspecting them as he spoke. "And he grew angry, saying that he had liked you first. That he was just waiting for the right time to tell you. Then he started reminding me of my engagement, stating that I had no right to think about you that way, and I admit I grew defensive. I didn't want him reminding me of my duty, one that I was all too aware of. And dreading, might I add. When I first met Lena, I didn't know how I was going to survive. I think that's why I started going to so many parties and running away on adventures. I wanted to experience as much of life as I could before I was tied down. Especially considering who I would be tied down with.

Well, I guess I have to be fair. I would probably hate Lena regardless of how rude or nice she was. Just the idea, being forced to marry someone, not out of love but out of politics. Honestly, I think that's how my mother died. Out of sorrow of being married to my father." He said it quietly, his love for his mother as evident in his voice as the scorn for his father. He massaged the back of my hands with his thumbs, thinking. Finally he admitted, "This is why I grew so angry at Croxley. I've always been jealous of his ability to go wherever he desires, no life predetermined for him."

"But you're the Prince! Don't you know how many people would dreaming of being you?"

"If I could, I would gladly give it. People wish they could have my power, I've spent my whole life wishing I could be normal. Unremarkable. But when I met you, when I saw your passion for justice, I realized that I could use my circumstances to my advantage."

His words hit home. I remember lying on the floor when I was younger, scrubbing dirt into my face or rubbing oil over my skin trying to make myself look more like everyone else. To anyone watching, it seemed ridiculous, ungrateful even. As if I couldn't appreciate the gifts I'd been given. But the thing was, I'd never asked for them. Now, however, I know they were given to me for a reason. Erik as well. We were both graced, and cursed, with a greater destiny in mind.

I thought back to Croxley and all the adventures we had. Looking back on it, I realized how much he risked for me. From the start, he had shown me a kindness I never could have expected. Little things like giving me a name, sharing his food, actually talking to me, all made the situation a little less traumatic. In the servant's quarters, I heard other girls' stories about their journeys. Some had to travel in harsh weather, others were forced to carry the supplies like a pack mule and cross rivers on foot while their escorts remained on their horses. One girl said that she travelled in a group of three others from her colony, a younger girl and her older brother. The guards wouldn't let them sleep around the camp-fire, rather forced them all to sleep separately on the outskirts of the camp. One morning she woke up and the other two were gone, taken in the dark of the night. The guards didn't even bother looking for them. They just made her carry what was left of their supplies and continue the journey.

It all made my trip sound like a vacation. Sam carried me through the forest, we were blessed with nice weather, and we even made a stop at the inn, where I was able to sleep on a real bed for the first time. When we got to the castle, Croxley made sure I ended up in a safe place, and has done everything he could to support my plan. I owe so much to him. More than that, though, I miss him, his teasing and his wit, his crooked smile. I can't imagine not seeing him again. But did I ever love him? Not in the way I think he wanted me to. Not in the same way I felt for Erik.

I looked at him, sitting there running his fingers slowly along the contours in the table, feeling the knots and bumps, the ridges and lines, that marred the surface. Not marred, I corrected myself. Made unique. "What are you thinking?" I asked.

"This table reminds me of people. All the little bumps and scratches give it a personality, a story. In Ahrenia, we only make tables out of perfect wood. One year, my father cleared down a whole forest in order to find the perfect tree to make into a footstool. In the end, it fell apart on evening during a feast, its wood weakened by disease. But this," he rubbed his hand up and down, "despite all the furrows and nicks, it is sturdy and strong. I'd guess it's been in your family for generations."

"You'd be correct," I said. "My great grandfather made it as a courting gift for my great grandmother. This was before they stopped the flow of wood into Cethin. Now, if we need to make anything, we have to take apart the furniture we already have."

"How strange," Erik said.

"What? That we have to take furniture apart?"

"No, that your great grandfather made your great grandmother a table." He smiled and continued, "I'm sorry, but I don't know how to make tables. Would you still consider courting me even if I were table-less? I might be able to find some other way to sweeten the deal."

"You better, because I definitely need some bribing if I'm going to be stuck with you," I teased back. Before I could come up with another jest, Erik's face turned serious.

"But honestly, Fara, what would you say if I offered it? A marriage to the kingdom?"

Part of me wanted to continue jesting, as if I didn't realize the sincerity of the question. The other half of me was focused on this new feeling in my stomach that accompanied his words. It wasn't a flighty, nervous feeling that often comes when I'm around the guards, nor was is that sick, heavy feeling that came when I was with the merchant in the bedroom. This one felt light, airy, like I had butterflies in my stomach flying to my heart, spreading warmth through my body.

So I sat there, lukewarm, not knowing how to respond. My internal struggle was interrupted when my father walked into the room. Erik jumped up and he and my father gave each other slight nods, in the same manner as a regional lord would give to a King. With this simple action, I saw a future in which the citizens of the colonies and the other citizens of Ahrenia were on common ground, and all the leaders were united under a single, just King. Could Erik be this King? I hoped so. I earnestly hoped so.

"What is the news?" Erik asked my father, successfully disguising his eagerness.

"After much discussion and deliberation, we have decided that it would be in the best interest of everyone to assist you in your efforts. Or, rather, accept your assistance for our efforts, as it seems we are both working for the same goal."

I could almost feel Erik sigh with relief. I couldn't believe that this was really happening, that the plan was finally in action.

"So now I ask you, what do you need us to do?" My father took off his cloak and put it over the doorway, as he does every night, and took a seat at the table.

"The commander said that the guards would be gone by tomorrow morning. That means that Fara and I will leave with them, so as not to arouse their suspicions. After we are far enough away, we will leave them and head on to the next colony. Here," Erik said and handed my father a map of all the colonies. "We need you to send a messenger the other colonies in order to spread the news. We already have someone heading over here," he pointed to the east-most colony where Mr. Harris and Heath had headed, "if you see them, tell them that you have received us and are ready to act. Fara and I will be heading towards Grundale, so you don't need to go there." My father studied the map, a crease in his brow.

"You and Faradene will be traveling together?" My father finally asked, raising his gaze from the map.

"Yes, sir. I will keep your daughter in the best care I can give."

My father inspected the Prince, and I could almost see the thoughts bouncing back and forth while his mind worked over the situation before him.

"Faradene, can you keep this man safe? I don't think he knows what he just agreed to. " He finally said, and I laughed.

"I'll try my best, father," I said as I leaned in and hugged him, warm in his embrace. I wanted to stay there forever. The months away from my family made me cherish every moment I had with them now, and my heart ached to know that Erik and I would have to leave them behind tomorrow. I squeezed my father hard, trying to communicate all of my gratitude and all of my love to him through that basic human contact. When I finally pulled away, he looked at me, and I thought I saw tears in his eyes. He coughed, and then stuck his hand out towards Erik.

"Good luck, son. You and Faradene may rest here overnight. I myself have to take care of some preparations. "

"Thank you, sir," Erik said, shaking my fathers hand. My father left the room, leaving his cloak up over the door and Erik and I to ourselves. Erik then looked at me, a successful smirk on his face, and I realized that my father essentially just gave Erik his blessing.

My heart fluttered, but I sternly put it to rest. Any feelings I had would have to wait. I couldn't afford to lose myself to any confusion, to any distractions. We had a plan now, a goal that was more important than myself or Erik or Croxley. It included the fate of all my people. Anything that happened afterwards, well, I can't say I plan on fighting it. But for now, I was content to let Erik's hand warm mine as we lay on the ground, the same ground that I had slept on my entire life, and fell asleep.

CHAPTER 31

Croxley emerged from the forest, Sir Thunder and Sam in tow.

It's been weeks since I've last been here, he thought to himself. He had been charged by the King to send a message to the border, warning the neighbouring country of Bastland that if they refused to trade with Ahrenia, the King wouldn't hesitate to send an army to invade.

He sighed, weary from the travelling, and thought back to all the times he had delivered similar messages to small, defenseless countries, with no way to protect themselves from the King's wrath. They always ceded to the King's will. Really, they had no choice.

This time was little different. Croxley remembered how the King of Bastland had read the message, a frown carving itself into his forehead as he translated the diplomatic message into the warning it was. He grew angry at first, they all did. But after a day of deliberation with the council, he called Croxley back to relay the response to the King, that they would accept and open their borders to Ahrenia's products once again.

Croxley understood why Bastland, and all the other small border nations, hesitated to trade with Ahrenia. With the Nethers constantly slaving away, Ahrenia had a surplus of products that invaded the markets of the other countries at much lower prices, and eventually their economy became completely dependent on Ahrenia.

But Croxley had long-since removed himself from this world of economics and politics. Normally, on such missions, he would deliver the message, and then leave to some tavern somewhere, using the King's money to find women and get drunk. This time, it wasn't much different. He still went to the tavern, he still spent the night with some very talented women, but he didn't enjoy it as much as he had before. He couldn't help but feel like he was trying to replace something, to nurse himself from his wounded heart.

Blast it, he thought as he absent-mindedly guided Sir Thunder and Sam through the gates. Lost as he was in his memories, he didn't notice that there weren't any guards at the gate, only the gatekeeper, who called out a brief, "Ho, Croxley."

But Croxley, his mind still stuck in the past, didn't respond. As much as he wanted to ignore it, he knew that he had been trying to nurse himself back in Bastland. Normally, he would drink with the gay spirit of adventure, and enjoy his women with the pride of a conqueror. But this time, he couldn't help but think of Fara. Fara and Erik. Damn, he cursed inwardly. Every time he thought of either of them, the other accompanied, always together as a pair in his head, a painful reminder that he wasn't a part of them. They were each other's, and he was alone.

He had thought that, with Fara, he had something. Most of the girls he had known before were shallow, self-centred. But Fara, she showed spirit, she had a passion for the future that exceeded that of what she was going to wear the next day. It didn't take much for him to fall in love with her. And he had thought, hoped, that the world above she was so obviously falling in love with, the nature, the people, everything, had also included him.

But then she met the Prince. How had that even happen? Erik was never interested in the slaves. What were the chances that he would be sitting in on the council when Croxley brought Fara in for evaluation? And he couldn't just let Croxley save Fara from that merchant. No, he insisted in helping, saying he wanted something "exciting" to do that night. Because saving a woman was just another form of entertainment for him.

Fate didn't seem to smile upon Croxley, but it always smiled upon the Prince. Erik had gotten everything he wanted, his whole life, while Croxley had to work behind him to keep up. Any trouble they got themselves into somehow ended up Croxley's fault. Erik, on the other hand, always ended up scotch-free. Any girl that Erik lay his eyes on would end up his by the end of the night, and Croxley would end up with the rejected girls, forlorn at being overlooked by the Prince. Upon finding Fara, Croxley finally had something that was his, untouched by the Prince. So when Erik told Croxley that he loved Fara, it stung like a betrayal of the worst kind.

Croxley stopped and exhaled, feeling some of his anger leave him with his breath. As much as he begrudged Erik, they had always been best friends. They've gone through too much to let something like this tear them apart. Eventually, Croxley may even feel happy for Erik and Fara. I doubt it. The best I'll be able to do is tolerate it, Croxley thought. But for now, Croxley was bitter, holding on to his anger and avoiding thoughts about Erik and Fara by finding solace in drink and women. And yet, no matter who he took to bed, he wasn't able to find satisfaction, because his heart now knew what it wanted, and primal lust was no match to the longing for love.

After coming to agreement with the King of Bastland, he didn't come straight home. Despite the pain of unrequited love, he still had honour, and he was going to stay true to the plan of rescuing those condemned to the colonies. And if there was a chance to prove himself to Fara, there may still exist the possibility for her to change her mind. With this in mind, Croxley had made a detour to the nearest colony, the northern clan of Fyzen. It was the smallest colony, and it had little protection from the guards because it was also the least productive. The only thing it could produce this far north in the mountains was granite, which was difficult to transport, thus the King arranged two large caravans a year to collect the gathered stone and otherwise left the Nethers to themselves.

Croxley knew that the last caravan left a few months ago, so there wouldn't be very many guards around to challenge his appearance.

Overall, his mission was successful. He met with the Fyzen leader, an old woman named Thylora, who despite her many years, was strong and stubborn. He had a friendly relationship with her. They enjoyed to bicker back and forth, and she found his youth refreshing. Fyzen hadn't had much success with children because all the mountain dust was hard on infants' lungs, so there was rarely a child to fuss over.

Croxley laughed to himself as he remembered what she had said to him when he first asked for her help. "Have they bred all the brains out of ye in place of a pretty face? I don't know if ye can tell, but we be stuck under miles of rock. 'Ow do ye think we can get to the royal city without those fancy wagons and riding animals you've all got to carry your lazy arses around on land? By the time we got there, me grandchildren would be needing canes to walk."

"I hate to break it to you, Granny," Croxley had said, and she squished her face together in an effort to hide her grin at his playful flirting, "but the 'stinking city', which is my home, by the way," he mocked good-naturedly, "isn't as far as you think it is. Those merchants and guards who say they've been travelling for months, well, it's only been a week, two at most. It's just one of the lies they tell you all to keep you here." He watched her expression, a mixture of disbelief and anger, and went on.

"I'll let you in on another secret, too. You aren't alone. There are more colonies. If we can get them all together, we could actually have a chance."

Thylora set her mouth in a tight line, thinking. Croxley waited patiently, knowing that, like the mountains themselves, her mind would change slowly and steadily. But once it did change, it would stand firm.

He waited for what felt like hours, Thylora only breaking the silence to let out a hmmm or haw. It wasn't long before he felt his eyes grow heavy in that dimly lit cavern. Eventually, she let out a decisive grunt and stood up.

"Al-right," she said, standing and crossing her arms, starling Croxley out of his doze. "If these words ye say are true, my people and I will give you aid. To be true, a lifetime of work in the mountains have made us strong and tough. If all ye surface-dwellers are as scrawny as you are, sonny, the King and his men don't stand a chance!" Thylora gave a firm nod and stuck her hand out to shake Croxley's, laughing when Croxley whimpered as his hand was crushed in her firm grip. He pulled it back and shook it in the air while grinning at his success and knowing that now, it had begun.

He made his way through the outskirts of Stonewall, noticing that things were much quieter than usual. Normally, in the middle of a sunny day like this, the streets would be full of merchants trying to peddle their goods, wives hustling through the streets to get back to their homes to cook supper, and petty thieves sticking their hands into every pocket that had the slightest bulge.

As Croxley approached what used to be the stables, he slowed down and led Sir Thunder and Sam to the shadows to watch the scene unfold before him.

Only half of the stables remained standing, and it was so badly burned that it looked like it would soon collapse and join the other half in a pile of rubble and ash. Around it stood the kings guards, poking through it as if they were searching for something. Croxley felt his stomach lurch as they pulled out what looked to be human bones. Did they belong to

Heath? A dreadful silence filled the air around him, and he flinched with every clack of his horse's hooves. As he came closer, the guards heard him, and a few of them ran his way.

"Sir Croxley," a guard with a thin mustache, if one could even call it that, greeted him.

"What happened here?" Croxley asked, adding the weight of authority to his voice.

"Arson and murder, sir."

"Murder? By whom?"

"By the Prince and his accomplice, me thinks, my lord-" the guard to Croxley's right didn't get a chance to finish, because the peach-fuzzed guard hit him on the back of the head.

"What he means to say, sir, is that we don't know yet, but the Prince has gone missing and some say they saw him enter the barn."

"The Prince has left? Where has he gone?" Erik, what on earth have you done?

"Nobody knows, sir. But the palace is in a riot."

"I'm sure it is. I'd best be heading there myself, then. Thank you for your report." The guards saluted Croxley, and he quickly walked the rest of the way to the castle. He found a servant and told him to take his horses to wherever they were keeping the others now that the stables had burned down, and headed into castle.

If the streets were unusually calm, the castle was unusually busy. Servants were running around, nobles were chattering to each other across the hallways, and guards were storming through in waves. What on earth is going on here?

For a few moments, Croxley just stood and watched the hum of the castle. He didn't know just what he had meant to do standing there, but he couldn't think of anything else to do at the moment.

After a few breaths, he decided to go to the servant's quarters. If his suspicions were right, Fara was the accomplice who fled with the Prince, but it wouldn't hurt to check. Even if Fara wasn't there, the servants always seemed to know what exactly was going on.

He carved himself a path through the hustle and bustle of the hallways until he found his way to the servant's quarters. In the main room he saw Mathelda calling out orders to the girls who were sitting at the tables. He scanned all the faces there, but he couldn't find Fara. He did see a familiar face, although it was hard to recognize her without her characteristic smile. What was her name? Mary? No. Sophia? Lydia? Ah, yes, Lydia.

She met his eyes and a shock of recognition flashed across her face. Mathelda must have noticed it, too, because she followed Lydia's gaze to

Croxley, who was still partially hidden in the doorway.

"Sir Croxley?" Before Croxley could creep back into the stairway, she was walking his way, determination in her step. He sighed and entered the main room. He noticed Lydia sit up from the table and leave the room as he entered. His eyes followed her out, but they were blocked when Mathelda moved in front of him. "Ah, Sir Croxley. I must say, I'm surprised to see you here."

Croxley raised an eyebrow, "Why is that?"

"Well, with the Prince having ran away from the castle for who knows why, we all assumed you would be by his side. You two are practically inseparable."

Croxley didn't say anything. He simply stood there looking at her until she cleared her throat and looked away.

"Ah, yes, well. In any case, I have something I need you to do. I'm too busy to do it myself. I just recently had a few, erm, rogue slave girls who caused quite a bit of trouble down here. It seems they were trying to hatch some rebellion plan, if you can believe it. Ha!" Mathelda laughed scornfully. Croxley tried to keep a straight face, but underneath the facade, his mind started racing. He tuned out what Mathelda was saying, trying to figure out what exactly had happened while he was gone. The Prince had left, and apparently Mathelda knew about the planned uprising, although how much he didn't know. He wondered if she had connected the Prince to the plan. "And with some of my girls locked up in the dungeon, I have even less hands to help around here." This pulled Croxley from his musings, and he paid attention to the rest of Mathelda's grumbles, but she said nothing more of the girls in the dungeon. "That is why I need you to run this message to Princess Lena." Croxley looked down to see Mathelda holding a letter out towards him. He took it, and after he exited the room, he stopped and stared at the letter for a moment, wondering why Mathelda was writing to Lena. Other than attending the slave evaluations when a new female was brought in, Mathelda didn't have much of a role in the castle. Likewise, without Erik here, Lena shouldn't have much to do with anything.

No matter how one looked at it, the fact that she was writing to Lena was suspicious. To be honest, he was suspicious about the whole damned thing. This castle is in an uproar, the Prince is missing, and I have no idea where Fara is, he muttered to himself. Then a thought struck him. What did Mathelda say? That she had to send some of her girls to the dungeon? Perhaps Fara was there. He made up his mind to check the dungeons after he delivered the letter to Lena.

He arrived at Lena's room and raised his hand to knock on the door, but stopped when he heard the bark of a sharp command.

"What do you mean you couldn't find it? It has to be there! The high priests said it was there! It's the only reason I came to this wretched country!"

"But your highness, that room is heavily guarded. It was hard enough to get in once. It would be highly suspicious if I were to go again,"

"Don't tell me that it's heavily guarded. You're a guard! Figure it out! And with the castle in the state that it is in at the moment, nobody would notice that you've been there before. Bentley, the moment is perfect. This must be done now, before the Prince returns from wherever he's gone off to."

Suddenly, the door flew open, and Croxley had to jump back to avoid being hit. A guard, whom Croxley assumed was Bentley, looked at him with wide eyes. Before Bentley could say anything, Croxley said, "I'm here to deliver a message to Lena. From Mathelda."

Lena, who must have been standing near the door, pushed the guard aside.

"I'll take it," she said, coming from behind Bentley. "Oh, Croxley!" Her voice went from harsh to a near purr when she saw Croxley waiting at the door. "You've returned! I'm so delighted to see you!" She gave a stern glance to Bentley, and he quickly walked down the way Croxley had come. Watching him leave, Croxley realized that he always seemed to be with Lena. Did she bring him here from her country, or was he already a castle guard? He couldn't remember seeing him before, but then again, he never really paid the guards much attention unless he and Erik had gotten themselves into trouble. He returned his eyes to Lena, who was wearing a deep purple gown with an even deeper plunging neckline. He traced his eyes down, following the lace embroidery as it hugged her curves. When he made his way back up, he saw amusement in her dark brown eyes. They almost look black, he thought to himself. She took the letter from his hands and then motioned inward.

"Won't you come in and sit down?" Croxley entered the room, and was immediately assaulted by a sweet perfume. It wasn't too strong, just enough to notice, and he definitely noticed. He took a seat down on the couch in the centre of the room. He looked around the room as Lena went to grab a wine bottle on the table next to them. She offered Croxley some as she sat down beside him. He noticed that she had put the letter away after reading it, and wondered what exactly was on the paper.

"I normally don't serve the wine myself, but what with the castle in a huff, my normal servant is gone at the moment. I don't drink the hard liquors you have here. They are a bit too strong for me. So I've taken to importing my own wine. I apologize if it tastes different," she smiled and handed it to him.

"Thank you, your highness," Croxley said, as he took a sip. He tried not to gag as it reached the back of his throat, the sweetness overpowering his senses, and forced it down. She watched him for his reaction, and he tried to assemble his face into a reasonably pleased expression. "Worry not, your highness, it taste's fine," he encouraged as he set the wine glass down.

"Oh, I'm so glad you think so," she said, obviously pleased with herself. "To be completely honest, I think it's much better than the drinks offered here. They are so bitter, and they always give me a headache. Back in Ethera, we drink only the finest wines, made with the sun-sweetened grapes of our vineyards." She sighed. "I guess I miss home. I haven't really found anyone here to call a friend yet." She slid her eyes down, and looked into her glass. After a melancholy sigh, she looked up at Croxley, her eyes half-shut under heavy eyelids, thick with lashes. "I can find a friend in you, right, Croxley?"

He wondered what to say, wondered why he was in this situation, wondered what exactly she was planning. Going off of what he had heard, she was a spoiled, selfish individual. But then again, he had heard most of this from Erik, and he couldn't figure out exactly how he felt about Erik at the moment either. He decided he would make up his mind for himself just what Lena's true character was. "Of course, your highness."

She smiled and put a hand on his leg. "You don't need to call me 'your highness', Croxley. Lena is just fine."

He shifted under her and she removed her hand. "So, Croxley, you are good friends with Erik, yes?"

"We were close, yes," he said, gruffly. If she was going to use him to talk about Prince Erik, then it was time for him to go.

"Were?" She asked, "Well, I was just going to ask if this kind of irresponsibility was normal for him. To just leave the castle at the same time that the servants try and revolt, it borders on cowardice." She swished her wine around in its goblet, and as she watched it swirl around, she commented, "I heard tales about him back in my country. They said he was boyish, spontaneous, and handsome. That he shirked his responsibilities in favour of parties and woman. Well, I would say it was all true. Except the part about being incredibly handsome. I think that they may have confused him with you on that point," she lifted her wine to take a sip, and peered at him over the rim of the glass.

"I thank you, your highness. Or rather, Lena," he corrected himself when she frowned. "But yes, I must agree that those traits are very accurate. He always tends to get himself into what he sees as grand adventures, but once things turn serious, he doesn't hesitate to leave. And yet he always seems to get things to turn out his way. I'd say it's his most impressive skill."

Lena just nodded and sipped her wine. When the silence had nearly reached the point of discomfort, she said, "Do you want to know a secret?"

He looked at her, surprised. Not sure how to answer, he played around with words in his mind until he decided on, simply, "Go on."

"When I first saw you, I had hoped that you would be the one for me to wed. You looked so much more serious, responsible. Like you could really go far in life." She leaned in closer and ran her hand down the side of his face gently. He couldn't look away from her eyes as her hand made its way from his cheek to his chest. "I can tell you another secret," she said, her voice low and sensual. "I know where the Prince ran off to. And I know that you probably were going to help him. But I can make you an offer, and I think it would be in your best interest not to refuse."

Croxley said nothing, and deciding that he needed a drink, quickly downed the rest of the wine in his glass, grimacing at the taste but welcoming the numbness.

"If you tell me what the Prince is doing, and exactly where he is, I can make sure to have him arrested. Don't worry, we will keep him alive, but he won't be able to live the frivolous life he did before. While you, Croxley, you will be the man I choose to marry. And with me you can rule the kingdom! Is that not what you have always wanted?" Lena set down her wine glass, and took his as well, noting that it was empty. She motioned to refill it, but he shook his head.

"Um, no thank you. Your highness, I don't know where the Prince is-"

"Liar!" She said harshly, her mask slipping for a few moments before she recovered her temper. Her voice resumed its low, sooth cadence. "You must know where he is. My sources tell me that you were in on the plan. And by plan, I mean the upcoming revolt."

His eyes widened when he thought about just how much she might know. He decided not to completely contradict her, but rather to give her vague answers until he figured out exactly what she was looking to hear. "Yes, but I don't know where he has gone off to. There are many colonies. He could have started at any one of them first."

"Well then, you will just have to make me a map of where all these colonies are, so that we can send guards to them promptly."

"Your Highness, I can't-"

"Croxley," she said, her voice all business. "You don't seem to understand. Either you help me find the Prince and bring this absurdity to an end, before all those Nethers get slaughtered by the King's army, or I will send you, as an accomplice to the rebellion, to the dungeons, where you can listen to the sounds of their screams as their hopeless rebellion is put down."

"Your highness," Croxley sighed, wondering how the simple errand of delivering a message for Mathelda turned into this, "all I can tell you is that Erik was going to the colonies. I can make you a map, but I can't give you any more information than that, because it is all I know. Wherever Erik and Fara went,"

Lena cut him off at the mention of Fara's name. "Don't mention that little wench. Why Mathelda assigned her as my personal servant girl, I'll never know. She was a bumbling fool who knew next to nothing about waiting on royalty. Not to mention the infuriating way she always looked at Erik. I wanted to wipe that silly love-struck grin off her face." She turned her venomous glare towards Croxley and he felt a chill as her lips curled into a wicked smile."I also saw the way you looked at her. It was slightly entertaining, to see you follow her like a puppy, only to see that she only had eyes for the Prince, who in turn only has eyes for himself."

Croxley's face flamed, and he cursed himself inwardly about being so obvious. He was a fool. But he wasn't fool enough to trust Lena. He could see now just how manipulative Lena could be in order to get her way. He just had to convince her that he was on her side until he found a chance to warn Fara and Erik.

Croxley stood and announced that he was going to return to his room. "As much as I wish to remain in your company, I have just returned from nearly a month of traveling under the King's demand, and I am quickly growing weary. I will get you the map you need tomorrow morning. Shall I give it to your guard?"

Lena shook her head no but remained on the couch, spreading herself out into the space that Croxley left open when he had stood up. Her gown slid up to reveal delicate ankles and smooth, soft calves that seemed to glow in the firelight. "I would rather see you again, Croxley. I want you to bring it to me yourself."

Damn, Croxley thought. This woman is dangerous in more than one way.

He felt empathetic towards to all the men she had chosen to manipulate, understanding now how difficult it is to refuse her. He had to give Erik some credit for so easily being able to overcome her temptations. But Croxley, he was a man all too easily tempted by feminine talents. Before she could pull him back in, he bid her goodnight and shut the door behind him, sending a small whoosh of perfume that followed him out into the corridor.

CHAPTER 32

"Oomph!" Croxley ran into someone as he was distractedly walking away from Lena's room. Before he could apologize, the woman he had bumped into was on her knees, bowing before him.

"Forgive me sir, that was my fault. I wasn't watching where I was going." She looked up, and Croxley saw that it was Lydia. "Sir Croxley!" She looked at him, then past him to where he had come from. "Oh no."

"What is it?"

"You've already given the letter to Lena, haven't you? I thought I would be able to stop you from delivering it, but before I could leave, Mathelda caught me and sent me to do some, erm, chores." She sighed and looked worried.

Croxley helped her up, but she kept looking down. "Lydia, what was in that letter?"

"Everything. Absolutely everything."

"Lydia, what are you talking about?" Croxley looked at her with concern.

Lydia said in a quiet whisper, "I told her. Well, rather, I told Mathelda. About Fara's plan. About your plan. That's how she knows about where the Prince is, and what he is doing." Croxley stepped back, taking his hands off her. "I did it to protect you! I thought that Fara would just be risking her life, the Prince's life, everyone's lives by starting a rebellion. I just wanted to keep everyone safe." She looked up, despair in her eyes.

"At first, I didn't tell them everything. I just said that the Prince was going to run off to another adventure. But I guess that was enough to have the King send guards after him, worried that he was trying to evade the marriage with Lena, I guess. But then the barn caught on fire, and after the guards lost sight of Prince Erik and Fara in the forest, Mathelda came back to get the full story. By then, I knew that I made a terrible mistake in telling her. But it was too late. She held me down, forced me to tell her everything. And now Lena knows, so pretty soon the King will know too."

"Why would't Mathelda go straight to the King? What does Lena have to do with any of this?"

"I don't know. I think they have some kind of plan in store. Ever since a few weeks ago, Lena has been having private meetings with Mathelda. I stumbled upon them once when I was coming back from a job late at night. They were huddled together over a table in the kitchen, discussing something in excited whispers. When Mathelda saw me, she grew angry and sent me straight to my room. After that night, I stopped seeing Lena, but her guard was often coming down to bring messages back and forth."

Croxley just stood there, silently going over in his mind everything that had happened since he set foot in Stonewall. He sat down on the stairs and rubbed at his temples. He was suddenly very tired. "Well, damn. What am I supposed to do now," he asked himself. Lydia didn't respond. After a while, she sat down beside him.

"Croxley, the girls they arrested, they are torturing them down in the dungeon. If I feel terrible about anything, I feel terrible about that. These girls did nothing but hope for freedom, and I was too scared to let them. I need you to help me rescue them."

Croxley rolled over in his bed, rubbing his eyes groggily and scratching his cheeks. His recent travels left a thin layer of stubble on his chin and cheeks that he had yet to trim off. I probably look like an outlaw, he thought. He walked to his restroom and saw the bags under his eyes. Correction. I definitely look like an outlaw. I could really use some beauty sleep. At least three days worth. After camping out in the woods night after night, sparsely interrupted by an inn every now and then, his bed had felt like heaven. He looked back into his main room, wanting more than anything to just lay back down and forget all that had happened since he returned to Stonewall.

He had been up late last night, talking with Lydia about how to go about rescuing the girls from the dungeon. Luckily, he had a reason to visit Lena, because she would be instrumental to their plan. He would bring her a map of the all the colonies, with labels telling her where the Prince and Fara would be most likely be. Of course he didn't know where Erik and Fara actually were, but he wanted to keep Lena and the King off their tracks for as long as possible. And it would be futile to make a fake map of the colonies. It may trick Lena, but if she brought the map to the King, as Croxley expected she would, the King would quickly see through the farce and Croxley may be arrested before he could escape the city.

After giving Lena the map, he hoped to convince her to send him to the dungeon in order to interrogate the prisoners. Perhaps he could make up some ruse about needing to get more information. He just needed a letter from her in order to get into the dungeon. If all goes to plan, he will make his way down later tonight and give the guards the message.

If he managed to get the guards to leave the dungeon, Lydia would be there to intercept them. She was confident she would be able to distract them long enough for him to get the job done. How she would do that, he left up to her.

Once they got everyone out of their cells, they would use the servant's quarters to leave the castle. There shouldn't be too many people using them late at night, but if there were, Croxley just had to hope that they wouldn't cause them any problems.

After shaving his face and getting dressed in more appropriate attire, Croxley headed out towards the kitchen.

He couldn't remember the last time he had eaten, and he was ravenous. He snuck into the kitchen, hoping to get in and out without being seen. He opened the door slowly, peering around and finding it empty. He dashed in and found some leftovers of what must have been yesterday's feast. He grabbed a leg of turkey, an apple, some cheese, and a large piece of bread. He shoved the apple in his mouth and piled the rest in his arms. He was looking for some pastries when a deep, rolling laugh echoed throughout the kitchen. He slowly turned around and saw none other but the King standing in the kitchen, with an amused smile on his face.

"Still snatching food from the kitchen, I see? You haven't changed a bit, Croxley," he said, shaking his head.

Croxley attempted to protest, but he couldn't around the apple in his mouth, so he just raised his shoulders in a shrug as if to say, it can't be helped.

"Come, boy. Let's sit at this table and eat like civilized human beings. You aren't a Nether, mind you."

Croxley nodded, remembering how much the King hated the Nethers. His great great grandfather was the one who created the system. It seems as though the prejudice against them had increased as it passed from generation to generation. If anything, the man sitting before him was responsible for the current hatred of Nethers in Ahrenia. The King made it seem as though they were all prisoners, the scum of society sent to live underground so as not to pollute the utopia above. Croxley, among most other Ahrenians, fully believed this. And for a while, whenever Croxley had to deliver messages to the lieutenants and captains underground, he got in and out as quickly as possible, never taking the time to get to know its actual inhabitants. But when he met Fara, he was surprised by her curiosity, her intelligence, her overall enthusiasm for life. She wasn't a deadbeat, a worm to spoil the pristine society above.

If anything, after returning back to Stonewall with her, the city lost a certain kind of luster. He even found himself bristling every time someone made a jab such as "dirt brains" or "mud eater", supremely uncreative insults stemming from the ideas behind how Nethers were forced to live their lives.

Musing through this as he chewed on his turkey leg, he saw the King through new eyes. This powerful man was more of a father to him than his own father. Or rather, Croxley always imagined it as such. His own father was never a source of pride to Croxley. Skinny and quiet, he always thought his father was weak. Instead of growing strong from years of delivering messages like Croxley had, his father had nearly withered away, claiming that the forest caused him to grow ill, making his eyes water and his nose run. How his mother could stand his complaints, Croxley never knew. He supposed that was why his mother had such a strong personality. She had to make up for what his father lacked. She was outspoken and honest, big-boned and strong. Thinking of his family stirred unwelcome emotions. Croxley couldn't remember the last time he stopped to visit his family. After he replaced his father as messenger, his family left the castle to live in the hills of Farthenburg, a small town in the east with rolling green hills and peaceful, easy living.

When this is all over, I should visit them.

"So how have your journeys been, Croxley?" The King asked, interrupting Croxley's musings.

"It's nice to be back. Also, the King of Bastland sends his regards and apologizes for their temporary lapse in trade."

The King chuckled. "I'm sure he did." He folded his hands and leaned forward on the table. His body looked relaxed, but his eyes were intense. "So, what else did you hear on your travels?"

"Not very much, my lord. There were only a few inns along the way, and most of them were uneventful. Dreary food, hard beds."

"And the colonies?"

Croxley nearly choked on his bread. "I'm sorry," he said, coughing to clear his throat, "um, I didn't pass through any on the way back. Was there something you had wanted me to do?"

The King looked at Croxley for a few moments, and then leaned back in his chair. "No, not quite. Well, now that you mention it, I do have one message. When you see Erik, tell him I said hello." And with that, the King stood up, leaving Croxley with his mouth hanging open, a piece of bread sitting in his mouth mid-chew.

He didn't know how much the King knew of the plan, nor did he know if he had found out from Lena and Mathelda or from other sources. Either way, the King definitely knew something was happening. Pretty soon he will know everything, Croxley thought, aware of the fact that Lena would have to explain to the King what she knew as soon as he and Lydia left Stonewall with the prisoners. He shuddered at the thought of how the King would retaliate. The mild-mannered man he had been scared Croxley more than the moments when the King was in one of his rages. It meant that he was thinking, planning, waiting.

Unable to shake the foreboding now resting upon him, Croxley finished the rest of the food without tasting it and hurried to Lena's room. The sooner he got this over with, the better.

He stood before Lena's door and knocked a few times. He waited and was about to knock a final time when Lena opened the door. Once again, he was struck by how beautiful she was, her dark brown eyes nearly glowing against a rich green dress, this one leaving more to the imagination than the purple number the night before. But today he wouldn't be trapped under her spell. Instead, he was going to manipulate the manipulator, outmaneuver her plots to succeed one of his own.

"Sir Croxley, back so soon! What a delight to see you again." She smiled, but didn't invite him in.

He stood awkwardly at the doorway for a few moments, and when she failed to say anything else, he leaned in and whispered close to her, "I have the map you needed. I was hoping we could further discuss things."

She stood stationary for a few moments, peering down the hallway, as if looking for someone, and then invited Croxley in. "Well, I guess that means you should take a seat. Come in," she motioned. He noticed that she seemed a little anxious, and he suspected it had nothing to do with the map he was about to give her. She sat across from him, smoothing imaginary wrinkles on her dress a few times, and then tucked her hair behind her ears. "Well? What do you have?"

"Here is the map," Croxley said, pulling it out of his vest. He rolled it out, flattening it out on the table in front of them. "The colony I circled is the one that Prince Erik is most likely staying in at the moment. We had planned to start at the top, and then work our way down." He had purposefully circled the one colony he knew Erik would not be, Fyzen. He had already visited there, and by now the colony should be evacuated, heading towards Cethin, which they had agreed early on would be the congregation spot. "If you send guards that way immediately, then you should be able to cut him off before he reaches the next colony."

She didn't tear her eyes away from the map. "There are so many colonies," she said, almost to herself. Croxley wondered what she meant by that, but before he could reach a conclusion, she stated, louder and obviously for him to hear this time, "I shall inform the King that you have aided in the capture of the Prince. And of course I'll leave out the fact that you were involved in the immediate planning of the same rebellion we are now working to prevent. I thank you for your help. Now, if you excuse me,"

Lena stood up to escort him out, but before she could push him out the door, Croxley interjected, "Your highness, if you would give me just a few more moments of your time." He took her silence as agreement and continued on. "Due to my recent travelling, I admit that I do not know the last of the Prince's plans. If any aspects may have changed, I would like to find out promptly so that we can respond accordingly. Therefore, I request that you give me written permission to visit the dungeons and question all the prisoners."

Lena stood there for a few moments, tapping her heel on the ground. With a sigh, she nodded and grabbed a piece of paper. She scribbled quickly, signing her name at the bottom, and handed him the folded note. "Here. This should suffice. Now, be on your way. I will hear from you later," she said, practically shoving him out the door.

He felt it close behind him, and he silently thanked whatever it was that had her so distracted. Getting the note was much easier than it should have been, and it was because her usual calculating mind was occupied with something else.

As he left the corridor and entered the main hallway, he saw the same guard from yesterday, Bentley, hurrying across the courtyard and up the same corridor Croxley had just exited. His curiosity ached to find out just what had Bentley in such a hurry, but he would have to wait. He had a plan of his own he had to deal with.

He met with Lydia back in his room. She edited Lena's note, carefully copying her handwriting. After she was finished, she handed it back to Croxley, which he put in in his vest. Lydia had to return to the servants' quarters, leaving Croxley alone to prepare everything. Finally, he left his room and headed towards the dungeon. The sun was just setting, leaving a gap in time before the moon would rise. Lydia said she would wait at the entrance and watch for the guards, where she would distract them and lead them to the garden while Croxley helped the girls out of the castle.

Croxley stopped at the entrance to the dungeon. Checking his boots, he ensured that the daggers weren't visible. He felt for the long blade hidden under his vest, slung against his waist. After adjusting his jacket to make sure the weapon was concealed, he pulled out his note from Lena and approached the entrance.

The dungeon was heavily guarded, for no reason other than the King had many enemies, and wanted to make sure that none of them ever had the chance to see the light of day again after doing him wrong. The further down into the dungeon you descended, the more criminal the prisoners were. At the very bottom were the murderers, the traitors, the King's worst enemies. Near the middle were the war hostages and innocent travellers kept for ransom, should the King ever need to deal with surrounding countries. Near the top were the petty street thieves and the protesters who spoke out against the King. He hoped that the girls would be on one of the top stories, not wanting to delve too far deep into the dungeon.

Each story was like a maze, and it spiralled around and around, with multiple guards on each floor. Croxley had only been there once before, and that was when he and Erik, young, bored, and mischievous, decided they wanted a thrill and snuck in to the dungeon to see a recently arrested war hostage. He was said to be one of the greatest generals of all time. He was captured during a great skirmish on Ahrenia's southern border, only surrendering after all of his men had been taken down and he found himself surrounded by Ahrenia's troops. Croxley and Erik were eager to see him, hoping to find some kind of mighty barbarian, with tattoos, piercings, wild hair, or other foreign embellishments.

Upon entering the dungeon, Croxley and Erik were hit with the smell of eternally wet stones, mildew, bodily fluids, and fear. The smell made them gag, so they plugged their noses and continued on, their boyish sense of adventure overriding all warning signals.

However, once they reached the general's jail cell, they instantly wanted to leave. The once mighty general sat in the corner, a bloodied, beaten pulp of a man, shivering and muttering to himself like a madman. He clutched his wrist against his body, rocking back and forth, and the two boys fought to tear their eyes away from him. His cell was decorated with blood and vomit. Erik retched, only adding to the collection, and the general looked up at them. His eyes were dark red, one nearly swollen shut, while the other was so wide in contrast it looked like it might fall out. His expression was a combination of fear and grief, and it hovered around him, the aura nearly overwhelming. Suddenly, he let out a deep inhuman moan, which sent the boys running as fast as they could out of the cell room and back to the safety of the castle. Neither of them ever mentioned it again.

This memory came flooding back to Croxley, and he was shamed to admit that, even as a grown man, it still gave him goose bumps.

He walked to the door, where a guard stood with a sword at his side. Croxley showed him the note, and the guard nodded, standing aside and opening the door. Croxley stepped inside and was immediately overcome by a wave of moldy, damp air that was heavy laden with years of suffering. He wrinkled his nose and walked down the stairs, the stairway dimly lit by lanterns on the walls. At one point, he nearly slipped down the mildewed steps. Cursing loudly, he caught his balance on a light mounted on the wall. Muttering to himself, he pulled the lantern out of its holder and carried it in front of him, treading more carefully now.

He finally reached the first platform, where two guards were talking quietly to each other. Croxley announced his arrival with an "Oy" and walked up to the two. They looked at him suspiciously for a few moments until one of them graciously asked,

"What the 'ell you doin' down here?"

"I was sent here by the Princess Lena. She wants me to question the prisoners brought in from the servants' quarters. She also asks that you meet her in the garden so as not to threaten the prisoners from answering."

"She does now, does she? I don't think I believe you." The guard who spoke had a gristly beard and foul breath, which crossed the short distance between his and Croxley's face, and Croxley tried not to grimace. The other just stood at his side, his arms crossed and his left eye drooping.

Croxley showed the two the letter, wondering for a few moments if they could even read, and eventually the droop-eyed guard nodded and said to the other, "Let 'im pass."

The other scowled as he stepped aside, spitting into one of the cells before he turned and went up the stairs. As Croxley continued down the next maze of tunnels, he peered into the cells of the prisoners. Most had chamber pots in the corners, and the prisoners either slept on the hard ground or were sitting against the wall. Croxley passed by a cell in which the prisoner was singing quietly, and as he got closer, he could just make out the words.

I once was a jester, a King of the court
Making a laugh was my favourite sport
But I told a bad joke, and before you know
I'll be swinging the gallows at the end of a rope

The man looked up at Croxley while he continued singing through a toothless mouth, the corners of his lips turned up into an eerie, crooked smile. Croxley turned his eyes away and focused on the path ahead.

When he made it to the next set of cells, he showed the guards the note and received a similar response. This time, he asked where the girls were, and was told that they would be three more floors down.

As he descended through the floors, he trained his eyes to wander less and less. The sights grew increasingly gory with each passing cell, and the smells even worse. Finally, he made it to his designated floor. There were three guards on this level, signifying that they had to increase the security for the more dangerous criminals. He gave them the letter, this time explaining, "Our Highness Lena sent me down here to question the rebel slaves. While I'm questioning them, she asked that you meet her in the garden to assist her with some tasks."

The guards looked at him skeptically, and he didn't blame them. He expected that this was the first time any such request had been made, and knew that they wouldn't leave without an explanation. If the plan were to get tricky anywhere, it would be here.

"What would she need with us?" One of the guards questioned.

"I'm not too sure, but you know the rumours. When she wants something, there isn't much you can do to change her mind. I would think that you would prefer to help her with whatever task she has than to deal with the King once she complains that you have disobeyed the future queen's orders." They guards all looked at each other, wondering what to do with this. Croxley added, "And I will be here to watch the prisoners. You have nothing to worry about. Unless, of course, you don't follow Lena's commands. I wouldn't keep her waiting, if I were you. And you may want to ask for some of the guards' upstairs to help you out." They still didn't budge, so Croxley added, "Take it from me, if you get on Lena's good side, she will definitely ensure that you are finely rewarded. Especially now that the Prince is no longer by her side, I would imagine she is feeling quite lonely□" Croxley drifted off, giving them time to realize his implication. He raised his eyebrow in a semblance of false confidence, while inside, his gut was in turmoil, roiling with nerves and the smells of the dungeon.

Apparently his farce was a good one, because the guards hastily agreed that they would hand the watch over to him.

"Oy!" Croxley called, before they could leave all the way up the staircase. "I think it would be best if you left the keys with me. That way, if one of the prisoners starts acting up, I can take care of it."

The guard with the keys, a skinny lad with a whitish pallor from all the days in the dungeon, tossed them to Croxley and headed up the stairs. When they were out of sight, Croxley let out a sigh of relief.

He began searching through the cells, which proved much harder than he thought. Every time he probed them, he would stumble upon a barely moving body, a beaten figure crouched in the corner, a thin, wasted frame crouching over a chamber pot. When his search finally brought him to the slave girls, he didn't have a problem recognizing them among all the other prisoners. Rather than having their colour robbed from their skin after years in the dungeon, they were tanned and still had some meat on their bones. But the heavy bags under their eyes suggested that it wouldn't be much longer before they started to share the same appearance as their floor-mates. Croxley rushed over to their cell, startling some of the girls closest to the gates. They ran to the far side of the bars, huddling up as if trying to protect themselves from him. Croxley could make out twelve girls total.

"Don't worry, I'm not here to hurt you." They stopped their jagged whispers and eyed him warily. "My name is Croxley. I am a friend of Fara's. I am here to get you all out of here."

A young woman a little older than Fara, tall and lean with long, braided brown hair, broke from the group.

"Did you say Fara?" Croxley nodded, and she came closer to the bars in front of Croxley. When she was near enough to the flame he still carried in his hand, Croxley could see that her shoulders had deep purple bruises on them. She walked stiffly, telling of other bruises not visible to him. "Did she make it? Did she escape?"

"Yes, Fara escaped. Or at least, I think she did. I'm not sure I know the whole story. All I know is that when I came back, Fara and the Prince were gone and the palace was in a ruckus."

The woman sighed with relief. "Thank goodness," she said.

"Do you know her well?"

"Yes. Fara was my room-mate. I helped her escape after Mathelda realized what we were planning. Her and I met with Heath and solidified the plan you had helped come up with earlier. The Prince and Fara were planning on using Cethin as the congregating point for all the colonies from which they would then set up a blockade around Stonewall." Croxley nodded, relieved that the plan hadn't changed much from the original. "At least, that's how it was supposed to go, before that traitor Lydia betrayed us all to Mathelda, who sent the guards chasing after Fara and the Prince and promptly sent us to the dungeons," she said, spitting Lydia's name.

Croxley bristled in defense of Lydia after hearing this. "It's because of Lydia that I am here. She feels terrible about the whole thing, especially about you all being arrested."

The woman shook her head, not wanting to believe it, wanting more to hold her grudge than forgive Lydia. She wrapped her arms around her body, as if cradling herself, and replied, "I don't care how bad she feels about it now. The damage is done." The tone with which she spoke carried the weight of one who been betrayed and disillusioned too many times.

"You might change your mind after I get you all out of here," Croxley said, dangling the keys in front of her face. She leaned in close to inspect them. This close to her, he realized that she was awfully pretty, in a no-nonsense, very natural way. Croxley, this is no time for flirting, he chastised himself.

"Once I let you all out, you have to be quiet and follow me. I can get us through the servant's quarters, but first we have to go back up through the dungeon. The guards should all be gone. Lydia is taking care of them." Croxley spoke as he undid the lock of the cell. The nearby inmates started to clamor, begging Croxley to release them as well. He tried to tune out their desperate cries, some pleading, some threatening, and others downright vulgar. He herded the group of girls quickly out of their cell, and they remained in their huddle, holding on to each other's hands, moving as a single unit.

"This way," he urged as the last one joined the group. They walked in the middle of the lane, trying to stay away from the hands reaching out of the bordering cells.

Croxley heard heavy thudding, but amidst all the noise, he couldn't locate the source of the sound. He was on alert as they approached the staircase, and he saw shadows coming down the stairway. "Damn," he whispered, among other, more uncouth curses. He held his arm out to stop the girls, looking for a way around the guards. He spotted a dark corner near the base of the stairs, and hustled the girls to hide over there. He watched as a stream of guards ran past them, towards where they had just been. After the last one ran out of sight, Croxley hurried the girls up the stairs.

A frustrated oath and a sharp command signalled to Croxley that the guards had found the empty cell. He pushed them on, faster, and they had made it up two flights of stairs when one of the girls tripped. Her hand cradled her ankle, and Croxley could see it was twisted and already swelling quickly. Her friend pulled her up and shouldered her weight, but still the pace was too slow. Croxley grew natsy and he could hear the guards growing closer, so he stepped under her other shoulder and propped her up. He knew that eventually they would be caught, but he couldn't give up, not after making it all this way.

They had almost made it to the last floor when Mathelda came around the corner, more guards in tow. She pointed at Croxley and barked a command, but Croxley wasn't able to hear it. The girl he was helping was crying, begging for them to stop. Croxley could feel their energy failing, finding that many of the girls were too tired from their time in the dungeon to keep up.

"Keep going!" He yelled, but the guards quickly overtook them.

Croxley had to release the girl at his shoulder to fight the guard at his right. He ducked under a swing and gave a hard punch to the gut, satisfied to hear the wind escape the guard's chest as he fell. In the same breath, another came up behind Croxley, and he dealt a firm kick that sent one guard tumbling into the other. On and on it went, the staircase working in Croxley's favour, as it only allowed a few guards in at a time.

The slight advantage only lasted so long, as Croxley grew tired. But he didn't want to pull his daggers because he was afraid he might hit one of the servant girls in these close quarters. There was a brief lull in the onslaught of guards. Croxley took this moment to look around, and realized that he had been separated from the rest of the girls, who were now being taken back down the stairs.

After dodging a blow to the chest, he stumbled back and ran into someone. He turned around, just in time to catch a fist heading towards his face. It belonged not to a guard, but to the woman he had been speaking to earlier. She looked slightly crazed, adrenaline hazing her vision. Her brown hair was wild, and her cheeks were flushed. She recognized Croxley and withdrew her fist. After working together to take the next guard out, he told her in between breaths, "We've lost the rest of the group." She looked around, her eyes widening, obviously having been too caught up in the fight to notice that they had been separated.

"We've got to get back to them!"

"We can't. We have to keep going. We wouldn't be able to make it through with all of them. If we go now, we might be able to get out of Stonewall and reach Fara and Erik. And if all is successful, they will be free soon. That, or we all will end up in jail. Either way, it's our only hope to rescue them now."

Croxley could see the battle in her eyes, and knew which side won when she looked away from where the rest of the girls had been taken. He stood in front of her, and pulled out his daggers, giving one to her. He held his out in front of him, warding off the guards still coming up towards them. Croxley backed up the stairs with the woman looking over his shoulder, facing the guards coming at them. Suddenly, Croxley felt the pressure change from behind them, and he spun around to see Mathelda grab the woman by the arm. She tried to fight Mathelda off, but Mathelda had the advantage of surprise and wrestled the knife out of the woman's hand, flipping it around and holding it against her neck.

"Put your weapon down or she gets it," Mathelda threatened. Croxley immediately put his dagger down, and as he stood up he felt some guards come up and grab him from behind.

"Sir Croxley. I would have thought that your conversation with Lena had convinced you of the recklessness of your plan. You could have been such a help in capturing the Prince. Ah well, you are replaceable. And so are you," Mathelda said, piercing the base of her captive's throat. The woman cried out, and Croxley struggled against the guards holding him down.

"Stop!" A cry rang through the dungeon room and everyone turned to look at the entrance. Lydia stood at the entrance, her arms bracing the sides of the door. Croxley saw that she had been beaten, blood dripping down the side of her head and staining the front of her dress.

"Lydia!" Croxley gasped as the guards tugged his arms behind his back.

Mathelda snarled, "You've done more than enough, Lydia. Get out of here."

"No! I'm not going to let you rule over my life anymore! I've been your puppet for too long, Mathelda. I'm not going to play your game!"

"Then you will lose!" She threw the woman in her arms down to the ground and rushed towards Lydia, the dagger held high. Croxley, adrenaline coursing through his veins, wrenched himself free from the guards. He saw Lydia and Mathelda struggling, and wanted to go and help her, but first he had to check on the brown haired woman, who was motionless on the ground. Sprinting ahead of the guards, he reached the woman and checked her for wounds. She was unconscious and had a gash down her arm, blood pooling thick around her. That and the small slit in her neck were changing her tan shift into a deep crimson. He picked her up, planning to get her to the exit and come back for Lydia, when he heard a cry of pain.

He turned around to see Lydia in the hands of the guards, her head hanging, while Mathelda was doubled over, her hair lose and draped over her face as she cradled her side.

"You whore!" Mathelda cursed, breathing heavily. "You will rot in your cell!"

The guards starting pulling Lydia down the stairs, and Croxley called after her, "Lydia! Let her go!" But with the woman in his arms, he could hardly fight off the guards heading towards him.

"Go! Croxley, go now!" Lydia yelled, and though it pained Croxley to leave behind Lydia and all the other prisoners, he knew that the tables had turned, and his chances for escape were getting smaller and smaller the longer he waited. He tore away from Lydia, Mathelda, the guards, the prisoners, and covered the rest of the distance to the exit as fast as he could.

After he bolted out the door, he found himself back in the castle. Some nobles standing nearby were startled and began chattering anxiously in the hallway, watching him with wide eyes that only grew wider when they noticed the bloody woman in his arm. He tore past them, and understood that the transition from chatter to gasps of surprise meant that the guards had appeared out of the dungeon.

He pushed himself even harder, running through the castle at full speed. He took some short-cuts through different rooms, and by the time he ran through the kitchen, which was, thankfully, empty this early in the morning, he had put enough distance between him and the guards to rest for a few moments. He looked down at the woman in his arms and found her awake, looking around.

"How are you feeling?" He asked, setting her down gently on the kitchen table.

"A little dizzy," she said, cradling her arm. He located a dish rag that didn't look too dirty and used it as a tourniquet for her arm. He used a little bit of brandy from the nearby shelf to clean it out, impressed that she gave only the slightest whimper at the pain, and then bandaged it tightly. He could hear some commotion outside the kitchen and knew that they were running out of time.

"Can you run?" He asked, and the woman nodded. He went to exit through the opposite kitchen door, but she shook her head.

"Not that way. There's a servants corridor that connects to the kitchen closet. It will lead us out of the castle. This way," She pulled him by the hand through the kitchen and down the corridor. They emerged in the back of the castle where the garbage was thrown, and the woman gasped in surprise when a swarm of rats darted from the trash that she and Croxley had displaced. They worked their way around to the front of the castle, and Croxley left the woman hidden in the shadows for a few moments in order to grab Sir Thunder and Sam, who he had tied out next to the steeds of visiting nobles in order to not seem suspicious. He had muffled the horse's shoes so that they wouldn't clack against the cobblestone and announce their escape. Lydia and Croxley had already packed all the supplies beforehand, but now there was more than enough since only two of them had made it out. After lightening their load a bit, they took off, weaving silently through the dark, empty streets. They didn't slow down until the city's walls were out of sight.

"Croxley, I need to slow down," the woman said. He stopped and got off his horse. "It's my arm," she explained, "I think it needs to bandaged again."

"Okay, just give me your hand and I'll help you down," Croxley offered his hand, but when she leaned forward, she did so too quickly and fell into Croxley's arms. The weight change threw him off balance and they went tumbling down. Croxley turned himself to make sure that he landed underneath her, and in doing so landed with a loud "oomph" as the wind was knocked out of him.

She chuckled at the sound and then apologized. "I'm sorry. To be honest, this was my first time riding a horse. He's quite large and intimidating."

Croxley found this hilarious, and when she looked at him perplexedly, he explained, "Sam isn't a horse, he's a mule. Sam-mule", he said with emphasis on the "mule". She understood the pun immediately and joined him in his laughter. Soon they were laughing with near hysteria, still on the ground. Finally, they calmed down, and the woman said, in a near-whisper, "We made it."

"Yes, we did," Croxley said, suddenly aware of her weight on his chest. He looked into her warm hazel eyes, their light nearly cutting through the darkness of the forest, and pulled her in, kissing her soft lips gently. He felt her stiffen slightly, and saw shock on her face.

"I'm sorry," he apologized.

"No, it's okay," she said, "it's just, well, after so many forced nights with strange men, I never thought I would want to, well, kiss back." And she pressed her lips on his, a light, hesitant touch. She left them hovering over his, as if testing it. Croxley waited a few moments, tasting the air between them, before bridging the gap and kissing her for a third time.

She was more confident this time, pressing back harder, and soon they were enraptured with each other's presence, gasping for breaths between each kiss in which they found solace from the harsh reality around them. It wasn't until the woman yelped when Croxley had moved slightly on top of her that they stopped and broke apart.

"Sorry, your arm," Croxley breathed, picking it up and kissing it along the bandage until he made his was up to her forehead.

"That's okay," she whispered, and Croxley could feel the smile on her lips. "By the way, my names Jean."

"Hello, Jean. It's very nice to meet you."

CHAPTER 33

"I can't help it, I'm just so excited!"

I was practically skipping through the forest as Erik and I led our horses through a particularly thick patch. As we headed south towards Grundale, it grew warmer and the foliage thickened.

"I don't think the situation calls for excitement." Erik said, grumpy because he had collected multiple itchy bumps from the insects of the forest. He was a ways in front of me, having to clear a path with his knife, and I was enjoying the view of his tanned, muscular back, revealed to me when he first removed his shirt a few hours ago after the temperature grew too warm for long sleeves. I myself had a loose shift tucked into a pair of trousers I had borrowed from Erik. At first, I was appalled to be wearing men's pants, but after snagging my frock on stray branches and thorns, nearly tripping multiple times, I eagerly changed into more functional apparel.

"Okay, I'll admit that asking their colony to follow us into a potential war isn't the most pleasant of terms, but still. I've never been to another colony! Look at it from my point of view," I explained, and Erik stopped plowing ahead to turn around, catching his breath. "Before this year, I didn't even know what colour the sky was. I didn't know that there were so many different types of animals, some that could fly, some that could swim, and I certainly did not know that there were other Nethers living the same way I did. I could have never imagined that I would be living on the surface of Ahrenia, let alone leading a revolution among all the colonies with the Prince of Ahrenia at my side. So forgive me for being excited about spreading this news to other colonies and finally freeing my people," I huffed.

Erik smiled and pulled me in to him, kissing the top of my head.

I squirmed out of his grip and complained, "Gross, you're sweaty."

He laughed and continued chopping away. I went over in my head what I was going to say upon arriving to Grundale. My name is Faradene. On the surface, I am known as Fara. I am from Cethin. Cethin is another colony. Actually, there are multiple colonies, and for ages we have been suffering under the harsh sentence of the King. But today, we will change that. Together, we are going to get our freedom. I giggled, exuding nervous energy.

"Going over your speech again?" Erik asked, teasing. I had already asked him to listen to it four times today, and had been doing so every day since we left Cethin.

"Yes I am," I admitted, not even denying it. "How much farther do we have to go?"

"If Croxley's directions are correct, we should be there soon. I just have to hope that we haven't lost our mark travelling through this jungle." Erik pulled out the map, consulting it.

"At least we haven't seen any guards," I offered. In fact, we have been traveling for nearly a week, and we haven't seen many people at all. The few towns and villages we had passed we were sure to avoid and leave a wide distance between them and us. I was still trying to grasp in my mind just how large the outside world really was.

Erik nodded in agreement, studying his map. I distracted myself by looking at the flowers nearby. Even after being on the surface for half a year at this point, I still haven't grown used to the beauty of flowers. They seemed to come in an endless variety of colours, shapes, and fragrances. And sometimes if you were lucky, a butterfly or bumblebee or hummingbird would join you in your appreciation of the flower and bring its own colours to the scene. The beauty was astounding, and I couldn't help but yearn to share this world with my people.

"Fara, come here," Erik called me over and showed me the map.

"If I'm right, we are currently heading this way, towards Grundale. Not too long ago, we passed by a small town, here," he indicated on the map, and I wondered how a whole town managed to go unnoticed. Then again, the foliage is so thick, if I didn't have Erik in front of me at all times, I would easily get lost. I hoped that this would play in our favour upon our return to Cethin. If we do manage to get a large group of colonists from Grundale to follow us to Cethin, it would be better for the thick green curtain to muffle the sounds of our parade. I refocused back to what Erik was saying, which was that we were approaching the entrance to Grundale. I felt a small jolt of excitement course through me when I saw how close we were.

Erik rolled the map back up and we closed the rest of the distance between the colony and ourselves. Eventually, we made it to the base of a mountain, water cascading down its face into a small pool.

"This is it," Erik signalled, once again consulting his map.

"What is what?" I asked. I was still entranced by the wall of water roaring next to us, my eyes trailing up the mountain, trying to find its source but to no avail.

"This waterfall is the entrance to Grundale. Or, rather, it hides the entrance. Just behind it is the cavern that runs deep into the ground and eventually winds into the colony."

I stared at him in disbelief. "How are we going to get through it?"

"Easy. As far as waterfalls go, this one isn't too heavy. If we approach it from the right angle, there shouldn't be any problems."

I watched what was essentially a vertical flowing river pounding on the surface of the pool at the bottom, sending droplets of water into the air. Erik must have seen the doubt on my face because he shook my shoulders, as if to shake me from my awe-induced stupor. "Just trust me."

I don't think I have much of a choice at this point, I thought to myself.

We changed back into more acceptable clothing, which meant that I had to shed my trousers and dawn my gown. I found myself missing the freedom the trousers had brought.

"Erik, were you serious?"

"About what," he asked, still changing behind a bush.

"About marrying me. If we make it through this alive, I mean." I stated it simply, as if it were a business offer. He was silent for a few moments, and I pulled at the threads of my sleeve, waiting for an answer.

He came out of the bushes, dressed in much more formal attire, and took my hands up in his.

"Of course I was serious. What made you ask?" His deep green eyes were filled with concern as they searched into mine.

"Well, if we do get married, that would make me queen, right? I was just thinking, if I were queen, I would make it a law that women could wear trousers."

He sighed in relief and pulled me in to his chest, resting his cheek on the top of my head. "Fara, you have my heart in your hands. You need to be more careful with it!" He pulled back and brushed my hair behind my ears, leaving his hand on my cheek. I enjoyed its warmth and pressed myself into it. "When all this is over, you can wear men's trousers any time you like." He smiled, but then paused to consider what he had just said. He opened his mouth to clarify, but I laughed and closed it with a finger to his lips. This close to him, I could feel his heartbeat, and mine seemed to beat in time.

"Don't worry about that right now," I said, looking up at him. Slowly, almost lazily, he closed his eyes and kissed my lips. I kept my eyes open, watching my hands wrap around his neck on their own accord, my fingers getting tangled in his auburn hair, glowing in the light of the sun. I closed my eyes and let myself get lost in his kiss, gentle and sweet with an undercurrent of nervous energy pulsing through between us. Before it could take over, turning our sweet moment into something more frantic and impassioned, we broke apart. He smiled slyly, as if at some private joke, and I felt some heat rise to my cheeks as I turned away and packed the rest of my items in my bag and slung it onto Misten. When we finished packing, Erik looked at me and motioned towards the waterfall. I swallowed, my mouth dry with nerves, and watched as Erik and Elana disappeared through the curtain of water. Closing my eyes, I followed behind, Misten in tow.

We made it through slightly damp but unscathed nonetheless. Erik removed some cloth that he had soaked in oil from one of the packs strapped to Elana's back and lit it on fire, casting a glow around us as we moved further into the cavern. Where as the tunnel running through Cethin was primarily dirt, presumably man-made when we were first banished to live underground, this tunnel seemed to have been carved by nature itself. A river ran alongside us, lazily working away at the stone of the mountain. The flame of the torch was caught by clear stones in the walls, the light reflected and bent into different colours that danced across the cavern as we made our procession. I marvelled at beauty of it all, wishing that Cethin had more to offer than just dirty mines, which seemed to produce more lung-clogging dust than actual coal.

Eventually, the river left us, diving beneath the rocks and forking away in the opposite direction, leaving my ears ringing from the sudden silence. Erik and I tried to fill the silence by talking, but the echoes of the cave distorted our words and make conversation difficult, so we stopped. Besides the pitter-patter of our footsteps and the clip-clop of the horse's shoes, the only other sounds were the drip-drops of water falling from pointed structures hanging menacingly from the ceiling and landing on the tips of similar points on the ground. I felt as though we were entering the mouth of a giant, sharp teeth ensconced with thick, bumpy enamel from years of eating lost travellers. I thought of all the guards who had made their way down here, undoubtedly cursing their luck the whole way. I also thought of all those who were taken to the surface, either by force or by choice. I though about Jean. Rather, I worried about Jean. I reached down into my shift and pulled out the small doll she had given me, which I had promised to give to her parents. I looked at its small purple dress, probably cut from her family's cloak, and rubbed my thumb over the worn fabric. Parts of the doll were soaked in blood. Brussel's blood, I reminded myself. I tightened my hand around it and put it back in my shift.

After a while, my eyes began to grow tired from the strain of trying to see in the dark, so I rested them on the small bit of light outlining Elana's head as she walked behind Erik. My feet were beginning to throb from walking on the hard, uneven cave floor, and I couldn't help but hope that every turn we rounded would be the last one. I felt like Misten was pulling me along rather than the other way around, and it was all I could do to not stumble and fall. I wondered why I had suddenly gotten so tired, why my endurance of years of living in the same style of caves was leaving me.

"Erik," I finally said, weakly. "How much farther? I'm so tired."

"It's the gas," he said. "These caves must be filled with gas that are causing us to lose our breath. I've heard about this from the guards, but I've not experienced it before. Try breathing through your shirt, using it as a mask. But don't stop moving. We are almost there, Fara."

I found a strip of fabric in one of Misten's bags and tied it over my nose, but I couldn't stand the warm, thick air I was forced to breathe back. I almost preferred the stale, sulfurous cave air.

After a few minutes, I couldn't stand it, and I tore the fabric away from my face. I had only taken a few deep breaths in before I saw spots dance around from the corner of my eyes, and my head started to feel light. I opened my mouth to call for Erik, but before I managed to get a word out, everything turned black.

"Where am I?" I groggily murmured. The words came out in a jumble. I cleared my throat and tried again. "Where am I?" I was laying down in an unfamiliar room, the ceiling comprised of purple stone with small holes riddling the surface.

I tried to lift my head to look around, but it started to pound so hard that I had to close my eyes and lay it back down before I vomited. I tightened my eyes against the spinning, and felt tears leak out the sides. I was scared, but I was also tired. Slowly, I calmed my breath and was able to relax and fall back asleep.

The second time I woke up was to the sound of someone shuffling around. Learning my lesson from last time, I didn't try to raise my head, although the pain had slightly gone away. I called out again. "Hello? Is anyone there? Where am I?"

I heard the shuffle quicken and felt someone grab my hand. "Don't worry, child, you will be al-right. You just took a fall and hit your head a little too hard. Once we get you on the mend, you should be fine." An old, wizened face leaned into view, and she smiled at me as she began to check my head, which I now realized was wrapped in bandages.

"I don't remember falling," I said. I thought back to the cave, how it was so hard to breathe, and how everything went black. I must have fainted, I thought.

"That big nasty bump on the side of your head tells a different story," she joked. I reached up to feel my head, and was shocked to feel a massive lump. No wonder my head felt heavy-it was two times larger! I sucked in a sharp breath, and the woman took my hand away and set it back down in my lap. "Hush, child. It's al-right. The worst has passed. You just have to take it easy for a few days and you should be good as new. The gases of the cave must have been too strong for you, a surface-dweller. I always said that Ahrenians had weak constitutions. All that life in luxury makes you weak." Before I could correct her and tell her I wasn't from the surface, she was moving me around. "Now, let's see if we can sit you up and get some food in you." She gently eased me into a sitting position, and I once again fought the urge to vomit. I pressed my eyes closed to stop things from spinning, and when I felt like I had my stomach under control, I slowly opened them.

Around me was a small room seemingly made of the same porous stone that acted as the ceiling. In the corner sat a fire, and on a small chair in front of the fire hung my dress and my shift. I realized in horror that I had on only the thinnest of undergarments. I pulled the blanket up over myself, suddenly self conscious. The old woman laughed, and I could see now that she was short and plump with dark skin. In this room, she looked like she was the same purple as the walls. She went over to the fire and scooped some soup from the cauldron sitting above it.

"You don't have to be shy, child. I've seen quite a few naked bodies in my time. As healer, it's part of my job. That's one of the reasons everyone calls me Ma. I've done helped their mamas give birth to them all. "

"But I thought I only had a head injury. Where are the rest of my clothes?"

"I had to make sure you didn't hurt anything else on your body when you fell down," she explained as she carried the soup over to me. She scooped up a spoonful and blew on it, and then held it out to me. I accepted it and was surprised by the pleasant taste. It was familiar, with the earthy taste of the tubers found in in the caves, but it was sweeter and had more of a spice to it. I wanted more, but she was feeding it to me slowly.

"Now now, child, take it easy. You've been in and out of consciousness for a few days. This is your first meal for a while, and I wouldn't want you to lose it."

I went over what she said in my head with distress. A few days? I opened my mouth to ask exactly how many, but she shoved a spoonful of soup in it before I could say anything. I swallowed it quickly and then spoke. "Where is the man I came here with?"

"Oh, you mean that handsome fellow who carried you here in his arms? He refused to leave your side until I shooed him out so that I could conduct a proper physical examination. He is addressing some matter with the council. I haven't seen him much since he left, but he has come in to check on you frequently. Actually, he is due to come by around this time."

"I need to speak to him," I told her. I didn't know how much of our plan he was carrying out alone, if he was at all, and if he was finding success or not. Thinking back to what happened in Cethin, I didn't think the odds were in his favour. As Prince of Ahrenia, he may as well of sentenced everyone to their fate down here himself, and I'm sure they weren't taking it well. Suddenly, the blanket felt suffocating, and I squirmed out of it, refusing more soup. But shaking my head made it swim, and I had to lay it back down to keep it from pounding.

"What did I tell you, child?" Ma tsked her tongue in chastisement. "Just relax. He will be here soon. And besides, you need to get some real clothes on before he sees you, anyhow." She raised her eyebrow suggestively and I flushed, remembering my current state of undress.

"Okay," I relented. I finished eating the soup, and she had me digest it for a while before standing me up and helping me put on a loose gown. Meanwhile, Ma chatted away about menial things, sometimes talking about chores she had to get done, sometimes gossiping about "my handsome man", and other times reflecting on the general state of the colony. From what I could gather, they were suffering from a famine, and their stores of tubers and roots were depleted. "The only ones we can seem to dig up are thin and bitter. We are running out of food, and we can't seem to find a way around it. Even our goats are drying up," she expressed, concern pressing her lips together. I listened intently, looking for things I could use when I spoke to the council, hoping to get them on our side. Suddenly, a thought struck me.

"Ma, do you know of a girl named Jean?"

The old woman's cheerful face suddenly grew solemn. The deep groves near her eyes sunk as her eyes fell downcast. That was a good enough answer as any.

"Jean, she was a good girl. I helped her mama deliver her, you know. She was such an awkward little child, her legs too long for the rest of her body. But she grew into it. Boy, she did grow into it. She was a source of beauty in this place. But more than her looks was her voice. Clear as a bell. I remember she used to sing me a birthday song every year in her sweet, bright voice. Always brought tears to my eyes, it did. Such a good girl," she said morosely.

"But then those guards came. True, we've but grown used to having guards around, but normally they would just mind their own business, only stirring up trouble every now and then. It was nothing too bad. This group, though, this group was barbaric. They seemed to live off of punishment, to feed from our suffering. One day, they noticed Jean. She had successfully stayed out of their sight for nearly a month, but eventually they saw her. She was singing for a small festival we were having. We tried to keep things light by celebrating the small things, such as the birth of a new goat. I'm sure I don't have to explain what happened next. Them boys, for they surely weren't acting like men, kept her in their barracks for nearly a week before she managed to escape. When I saw her again, she was battered and bruised, nearly torn apart. She could hardly speak, let alone sing. I had never seen anything like it." Ma paused, and a large tear rolled down her cheek. We sat in silence that moment, sharing our unspoken grief. I remembered the song Jean sang for me the first night I was in the servant's quarters. Her voice was clear and strong, but out of practice. I wondered how it must have sounded before life took its toll on her.

"I don't want to know how much longer this would have gone on were it not for the new captain," Ma continued. "He came in about two months after the arrival of that terrible troop, and he straightened those boys out. When one of them tried to bring Jean in, he saw her beauty and instantly arranged for her to be sent to the surface so that she could serve the kingdom. I remember the cries of grief that came from the den of her family that night. Their wails shook the walls of this entire place. But they knew that it was probably for the best, that Jean was safer on the surface than she ever would be down here. Beauty is as much a blessing as a curse, you see."

I didn't need her to tell me. I've lived my entire life at the crossroads between prejudice based on my home and attention drawn by my appearance.

Ma sighed and sat down, and I regretted opening an old wound. I hoped that my next news would be taken better.

"Ma, I can promise you that Jean is one of the strongest people I know." She looked at me with confusion on her face.

"How do you know about Jean?"

"She is my best friend. She helped me survive my first days on the surface after I came from my colony."

"But I've not seen you here☐" she pondered quietly.

"That's because I'm not from Grundale, I'm from Cethin. Ma, there are more places like this throughout Ahrenia."

"Well would you look at that," she said quietly, and I was glad she was already sitting down. By the look of revelation on her face, what I told her surely would have knocked her down. "I always liked to think that, even though we suffer here, there aren't that many of us. The universe couldn't be so cruel as to make more than our small group suffer so that others may prosper. But to hear that there are more colonies who have to deal with this curse☐child, that just saddens my heart."

CHAPTER 34

Prince Erik came by a little after that. The air was warm and moist, very different from the cool air of Cethin. Ma told me that it was because Grundale wasn't very deep down, it was just deep in the mountain. Either way, it had me sweating through the gown, causing the light fabric to stick transparently to my skin. I may as well not be wearing anything, I thought, when I saw Erik noticeably blush upon entering the room. Ma winked at me as she left the room to give us some privacy, and I rolled my eyes.

"How are you feeling?" He asked, and I pulled my covers up a bit to cover myself.

"I'm feeling better, thanks. Well, that's not entirely true. Before, I was asleep, so I didn't realize how much my head was pounding. Are you sure you didn't hit my head against anything when you were carrying me around, trying to be my knight in shining armour," I complained good-naturedly. "So fill me in on what happened after my, uh, incident," I asked embarrassedly. I silently pledged to myself that one of these days, I was going to rescue him and make things even between us. I was sick of playing the damsel in distress.

"It was pretty uneventful. I found the general and gave him the letter, and he didn't challenge it. I think at this point he would have taken any excuse to get out of this place. He looked pretty miserable. They were out of here in a few hours. Then I found someone to tie up the horses. Misten and Elana are in the stables with the goats and the sheep, and I've made sure to check on them every now and then. You should've seen the reaction of the people when they first saw Elana and Misten. You'd have thought I brought a dragon into their home! They were terrified and mystified by them at the same time!"

"What's a dragon?" I interrupted.

Erik looked at me with disbelief. "It's um☐well☐that doesn't matter. After that, I asked around until I found the chief, and he got things together for the council meeting. I have to say, he took a lot more convincing than the general."

"Even with your good looks and charm," I teased. He sighed and lay his head in my lap.

"I often think that sometimes my looks do me more harm than good. If I were hideous, he probably would have listened instead of taking a swing at my face. Or maybe that was because I told him I was the Prince. Either way, it took a while to get him to listen to me."

I combed my fingers through his hair absent-mindedly, wondering how different my life would have been if I had been born normal. Would I be the same person? Would I have been challenged to fight for my people if I didn't have anything that made me stand out? I would like to think so.

"How are things going with the council?" I asked him after a while.

"They are moving slow. Slower than in Cethin, that's for sure. These people seem to have given up, to 'accept the role bestowed upon them' in their words."

"That makes it sound like it's an honour," I told him. He nodded in agreement. I thought back to what Ma had said, about suffering for the good of everyone else. It seemed as though she thought that if they anguished enough, then other people would be saved. This completely contrasted the fiery spirit of Jean, who sought justice and equality for everyone. If anything, that contrast alone gave me hope that if they learned the truth, they would be able to fight with the same spirit.

"I can't wait to get out of this bed so that I can help you," I told him. Not being able to move around drove me insane, especially considering how pressing our time frame was. "Time is of the essence, and I can't afford to be laying in bed while the King might be mobilizing troops against us already."

He put his hands on my shoulders as if to hold me in bed, and I scowled at him. "Don't worry. Even if I tried, I don't think I could make it a few steps without getting sick or falling down. I'm not going to try anything dangerous."

"That's a first," he said with a smirk, and to be honest, I didn't blame him for not believing me.

We talked some more about how his appeal was going, and he told me that they had initially refused to hear him, being the Prince and all, but Ma was able to talk them into it.

"She's a character, she is," he had said, and I laughed in agreement.

He said that they weren't completely opposed to the idea, but they didn't want to cause more trouble, didn't want to jeopardize their people. "I don't think they believe we have a chance," he confessed.

We brainstormed some different arguments we could use to get them on our side, but eventually we started talking in circles, so we changed topics. I could tell that he was tired and tense, and I was grateful that he was here to keep me entertained while I recovered. Eventually, though, Ma came back in and shooed him out, saying that she needed to check my head and take care of me, which was impossible with him here to distract her. After he left, she looked at me, and I was slightly frightened by the hungry look in her eyes.

"So, what did you talk about?" She asked as she unwound my head, reminding me of the servant girls begging to hear the latest gossip.

"Nothing," I laughed, and then clarified, "well, nothing you would be interested in hearing."

She groaned and I caught a murmur that sounded something like, "You kids don't know how to have fun nowadays".

She didn't wrap my head back up, saying that all the wound needed at this point was some fresh air. And for myself, she thought I could use some more soup.

While we ate, and I was able to feed myself this time, I asked her if she knew anything about what Erik was discussing with the council.

"Well, before you told me about the other colonies, I hadn't heard anything at all. But it had me thinking, so I went to the council while I was out and talked to them."

"Really? And what did they say?"

She was silent for a few moments, simply sipping her soup. Eventually, she reported, "Not much. They really don't know what to think of things at this point."

"But we can't wait for them to decide! They need to make up their minds before it is too late!" I said, my voice rising in volume.

"Child, you don't seem to understand how things work around here. It has been the same routine day in and day out, and suddenly you two appear, somehow convince the guards to leave, speaking some crazy that there are more colonies in Ahrenia and that you want us all to join together to fight against the King. It'd be crazy if we accepted it without thinking about it first."

I sighed. I knew she was right, I just didn't want to come to terms with it. "Okay, I'm sorry. But if you could think of any way to convince them that this was the right thing to do, what would you do?"

She looked up from her bowl, having finished all her soup, and stared into my eyes. "You can't convince people to do something they don't believe in. You have to prove that it is worth believing in." With that, she stood and took my dish, which wasn't quite empty, but I didn't complain.

As she walked away to set down the bowls, a woman came rushing in, nearly hysterical. Her face was tear-streaked and her eyes were frantically searching around for a target. I was surprised when they finally found their mark, me. She rushed towards me, and started shoving something in my face.

"Where did you get this? Where did you get this!" The question sounded more like an accusation, and I shrunk away from her as much as my position would allow.

Ma, meanwhile, had dropped her dishes with a clatter on the chair and came rushing towards me, pulling the woman off. "Yasmia, stop it! Get a hold of yourself!" She grasped Yasmia's shoulders and held her back, and slowly Yasmia sunk to the ground, pulling Ma into an embrace as she sobbed into her shoulders.

With the attack over, I was able to focus on what it was the woman was pressing on me. I instantly recognized it as Jean's doll, because its purple dress was stained with blood. It must have fallen out of my shift when Erik was carrying me.

"Are you Jean's mother?" I asked, coming to the only logical conclusion I could make about the situation before me.

Yasmia turned her puffy eyes up towards me. "How do you know her name?"

"She was my best friend," I stated, but before I could expand, Yasmia started to wail again.

"My goodness, child, what has you in such a fit?" Ma asked the woman.

"My sweet Jean is gone! Forever, gone!"

"What led you to believe that?"

"The doll, her doll, the one I made for her when she was a child out of her father's cloak, the one I sent with her when she was taken to the surface, is covered in her blood! And now this girl," she wept, pointing at me with a shaking finger, "she says that Jean 'was' her best friend. Was means she no longer 'is'. Don't you see? Jean is dead!"

"That's not true!" I had to repeat it three times before I could be heard over the sobs of Jean's mother. She sniffled, quieting a bit.

"What?"

"I said, it isn't true. Jean isn't dead. Your daughter, your strong, brave, inspirational daughter, is very much alive."

Yasmia's chest was still jumping with the erratic breaths that come from crying too hard, but she no longer had streams coming from her eyes, which I could now see were the same hazel as Jean's. I could only imagine the intensity of emotions she must be feeling right now.

"Jean is alive?" She asked, and then repeated it to herself quietly, over and over, as if trying to convince herself it was true. "But the blood, on the doll," she protested.

"Doesn't belong to her," I explained. "I promise you, Jean is alive and fighting." I paused before I went on, considering what I was about to tell her, but I realized that, at this point, the truth would be the best for everyone. "At least, last time I saw her she was. She was helping me plan the rebellion. Actually, she gave me the idea. But someone betrayed us, and she was captured before she could escape." I watched her mother carefully, not wanting to send her back into hysterics. "She believed in what we were fighting for, and she didn't hesitate to stand up against the King. I know that she expected Grundale to fight as well. But each day that you all wait and deliberate, she sinks deeper and deeper into trouble. To rescue your daughter, we need to act quickly." I felt guilty for manipulating a mother's grief in such a way, but there was no way around it. It was the truth.

Suddenly, Yasmia's face grew hard and she looked straight at me. I watched as her eyes strengthened, and I suddenly knew where Jean's fighting spirit came from.

"I'm not going to let them take my daughter away from me again," she said, gripping the doll tightly. She stood, Ma helping her up, but Yasmia was no longer shaking. She walked to the edge of my bed and pulled me into her arms. I could feel every ounce of worry, relief, and determination in that embrace, and it brought tears to my own eyes. "Thank you for bringing a part of her back to me," she whispered. She released me and strode out of the room.

As soon as she left, I felt my body slump with exhaustion. My head pounded and I couldn't seem to keep my eyes open. Ma helped me lean back and pulled the blanket over my chest.

"Now you rest, child. Things will be different in the morning. I can feel it."

"Fara," I felt someone gently shaking me. "Fara, wake up." I blinked my eyes open and saw Erik standing before me.

"What is it?" I yawned, sitting up slowly. I noticed that my head was much improved, and that the motion only made me slightly light-headed.

"I don't know what you did last night, but you saved us!" I looked at him in confusion, not understanding. "That woman that you spoke to? She came storming in to the council meeting last night and practically demanded that her people get up and fight. Her rally was incredibly effective. After about an hour of deliberation, the council decided that they would join us."

"Erik, that's great!" I was thrilled at the news, and I marvelled at the power of a mother's love for her child, for that is what truly turned things around to our side.

"Now, they didn't agree to send everyone. The children and elderly will of course stay home, so some of the women will have to care for them. But these people are strong, Fara. And I can see it in their eyes. Once they pick up a cause, they won't stop fighting for it." Erik sat down next to me. "Fara, we are going to leave around mid-day."

"What time is it right now?" I asked.

"It's early in the morning. At least, according to them. I'm not sure how you all can keep time down here."

"We've had to adjust."

He winced. "Sorry, my bad. So, do you think you can get up?"

I rotated my head around to test it out, and I found that as long as I kept it relatively straight, it was fine.

"Yes, I think I'll be okay." I gave him my hand, and he eased me out of the bed one foot at a time. I was a little wobbly on my feet, but otherwise I felt much better. My stomach growled, and I found that I was hungry for something much more substantial than soup.

Erik must have been reading my mind, because at that moment he offered me some bread. I looked at him questioningly while chewing on it, relishing the feeling of something with actual substance. He pulled off a piece, and while he ate, he explained, "I got it from the storage. I've been helping them all night with the packing and preparations for the trip." As if to emphasize his point, he yawned and I got a nice glimpse of chewed-up bread mush in his mouth.

"Yuck," I said, jokingly nudging him, but I overestimated myself and lost my balance, ending up having to hold on to him for support. I tried to steady myself, but before I could push away, he had me wrapped in his arms, kissing my forehead, then my cheeks, then my lips. I looked up at him, dazed for a few moments, when suddenly a voice interrupted my trance.

"What do you think you're doing out of bed?" I gasped and turned my head to find Ma standing with her hands on her hips, looking cross. I quickly squirmed my way out of Erik's grasp, and he just chuckled, keeping a hold on my hand. He let go, however, when Ma walked up and gave him a resounding clunk on the head. She pointed her finger at me and threatened, "If I wasn't treating you for a head injury, you'd be getting one too!" She reached for my face and I flinched away, but she was too fast and quickly had it firm in her hands. She yanked my head down to inspect it, turning it from left to right, clicking her tongue as she did so.

"Al-right, fine. I guess it isn't so bad," she finally relented. "If the situation were any different, I would keep you in bed for another day or two, but with things as they are☐hmphh. I still don't like it. After all my years☐" she mumbled as she walked away towards her supplies. Erik looked at me with a mock crazy expression on his face, and I shushed him before Ma turned around.

She returned and handed me a small, scented satchel. "Put this on your head if it starts acting up. You might get a few headaches during your journey. If that happens, this should help keep some of the pain away." She turned back around and rummaged through her supplies some more. I left Erik's side and joined her.

"You aren't coming with us?" I asked, waiting for an answer while she sorted through an assortment of intimidating instruments. I tried not guess what they were used for.

"No, child, they need me here. I have to look after all the young'uns and the elders while everyone else is gone. But don't you worry. I'll send some of my apprentices with tools that should prove useful on the battlefield."

"Ma, we aren't going to battle. We are going to negotiate with the King."

Ma stopped her sorting and looked at me with sad eyes. "I hope that's all, child. I truly hope so."

"No, we can't bring that," Yasmia was directing a younger boy around Conor's age, who was trying to drag a goat along with him. I watched on the sidelines as the adults gathered everything together, sensing the rhythm that ebbed and flowed between them all without any spoken command. It made me slightly homesick, the dynamic that held them together. It represented a group of people in which each individual had their own role, their own contribution to make, and together the community thrived as a single unit. I could only hope that all the way out here, so far from my family and my home, I was serving my role and making my mark.

From across the room, Erik was guiding a tall man my direction. Unlike my father, who was thick, this man was spindly, his limbs appearing as though they would snap at any moment. But his face, in contrast, was firm and set, his eyes strong and bright. I watched as he and Erik navigated around the business going cn in the cavern and make their way towards me.

"Fara, this is Alonso. He is the head of the council of Grundale."

I folded into into a slight bow, keeping my head low out of reset.

"Fara, I am pleased to meet you." Any skepticism I had about his ability to lead the council was shattered as soon as I heard his voice. It was clear and strong, not too low and not too high. It commanded your attention from the first syllable, and you knew that whatever this voice had to say was important.

"This young man," he continued, "has told us an extensive amount about you and your plan, and I must say your bravery and tenacity are inspiring. I hope that we may prove worthy of this alliance in the grand scheme of things. But for now, know that you have my support, which, I must admit, I was reluctant to give it at first. It took a bit of, ah, convincing." he said with a glance in Yasmia's direction. Yasmia returned it with a slit-eyed scowl. "Hmm, yes. Convincing, indeed. Regardless, we will follow you to Cethin and hope to convene with the other colonies before venturing towards the royal city."

"I'm honoured to have your support, sir," I said, slightly dipping my head again. He nodded in return and then left to help delegate the preparations.

"It's really happening, Erik. I can't believe it," I told him as I watched my plan unfold. Sudden pangs of anxiety gripped my stomach as I realized that I was now responsible for these people, and my people, and all the other colonies who choose to join us. If something goes wrong, if something happens to any one of these people, it will be my fault. If someone dies-I wouldn't let my mind wander down that road. I needed to remain strong and lead with assured steps. I couldn't do that with my concentration wavering, second-guessing myself at every fork in the road.

Erik must have sensed my stress, because he laced his fingers through mine and squeezed my hand. "Don't worry, Fara. We can do this. These people, your people, are strong. Together, they are much stronger than any army my father could assemble. We will change his mind. You'll see."

I looked up and kissed him, finding courage in his bright green eyes. He kissed me again, and I felt my heart swell up with strength and a determination to make things right.

CHAPTER 35

"I have to thank you again for keeping an eye out for Fara." Croxley and Jean were walking through the forest with Sir Thunder and Sam in tow.

"I didn't have much of a choice. That girl practically threw herself into harms way, and I was the only person around at the time to keep her from doing it again."

Croxley chuckled, "You don't have to tell me twice. I felt like half the time I was watching a child take their first steps right into a lion's den."

"Aren't you the one that brought her into the lion's den?" Croxley turned to look at Jean. She met his gaze and he couldn't tell if he saw blame and anger in her eyes or grief and pain. Probably a mixture of both, he thought to himself. He turned around and replied into the foliage, "Yes, I guess that's right. But she would've made her way up here one way or another. I guess that fate smiled upon her and made sure she got stuck with a softy like me to take her up here."

"You care for her, don't you?" Jean asked.

"I did, yes. A bit too much, if you ask me. But I couldn't measure up to the Prince. I mean, he's the Prince. That pretty much entitles him to any girl he wants. Any girl in their right mind would chose him over me. Fara did."

"I wouldn't." Croxley stopped walking and turned around. Jean was braiding Sam's mane, her face turned away from Croxley as she spoke. "Just because Fara chose the Prince doesn't mean that she doesn't care for you. If I know Fara, and trust me, I think I do, she cherishes your friendship more than you could know, and the moment she realized that she was hurting you probably put her through a lot of grief. I know that Fara loves you, just not in the way you want her to. But you can't change the way someone loves you, you just have to accept their love in whichever way it comes, cherish it, and protect it." Jean looked up from her braid and met Croxley's eyes. "So don't give up on love, okay?"

Croxley gave a weak shrug. He didn't know how else to respond. After their kiss, they hadn't talked about anything but the logistics of the plan and what was going on in the castle. Every time Croxley tried to bring up whatever it was that was happening between them, Jean would change the subject. It has made for a very long trip thus far.

Before he could respond, he heard a crashing through the forest. Both he and Jean crouched behind the bushes and pulled the animals out of view.

"Why d'ya suppose the King is sending us out into the woods?" Just a few paces in front of the Croxley and Jean's hiding spot emerged two castle guards clothed in war gear.

"You heard 'im. We are supposed to keep watch for the Prince."

"Ay, I know that. But why would the Prince be coming out of the forest?"

"You didn't hear it from me, but some guards were talking that the Prince up and gone rogue."

"What does that mean?"

"Rogue? I think it's when a man decides to fight against us instead of with us."

"I know what it means, you dimwit. But what about the Prince?"

"Oh,that. Well, I heard he ran off with a slave girl and now he is gonna try to free the Nethers." "Now why would he wanna go an' do that?"

"Don't ask me. I say good riddance to the Nethers. If I were him, I would pretend to help 'em and then lead them straight to the guards surrounding the castle. Then we can wipe 'em out for good this time."

"That's a good plan."

"It is, ain't it? I should tell the general. Then maybe he'll stop sending me out on border control."

"Not if I tell him first!"

"Blast it! Hey, get back here!" The sounds of crashing steps reverberated through the forest until they faded into silence and were overtaken by the resuming birdsong.

Croxley heard Jean suck in a breath and realized that he was holding his own.

They looked at each other, eyes wide. Jean was the first to break the silence. "So the King knows."

"That's not much of a surprise. When I told Lena I knew it was only a matter of time before he found out."

"What do we do? If the Prince and Fara lead everyone to Stonewall, they will be ambushed. It's a sure death."

"That just means we have to get there first. Come on," Croxley stood up dusted off his hands. Before he could help Jean up, she was already standing. She looked at him and shrugged.

"What? I'm used to doing things myself. You can't wait around for people to pick you up. They just let you fall in the end." She shouldered her pack and made her way back to Sam who was still tied behind the tree cover.

"I'm sorry for whatever it was you had to go through that made you think that way," Croxley said. She didn't turn around, but instead mounted Sam.

"Don't be. It isn't your fault. You've got your issues and I have mine. That's just the way it is."

"But no one should have to suffer alone." Croxley stepped towards

Sam but Jean kicked him into a walk."

"Come on, we have to go," she said behind her, leaving him and Sir Thunder behind.

Women. Why do they have to be so difficult, he thought to himself. He gave Sir Thunder a few pats, mounted, and followed in her wake.

"Wow. Would you look at that. Oh my, and that too. All of this is just too much! It's so amazing!"

I rolled my eyes and looked towards the canopy, trying to hold my tongue from saying anything mean. We've been travelling through the jungle for a few days now, and while at first it was amusing to see everyone's response to the surface, it's gotten to the point that I just wanted to shout "Yes! It's a flower! And that over there is also a flower! We are surrounded by flowers! And animals, and trees, and dirt, and a whole bunch of other things. Now get over it!" But instead I just bit my tongue and counted the steps until we reached Cethin. We were making much slower progress than when Erik and I were travelling alone, which was to be expected, but all the stops along the way to smell a flower here and there, to taste the water of this stream and compare it to the other stream, have taken up a lot of our time.

But I shouldn't complain. For the most part, everyone has reacted very well to the surface. We've only had a few individuals who suffered from what could only be called panic attacks. I could relate. The surface could be large and overwhelming, and after living in the tight, underground caverns, even the cramped foliage of the jungle could be too open of a world to handle.

"I just made a head count and we still have everyone." Erik jogged up behind me. "Well, almost everyone. Jovan had a few leeches on his back and legs that looked like they had sucked him dry. Don't worry, he seemed more interested in what I pulled off of him than about the blood loss. So I'd say the head count totals at forty and a half."

I frowned at Erik's attempt to make a joke. He winced and said, "Sorry, bad joke. How's everything going up here?"

"How is everything? I'd say everything is amazing," I said with fake enthusiasm.

"Really, Fara, you shouldn't be one to judge. I'm sure you drove Croxley insane with all your 'amazement' at the surface. You should know how it feels to be in their place."

I sighed and admitted, "I know. I'm sorry. It's just, every step we take closer to Cethin, the more nervous I get."

"I'm not going to say 'don't worry', because that would be useless. But don't let your nerves take over. You literally have an army standing behind you."

"Which I may be leading straight towards danger," I replied, my gaze directed downward, focusing on kicking a pebble through the red dirt until it got stuck under a raised, gnarled root.

"That may be so. But regardless, you are leading us towards something. It may be better, it may be worse. However, we'd all be fools not to follow you. And I think, well, I hope, at least, that I'm not a fool." Erik's feet entered my field of vision, and I watched as his fell in step with mine.

"Speaking of fools, I hope Croxley is okay."

"Me too. Knowing him, he's probably stirred up things at the castle, gotten himself in a heap of trouble, and then somehow managed to get himself out of it."

"Do you think he'll make it to Cethin?"

"I hope so. By now, everyone should be there waiting for us. Heath and Mr. Harris, if they had any luck, would have arrived a few days ago. I doubt that their group is taking as long to move as ours."

I nodded assent, and was about to open my mouth to comment but was interrupted by a loud "Wow! That spider is so big! It's amazing!"

I looked at Erik in exasperation. He rolled his eyes and shrugged, grinning. I leaned into him as he wrapped his arms around me, my head curled into his chest. At few moments later, we heard a shout. "Wait, what's it doing? OW!"

I felt Erik exhale and we pulled apart, looking at each other with a mixture of concern and exhaustion in our eyes. "I've got it," Erik said with a sigh.

"This is it." Croxley and Jean stopped their mounts. They had reached the entrance to Cethin. Croxley dismounted Sir Thunder and held out a hand to help Jean down, but rubbed it awkwardly through his hair when she didn't take it.

"This is Cethin? It looks so, obvious." Jean walked around the cave's mouth, circling it as if it were a strange animal.

"You mean there isn't a giant waterfall blocking the entrance?"

Jean turned back to look at Croxley with an ornery grin. "I'm just saying, compared to Grundale, it's a tad dull."

"You'll see though. While Grundale is protected by the water and the gas, Cethin is a series of mazes that can easily drive a man mad." Croxley took Sam's reins from Jean and led Sir Thunder and Sam into the cave. He tied them to the post and bundled his gear into his pack. He shouldered it and began to make his way deeper. When he didn't see Jean follow him, he turned around.

"Well? Are you coming?"

Jean hesitated, looking into the depth of the cave. She paced back and forth across the entrance before taking a deep breath and crossing into the cavern. "Yeah, I'm coming." Croxley gave her a curious glance, and she shrugged. "What? Come on, let's go," she responded as she went ahead.

"Jean. Jean, wait." Croxley had to jog to reach her, and only managed to grab her arm before she tried to speed up. She tugged her arm from his grip but he held it tight.

"What?" She spun around, angry.

"What's wrong?"

"Nothing!"

"Jean, I'm not stupid. I can tell something is bothering you. And I don't want you to have to suffer it alone. Plus, this will be a long trip if you give me the silent treatment. Trust me, I know."

Jean kept her head turned down, her eyes pointed towards the ground but unfocused. Croxley slid his grip from her arm to her hand and held it, squeezing gently. She looked up at him and he saw a tear drip off her cheek. "Jean," he said, softer, and leaned in to wipe it off. She flinched away and he paused, then continued to reach until his hand was resting on her cheek. He thumbed the tear off but kept his hand there. Closing her eyes, she leaned into it.

"I'm just☐scared," she exhaled, keeping her eyes closed.

"Scared of what?"

"I'm scared of letting people too close. I've kept a wall up for so long that I'm not sure how to let it down. Or if I even want to let it down. Let people in and they hurt you. That's what I've come to find." She opened her eyes and leaned back, pulling away from Croxley's hand.

"I'm also scared of seeing my family again, if they are still alive, that is. I'm scared of what they will think of me, what they will say to me, if they will still love me," her voice broke on the word "love" and another tear trailed down her face, which she made no effort to wipe away. "On top of it all, apparently now I'm afraid of dark tunnels, because they remind me of that prison. What those men did to us down there, I thought I had shut it all out from my mind. But it seems I'm not as good at that as I used to be."

"Maybe it's a good thing your walls are coming down. Otherwise nobody would be able to reach you." He pulled her into his arms, and she leaned her head against his chest. He felt her shaking, her silent tears soaking his shirt.

When they finally slowed, she pulled herself away, placing her hands over the tear stains. She looked up at him, and despite her red eyes and runny nose, Croxley thought she looked beautiful. I better keep that to myself, he thought as he leaned in to kiss her cheek. But Jean surprised him by turning her face so that her lips met his. The kiss was gentle and sad, but also healing. They broke apart, Croxley releasing Jean's hand, and together they walked side by side down to Cethin.

"Hurry up, hurry up!" I was packing up camp, throwing everything into sacks as quickly as possible. We were almost to Cethin, and I could hardly wait.

"Fara, calm down. It's going to take some time for everyone to get going." Erik was helping a few of those from Grundale roll up their bags, and it was all taking far too long. "You need to remember, these people have never travelled before. They are tired and stressed, and if you push them too hard you may lose their loyalty."

These past few days, Erik has really surprised me. At the castle, I never had a chance to see him interact with anyone other than Croxley, Lena, and the occasional servant. But here, with these people, I've gotten to see a whole new side to him. He knows how to lead people, but in more ways than just telling them what to do. He knows what they need, and how to give it to them. He knows how to be patient, how to tolerate their mistakes, and he knows how to make each individual feel important. For the first time, I saw him as more than a Prince, I saw him as a King. There was no doubt in my mind that, under his rule, Ahrenia would be changed for the better.

"I know, I know. Im sorry." I approached one of the groups and helped them pack their things. They mostly chattered amongst themselves, talking about family they left at home, the magic they've seen on the surface, and all the other things that you talk about with people you've known your whole life. I enjoyed listening.

"Miss Fara, how much farther do we have to go," asked Wilson, an older gentleman whom I was helping roll blankets.

"We are almost there. I would say we are going to reach the entrance to Cethin around mid-day. Once we get there, it's a long trip through the tunnels. All in all, we should be in the meting hall by the end of the evening."

"Ah. I see. I'll admit, I'm very excited to meet other Nethers."

I smiled at him. "I am too," I agreed. But if I was honest with myself, I was much more nervous than I was excited. But I remembered what Erik had told me, about keeping a brave face, and I made sure to hide my fear.

Wilson, however, must have seen through the facade, because his next comment was, "If I were you, I would be nervous. You are a very brave young women."

"Thank you," I said, looking at him as I tied rope around my blanket. "That really means a lot to me."

He put his hand on my shoulder and smiled, then left to join the rest of his group. I remained kneeling for a few moments, watching as they interacted, noticing the new confidence they showed out on the surface, the sureness with which they walked replacing the uneasiness that caused them to stumble in their first few days on the surface. I hoped that this was a sign for the future, one in which the Nethers from Cethin, Grundale, and all the other colonies, could adapt to live comfortably together.

I stood and took my blanket to the back of the group, where Misten and Elana were being loaded with the supplies. I gave them some herbs I found growing in the forest, rubbing both of them absent-mindedly. When all of this is over, I thought to myself, I just want to ride Misten all over Ahrenia. Maybe even further. I'd love to see the world. As I trailed behind the group, I daydreamed about the places that Croxley told me about, like beaches and deserts, snow and ocean. I couldn't imagine what half of it looked like, but that was half the fun. Right now, my future was limitless, the possibilities endless. That is, if everything goes according to plan.

CHAPTER 36

"Everyone quiet down!" A large man stood in the middle of the cavern, the walls of which were practically vibrating from the echoes of his voice. Croxley and Jean had made their way through the tunnels and into Cethin, but as they came through the last of them, they were shocked by the chaos gripping the cavern, made even more apparent in the juxtaposition between the silent tunnels and the raucous room.

Crowds were gathered in various corners of the room, and people were hustling among them, coming from different openings to the cavern, some with their arms overflowing with supplies, others empty-handedly storming towards their destination. Amidst this was a constant underlying chatter that maintained at a dull roar. All of this came to a sudden stop at the command made by the large man in the center. Croxley assumed that this man was Anso, Cethin's leader.

"Now then. I know that everyone is anxious and eager to get a move on. I assure you, I feel the same. This cavern is by no means large enough to suit all of us, and while Cethin doesn't mind providing refuge for their Nether brothers and sisters for the time being, we simply do not have the resources to supply for everyone."

"Are you kicking us out?" An accusing voice rang out amongst the crowd. The suspended silence fell and the clamour resumed, anxiety and anger now underlying the chatter.

"Quiet down, quiet down," Anso boomed again. "There is no need for this disorder, nor is there need to worry. I only say this because it needs to be addressed. My daughter and the Prince should be returning soon with the remaining Nethers, but until then we have to wait for them. If they don't return soon, however, we may need to set off on our plan without them. So you see, my brothers and sisters, I am not kicking you out. Rather, I am warning you that we may need to band together earlier than expected and take charge of this rebellion. I will give my daughter till next morning and, if they haven't returned by then, we will have to leave without them."

Right into a trap, thought Croxley. He knew that Jean was thinking the same thing when she looked at him with wide eyes.

"Croxley, you have to do something," whisper Jean.

"What do I do? I'm not the Prince. Who am I to take charge of this?"

"Who says this is the Prince's job? You came up with the plan alongside him, didn't you? Not to mention, you've been to more colonies than he has. You know most of these people, you know their customs, you know how they've been mistreated and abused. You know best of all how to appeal to them." Croxley remained unmoved, his gaze concentrated on the man standing in the middle of the room. "Croxley, I know you can do this."

He kept his gaze focused, his mind running through all the possible scenarios and outcomes. . Eventually, he knew that he couldn't wait any longer and decided he had to listen to Jean and take charge.

He clenched his fists as he approached Anso to hide their shaking, and focused on planting each foot in front of the other. He couldn't understand why he was so afraid. He's spoken to plenty of the Nether leaders before, and he has had audiences with the King and other nobles back at he castle. So why am I so damn scared, he cursed. Before long, his feet had taken him to the middle of the room, and he cleared his throat to announce his presence to Anso, who was facing the other side of the cavern and had his back turned to Croxley.

He spun around and a looked surprised, having to look down to make eye contact with Croxley. "Who are you?" he asked.

Croxley opened and closed his now sweaty palms and announced, "I am Croxley, the messenger of the King's court and the intermediary between the colonies and the castle."

"Croxley, eh? And what are you doing here?"

"I've come to warn you of the King's trap."

"Trap? What trap? How would the King know to set up a trap?"

"Well, er☐I had to tell him the plan." Croxley squirmed under his glare, and knew what was coming. He tried to hold his ground but was still startled when Anso boomed, "You mean you told him the plan? You traitor! And now you have the nerve to come down here and tell us what we ought to be doing?"

"No, sir, you don't understand," Anso cut him of before Croxley could finish.

"Don't tell me I can't understand. I know about you. You did all the King's dirty work, bringing the commands back and forth between the King and his guards, sometimes taking our men and women back with you to become slaves for the King. You were the one to take my daughter. And now you have the nerve to come and ask me to listen to you?"

"Sir, I," Croxley tried again to get in a word, but this time Anso looked like he was going to take a swing at Croxley. However, Croxley wasn't about to back down, and after taking two solid hits to the stomach, right before a strong blow was heading towards his face, a voice cried out.

"Stop!" Jean stepped out of the group and stood in between Anso and Croxley. "Stop! You have to believe him! He is only here to help!"

Anso didn't seem convinced, but Jean's outburst gave him just enough pause for Croxley to squirm out of his grip and stand a few steps away, his chest rising and falling with his panting. Before Anso could reach out for him, another hand gripped his shoulder. He turned around, red in the face, but all the color drained when he saw who it was.

"Father, stop." Anso turned around to find Fara standing behind him. She smiled, but only for a moment before she saw Croxley grimacing in pain. "Father, really? I'm not going to bring any more friends home if you don't stop trying to beat them all up." Anso shrugged apologetically, and Fara continued her gaze from Croxley to Jean, her eyes widening and a small cry escaping her mouth as the realization crept in. It only took a few seconds for her to cross the distance and pull Jean into an embrace.

Croxley was watching this unfold when he received a solid punch to the arm.

"What the," he turned around, only to find the Prince standing next to him.

"Hey, Croxley," was all Erik said. He stood at Croxley's side and watched as Fara and Jean talked non-stop about what each of them had been up to. At one point, Fara leaned back with surprise and looked at Croxley with wide eyes, back at Jean, then back to Croxley. He reddened slightly, only imagining what Jean must have told her.

Suddenly, Fara disappeared and ran out of the cavern. Croxley looked questioningly at Jean, who just shrugged. The Prince, likewise, gave no hints. Just as swiftly as Fara left, she reappeared, this time with two people in tow. Behind them, a crowd of individuals came through, filling in the rest of the tight Cavern, but Croxley kept his eyes on the couple following Fara. When they got close enough, he was able to make out on their faces expressions of nervousness riddled with sorrow, but also small glimpses of hope. When they saw Jean, they both stopped. The woman was holding a doll in her hand, and Croxley saw it fall to the ground, forgotten in the dust.

Croxley looked back to Jean and saw a look of disbelief on her face which mirrored that of the couple standing in front of her.

Slowly, Jean took a step forward, then another step. Closing the distance, the couple came forward until they were at an arms reach. The man held out his hand and placed it on Jean's cheek, and Croxley watched as a tear rolled over his hand from Jean's eyes. All was frozen for the next two breaths, when abruptly the still frame was broken and Jean was pulled into an embrace. More tears came spilling forth, and Croxley felt his own face dampen. Jean and her mother were speaking in quiet, disjointed sentences, broken up by both sobs and laughter, while her father stood with his arms around both of them, like a sentry, making sure nothing would happen to his small family again. After a while, Jean's mother left the group and walked towards Croxley.

"Are you Croxley?" She asked.

"Yes, ma'am."

"Thank you for keeping my daughter safe," she said simply, her words filled with emotion and gratitude.

"Of course," he replied, and she returned back to Jean.

Croxley made his way back to Anso, Fara, and Erik, who were deep in discussion.

Standing right next to each other, he amusedly noticed that Anso and Fara looked extremely similar. He decided that now wasn't the best time to mention this.

"This is everyone?" Fara asked, scoping the room.

"Yes. Your friends Heath and Mr. Harris are down in the supply room, helping everything get organized. Your mother, likewise, is having the children and the elderly help repair any shoes, cloaks, and other equipment so that we may be best prepared for the journey."

"What about weapons?" Croxley added. Everyone looked at him incredulously. Fara was the first to pipe in.

"Why do we need weapons? We aren't going to fight. We are going to convince the King to give us an audience."

Croxley shook his head. "Fara, listen to yourself. You know the King.

You know what he is capable of. Do you really think he will listen to you and your people? I can tell you the answer. No. In fact, he is setting up a trap with which he intends to kill all the Nethers you bring to him. Right now, as we speak, he has an army positioned around Stonewall, told to fire on-sight at any Nethers they meet."

Fara and Erik looked at each other with concern on their face.

"How could he have set up an army? We sent all of his guards to the northern border." Erik said.

"Because he knows our entire plan." Croxley paused and gathered his thoughts, calming himself before the inevitable storm. Might as well get on with it. "He knows because I told him. Rather, I told Lena, who told him. And Mathelda probably knows as well."

"You what?" Fara asked incredulously. Before she could say another word, Erik interrupted.

"Go on," he told Croxley. Croxley nodded and continued.

"I had no other choice. After returning to the castle, everything was in shambles. You and Fara were gone, most of the servant girls including Jean were in prison, while Mathelda and Lena were running the castle. The only way to get any information was to get close to Lena, which meant giving her some information. Don't worry, much of it was false, but I had to give her some basic truths for her to believe me. As expected, she went and told the King, and now he has an army waiting for us at the castle, read for an ambush."

Fara looked distraught, bitting her thumb and thinking hard.

"What are we supposed to do?" She whispered.

"We need to fight back."

She looked at Croxley with fire in her eyes. "I can't put these people at risk. They didn't sign up to fight. If anything happens to them, it's my fault. I can't take that chance."

"If I may," Anso spoke up for the first time, "Faradene, I've seen you grow so much since you've left Cethin. You've become a strong, mature, passionate young woman. But nobody expects you to take responsibility for all these people. You are still too young for all of this to rest on your shoulders alone. I've been a leader for many years, and I agree with you, a leader is responsible for their people's safety and should always protect them. But a leader must also know what his people are capable of. My people, your people, all those that you have gathered here, are a strong people. We have been fighting with our lives for the past centuries just to survive in these caves. I think I speak for everyone when I say that, if you ask us to fight, we will fight. Some losses may occur, and if that happens, it happens. Sacrifices must be made for the greater good. But you can't let fear rule your decisions. Rather, a leader needs to always rule through faith."

As Anso was speaking, the cavern grew quiet. Croxley didn't notice until Anso was finished that the entire room was now focused on them.

He watched with astonishment as he saw leaders from each of the groups step forward and make their way to the centre of the room. They congregated around Anso, Fara, Erik, and himself. Croxley scanned their eyes, seeing in each of them a wisdom and a determination not found on the surface. He knew, without a doubt, that their support would be unwavering. Croxley recognized Thylora from Fyzen as she spoke to them.

"I know my people when I say that we are willing to fight for our freedom, Miss Fara. And I put my trust in you that you will lead us to victory. If you ask us to fight, we will follow you. We may not have formal training, but years working in the mines have made us strong, and years struggling under oppression have given us a fighting spirit."

The others nodded in agreement, adding in their own vows of loyalty and determination. They each returned to their respective groups, telling their people of the new plan.

From the centre of the room, Anso rallied, "We will fight for the freedom of ourselves, we will fight for the freedom of our families, and we will fight for the freedom of our future!" The whole cavern responded with a loud cheer. Croxley saw Fara's eyes water up as she tried to stay strong, and knew that inside she was struggling to keep a brave face in the midst of these people's unfaltering faith in her. At the same time, he saw Erik's hand form around hers, and he felt a small jolt in his chest. He expected to have this reaction, and was curious to feel that it wasn't as painful as he expected. Yes, it was there, but only as a small reminder of the feelings he had for Fara. Has, he corrected himself. If he was going to be honest, he figured he would always love Fara in some way. But now, with Jean, well, he was just going to let things happen. After the battle, then you can try and figure things out, lover boy, he chastised himself.

CHAPTER 37

I watched as Nethers all around me rallied and cheered, ready to give themselves to the fight. I felt a mixture of pride and fear. Pride in my people, in their strength and in their power, but also a fear in myself and my ability to lead them safely. But looking around me, I realized that I had little reason to be afraid. I had my mother and father, Erik, Croxley, Jean, Conor, and so many other people to support me. Yes, there was a chance people could die. Yes, there was even the chance that I could die. Yes, I am responsible for bringing these people together, and I am equally responsible for whatever may happen to them. But I know that I am not responsible on my own. With all this weight on my shoulders, I know that, should I begin to grow weary, I have people I can depend on to help me remain standing.

Eventually, the hollering quieted down, and the cavern emptied out as people took up their chores with a renewed vigour. I put Croxley and Erik in charge of weapons, although I wondered just what we could use. Other than the pick-axes from the mines and the shovels and pitchforks from the gardens, we had very little that could function as weapons.

"Do you think we might be able to☐" Croxley looked at Erik, and Erik replied,

"No. Well, it would be risky, but☐"

"I could find us a way in," said Croxley.

"I'm sure you could. It's finding a way out that's the hard part."

I was growing irritated by this conversation of which I was completely clueless, and after the passing of a few more vague lines, I finally exclaimed, exasperated, "Would you guys please clue me in as to what you are talking about?"

"Well, Croxley has the idea that we might be able to raid the city's weaponry. Normally the guards at the wall keep weapons stocked so that, should the event arise, they would be ready to defend the city. Now, if we could find a way to get into the weaponry, take a load of weapons, and then get back out, we could give them to our army." I inwardly cringed at the word "army", but I knew that I had to get used to the term.

"The problem," Croxley continued, "would be getting through all the King's troops in order to reach the wall. Getting yourself in is one thing. After we get all the weapons, it will be difficult to bring them back unnoticed. I would need two or three strong men at the least to help me carry things back, but they would also need to be stealthy enough to remain unseen."

"I can ask my father and some of the other Netherleaders to choose their best men for the mission," I offered.

Croxley nodded his head in assent. "That would help. Another thing. If we want to have any chance, we need to leave as soon as possible. The more time we give the King, the more time he has to prepare his forces. I'm thinking that we should leave by tomorrow morning."

"Tomorrow morning? Are we ready?" I looked back and forth from Erik to Croxley, and they both seemed resolute.

"Fara, your father was planning on leaving soon any-ways. We have everyone working at top speed to get all the supplies together, and it seems that everything has nearly been completed. We can't afford to wait any longer," Croxley added.

"Listen, I know you are scared. But the longer you put this off, the more damage you might do to your people. It's in everyone's best interest to leave as soon as we can, and if there's a possibility to leave tomorrow, we need to take advantage of it," Erik encouraged.

"I know." I took a deep breath, exhaling slowly through my mouth. "I know," I repeated. I looked at each of them, going from Croxley to Erik and back, and after a moment's pause, put out my hand and said, "Let's do this." They put their fists atop mine, and we stood together, joined as three. Another hand came in and joined, and we open the group to make room for Jean.

"Al-right guys. So what's the plan?" She asked.

"We are going to leave in the morning. Jean, if you want to help me, I need to tell the other colonists to get ready to leave. Erik, Croxley, you two try and assemble all the weapons you can here, and I'll attempt to bring you some men to infiltrate the gates."

"Sounds good."

"Got it."

"Al-right."

We all broke apart and set off to our tasks, joining the ordered chaos around us.

The next day, we made it out of the tunnels on schedule, and our journey was mostly uneventful. All the other Nether colonies had already been above ground, but Cethins were still new to the surface and all its stimuli, so we had to go through much of the same experiences as we did with Grundale. With the other Nethers there to help them adapt, things moved much more rapidly.

We relied on our goats and sheep to carry most of our supplies on their backs. Croxley and Erik thought it was the strangest concept, war goats. But with only Misten, Elana, Sir Thunder, and Sam, we needed some "backup troops" to help carry the load. With high spirits, the people talked about painting the goats' coats and dying the sheep's' wool with war colours, gathering berries and flowers along the way for pigment. I was relieved that morale was still so high, and could only hope that it would remain so as we got closer and closer to the castle.

It was the fourth day that I noticed the overall mood starting to change.

"Give it back!" I was walking near the back of the group, talking to some of the older Ethers from Zen when I heard a deep, loud cry ring out from the front of the mass of people. I looked around in confusion until I heard another yell, this one high pitched, sounding as if it came from a woman. I rapidly made my way towards the source of the commotion, finding two large men circling each other in a larger circle of observers who were nervously whispering to each other.

"I saw you take it," one of the men said. He was largely built, his arms thick and his chest wide. The other man shook his head dramatically, appalled at the accusation. "I did no such thing! Besides, what would I want with your cloak-pin?" The accused was of a thin, wiry frame, and his fingers twitched at his sides.

"You tell me! You're the one who stole it! You were probably searching to sell it or trade it," the large man threatened.

"Even if I did, I wouldn't get anything for it. That pin isn't worth a steaming pile of goat's ah-," before you could blink, the accused was charged by his accuser and slammed to the ground. Everyone started shouting and hollering, small fights breaking out on the sidelines around the central fight, where the accuser was heavily beating down on his victim who was barely able to keep his hands up and protect his face.

I shouted once, twice, three times to try and break things up, but my voice was drowned out by the chaos around me. I desperately ran into the centre of the crowd, trying to pry the men apart, but I was too weak. I pulled on his arm, but he shoved me off, sending me to the ground. Frustrated, I felt hot tears come to my eyes. I wiped them aside and picked myself up, ready to try again, but was stopped by a hand on my shoulder.

Erik stepped past me, pushing me back sternly, making in very clear that I was not to move.

I watched in amazement as the crowd seemed to hush as he walked into the fray. It was if they could feel his command in every step, recognize his authority without him even needing to speak. As the crowd quieted, the accuser slowed his attack and looked around him. The man underneath him slowly made his way out, dazedly realizing that the attack had finished. I held my breath as he lifted his face towards the crowd, wondering just what kind of damage had been done.

I exhaled in relief when I saw that, despite a broken nose and the beginnings of a black eye, the man didn't suffer any major injuries. Once he got his wits about him, he tried to scatter off, but Erik grabbed him by the collar.

"Not so fast," he chastised. "I'm sure I don't need to inform you men that this behaviour is completely unacceptable. Now, in a more civilized manner, could someone please explain to me just what is going on here."

The large man seemed to wilt under the pressure of Erik's gaze. "Well, you see, your highness," he looked to the ground and lowered his head in a weak bow, "my family pin was stolen. My wife gave it to me before I left my colony, and I've worn it on my cloak every day of this journey. This morning I had to take off my cloak to help with the goats, and when I turned around, my cloak was in a heap on the group, and the pin was missing. I saw that," he pointing at the man in Erik's hands, "rat scurrying away."

"Who are you calling a rat," the man blubbered with his hand over his nose. Erik tightened his grip around his collar, not letting him get loose.

"Did you or did you not take the pin?" Erik asked, addressing the man in his grip. He squirmed around, not looking Erik in the eye, so Erik gave him another jerk.

"Okay, yes, I took it!" The man admitted, and luckily someone from the crowd pulled the accuser back before he could get his hands on thief again, who yelped and covered his face. Erik patted him down until he found the pin, which was intricately detailed in silver with precious stones placed throughout it. He gave it back to its owner, while the man in his arms seethed, "Can you blame me? I don't know what to expect in the future! This plan could go terribly wrong, and we could all end up scattered with nothing to our name. And if it works? Then what? We somehow find a way to start our lives over from scratch in a city where we have nothing of value to trade?"

Some of the crowd murmured assent, and I felt the spirit collectively fall as they realized the truth in his argument.

But then another spoke up. It was the older man from Grundale, Wilson. "That isn't true. Who do you think supplies the surface with all their necessities, like gold and granite, coal and silver, and all the elements in between? We are the only ones who know how to dig them up. If they were smart, they would try their best to get on our good side in case we do manage to succeed. And if we don't? Well, we've seen the surface, we've been shown a way out and I know I don't speak just for myself when I say that I don't intend on going back. If that King tries to send me back down to the ground, he'd have to do so after I'm dead." He stared across the crowd, as if challenging someone to argue with him. But the crowd remained silent, their eyes downcast. With my palms slightly sweaty, I made my way towards the centre of the crowd.

"I realize you all are growing nervous, and this is causing tempers to flare. But I know, I know, that we can do this. You have all proven yourself so strong. You've come to the surface, leaving everything behind and coming to an entirely new land, with new people, new plants, new adventures, new trials, and you have accepted them all. Alone, we have survived. But together, we can fight, we can win, and we can thrive."

The crowd cheered and raised their fists, and I felt something in me strengthen.

Later in the evening, we made camp. We were very close to the wall, so Erik, Croxley, and some others scoped around to find a place that would keep us close, but hidden. I noticed that Jean stuck near Croxley and volunteered to check the borders with him. I smiled as I watched them disappear into the forest together. The bushes at my back rustled as Erik joined me. I turned and leaned against him for a few moments before righting myself.

"I'm going to take first watch," he told me. I kept my gaze directed towards the forest as I said, "I'll stay up with you."

"No," he answered. "You need to get your rest. I'll be fine."

I was about to protest when a yawn took over, and I realized that I was exhausted. He was right, I hadn't been sleeping very well since, well, since I first left Stonewall. Everything has been so wild, so hectic, so crazy, that I couldn't wrap my mind around it all. Who am I kidding, I thought to myself, I still can't wrap my mind around it. But now I didn't have much of a choice;. Tomorrow morning, Croxley and Erik will infiltrate the gates and try to steal some weapons. If all things go according to plan, they will have the weapons back by midday and we can assemble around the entrance. I'm still hoping that we can settle things peacefully, that our mass presence alone will inspire an audience and convince the King to grant us our freedom, but I know that they weapons are needed as a back up. I admitted to myself that they might also add some weight to our argument.

"Fara, go to sleep." I swayed on my feet as Erik turned me around by the shoulders and pushed me gently in the direction of camp. I let my feet carry me as I went back to my sleeping arrangement, which I shared with my mother and father. My father was still up, no doubt checking on the last-minute details. I felt bad not being a part of the final preparations, but they surpassed my capabilities. I don't know anything about combat or battle. Then again, I don't know anything about assembling and leading people into rebellion, and I've seemed to do well so far. But something told me that this was different. It was time for me to let somebody else take the reigns for a change, before I ended up driving myself and everyone else off a cliff. My mother was already asleep, sprawled out with her face to the world, as if challenging it even in while she slept. I fell in beside her, the sound of her gentle breathing lulling me to the brink of sleep, but something kept me from drifting off completely. I tried to get a grasp on it, but with each breath I sunk more and more into the ground, until I lost the battle and let the darkness overcome me.

CHAPTER 38

"Let me come with you," Jean said. She and Croxley were discussing the plan to siege the gates and take the weapons, their quiet voices joining the sounds of the night-time forest through which she and Croxley were combing through. He held a branch for her to pass under, then followed behind her.

"And why would I let you?"

"Because I know Stonewall. And don't say you know it too," she said, holding her hand up to pause the argument Croxley had already opened his mouth to give, "because I've seen all of it. You've only seen the shining streets, the glistening ballrooms, the extravagant feasts. Me? Every moment I've spent up here has been in the background, cleaning up the skeletons in the closets, taking the dirty back-roads, fighting for a scrap of leftovers. I know how to navigate the ins and outs of the castle as well as all its in-betweens. Most importantly, I know how to get us into the weapon room."

"We already have a plan to get into the weapon room," Croxley replied, dismissing her, but Jean shook her head.

"It won't work. You're trying to get too many men in too fast. The guards will notice immediately. What we really need is just a two people, you and me, to open it from the inside. Once we get in and get to the weapons, we can bring in a few men at a time to help them carry everything back. But we only need two or three at most. Otherwise we will be noticed for sure."

"Why didn't you mention this earlier, when we were planning everything?"

"Because then I wouldn't be able to go. Admit it, you and Erik would probably end up going together, leaving Fara and I behind to wait for you. When are you men going to realize that women are just as capable as you are of making and carrying out plans?"

Croxley stopped walking, not sure whether to be embarrassed, ashamed, or offended.

He didn't have much time to decide, however, because at that moment, Erik stepped out of the bushes in front of them.

"Maybe when you start telling us the plans instead of always keeping them secret. Honestly, you women are so hard to understand sometimes."

Croxley and Jean looked at each other with bewilderment on their faces, both self-consciously taking a step apart.

"I want to help with your plan. Just tell me what part I have to do in order to make it work," Erik announced.

Croxley looked at Jean, and when she didn't say anything, he exclaimed with exasperation, "Come on, it's your plan. You can't expect me to be the one to explain it. What happened to women being equal?"

Jean scowled at Croxley before she began to explain her idea to Erik. "Well, it starts off with us going to the wall. Once we get in, I'll make sure Croxley and I get to the weapon's room. When we open it and the coast is clear, I can run back to the entrance. That's where I need you to be on the lookout for a signal. Once you see it, send some men to gather the weapons, and they will bring them back to camp so that everyone will be ready to fight, if need be."

Erik could tell that Jean was leaving out some parts of the plan, but decided not to push much further for fear that she would reconsider letting him in on the plan at all.

"Last question. When are we leaving?"

Jean answered, "We need to leave now."

Erik nodded, "Okay. I'll meet you there after I go back to the camp to get my men. Will that give you enough time to get in?"

"That should be fine. Just wait behind the cover of the trees for a signal from Croxley and I." She produced two small cuttings of mirror glass from her shift and flashed them, catching the starlight just right. She handed one to Erik and placed the other one back in her shift.

"Got it." Erik tucked the piece into his pocket and then placed a hand on each of their shoulders. "Good luck," he said, and they split ways.

"There they are," Jean and Croxley were crouched behind a hedge of bushes in front of the wall. They had followed the line of the wall in the direction of the gate until they spotted the beginnings of the troop's base. Set up between the hedge and the wall were a series of tents. A few men were pacing back and forth between the camp, while others were keeping a perimeter around the gate. Croxley and Jean ducked when one of the patrolling guards passed them, but they didn't have much to worry about, based on the glazed expression of the guard who was nearly dragging his sword as he walked by. After he passed, they slowly walked along the perimeter of the forest until they reached the end of the camp.

Overall, there were about 200 tents set up, and Croxley knew each tent could hold three to four men. This added up to a group of about 800, not including those sleeping outside of tents and those being housed elsewhere, such as in the wall itself or in the homes of citizens unlucky enough to have their home near the wall.

"I'd guess they probably have around 1,000 troops, give or take a few. We've got maybe 300, 350 max." Croxley said to Jean. She was scoping the outline of the base with squinted eyes, slowly scanning from left to right until she stopped. She peered closer, leaning so far forward that Croxley had to catch her before she left the cover of the forest.

"That must be it," she concluded. Croxley tried to follow her gaze but couldn't find what she was looking at.

"What," he asked.

"That's the entrance to the weapon room." She scooted closer to him until her eyes were at the same level as his. "There. See where those two walls meet? Right underneath there is a small trap door that leads to the servant runs."

Croxley wasn't looking at where she was pointing, however. He was too entranced by her presence, all too aware of how close she was to him, of her smell, of the heat coming off of her, of the way her hair was drifting into her eyes as she focused on the wall ahead. She stopped talking and looked at him, and it took a few seconds for him to shake out of his trance.

"Ah, yes, the trap door. Got it." She drew her eyebrows closer together but didn't say anything else. He cleared his throat and continued, "so, how do we get there?"

"I've been timing the guards and it seems that the longest gap between the rotations is right when the guard up ahead passes by. Either he is a bit faster than the guard behind him or the latter is slower, but either way, their spacing is uneven, which gives us the most time to pass through. Once we get past the border, we can weave through the tents. I don't think anyone is still awake, and as long as we are quiet, we won't wake anyone up."

"You know, I never would have expected you to be so covert. How did you learn about all this?"

Jean smiled mischievously with her eyes cast down as she explained, "Well, I told you I knew the ins and outs of the city, didn't I? After my first job didn't work out so well, I decided to take a break and live on the streets for a bit. I had my rounds with pickpocketing, never from any of the citizens, mind you, only the nobles. Actually," she said, looking up at him with an apologetic expression, "you were one of my first."

Croxley turned this over in his mind, trying to figure out what she was referring to because he knew it couldn't be what he immediately thought of. "Your first what?"

"When I was first learning how to pickpocket. You were walking through the street by yourself, I think delivering a message or something. Even though you weren't exactly dressed in a courtly fashion, the way you carried yourself made it all too obvious that you were from the castle. So, I decided to, ah, make a little mess of things and see if I could get my hands on some of the castle's wealth."

Croxley's eyes lit up as the memory flashed before him. "That was you? That day that I was walking through the city and a fruit stand fell over? The shop keeper accused me of bruising all his apples and wanted me to buy the whole stock. I was so busy arguing with him that I lost track of myself and thought that I misplaced my compass. But no," he leaned back from her, looking at her with amazement. "You took it!"

Jean looked at him nervously, not sure how to respond to him, when suddenly he burst out laughing.

"Hush!" She leapt towards him and covered his mouth before anyone could hear him.

"Sorry, sorry," he gained control of himself and settled down. "Sorry. I just can't believe that you took it from me. I was looking for that thing for weeks. When my father found out I had lost it, he gave me the worst beating ever. It was the first gift I had been given after officially becoming a castle messenger." He sighed wistfully, then asked, "You don't happen to still have it, do you?" He looked at her hopefully, but she shook her head.

"Sorry. I had to find a way to eat somehow."

"Oh, I see. Al-right."

"But if it makes you feel any better, I waited till the last minute before selling it. I really didn't want to. It was beautiful."

"Yes, it was."

They sat in a comfortable silence for a few minutes, watching as the guards passed by, until the guard Jean had pointed out earlier came into view again.

Now, she mouthed, and they burst out of the bushes. Sprinting through the opening, Croxley felt a burst of adrenaline rush through him, propelling him forward. He belatedly realized that he and Jean were holding hands, and gripped hers tighter as they ran at top speed towards the wall.

When they reached the tents, they wound through them carefully and swiftly, avoiding all the armour and weapons scattered outside. Croxley looked at Jean, pointing them out, and she understood the message. They could easily take these weapons back in addition to those found in the weapons room. He made a mental note to tell Erik when he came with the men to have him take some of the weapons outside along the way. Not only will it increase their supplies, but it will cripple their army. Okay, maybe not by much, but any bit can help. This internal monologue continued in his head as they ran to the wall. By the time they reached it, both Croxley and Jean were huffing and puffing, attempting to do so as silently as possible.

Once they caught some semblance of breath, Jean started pacing the wall, repeatedly looking up and down from the top of the tower to the ground. When she reached where the walls met, symbolized by a slight discolouration in the stones, she used her foot to push aside the leaves and dirt covering the ground. Croxley kept watch on the camp as she did so, hoping that the sound of her digging didn't wake anyone. Suddenly, he heard a loud creak and whipped around.

She had the trap door open slightly and was already climbing inside. She motioned for him, and he quickly climbed down the ladder to join her, letting the door shut quietly above them.

It was nearly pitch black. The only light came from small cracks in the trap door above, and since it was still night-time, that light did little more than allow Croxley to see the outline of their surroundings. As his vision adjusted, however, he realized Jean was walking down the hallway. He sped up to catch her, carefully putting his arms out in front of him in case he ran into anything.

"You need to work on this whole 'waiting' thing," he told Jean when he reached her.

"Sorry. I'm not used to having someone follow me who I'm not trying to lose." She slowed her pace down a bit and made sure Croxley was following before she turned a corner. "The weapons room is just on the right. There is normally a lantern lit in the room at all times, in case of emergency armament. It'll help us find what we are looking for."

They made it to a door at the end of the hallway, but Jean cursed when she saw it had a lock on it. "When did they put that there?"

Croxley went closer to inspect it. He picked it up and rotated it around, measuring its weight in his hand. Dropping the lock, he put his hands on the door, feeling the material. The wall around it was stone, but the door itself was of wood. "It's pretty thick, but the lock is slightly rusted. It's worth a shot," he announced.

By the time Jean realized what he was going to do, it was too late, and Croxley had rammed his body into the door. The first time it barely budged, but before she could stop him, he rammed it a second and then a third time. She grabbed onto him before he could do it again, and felt his heart beating through his chest, which was moving rapidly with his breath. He was nearly panting, but didn't move his gaze from the lock. He studied it until he regained his breath, then looked at Jean. She nodded and released him. Stepping back, he planted his feet and released a roar as he slammed into the door, which swung open with a resounding thud. Jean blinked a few times, blinded by the sudden light of the lantern. As her vision adjusted, she gasped when she found Croxley precariously stopped a few inches in front of a rack of spears, their heads all pointing in his direction. She pulled him back before he could fall into them, and he leaned against her.

"Don't let me do that again," he panted. "I feel like I was just ran over by a horse-drawn carriage."

Croxley shook himself, stretching his limbs out and cracking his neck, before he took inventory of the room. Inside, there was a multitude of spears and swords, most of which were basic army standard. There were also a small selection of bows and arrows, as well as a few exclusive weapons, such as a mace and a flail. After he had made sure he had a good count of all the weapons, he signalled to Jean that they should leave the room. They ran back down the hallways and made it to the trap door, Jean climbing up first and slowly opening the door, peering out through the small slit to make sure the coast was clear. When she made sure that there were no guards in sight, she climbed out, holding it open for Croxley while he came up.

Croxley looked at the forest across the way, searching for some sign of Erik and his men. His eyes scanned through the trees until they found what they were looking for, a glint of moonlight off of Erik's mirror piece. Croxley waited for Jean to flash her piece, but she held up her hand, mouthing the word no. She pointed to the guard walking the perimeter, and he understood that she was waiting for the gap again. But after waiting for a full rotation, he realized that the guards must have switched while they were in the weapons room, because the gap no longer existed. He looked back at Jean in alarm and saw that she was biting her lip, obviously trying to come up with a plan. But time was short, and Croxley knew that the more time they spent trying to come up with a plan, the higher the chance that they would get caught.

"Jean, we need to risk it. If we time it just right, we might be able to get through."

She frowned but nodded in agreement. After the next guard passed by, Jean flashed her glass. Bursting through the forest came Erik, followed by three other strong men, moving surprisingly fast for their size. They made it nearly all the way when Croxley heard a shout. He saw the men's eyes widen as they realized they were spotted, but they kept running at Erik's command.

By the time they reached Jean, she was ready and had the trap door lifted. The men nearly jumped down the hole, Croxley and Erik close behind. Jean pulled the door down above her head, and the last thing Croxley saw before it closed was a group of troops running past the door.

They waited in silence, not even daring to breathe, as they waited for the men's shadows to pass by the door. It seemed like an eternity, but finally the guards moved on, apparently not knowing to search the ground for the entrance. Croxley blessed the slaves and all their secret passages. When they could no longer hear any sounds coming from the guards, Croxley turned around and looked at the men Erik had brought with him.

"This is Knox from Weldar, Garvan from Laurevell, and Calder from

Sprokil," Erik introduced the men with him, and they all nodded successively.

"Glad you could make it," Croxley joked. "There are plenty of spears and swords in the weapons room for us to use. I don't know how many you can carry," Croxley's statement was met with an amused look from each of the men, so he decided to keep going, "but there are nearly enough weapons for all of our people. Jean and I saw some weapons scattered throughout the camp that we can pick up on the way out, but I don't know if we will get a chance, now that they know we are here.

Erik nodded, "I will keep that in mind. Now, where is the weapons room?"

"This way," Jean said, taking them through the corridors until they reached the room. Croxley saw Erik stop to study the door, and when he looked back at Croxley with his eyebrows raised, Croxley just shrugged.

As soon as they entered, the men didn't waste any time piling up the weapons. Croxley noticed that they brought with them large pieces of fabric onto which to lay the weapons down, and when the pile was large enough, they wrapped them up and bound them with some animal skin. Smart, Croxley thought. Each man would be able to carry around 50 spears or 30 swords, so between them all they should only have to make one trip. In a short matter of time, they had all their weapons loaded and began to make their way back to the entrance.

"I'll open the door and make sure the coast is clear," Jean said, climbing the ladder and silently pulling herself up and through the door, closing it behind her. They all waited in silence until she pulled the door open again a few moments later.

"Go now," she whispered down. "They sent a search party out for us, but they haven't yet woken up the rest of the troops. I think they are still trying to figure out who we were and if it's worth it to sound the alarm. We should consider ourselves lucky. Right now, they are on the southern edge of the forest, pretty close to our camp, which means as soon as we clear the opening, we need to steer them in the opposite direction. We should run north east. Once we reach the thicker parts of the woods, it should be easy enough to lose them. We can reconvene at the camp and then distribute the weapons."

Croxley had to admit, she came up with a good plan, and he couldn't think of any immediate faults. He didn't know how the other men felt about following her command, but no one spoke up against her.

They all handed her their packs and she pulled them up, leaning them against the wall. As each man made it up, they put their packs back on and made their way through the camp. It was much harder to be both swift and silent due to the heavy load of clanking weapons on their backs, so they had to sacrifice speed for silence. They decided not to risk their lot by trying to take all the weapons they came across, but any notable weapons, such as a large mace and pointed club, were added to their numbers. Erik and his men were leading the way, and when he turned around to check on Jean and Croxley, he noticed that they weren't carrying any weapons. Why didn't they pack anything, he thought to himself. He wondered what they were up to, knowing that they hadn't conveyed to him the whole of their plan earlier this morning in the forest.

As soon as they reached the clearing, Knox, Garvan, and Calder all sprinted to the opposite end of the forest. As was expected, the guards took immediate notice, and after they realized what was on their backs, they sounded an alarm and started chasing after the men. Erik turned to Croxley, and told him, "Whatever you are up to, I wish you good luck," before sprinting off to join his men. When he reached the border, he turned back to see Croxley and Jean dash out into the open. They succeeded in distracting some of the guards trailing Erik before running off back towards the gate, making a ruckus and calling for the attention of all the troops. Men came rushing out of the tents, causing chaos as the guards who were chasing Erik and his men suddenly had their view blocked by a crowd of confused, adrenaline-pumped soldiers, and the guards quickly lost track of their target as they wove through the masses of people. It didn't help that it was approaching dawn, so the moon was lowered and the stars fading, making it nearly pitch black outside, the flicker of their lanterns swallowed by the darkness. Erik lingered a bit longer, hoping to know the fate of his friends, but Knox put a hand on his shoulder, urging him to leave. He gave one last glance back before he turned and ran into the darkness of the forest.

CHAPTER 39

This morning I woke in a panic. Having gotten use to waking with Erik at my side, I immediately noticed his absence as I groggily rose to the rising sun. A jolt of anxiety swept through me as I realized that he never came back from his morning watch. I frantically looked around, searching for his mat nearby, but it was still rolled up with the rest of his supplies, minus his sword. So he came back for his sword and then left without telling me. My mother must have heard my panicked breathing, because she rolled over and pushed herself up into a seated position, looking at me with half-shut eyes.

"Faradene, what's wrong?" She asked me.

"Erik didn't return from watch last night," I choked, fear tightening my throat.

"Now Faradene, don't work yourself up. He may have decided to rest somewhere else, or perhaps your father has already snatched him up to get things ready. I'm sure he is fine." I highly doubted that what my mother said was true, but it was calming to hear her words none-the-less.

"I'm going to find father," I told her, running off in search of my father in the hopes that Erik would be with him.

After a few moments of franticly dashing around the camp, I found my father speaking to one of the elders from another colony.

"Father," I ran up to him, breathless. I'm sure I looked like a ragged mess, because the elder to whom he was speaking looked startled by my appearance and took a step back. I ignored this and continued my interrogation. "Father! Have you seen the Prince?"

"Faradene, calm yourself. What has you so worried?" My father put his hands on my shoulders to steady me, and I sunk into their strong grip until he was nearly holding me up.

"I can't find Erik!" my father raised an eyebrow and I realized I was still speaking quickly. I took a breath and started over. "I can't find Erik. I was hoping that he would be with you."

"He isn't with me, but I can tell you where he is. He left early this morning with three other men. They went with Croxley and Jean to retrieve the weapons." I looked incredulously at my father and the absurdly calm manner in which he said this. I opened my mouth in protest but closed it when he narrowed his eyes. "Their plan was strong and the timing was perfect. It would have been wrong for me to not allow them to go. Regardless, they would have gone any-ways. This way is safer, I assure you." He let go of my shoulders and pulled me into an embrace. "Have faith in your father, have faith in your friends, and have faith in Erik. We all have to make sacrifices, Fara. Trust me when I tell you that Erik will do everything that he can to make it back to you." I let a few silent tears fall into my fathers broad chest, inhaling the familiar scent of his cloak. Smoke, dirt, and sweat. When I had control of myself, I pulled away and smiled at him.

He turned his body to the side and I noticed the elder was still standing there, looking impatient. My father extended his arm in my direction and introduced me as his daughter. "Faradene, this is Enric, one of the councilmen from the Dirskin colony."

I extended my hand to shake his, while at the same time sniffing my nose, and he recoiled. My father winked at me and my still racing heart slowed a bit in ease.

Erik and his men came loaded with weapons in the early morning. I was running out to greet them when I noticed that Jean and Croxley were missing. I slowed down to a stop while my mind ran over all the possible explanations for their absence. I had to stop it from wandering too far before it took me down a dark path. I was sure that Erik would have a good explanation. That they had to take a different path back, that they were just behind them. Anything would do.

When Erik came close enough, he wrapped his arms around me in an embrace but I remained stiff. "Where are Croxley and Jean?" I asked.

"They had a plan of their own. I'm not sure where they are right now, but if I had to guess, I would say they were in the castle."

"What do you mean, in the castle?" I couldn't believe him. How did he not know where they were? Weren't they together?

"When we were running away, they left the group and went their own direction." I was ready to unleash a stream of rather impolite words, but he put his hand up to stop me. "I didn't know what they were going to do until the last minute. And without them, I don't think we would have been able to escape and make it back."

That reminded me of the other reason I was angry at him.

"Why didn't you tell me you were leaving?" I accused as I hit him repeatedly in the chest. He took it all unflinchingly until I was finished, my shaking hands resting above his heart, the beat thudding under my touch. "I didn't want to wake you. Now wait, before you get angry, you have to admit, if I woke you up and told you where I was going, you would have insisted in following. Not only that, even if I convinced you to stay here, you would've been up all night with worry. You needed the rest. And I knew I would be back." I pulled away from him but he pulled me back in and planted a kiss on the top of my head before letting me go.

I clamped my mouth shut to keep my thoughts from escaping, trying to convince myself to hear what he was saying. We walked back in silence as I wrestled over this in my mind, finally coming to terms with the situation. I wasn't okay with it, but at least I understood.

We met my father among the goats and sheep, going through the supplies to prepare for the day. With him were Heath and Mr. Harris. I haven't seen them much since we returned to Cethin, although I've had a few chances to talk with them while we were travelling from Cethin to Stonewall. Mostly they spent their time with the other Nether leaders. It turns out they made fast friends with the leaders of the colonies they had to recruit, which doesn't surprise me in the least with Heath, but I was a little surprised that Mr. Harris was so amicable among the Nethers.

"Looks like you had some luck," my father joked in reference to the weapons as he dusted off his hands and approached us. I was always amazed at the way my father handled stress. He was able to make jokes in the worst of it all and make everyone feel safe. I, on the other hand, seemed to forget how to swim when the water turned rough. "Did we get enough for everyone?"

"I'd say they did! Look at all them swords! And that mace," Heath eyed the mace longingly, and I figured that we'd be seeing him wield it later on in the day. I had no doubt that he knew how to do some real damage with that weapon.

Mr. Harris stood by and ran his finger down the blades of one of the swords and said simply, "These are fine weapons. Army grade."

My father inspected the spears and the bows, kneeling down to feel the points. He stood up and asked, "Should I gather everyone together?"

Erik nodded, "Yes. We will stay here and organize all the weapons."

"Here, Father, I'll help you," I said, joining his side. I felt useless for having slept while everyone else was busy getting things together, and although I knew I needed the rest, that didn't give me an excuse to slack off now.

My father and I made our way through the camp, sending everyone to where Erik and his men had unloaded the weapons. It took us a good two hours to get to everyone, as we were frequently having to stop and answer questions, ease people's worries, and size them up to make sure they got the appropriate weapons. Erik was giving basic instruction on how to use the weapons, but with such little time, we would most likely end up depending more on strength than skill. Years in the mines made for thick bones and strong muscles, and an ability to wield tools with ease. In a sense, our oppression might very well lead to our success.

"No, that sword it much too large for you. Yes, you may be able to carry it, but how does your swing look? Exactly," my father was trying to convince a the young, rather thin man to switch out a sword nearly as large as himself for a smaller dagger, but the young man seemed to have his sight, and pride, set on the larger weapon. However, when he tried to swing it, he could barely heft it off the ground, and the swing was so wild it left him off balance. I had an idea, and returned from the weapons pile with a bow and arrow.

"Why don't you try this," I offered the bow and arrow up to him, but he just looked at it skeptically. We hadn't had many people take up the bows and arrows, because other than the occasional slingshot toy that the younger boys fashioned out of leftover scraps of leather, there wasn't any equivalent to bows in the colonies.

"What's your name?" I asked as the man inspected the weapon and played around with it in his hand.

"Derrin," he said, slinging the arrow and pulling the bow back. I ducked as he slid his aim over my head, but slowly rose in astonishment as I watched the arrow sail across the field and into the trunk of a tree. "Wow. That felt good," he said, putting the bow down.

219

"How did you do that," I asked, still shocked that his arrow ran true.

"Well, I'm from Weldar, and in the centre of our colony is a large harp. I used to play around and use the strings to fire rocks and such at my brothers. When I got older, because I was a bit, well, scrawnier, than the other boys, I was trained as the colony's musician. The shape of the harp is very similar to this bow," he shrugged, embarrassed.

"Do you know if anyone else who came with you would know how to use the bow?" I asked, suddenly excited.

"Most of the women of my colony were trained on the harp. Many of them remained home to care for the children, but I can find the ones who came with me," he offered.

"That would be very helpful, Derrin. Thank you!" I smiled at him and he blushed, nearly sprinting away from me to find the women.

"I think he likes you," Erik teased, doing up from behind me.

"Does that make you jealous?" I teased back. I leaned into him, feeling safe in his warmth.

Is this the calm before the storm? I thought to myself. In just under an hour, we would be at the wall, either fighting for our lives or negotiating with the King. It's really the same thing, isn't it? We would still be fighting for our lives, just with words rather than weapons.

"If everyone could gather round," my father called us all together, and the crowd quieted. I looked around to see that everyone had a weapon of some kind in their hand. Heath was lovingly caressing his mace, while some of the less mature men were aiming their swords at each other, play-fighting with their new weapons. The older members of the group looked more solemn, some even holding their spears and swords away from them as if they could separate themselves from the violence their weapons would inevitably bring.

"We've been brought together here for a purpose greater than ourselves," my father begun. His voice carried over the crowd, taking his message to each individual. "Centuries ago, we were forced to live underground, exiled from society on the basis of our wealth, our jobs, our appearance, our disabilities. While those on the surface have prospered, we have toiled away underground, making the best out of the worst situation. We have been beaten and abused, mistreated and taken advantage of. But now, because of my daughter, Faradene," he extended a gesture in my direction, "we have all been brought together to fight for a better future." My father called me to the center, but my legs didn't seem to be able to carry me. I felt a hand take mine, and I looked to see my mother holding my hand tight, tears in her eyes.

"I'm so proud of you," she said, and holding my hand like she did when I was still a child, she brought me to my father in the centre of all the colonists. Although my knees were shaking, I walked with my head held high, and when I spoke, I was relived that my voice was strong.

"Over half a year ago, I was brought to the surface as a slave. It was there that I learned that I wasn't alone, that my people weren't alone. There were many others like us, who suffered at the hands of the guards, who toiled away in the name of the King, who never got to see the light of day because we were deemed unworthy. Although I grieved that there were so many others who shared our fate, I also found hope. I knew that, if we all found each other, we would have a standing chance against the King and his men. We could make a case against him and earn our freedom. Not only will we win the right to live on the surface, where we belong, but we will also have the opportunity to mend the broken bridge between ourselves and our brothers and sisters on the surface. We will replacing all the prejudice, the lies, the stereotypes, with the truth.

It is my wish that we may achieve this without ever drawing our swords, readying our arrows," as I said this, I looked at Derrin and the group of women he had organized, all armed with bows and arrows. I looked at Heath with his mace, Erik with his sword, my father standing with our family's staff, and everyone else with their weapons in hand. "In a perfect world, it would be so. But this isn't a perfect world, which is why we are now prepared to fight. I thank each and every one of you for putting your faith in me, and I can only hope that I will prove to you that it was worth it. So today, may we fight for our rights, may we fight for our honour, and may we fight for our people!" I raised my sword and everyone around me did the same, cheering.

We were ready.

CHAPTER 40

"Wow. That's a lot of soldiers." We had made it to the border of the forest, and I could see the camp of the King's army. Along the way, Erik had filled us in on some of the information he gathered during his weapon run, and although he told me that there had been around a thousand soldiers, the number didn't look so overwhelming in my head.

"We should still stick to the plan," I asserted. Earlier on, we had agreed that we would first send out a small party made of myself, Erik, my father, a few other Nether leaders, and some of the newly farmed archery unit. We would present our case, ask for an audience with the King, and hopefully everything would run smoothly after that. If not, well, that's why we have the weapons. Hopefully the element of surprise will give us some advantage, being that there were at least three times the amount of soldiers as there were Nethers.

"Faradene, before you go," my mother came up to me through the crowd, "I have something to tell you." My mother took my hands in hers and looked at my father, who nodded at her.

"I wanted to tell you the origin of your name," she said to me. I was confused at her timing. Couldn't it wait for when we weren't heading straight into battle? But knowing my mother, she had a reason for telling me this now. "Faradene is a name that has been passed down from generations on my side of the family. It was the name of your great, great, great grandmother, a powerful warrior from before the Purge. The storytellers refer to her as Fara. She fought against invaders trying to enter Ahrenia, back before we had all been sent underground. She never failed to fight for justice, and when the King decided to banish us all to the colonies, she stood up against him. Because of this, her entire family was sent to live in the colonies alongside the people she so courageously sought to protect.

She was a war hero, known for her beauty, her loyalty, and her strong will. From the moment you were born, your father and I knew that you were something special. And I am so proud to say that you have earned your name, that you have lived out Faradene's legacy." My mother had tears in her eyes at the conclusion of her story, and I couldn't help but feel mine water as well. She gave me a strong, firm hug, and I held on tight, knowing this may very well be the last time I saw my mother. When she released me, we both had tears streaming down our faces, contrasting the smiles on our lips. She kissed the top of my head, wished me luck, and went back into the rest of the group to finish the last preparations.

As I geared up to enter the field, I couldn't help but feel my heart swell. This whole time I had thought that my parents had always bemoaned having a daughter like me, who couldn't contribute to her fair share of work, who couldn't seem to do anything but get herself in trouble and make trouble for everyone else, whose mouth seemed to run faster than her mind and somehow managed to find the perfect words to cause harm to those she loved. But I could see now that all their punishment, all their admonitions and overprotection, came out of their love for me, their concern for my safety, their belief that I was made for something more. I wasn't going to prove them wrong.

I walked into the field with my head held high, Erik in step next to me, my father and the Nether leaders behind us, and the archers in the back. It didn't take long for the soldiers to spot us, and in just a few moments we were surrounded by weapons. We made no motion to draw our own, kept partially hidden in order to not appear as threats as well as to keep them from being taken from us immediately. A man on a horse approached us, and I assumed he was a general of some sorts by the proud way which he carried himself.

"Ah, Prince Erik. So you have come to turn yourself in?" He said to Erik, and then turned his eyes to me, raking them up and down my body in a way that left me feeling utterly violated and had my father in the background growling angrily. "So this is the wench that convinced you to leave to castle, abandon all of your people, and become a traitor to your kingdom? I think you could have chosen better," he laughed, keeping his eyes locked on mine. I kept my face hard, refusing to let his comments in.

"We have come for an audience with the King," I announced, my voice unwavering and hard. I have lived with this kind of abuse my entire life, and I wasn't going to let this man, or any man, for that matter, scare me any longer.

The man looked amused by my demand. "Do you honestly think the King would waste his time with you?"

"I'm sure my father would want to hear what his people have to say. And if not them, at least the words of his son, the Prince of Ahrenia," Erik said.

"Ha! You don't have any right to call yourself a Prince now. You are no better than the Nethers themselves, just as dirty and stupid as the rest of them. Besides, the King has no regard for you as anything more than an enemy of the nation. In fact, he has put a ransom on your head. 100,000 gold coins for anyone who brings you in, dead or alive," the general threatened. "And I'm pretty sure he would prefer you, well, dead, more than alive." As he said this, the troops surrounding us closed in, pushing us tighter together. The archers all faced outward, their backs to us and their bows towards the guards, while the rest of us drew our weapons.

"How amusing. You think you might stand a chance. Well, I've been out here for a week with nothing to entertain me, so go ahead. I could use some entertainment. Men, attack!"

At that same moment, Derrin blew on the horn he had carried with him, the signal that called the rest of the Nethers out of the forest. In seconds, the field was flooded with troops of both sides, and the fighting began. I watched as swords swung, arrows flew, and spears stabbed at warriors all around me. I had never before seen such a scene of violence, and it had me rooted to the ground. I couldn't seem to tear myself away from the bloodshed unfolding before my eyes.

"Fara! Watch out!" I turned around just in time to see a guard running at me, his sword drawn and a sick smile pasted on his face. I blocked his strike just in time, and parried his offensive swings until an opportune moment came for me to lunge, slicing open a long gash down his side. He staggered for a few moments, giving me an opening to deliver a death strike, but I couldn't bring myself to do it. As he righted himself, he brought his sword down on me with such force that I barely had time to block it, and I had to use all my strength to keep his blade from reaching my chest. He pushed down harder and harder, and I howled in pain as my muscles ripped, pushing back with all my might. My trembling arms were about to give in, and I knew he could tell by the fire in his eyes, the sudden increase in his focus. Then, without warning, the light went out, and he slumped forward, nearly landing on me before I leapt out of the way and he hit the ground. My heart was racing and I wasn't able to make sense of what just happened until I saw Heath standing where the man had just been.

"Fara, are you okay?" He shouted over the clanging of weapons.

"Yes, yes!" I had to repeat it a few times before I could get the shaking answer out of my throat, which had been sealed in fear.

He nodded and focused his sword on a man lunging towards him, and I shook myself from my nerves, berating myself for my cowardice. Fara, this is war. You can't be soft. As soon as I told myself this, I was charged by another man, this one smaller, and I planted my feet firmly in the ground, ready to fight.

"Come around this way." Croxley was following Jean as she navigated through the tunnels of the castle. After ditching the guards that were following them, they made their way towards the castle to see if they could find the servants and release them.

"You never know what the King is capable of," Jean had told Croxley when she was explaining her plan to him earlier. "He might just decide that the best way to end the revolt is by taking it out on all the servants from the colonies. I want to make sure he doesn't lay a hand on any of the girls that were with me."

They had been navigating through the tunnels for a few hours, and Croxley was amazed at the network that had been underneath Stonewall this whole time. The mischief Erik and I would have gotten into if we would have known these tunnels were here, he thought to himself. He chuckled as he remembered some of the more dangerous things he and Erik had done, but stopped short when he saw Jean's hand shoot up.

"Shhh," she hushed, craning her neck around the corner, listening for anything that might be coming. After a few moments, she motioned her fingers towards her. "Al-right, this way. We are almost to the corridor that enter into the kitchen."

"Once we get there, we should have a straight route to the prison, where the girls will most likely be kept. I'm hoping that the number of guards here in the castle will be lower because of the rebellion," Croxley said.

They made the rest of the trip in silence, listening for any approaching footsteps, as well as the sound of people overhead. They were nearly there when they saw the flicker of a lantern.

Croxley and Jean searched frantically for a hiding spot, but there were no nooks or crannies that could protect them from the lantern's revealing blaze. They backtracked a bit so that they were concealed behind the corner of an intersection between two tunnels. This hid them well enough at the moment, but if the lantern-wielder decided to go down their tunnel, they would be spotted.

The lantern made its way to the centre of the intersection, and the sudden bright light blinded Croxley momentarily. He blinked his eyes rapidly to adjust, and as they cleared, he was shocked to find Jean running towards it. A few moments later, when he had regained full control of his sight, he was equally shocked to see that it was held by an old woman wearing the basic garb of a laundry maid.

"My goodness, child, what are you doing here?" The old woman asked Jean.

"Winnerva, I could ask the same of you!" Jean answered in a hushed voice.

"You know me. I always try to come down here. I've been so busy running back and forth between the nobles that I haven't had a chance to check on the tunnels. Honestly, why they have to change their gowns three times a day is a mystery to me."

"Croxley," Jean said, turning back to him, "this is Winnerva. Remember when I said I was living on the street? Well, after I discovered this tunnel system, I decided to make it my home and live down here. I mean, I'm from Grundale, so it fits, right? Well, one day I was wandering the tunnels and I ran into Winnerva. She took me under her wing and helped me find a better way to live, one that didn't involve stealing or beatings or any of those other things I've had to go through. She's done this with a lot of different people she's found under here. She's made it a kind of refuge."

"Ah, the girl flatters. I'm just an old croon that can't seem to stop getting involved in other people's business. Well, that, and I happen to have a direct line to the castle. I'm on good terms with most of the staff there, so sometimes I can convince the cock to give me leftover scraps every now and then to feed to all the scrawny misfits I find down here, like Jean. And every so often I meet a semi-decent noble that wouldn't mind a foot servant or assistant, so I help these young's get back on their feet with a respectable future. How did Madam Thrope treat you, by the way?" She asked Jean.

"Very well, Winnerva. I was her foot servant for quite some time, but sadly she fell ill and passed away. After that, I found a job at an inn, but that didn't work out, so I ended up back at the castle."

"I'm so sorry to hear that, child," Winnerva expressed, putting her hand on Jean's shoulder for a few moments before she turned to Croxley. "I know you. You're that messenger boy, the Prince's best friend. Everyone up there is looking for you," she said.

"I know. That's part of the reason we are sneaking around down here. Do you happen to know what's going on? Regarding the King and the rebellion," Croxley asked, hoping to get any inside information that might make their near-suicide mission a bit easier.

"Well, nearly all the guards have been sent to the gate, so the castle is relatively peaceful, except for the nobles who think they can raid the wine cellar and drink themselves beyond reason. Mathelda and the staff have been kept busy cleaning up after these parties, so some of the older servants like myself are stuck doing all the rest of the work in the house."

"What about the girls who were imprisoned? The ones who tried to escape?" Jean asked anxiously.

"They were taken out of the jail and moved to one of the rooms in the eastern tower, where guards are always on patrol in front of their room."

"That could make things a lot more difficult, or a lot easier," Croxley mused.

"Well, there is only one way to find out," Winnerva said, slowly turning herself around. Croxley wondered how old she was, and just how much she had seen here at the castle.

He followed in the wake of this mysterious little woman and her lantern as she guided he and Jean out of the tunnels and into the castle.

Ascending into the kitchen, Croxley noticed that there was an absence of clacking utensils and cooking-ware. Normally, the kitchen was a cacophony of chopping and orders and hissing kettles. Today, there wasn't even the sound of soup simmering in the pot over the fire.

"What happened here?" Croxley asked.

"Well, after you and Jean left the castle, you started a small riot. When the guards were moving the the group of servant girls from the prison to the tower, one of them managed to get away and reach the servant's quarters. By the time the guards caught up with her, she had spread the news that Jean and Fara were going to liberate all the Nethers. After that, well, I'm sure you can imagine the chaos that ensued. You've given them hope.

Word travelled quickly through the castle, and soon all the Nether servants had gone on strike, and even some of the non-Nethers teamed up with them. Since this happened, there has been no one to help in the kitchen, no one to help do the laundry, no one to do any of the chores. A few of us older ones stuck around, because where else would we go? And besides, staying here allows me to keep an eye on everything."

"Where did they all go? After they went on strike," Jean asked excitedly.

"They took up residence in the old ruins of the stables. They've been camping out there for nearly two weeks. The King has sent a few rounds of guards to the stables to try and bully them into coming back, but they put up a good fight and the King just doesn't have enough man power right now in the city with almost all of his men surrounding the wall."

"Croxley, we need to join up with them," Jean told Croxley. He nodded.

"I know, I was thinking the same thing. But first, we need to save the rest of the girls in the tower." Croxley then turned to Winnerva. "Winnerva, do you know which tower the girls are located? And where we could possibly get a key?"

"They are in the north wing. As far as a key, I can't help you there. I wouldn't know where to look, but my best guess is that it would be with the King." Winnerva held up a hand to silence them, and cocked her head to the side. She listened for a few heartbeats, then said, "Hush now, you have to go. Someone is coming."

Jean took Winnerva's hand, whispered her thanks, and ran with Croxley towards the King's throne room.

"I haven't been to the throne room since my evaluation," Jean murmured quietly. "To be honest, it's making me nervous."

Croxley thought guiltily about all the evaluations he had attended, sitting through them with disinterest. For him, it was only a chore. But for those under inspection, it must have been nerve-racking. A simple wave of the King's hand could determine the job you had for the rest of your life, something that could make the difference between being a guard for the castle or being a garbage collector.

He remembered, as well, the pain he saw in Fara's eyes when he had to feign indifference to her fate. The way she had looked at him, as if he had turned her over to the wolves without a second thought. Well, it must have seemed like that to her.

He and Jean slowly made their way through the empty throne room, and Croxley wondered where the King was. He was almost always in the throne room. The only times he left was to sleep, dine, and fight. Oh no, thought Crolxey, he must've gone to the wall. Croxley made a silent plea for the health of his friends on the outside of the wall, then turned his mind to focus on where the King would place the key.

A distant memory tickled the back of his mind while his eyes scanned the room. They stopped at the foot of the throne, and although he couldn't see anything, he wasn't able to tear his eyes away from it. He simply felt like there was something there. He studied it, looking for some kind of clue, but the only thing out of the ordinary was the rug under the throne, which was a little crumbled.

Suddenly, the memory revealed itself, and he watched a faded scene play out in his mind of him and the Prince playing around the throne when they were children. The King had been busy at a council meeting, or rather, the time when the King told everyone what they had to do, and Prince Erik was sitting on the throne.

"This will be me one day," he announced in his high pitched, seven year old voice. "And I'll be the meanest, strongest, most powerful King there is."

Croxley was sitting at the foot of the throne, picking at the edge of the rug, when he noticed something underneath the it.

"Hey Erik, what's that," he had asked, interrupting the daydreams of his friend.

"What? I don't know." Erik jumped off the throne and knelt next to his friend. They both inspected what looked like a small door underneath the back leg of the throne. They looked at each other, their eyes ablaze, thrilled by the new mystery to solve. They ran behind the throne and tried to push it forward, using all of their seven-year-old strength, but it didn't move one budge.

They were huffing and puffing from the effort, but they didn't give up. They pushed once more, just barely getting the leg off the door, when suddenly the King appeared from behind them.

"What are you doing," he fumed, his eyes crazed and his face contorted in anger. He grabbed Erik by the arm and pulled him back, lifting him into the air, dangling him in front of his face. "Do not touch this. Ever!"

Croxley just stood nearby, watching Erik try to hold back the tears forming in his eyes. He looked away, not wanting to see his friend lose face. From that point on, Croxley was always wary of displeasing the King.

Now, in the room again, Croxley walked to the corner of the throne. He pulled back the rug, and sure enough, there was the door. The leg of the throne had already been moved, no longer covering the door.

"Jean, come here," he said, calling her over.

She wandered over, and looked in astonishment at the door. "Is that what I think it is? Where does it go?"

"I don't know, but whatever is down there is important. The key to the tower might be in there," Croxley told her.

She focused on it as she joined Croxley's side, as if trying to decide if it was real or not. Croxley opened it and saw a staircase leading down. "Shall we?" He stepped down into the room and was about to call Jean down when he noticed the flicker of a lantern.

"Wait up there," he whispered to Jean before quietly descending back down.

As he made his way around the corner, he saw a figure in the center of the room, standing next to a large pedestal. He couldn't quite figure out what it was on top of the pedestal, until the light from the lantern flickered across it. It was a jewel the size of Croxley's fist, a bright blue shade that seemed to radiate from inside. The figure's back was to him, and he was about to find a place to hide when they grabbed the jewel and spun around.

"Lena!" Croxley couldn't hold back his cry of astonishment. At the same time, Lena let out a hiss of anger.

"You! What are you doing here?"

"I should be asking the same of you!"

Lena shrugged. "Well, there's no point in hiding it. I'm taking the source of Ahrenia's wealth."

"What?" Croxley couldn't seem to find anything else to say.

"You mean you didn't know? Here, I'll give you a little history lesson. Throughout the neighboring lands, there are tales of Ahrenia's wealth, tales of all the different gems and jewels that have been found in your mines. A few centuries ago, Ahrenia found this beauty right here," she paused, rotating it in the lantern light. It caught the light and refracted it throughout the room, dancing across Lena's face like a mask. "Wrought with greed, the King at the time became obsessed with finding more jewels like this. And although they came up with many smaller, less impressive stones, he was never satisfied. So he sent all the poor, the disabled, the criminals, anyone he saw as expendable, to the mines in the quest for a jewel greater than this one. He told the people that it was a Purge of sorts, and he would only let them back on the surface if they could find a stone of even greater beauty. Obviously, it was never found, but he died before the mines were shut down, and all those people were left down in the mines, with no one bothering to bring them back up."

Croxley tried to wrap his mind around this. It went against all he had been told about the origin of the Nethers. Either way, no matter what the true story, sentencing a mass of people to life underground was wrong, he reminded himself. But to think that all of this prejudice, all of this war, was because of some greedy King's quest for more riches? And to be told this by a foreigner? "How do you know all this?" Croxley demanded.

"Everyone else knows it. But all you Ahrenians have been brainwashed into thinking you are better than everyone else, including some of your own people. It's a pity, really. Your country has so much potential, and its all wasting away underground." Lena put the jewel in her cloak. "Well, that's enough story time for now. I'm going to take this gem and go back to my home country. You all have fun with your civil war here."

"Wait, stop!" Croxley blocked the entrance and drew his sword against her. "I can't let you take that." He pushed her back against the corner of the room, and she put her hands up, fear in her eyes. But Croxley watched the fear changed into amusement as her gaze traveled over his shoulder.

"How about I offer you a trade?" She said, and Croxley turned around slowly, keeping his sword trained on Lena until his eyes found what she was looking at.

"Jean!" Jean had a knife pressed against her throat by a guard, the same one Croxley had seen going in and out of Lena's room before.

"I'll have Bentley release Jean if you forget this whole thing and let me, with the gem in tow, leave this country," Lena offered with a slick glean in her eyes.

Croxley looked between the gem and Jean. He felt as though he was being forced to chose between his nation and the girl he☐loved? His mind filled in the blank, and he realized that he did love Jean, just as much as he hated what the gem symbolized. If this was the reason so many people had been banished underground, if this was the reason Ahrenia had been split for so long, he believed that Ahrenia would have a better future without it.

Bentley pushed the blade harder against Jean's throat and she gasped. That sound spurred Croxley into making his decision.

"First release her, and then I'll let you go," Croxley told Lena, lowering his sword only slightly. She smirked in triumph as she motioned for Bentley to release Jean. He shoved her towards Croxley, who had to drop his sword in order to catch her from falling.

"I knew you would chose her over the gem. You always were a sap, Croxley," Lena said, picking up Croxley's sword and running to the exit. "Oh, and good luck with your little rebellion," she threw over her shoulder as she and Bentley ran up the stairs and out of the room. Croxley inspected Jean's neck, looking for any wounds, but only finding the scar on her neck from their encounter with Mathelda. "Are you okay?" He asked her, still holding her in his arms.

"I'm fine, I'm fine. Actually," she said, pulling something out of her pocket, "I'm more than okay. I think I got the key to the tower." She held up a key and smiled. "I snatched it from that guard when he had me in his grip."

Croxley could think of nothing to do but to kiss her. Yes, I definitely love this girl.

CHAPTER 41

I wiped the sweat from my eyes as I stopped to catch a breath. We were fighting in waves, and I had just been replaced, so I dragged myself back to our camp. It was now well into the afternoon, and still, there was no end in sight. In the beginning, we had been doing well off, surprise giving us the upper hand, but no matter how you looked at it, we were outnumbered. We couldn't keep fighting for much longer, and I didn't know how much more death I could handle. Every time I heard a scream or a shout, I cringed, hoping that it wasn't from any Nether. But that didn't mean I wanted the soldiers to die, either. With each soldier that I struck down, I felt myself grow heavier and heavier.

I tried to eat something to restore my energy back at the camp, but as I walked past scores of wounded Nethers, I decided that I couldn't stomach any food. Instead, sat at the edge of the camp, cleaning off my sword. I felt someone come up behind me and spun around, startled, my nerves still fried from the fighting. It was Wilson, holding some bandages and a water canteen.

"Miss Fara, are you okay?" He handed me the flask and I took a small sip, testing whether or not I could at least handle water. Finding that I was suddenly parched, I drank it down in one gulp, belatedly realizing that I was incredibly thirsty.

"Yes, I'm fine. A few scratches, but nothing too bad." He offered his bandages but I refused. "No, save your bandages for those who need them. I'm sure more will be coming in."

"Yes, I'm afraid so." He sighed and sat down next to me. "War is a terrible thing."

"And it could all be avoided if the King would just give us an audience," I announced dispassionately. It was taking too much strength to be concerned about anything other than survival at the moment.

"Things that are worth fighting for most often aren't easily won," he concluded, and we just sat in silence as I sipped the rest of the water from the canteen.

I was scanning the battlefield when my eyes caught movement from the left side. A large crowd was coming down from behind the gate. My heart sunk when it occurred to me that it must be more soldiers coming in. We can't handle any more soldiers, I thought. I stood up and watched them march down the hill, heading straight towards our camp. I grew alarmed at the thought of them attacking us here, taking out all the wounded and the tired. Even the worst war criminal would frown upon that tactic.

But as they came closer, I noticed that they weren't wearing any armour. What is going on? My battle-spent mind wasn't able to process what I saw before me, until it recognized Croxley and Jean at the front of the group.

I leapt up and ran towards them, somehow finding the energy deep within to spur me forwards.

By the time I reached them, I was panting heavily.

"Fara! Are you okay?" Jean checked my arm, which had stopped bleeding but looked admittedly angry.

"I'm fine, I'm fine," I gasped. "What are you doing here?" I managed to get out in between breaths.

"We started a rebellion. In the castle. After we left, all the slaves and servants, both Nethers and Ahrenians, stood up against the King and struck back!"

"Fara!" In the middle of Jean's explanation, I was charged and tackled into an embrace that sent pain shooting through my body.

"Ow!" I cried, and my attacker let go.

"I'm so sorry! Sorry, Fara!" Lydia stood before me, tears streaming down her face.

"That's okay," I assured her, but she shook her head.

"No, for everything! I'm sorry!" I stopped her before she could apologize any more.

"Lydia, really, it's okay. What happened is in the past. You did what you thought you had to do." She wailed and came in to hug me again, but this time I was prepared and able to position myself so that she didn't hit any of my wounds.

"Fara, how are things going out there?" Croxley asked me, indicating towards the battlefield.

"We don't have enough numbers," I replied. "We are growing tired and it won't be much longer before they overpower us."

"How many men do we have left?"

"At least a hundred have been killed or wounded, and another 50 are resting, trying to gather their strength before entering the fight again."

"Well, we should be able to help. There are about 500 of us here, and while not all of us can fight, we can help heal the wounded and get supplies ready."

I was taken aback by the number. "Five hundred? If we storm the field all at one time, we might be able to overwhelm the soldiers into submitting," I plotted. I looked at Croxley and Jean for confirmation, and they seemed in support of the plan.

"It would be risky. We don't want to lose all our numbers in one go. But then again, it just might work," Croxley mused.

"It's the last chance we've got. It's all or nothing, Croxley."

He nodded, and I rejoiced at our sudden good fortune.

We made our way to the camp to get everyone their weapons. Luckily, among the group were some old palace guards and other servants who had experience with weapons, so they knew exactly what to grab. As for the others, we didn't have time to get everyone matched up with the correct size and grip. I just hoped that our numbers would be enough to make up for the inadequate supplies. I could tell passing through our camp that the sight of fresh troops raised everyone's moral. I just had to have faith that it wouldn't be for nothing.

Once everyone was equipped, we lined up before the battlefield. Looking to Jean and Croxley, we exchanged "good lucks", and with our weapons raised in the air, we charged back into battle.

We were met with the clangs of swords and the shouts of men fighting with their last ounce of strength. I could see in the King's soldiers' eyes their disbelief at the sudden onslaught of opponents, and it didn't take very long before we had pushed them back to the edge of their camp. I watched as a fresh wave was getting ready to come in, and I steeled myself to prepare. But before they reached us, a stillness rolled across the field. Atop an armoured horse sat none other than the King.

Throughout the crowd, weapons fell to the sides of their wielders as he passed by. He climbed a mound in the centre of the battlefield and bellowed, "I heard you wanted an audience. Well, I am here. If you are brave enough, come and face me."

I stood there, disbelief and suspicion rooting my feet into the ground. But as I was watching the King, my eyes caught motion coming from the peripheral of the battlefield. It was Erik, weaving his way towards his father. This spurred me into motion, and I headed in the same direction, hoping to beat him. This was my battle, not his.

I caught eyes with Croxley as I made my way through, and he shook his head, warning me not to go any further, but I kept on going. I was past fear, I was past hiding, I was past letting everyone do things for me. This is what I stood for, this is what I have worked so hard towards. I needed to do this for myself as much as for my people.

When I made it to the bottom of the mound, I was faced by a group of guards. Some gave me dirty looks, while others looked at me in awe. To my amusement, a few even looked scared.

I pushed my way through the barrier and trudged up the mound until I reached the top. When the King saw me, he raised his eyebrows.

"And who are you?" He asked, contempt dripping from his voice.

"I'm Fara, and I am here to represent my people," I responded, my voice strong and steady. The anger I felt towards this man trumped any nerves I might have had. I wouldn't let him see me tremble. Not again.

"So you're the one who's causing all this trouble. I think I remember you. You're the one that shovels horse manure all day in the stables, right? With that bumbling fool, Heath. Pity, his mind was barely sharp enough to work with animals. I can't imagine what you had to go through, dealing with him all day."

I felt my temper flare, but I knew that was his intention, and I wasn't about to let him get to me now.

"I'm here for an audience," I demanded, cutting right to the point.

"Oh, that's right. You thought you and your people were important enough to take my time and complain about your lives. Well, I do have to say, you certainly know how to catch everyone's attention. I mean, it's part of your nature, right? You've always wanted to be the centre of attention. You just can't stand being overlooked, am I right?" He was fishing for that spot, the trigger that would send me over, but it wasn't there. Anything that would have been there for him to use against me had been healed in this past few weeks. "Well, you have my audience," he said, giving a mock bow.

"I ask for the freedom of my people. Not just of Cethin, but of Grundale, Fyzen, Weldar, Laurevell, Montill, and Sprokil, For all of those oppressed and robbed of the basic pleasures of the sky, the wind, the sun. I request that we are liberated from our underground prison, where we work and toil for the sole benefit of those who prosper above. I ask for a chance to join our brothers and sisters above, to reunite Ahrenia and pursue a new future." When I finished, the King said nothing, solely looking at me. I held his gaze, neither of us flinching, when suddenly he threw back his head and laughed a cruel laugh.

"How cute. That was a touching speech, I'll give you that. But I don't think I'm going to let that happen. As much as you all may want to come back and 'be free', as you say, have you ever thought about Ahrenians? They don't want you. They will reject you, scorn you, make your life miserable. You will suffer and live in such despair that you'd eventually go crawling back to your caves underground where you Nethers belong."

I stumbled at the thought. I knew that there was prejudice. I had encountered it more than once up above. But how deeply engrained was it? Could Ahrenians ever learn to accept the Nethers?

"That's not true," in the midst of my doubt, I whipped around to see

Erik standing before his father. He had a stream of dried blood trailing down his forehead and cheek, and streaks of blood crossing his clothes. Try as I might, I couldn't find their source, so I assumed they were from his opponents. Despite it all, I was relieved to see him relatively unharmed. But that didn't mean I wanted to see him here. With what was essentially a death warrant on his head, the most dangerous place for him to be was here in front of his own father.

"Ah, so the Prince finally decides to show his face," the King said, his eyes directed with deadly precision towards his son.

"Father, at least consider this. We need to think about a future with the Nethers."

"We need? How do you know what we need? Since when have you tried to lead the nation? You are not a King. I wouldn't even venture as far to call you a Prince."

"I'm doing more for our nation that you ever have. I'm trying to fix everything that was broken so many years ago. It's time for a change," Erik urged, motioning his arm over the battlefield, indicating the carnage that had been shed. I was following his sweep with my eyes when I caught sight of an archer taking aim. I traced his line of sight and before his target registered in my mind, I was being pushed to the ground.

"Fara, watch out!" Erik tackled me to down. I heard him grunt when we hit the floor, and I pulled myself up off of him, thinking it was my body weight that had caused him to continue moaning. It wasn't until I had pushed myself up when I saw the arrow protruding from his shoulder.

I gasped and tried to move him onto his side so he wasn't laying on top of it, but a soldier ripped me away from him.

"No! Erik! Let go of me!" I screamed as I fought against their grip, but it was no use. I was forced to watch him bleed from the sidelines as his father walked up to him, swinging a sword in his hand.

"She calls you Erik? You allow such scum to call you by your first name?" The King frowned as he stood over his son. "I was right. You no longer deserve to be called a Prince. What you've become now is no more than a public enemy. And as a King, I have to protect my people." He held his sword above the Prince, who was writhing in pain. I saw red spread from his shoulder blade, tendrils of blood spreading through the fabric of his shirt. Every moan that escaped through his lips sent a wave of pain through my body, and I was completely suspended by the guards who had me in their grip, my legs no longer able to hold my body up.

I watched in horror as the King dangled his sword over Erik's throat, Erik's fate dependent on the few inches between his neck and the blade. Its swinging became wider until it was a full arch, ending with its point directed straight at me. I felt my mouth go dry as I looked down the breadth of the sword to the King's hand, up his thick arm, and into his dangerous eyes. In them I saw so much hatred that I felt my stomach squirm.

"And yet, I would hate to waste all that time I spent raising you into a Prince, Erik. I think you, girl," he said, jabbing the sword towards me, laughing when I flinched away, "should be the one to pay for this. Maybe Erik would learn his lesson if he had to suffer the consequences of forgetting where he came from."

I felt the guards shift my position so that I was on my knees, my neck bared to the King's sword. But I was detached from my body, seemingly watching myself as the King ran his sword under the numbers on the back of my neck, 923, creating an underline of blood that trickled down my spine. I watched as Erik struggled to pull himself up, gripping his shoulder in agony every time he put weight on it. I could see him trembling, and yet I felt strong and steady. I looked over the field and saw from end to end the exhausted fighters of both sides, leaning against their weapons, the points stuck in the ground, Nethers and Ahrenians alike no longer wanting to fight.

I was pulled back into myself at the vibrations of a loud clack through the air. The King's sword fell to the ground, and I could make out from my position the end of a thick staff. I rolled myself out from the guard's grip, which had gone slack from shock. I found my father pinning the King to the ground with his staff.

"Faradene, get back," he demanded over his shoulder. The King rolled himself up, standing in front of my father and pulling a smaller knife from his belt. They circled each other, taking small steps, their eyes locked. I strayed my eyes from them just long enough to reach Erik, who had finally fainted from the pain. His forehead was glistening with sweat, and I saw that he had broken the shaft trying to reach me. I just kept brushing through his hair with my fingers, anxiously monitoring him while at the same time keeping watch on my father and the King in their deadly dance. The lives of two of the most important people to me were both suspended, and it was all I could do to hold the wave of anxiety back.

Suddenly, the King lunged at my father, who just barely was able to block the knife with his staff, thrusting the King away. He only had time to deflect all the quick, angry attacks the King was throwing his direction. Another few attacks and the King made contact with my father, his knife tearing deep across my father's chest.

Seeing his blood broke the wall I had built in my mind, and a scream ripped through my throat. There were no words, just a drawn out wail that filled with fear, pain, and sorrow. My father looked back at me in shock, and I watched his demeanor shift. He started to advance on the King, sending out attacks with his staff, which had a stronger reach than the King's knife. Though the staff noticeably wore the King out, it didn't draw blood in the same way his knife did, and my father was rapidly losing strength. He dodged a thrust by the King, but in stepping back, lost his balance and fell.

I rose from my crouched position, the stress of the fight filling me with nervous energy. My father got back on his feet just in time to avoid another strike from the King, but he was breathing much harder than his component, who had obviously been battle trained. Although my father may have been stronger, the King had more technique, with which he was winning the upper hand.

My father fell a second time, and remained kneeling, attempting to catch his breath. My heart stopped as I watched the King close in. I frantically searched around for an answer, for some way to help, when I saw the sword the King had dropped. I picked it up, my vision focused on my father while everything else was clouded out. With all of my strength, I ran to where my father was kneeling and, standing in front of him, I held the sword in front of me. I closed my eyes as the King lunged, and felt myself fall into my father as the King's weight pushed against me. After a few moments of stillness, I opened my eyes to find that my hands were nearly touching the King's stomach, the sword having gone all the way through and coming out of his back. I dropped the sword and watched as the King slumped forward, falling face-down beside me. I couldn't take my eyes off his body, the sword having been driven deeper into him by his fall, blood running down the sides. I was only slightly aware of my father as he reach around me, shielding me from the scene.

"It's al-right Faradene, it's over. It's done." I let him wrap his arms around me, closing off the rest of the world like he did when I was a child. "It's done. It's done."

EPILOGUE

"I think it looks nice, don't you?" Erik and I were standing in front of a small tree I had just planted in the garden. It was the one I had brought with me from Cethin nearly a year ago, having continued to grow in the windowsill of my room even after I left. Lydia told me that she had watered it every night, hoping that some of her love and care would reach me and help me stay strong no matter where I was. I can't help but think that it did.

It's been two months since the rebellion. After the King died, no one on either side knew how to react, and the fighting ceased. Soldiers from the King's army, along with some of the Nethers, helped us carry Erik back to the camp. We were informed that the King's general had been seen leaving on horseback with a few of the other higher-ranked men not far behind, leaving the soldiers to fend for themselves. We sent some Nethers to their camp to help heal their wounded, and they likewise sent some supplies our way.

By the next morning, we had all moved into the castle, rooms having been deserted overnight when the nobles heard that the King had been killed. Some fled out of fear of being punished for their relationship with the King, while others simply left, sickened at the thought of sharing a home with us Nethers.

Those who remained were genuinely interested in learning more about us and how we had survived so long underground. But our answers weren't as interesting as they had hoped. When one man asked my father if we ate giant cave worms, my father sprayed the ale he had been drinking across the room and exclaimed, "Are you joking? What in the bloody devil is a giant cave worm?"

I spent most of the first week with Erik in the healing room. Although we were able to take the remainder of the arrow out immediately after he made it back to camp, it had none-the-less been in there for too long and he grew fevered and sick, drifting in and out of consciousness for the whole week. I made sure that I was there every time he woke, even if it was only to see him blink his eyes in confusion, mutter a nonsense sentence, and slip back into unconsciousness. My mother and father tried to get me to retire from my post and get good rest, but I refused to leave Erik's side, so instead they would bring me meals. Some nights, I would fall asleep sitting next to him, and would wake to see Croxley sleeping in the chair across from me, on the other side of Erik's bed.

We were both in shambles until one morning, Erik woke up and looked around the room, actually seeing what was in it rather than whatever delusion his mind had supplied before.

"What smells so bad in here," he asked, his voice raspy from disuse. He looked back and forth between Croxley and I before surmising, "Wow, you guys look like hell. You could really use a bath."

I sprang from my chair and nearly jumped into his bed, tears streaming down my face as I wrapped my arms around his neck.

"Ouch! Wounded Prince, over here!" Erik cringed as I landed right on his shoulder.

"Sorry, sorry," I said, gently easing myself around it.

"Erik, did you really have to go and nearly get yourself killed?" Croxley asked, standing from his chair and looking over Erik. Erik just grinned and replied,

"It was all part of the plan. You know I have a flair for the dramatic. Besides, I knew my father's archers were never good shots." Croxley laughed and patted Erik's shoulder good-naturedly, receiving another groan of pain. "Really, guys, if you don't stop hurting me, I'm going to have to send you out of my room."

Croxley and I were eventually able to reign ourselves in, quelling our excitement, and managed to catch Erik up on what had happened since the battle. Erik had fainted before my father had entered the fight, so we had to fill him in on everything that happened in-between, including his father's death. I watched his face as it sunk in, and I knew that internally he was fighting between the victory of the people and the loss of his father. Understandably, he asked us for some alone time, during which I went to wash myself and raid the kitchen. Now that I wasn't so worried about Erik, I found that I was ravenous, as well as extremely tired. After practically gorging myself, I went to my parent's room and fell asleep.

After that, Erik was on a quick road to recovery, and managed to get himself out of bed by the end of the week. Once he did, he never got back in. Everyone seemed to need a piece of him, which shouldn't have been a surprise. After the fall of his father, he was, in effect, the new King. Not only did he have to deal with the consequences of the rebellion, but he also had to maintain all the current states of affairs and other daily tasks of a King. As busy as he was, I was caught up with my own business of having to find a way to help all the Nethers adjust to life above ground. After our victory, I sent some messengers from each colony back to their homes in order to confirm our victory. Almost immediately, Nethers began pouring in through the gates. I underestimated just how many people were in each colony, and after just two colonies came through the gates and into the castle, I realized that there was not only not enough room for us in the castle, but in all of Stonewall.

With the help of the council leaders from each of the colonies, we organized construction teams that helped build temporary camps on the outside of Stonewall for all of the Nethers until they decided where they wanted to go. I made sure that the gates were always open so that both the Nethers and Ahrenians could go in and out as they pleased.

As for the people of Stonewall, the lower class accepted us almost immediately. It was the middle and upper class who fought the hardest against our presence. However, once we began trading that which we had brought with us, such as wood and coal and precious gems, all of which the King used to have a monopoly on, we were easily able to win them over.

As it turns out, the gem that Lena had taken from the King's room was not the only gem of its kind. The greedy King that was responsible for sending us all underground was actually successful in finding more of the same gem, varying in size and shape, some even more impressive than the original. He hid them away in order to continue the mining, as well as out of fear that any potential rumors of the gem would summon thieves to Ahrenia. Jean found the gems when she and Winnerva explored the tunnels around where the secret throne room was located.

Apparently, this discovery set off a desire for exploration in Jean, and she and Croxley ended up leaving one night to "go adventuring", as she had called it in the letter she left behind to explain her and Croxley's sudden disappearance.

With all this going on, Erik and I rarely had a chance to see each other. It wasn't until one night, when I was speaking to some of the council from Monthill, when Darren came in and told me that I was needed in the garden. I was a little hesitant to leave,having finally made it clear to the leader why it wasn't okay to simply take food from any farm one happens upon, but Darren insisted that it was urgent, so I left what I was doing and made my way to the gardens. It was a new moon, so the sky was lit only by the stars, which sparkled in their reflection off the water in the small pool in which stood the statue and its adorning morning glories, all folded up for the night. I heard the crack of a twig and spun around, my nerves still on high since the battle. In the moonless darkness, it took me a few seconds to make sense of the figure approaching me.

"Beautiful night, is it not," Erik greeted, extending his hand out to reach mine. I put it in his, and he pulled me close to him, his body warm in the cool spring air. He started humming a quiet tune, guiding me in a sow dance around the pool. We twirled and stepped to our own music for what seemed like hours, but at the same time mere seconds, completely lost in each other. When Erik's tune came to an end, he stepped away from me and, keeping my hand in his, kneeled down in front of me.

"Fara, when I first met you I was a completely different person. I was naive, self-centred, arrogant, and I could care less about anyone but myself, let alone a nation. But after I met you, you inspired me to look past myself, to learn and feel and experience something other than what I was used to. You taught me compassion, dedication, and selflessness. Because of you, I feel I am ready to lead Ahrenia towards something better. Do you think you could lead along with me? I don't think I could do it without you by my side. Now, I know its no table, but☐" Erik pulled out a small ring, two thin, delicate silver bands interwoven around a small strand of diamonds. I looked back and forth from it to Erik, anticipation welling inside me. I had barely let him finish asking, "Fara, will you marry me?" before leaping into his arms and shouting "Yes!"

If things were easy, we would have been married the next day, but apparently, when you are royalty, marriages are much more complicated, especially when you are still technically engaged to someone who robbed your country of their crowning jewel and fled during the midst of a rebellion. We had to wait for permission from Ethera, Lena's home country, to end the engagement in order to prevent an all-out war before Erik and I could even begin preparing for our wedding.

Nevertheless, I found myself in a constant state of bliss. Not only did I have the promise of a future in which my people were free, but I had a future that I could share among the people I love.

Standing in front of the tree that came with me from Cethin, now planted at the entrance of the castle's garden, Erik's hand interlaced with mine, I couldn't believe everything that I had been through. "Do you think it will last?" I asked Erik.

"The tree, or this," he said, sweeping his arms in a motion that referenced all that was changing.

"Both," I replied.

"I think," he said, brushing my hair out of my face and kissing my forehead, "we have to take it day by day and just hope for the best."

I nodded and looked beyond the tree to the city of Stonewall before me, knowing that over the wall lay a brand new future.

"I think it's time we tear down that wall."

THE END.

ABOUT THE AUTHOR

L.T. Kenneth was born and raised in a small township named Botshabelo in South Africa, where he also studied in the local schools of his born town. He then began his relish passion of writing fiction from his early teen, which changed his life around. After publishing short-stories through small publications, he began writing novels because of the reception for his paranormal romance stories. Which he still writes today.

COMING SOON.
1. The Titanium (Destiny of Love part 2 and 3)
2. The Titanium (Gift of Love part 1,2 and 3)
3. The Titanium (Awe of Love part 1,2, and 3)